SKYSHIP THRIVE

THRIVE SPACE COLONY ADVENTURES BOOK 1

GINGER BOOTH

ISBN: 9781794556300

Cover design by www.rafidodigitalart.com
Skyship image © Freestyleimages | Dreamstime.com
Diagrams by Ginger Booth

This is a work of fiction. Names, characters, organizations, places, events, and incidents are either products of the author's imagination or are used fictitiously.

❀ Created with Vellum

PROLOGUE

Humanity spread to the stars on a shoelace.
We gained control of gravity.
We settled the Moon, Mars, and Ganymede.
The star drive was discovered.
Explorers sought out new solar systems.
The best were colonized. Terraforming began.

But behind them, Earth was failing.
Time ran out.
None of humanity's new homes were ready.

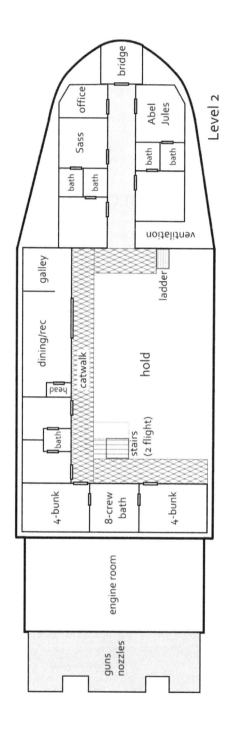

Level 2

bridge

office

Sass

Abel
Jules

bath

bath

bath

bath

ventilation

galley

dining/rec

catwalk

head

bath

hold

ladder

stairs
(2 flight)

4-bunk

8-crew
bath

4-bunk

engine room

guns
nozzles

2

Level 1

5 m

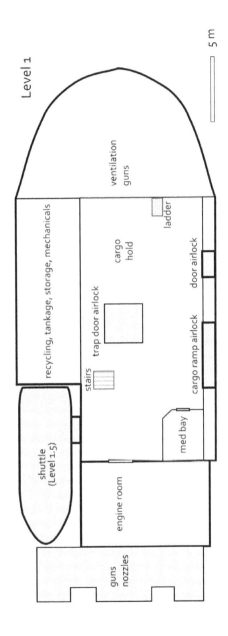

ventilation
guns

recycling, tankage, storage, mechanicals

ladder

cargo
hold

door airlock

trap door airlock

stairs

cargo ramp airlock

shuttle
(Level 1.5)

med bay

engine room

guns
nozzles

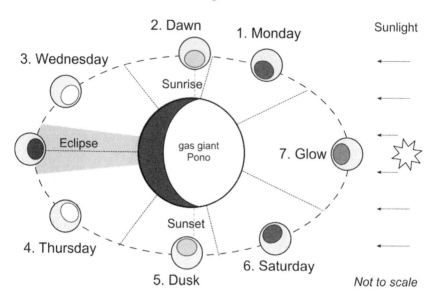

"Days" of the Mahina Week

Mahina 'week' is one orbit of Pono.
Most settlements face the gas giant.
They get sun for 3.5 days a week.
A day is 24.87 Earth hours (24 local hours).

1

Novice Captain Sassafras Collier brought her skyship *Thrive* to hover on station. Gearing up, and simpler tests, had gradually built up to this, her fledgling business cashing in nicely along the way.

The giant needle of an ozone generator spire impaled the view of the full gas giant planet Pono as it hung in the sky before her, bathing the moon below in the springlike green light of Glow.

Why this weekly 'full moon' could stir the human heart the way their primordial Moon once did, Sass didn't have a clue. But everyone's blood got up on Glow, final day of the local 'week.' Over her years in law enforcement, she'd experienced the phenomenon firsthand, busting up fights and ferrying rowdy idiots to the emergency room.

Statistics concurred. Glow was the day to do something stupid.

"Do you hear a hiss?" she asked her first mate Abel.

"I don't hear a hiss." He breathed deeply and checked a telltale on the control panel. "Atmo is within tolerance. Bit low, but we're at altitude."

5

Sass sighed. "Abel, with a positive seal it shouldn't matter that we're at altitude. Just keep her on station. I'll help Kassidy leap to her death."

"I wish you wouldn't put it that way. Are you sure we're not —"

"We're not liable," Sass confirmed yet again. "Kassidy signed a release." Sass squeezed the young man's shoulder and left, re-sealing the bridge door behind her.

She paused on the catwalk above the hold to listen. She couldn't pinpoint any hiss. But then, she was standing right next to the fan system. The machinery was blocked by the beautifully inlaid wardrobe cabinet their client Kassidy parked there. So the captain wouldn't be able to hear anything subtle.

"Are we ready?" she called down into the cargo hold. She hopped the slide down, lately simplified to a dogleg with a single banked curve. Only then did she notice Jules lurking at the galley door, Abel's young bride. "Jules, you should be in your sealed cabin."

"But Eli gets to watch!"

"Eli is a scientist. Who will wear an oxygen mask when the situation warrants."

Eli confirmed sheepishly, "I'll just go get that oxygen mask."

"Yes, you will. You'll seal those cabins, too, as ordered."

"Yes, ma'am."

Sass turned to Kassidy, encased head to toe in something black, much like a neoprene wetsuit, though who knew what material her urb costumer used. Her tidy athletic build looked great in the skintight outfit. The younger woman was most disappointed that her gorgeous hair couldn't fly free for the cameras.

But the outdoor temperature was -10 °Celsius, and woefully low on oxygen or any other gas pressure. Kassidy would have risked it anyway. But Sass insisted she was in training for a jump from 3,000 meters, nearly the top of Mahina's shallow atmosphere. Frostbite there would be nearly instantaneous.

Kassidy rolled her eyes while Sass worked through her checklist. She tested buckles and gauges, and Kassidy's backup gravity generator with its remote dead man's switch.

"You will keep up a running commentary at all times," Sass rehashed with her. "If you go silent for half a second, I abort remotely. And you flutter down like a flower petal."

"Yes, mom," Kassidy agreed. "Just make sure the cameras stick with me. While I flit and float."

Sass smiled as Eli joined them, now in goggles and oxygen mask. Sass was fairly sure Eli didn't need them any more than she did. But appearances must be maintained for the youngsters, lest they learn bad habits. She pulled her own roomy vacuum suit over her clothes, but didn't seal it yet, leaving her gloves and helmet racked.

"Eli, you stay here as my backup. I'm on the ramp with Kassidy."

Eli gave an exaggerated nod. "On a clamped line."

"Yes, dad," Sass quipped, earning a grin from the wet-suited daredevil. Sass was old enough to be Eli's grandmother, or Kassidy's great-grandma. Hopefully they didn't realize that. By Mahina standards, Sass appeared twenty-something.

She hauled on a lever to bring down the airlock wall in front of the cargo ramp. This extra door remained retracted in atmosphere. She accessed the ship-wide address system through her headset. "Captain speaking. Now testing cargo airlock. All hands verify pressure secure."

"Aye-aye, captain!" Jules returned eagerly over the intercom.

"Bridge secure," her husband Abel confirmed.

"Jules, confirm location," Sass prompted.

"In my cabin, where you sent me."

"Jules, next time I'd like you to say 'first mate cabin secure,'" Sass instructed.

"Yes, ma'am. First mate cabin is secure. Galley secure."

"Just like that," Sass encouraged. "Good job, Jules."

"My cabins and the engine room secured before I joined you," Eli offered at her elbow. "I didn't check your cabin."

Sass nodded. "I secured my cabin and the empties before takeoff. Abel sealed the engineering spaces." She took a mental stroll through the floor plan. "Abel, did you catch the med bay?"

"Sorry, captain. Didn't think of it."

Sass nodded to Eli, who scurried across the cargo bay to see to it. They tended to forget about med bay, down here in the hold by the dangerous stuff. Most of the living space lay upstairs along the catwalk or near the bridge. The large hold couldn't be subdivided for air pressure, though they could evacuate the atmosphere to restore later. These old skyships hailed from a time before Mahina hosted an atmosphere, designed for airless asteroids and the voids between.

Today was their first live test of the pressure seals on her new used skyship, not just Kassidy's ability to save her own skin with a grav generator. Sass was confident of the Kassidy part. The pressure seals, not so much.

"Med bay sealed," Eli reported.

"Pressure secure," Sass acknowledged. "Evacuating air from cargo airlock now." She pressed a button. A previously dead lamp blinked red over a lock the size of a barn door. Sass put her ear to the seal, waved her hand to feel for air currents, then repeated on the other side.

"Aren't we on the wrong side of the lock?" Kassidy inquired, fist on hip.

"We are testing the lock before putting our soft squishy bodies into it," Sass returned. "Do you hear a hiss?"

"I hear air pumps."

After a few more seconds the blinking stopped, leaving the tell-tale steady red. Another red light gleamed inside the airlock itself. The chamber stretched as wide as the ramp, but only a meter deep, like the space between a door and storm door. Not that anyone needed a storm door on Mahina. The moon's budding atmosphere didn't enjoy much weather. They took turns peering out through a window.

"Airlock evacuated," Sass reported. "First mate, pressure check."

"Interior spaces no change, captain," Abel reported. "Cargo lock 70% to match exterior air pressure."

Sass stepped to the control panel at the left. "Extending cargo ramp." She returned to join the other two heads watching out the window for fun. "First mate, we need to wash this window." Fingerprints and suspected nose smears fouled her glorious view. Her new old ship was just too much fun for words.

Abel chuckled. "I'll make a note of that, captain."

The ramp lowered beautifully to its horizontal position. With no ground to rest on, it formed a gangplank straight into the golden orb of the gas giant Pono stretching halfway across the dark weekend sky.

Abel prompted, "Captain, if you're done admiring the view?"

"Right. Closing cargo ramp.... Sealed. Restoring atmo to cargo lock... Green light. Pressure check, Abel."

"All same, except cargo lock a touch on the low side."

"How low?"

"Says 97%," Abel replied. "I'd risk it. Maintenance request noted."

Sass grinned appreciation of the first mate's self-ticketing system. "Alright. Let's do this. Kassidy and Captain proceeding into the airlock. Eli has lock-side controls." She donned and sealed her own helmet and gloves. Cool canned air tickled her hairline, smelling metallic.

"Eli at lock controls," the scientist offered, doubtful of his etiquette.

Sass shot him a gauntleted thumb's-up, and opened the door. Pushing down the door lever took more muscle than she would have liked. She asked Abel to note that for attention, too.

In a moment, she and Kassidy were in the skinny slice of lock space, door shut and sealed behind them. Her young client folded arms and tapped an impatient foot while Sass clamped their lines to a handrail with D-rings. Sass raised an eyebrow at the performer and received a confident nod in reply.

The captain punched the airlock evacuate button on the side control panel. She grasped the side bar and Kassidy clutched the bar on the door. A light blinked on the panel, then went steady red as the lurid no-pressure light bathed them in scarlet.

Sass pressed the cargo ramp button. The breeze hit them as the ramp extended again, her roomy suit flapping around her.

She wouldn't have missed this for the world. Nothing stood between her and the enormous gas giant. The thin air shouldn't make

9

much difference, but it did. The gas giant was clearer, brighter, as though she could reach out and touch it.

Sass shot Kassidy a thumb's-up. *Your show now.*

"Damn, this is too cool," Kassidy replied. "Give me a couple minutes to deploy my cameras and talk to my fans." Her drone spheres rose to take station, to either side and directly ahead for a closeup. She turned her blazing grin on. "Broadcasting *Now.* Hey, fans! This is Kassidy Yang, speaking to you from the tippy top of an ozone spire. I won't tell you which one! Right ahead of me is a full gas Pono on this brisk and gorgeous Glow. Aren't you glad you subscribed to my livecast now, huh?"

She continued in that vein. Sass almost wished the cameras weren't recording, so she could creep out the gangplank and gaze down. But they'd agreed she wouldn't appear on screen. She craned her neck to peer out the side crack. The moon's horizon felt unnervingly close. From this height she should see 75 kilometers. A single dark green settlement intersected her sliver of view, lonely against the gas-lit empty regolith — the original rock and moon dust of Mahina.

Kassidy subtly shooed her into the corner. Sass complied and lost her glimpse of the surface. But at this height, she saw a star, or maybe a moonlet, glimmering to the right. She never saw stars from the ground on Glow.

"Now I'm approaching the edge, fans. Oh, my, that's a long way down! I see Newer York, Albany, and Hutchins. I'm waving at you! That ghost town off to the left is Petticreek. Wow, this air is crystal clear!

"Gang, my heart is thudding a mile a minute! This is going to be great! OK, I'm unclamping my safety line — now! And ten. Nine. Eight. Can you stand it? Six. Five. I have backup safety measures. But nothing is sure but death and taxes! Three. Two. One. *Jump!*"

At Mahina-normal one-sixth gravity, Kassidy bounded upward in a graceful arc, reminding Sass of a slow motion replay of a diver off the high board. The stunt woman flattened as she disappeared below the ramp, her trio of cameras keeping pace.

Sass quickly hauled Kassidy's safety line in, and punched the ramp retract button. Gauntleted finger poised over the next button, and stabbed it as soon as the ramp sealed. *Thrive* began maneuvering at once. Outside the ship's interior gravity field, Sass swayed and held tight to the grab bar. She fidgeted with her D-ring and listened to Kassidy's steady patter. *Come on!* She wished she'd stayed inside to watch the show.

But she couldn't regret coming out to offer Kassidy emotional support. The young nut job probably didn't need it. But you never knew. Sass smiled to think she might have added some courage.

And the red wait light kept blinking. The lock wouldn't open.

"WOOT! THIS FEELS AMAZING!" Kassidy told her fans over the livecast.

From her falling vantage, the layout of the living towns in the distance was crystal clear. A tiny cluster of downtown buildings spread out to farm fields. The forested hedgerows staggered outward like the scales of a spruce cone, or the petals of a zinnia blossom.

Any neighboring atmo spires lay beyond the horizon. The barren moon regolith left plenty of room for expansion between settlements. Features that appeared random on the ground, showed as a worn crater from this height, with concentric rings and radiating fracture lines. The atmo plant itself, tucked in a ravine beneath her, included a green belt. Pono reflected off a deep reservoir, the largest outdoor water she'd ever seen on Mahina. A half dozen sequins of tree-rimmed fields spread toward her feet, a large solo farm flanking the atmo factory.

The curve of the horizon showed clearly, with a light band between moon and sky, like the thickened base of a glass bottle.

All this Kassidy drank in quick as breathing. She needed to keep up the banter.

"I'm falling belly-down to increase wind resistance. But that atmo plant is getting bigger fast! Deploying parachute." That gave her a strong jerk. The harness bit into her thighs and tightened across her chest, bobbing her upright to fall feet-first. The drone cameras briefly dipped below her, then adjusted to resume station-keeping alongside her.

"Grav generators control this fall, friends," Kassidy continued. "The parachute helps me steer. And a do-si-do left," she yanked on one line, then another, "and a do-si-do right. Very cool! Rapidly approaching the force field. The atmo plant is off-limits. Let's aim left toward that big farm, shall we? The fields look softer than bare regolith." She laughed and swerved.

"Guess I should have asked permission first, huh? Always easier to get forgiveness than permission. Watch that horizon get closer! Let's slow down. Yes! Floating in at point one g now. Gives me time to sightsee up here! What a beautiful little world you are, Mahina, under the light of full Glow!

"Coming in for a landing. Yeah, it's quick! And —" She hit the ground running a few steps through knee-high hay. "I'm down. Safe! *Woot!* I wanna do it again! Sass, Abel, you coming to pick me up?"

"Right behind you," Abel replied.

Kassidy continued chatting with her fans as Abel landed the ship.

Sass sighed. She stripped out of her vacuum suit and dumped it in a corner of the shallow vestibule. Once the ship settled, she stabbed the cargo ramp button to set it down, and stabbed another button to retract the airlock gate. "Abel, note pressure seals need maintenance on the cargo lock."

Abel laughed. "You were stuck in there?"

"Yup." She racked her pressure suit while Kassidy signed off with her audience. Sass supposed it shouldn't surprise her that the stunt woman chose to land in her old farm. Forb Turner's farm now. His fields were the only soft ground near the atmo plant. She just hadn't thought about it.

She jogged down to offer the triumphant stunt woman a hug and congratulations, then helped her tame the billowing parachute. "Can we offer the farmer a tip? Forb Turner. I have his contact info. We don't need to knock on the door."

"Sure! Offer him five hundred," Kassidy replied magnanimously. "Is he photogenic?"

"Not especially." *Five hundred credits? For falling on his hay field?*

"And twenty-eight thousand for us," Abel reported over the comms. "That right, Kassidy?"

"Round up," Kassidy replied with a grin. "Make it thirty thou. You've been awesome!"

Sass's eyes widened. Their negotiated base pay was 10,000c for stunt day for skyship rental, plus a modest cut of her audience take. The lady had generous fans. "Pleasure doing business with you! All hands, release from seals. That's a wrap. Let's fly. Any requests on where to park?"

"Par-ty, par-ty!" Kassidy replied. "Newer York looked good from the air. Drinks on me at the bar!"

The captain didn't need to call Forb after all. By the time they got the parachute folded into its pack, the man himself bounded into the field, his long slow strides bouncing him a meter into the air. He peered side to side, as though his eyes had trouble keeping a bead on the large skyship.

"He never wears gravity, does he?" Kassidy said sadly. His too-tall and spindly build made that clear. "Must make you crazy, Sass."

"It does that," Sass breathed. Sure was nice to have a new friend who understood. Kassidy's popularity didn't surprise her a bit.

Fortified, the captain turned to bellow a greeting to her old farm's new owner. "Sorry, Forb. If I'd known, I would have warned you ahead of time! Got those soybeans in alright?"

2

___

The first wave of star drive explorers set out in 2072. The terraformers left Earth only 12 years later. They expected 150 years before accepting colonists. They got 42.

— Quasar Shibuya, *The Early Diaspora.*

Two weeks before...

"A covered wagon?" Sass murmured, shading her eyes to gaze at the far hill. "You've got to be kidding me."

A cloud of dust showed the farm's new owners arriving ten days late. Well, one and a half sun cycles. They called a sun cycle a week here on the moon Mahina, and one-seventh of that was dubbed a day. Today was Dusk, the gas giant planet Pono looming at half-full beyond the closer ridge, the sun creeping toward the horizon to set in a few hours.

Pono never budged in the sky, from any given spot. Gravity tidally locked planet and moon to face off against each other across the eons. Though the weather on Pono changed. Currently one of the purple storms was visible on the giant globe in the sky, nudging apart brown striations that girdled Pono's yellow orb. Sass recalled that it was a great red spot on Jupiter, back in the Earth system. Pono and Mahina resembled Jupiter and its moon Ganymede, or so they said.

Like Jupiter, no one could live on Pono.

She turned to the graves to say her final farewell. Five of them were sentenced to this farm. Sass was the only one left. She inherited it all, and looked the same as the day she got here. The others died young of old age.

"Thanks," was all she said in the end. "Wish me luck."

She'd bounded up the hill off-gravity, but left her grav generator on for a slow hike down to the farmhouse, gazing around one last time. Denny, one of the dead, had worked hard to plant the ridges to look 'natural,' varying the three landscape species available — aspen, spruce, and hay grass. He mostly failed, because three kinds of plant and no animals looked repetitive no matter how you staged them. Sass managed better arranging the kitchen garden and the crop fields.

The farm was prettier than most. She liked the way the silhouettes of dark spruces loomed against the faint turquoise grid of the force field to the east during the dim twilight after sunset.

She'd be gone by then.

Now that the moment was upon her, freedom at last, anxiety took hold. She'd been hemmed in on this farm for twenty years. The two ridges, and the force field containing the atmo facility to the east, had formed the walls of her life. Agoraphobia set in.

That's ridiculous, she thought, then thought better of it. Even paranoids have real enemies. Every time in her life she'd come to the cusp, had to uproot herself, leave and start over, she'd met unmitigated disaster. And if that scenario has played out for 100 subjective years, while everyone around her grew old and died, even the world she were born on, then...

Yeah. Her anxiety was not unfounded.

Tough. My prison sentence is over. I'm out of here.

The farm buyers, Forb and Chicago Turner, weren't speed

demons at driving that wagon. Sass had time to wander through the house once more alone, saying good-bye. The place was immaculate as it had never been in real life, an artifact of the Turners being so late. Sass even washed the sheets and made the beds for them yesterday. Fresh cut flowers graced the tables, their fragrance wafting through the rambling one-story ranch. Sass left most of the furniture for the new owners.

She drifted through the rooms one last time, ostensibly checking for anything she'd left behind. But really she was letting go of her favorite bits. The master bedroom that had been hers since the last of the others died, rich in potted palmetto trees. The guest room her parole officer crashed in when he got too drunk to leave. The deluxe bath Sean had crafted so beautifully, walls tiled in native striated stone, polished to perfection.

They used to pile into the huge hot-tub together to celebrate sunset. Now it had been years since Sass did more than punch the auto-shower button, and be out of there clean and dry in under five minutes.

Earth years, of course. Even she hoped to be dead before the gas giant could complete that many astronomical years. She forgot how many Earth years it took Pono to orbit its sun. Mahina raced around Pono once a week.

Sass nodded approval to the auto doc med-bay. Decorating that closet had been one of her improvements. Her bedmate of the time had been stuck in there for a week once in its raw extruded form, and demanded company. Now its walls were a nicely textured sage, with varied art, plenty of plants, and a sky-blue ceiling.

Her original sky, anyway. Mahina's sky rotated through a pageant of greens.

She drifted into the huge yellow kitchen. She poured a tall glass of tea, twirling an ice wand to form a frozen helix up the middle, then added the wand to her last-minute carton. A screen on a cabinet allowed her to check on the wagon's progress, then she carried her tea out to the veranda.

She settled on the hammock and propped her feet on the porch rail to wait. This spot provided the best view for sunset, with the half-full gas giant hanging to the right of the peak. She snapped one last picture. *Damn them for being so late.* Her anxiety was gone now. She was impatient for this horribly protracted parting to be over, for the next phase to begin.

"Welcome home!" she called out, rising. Unused facial muscles protested her false smile.

"God bless and good evening!" Forb Turner called back, as he brought the wagon to a halt before the house. His wife Chicago chimed in more timidly, "Blessed be!" There were no children.

"Good to meet you in person! Say, I was hoping to leave before the sun sets. I'd offer to help put away your livestock, but..."

"Oh, I'll take care of that!" Chicago said. She leapt lightly out of the wagon.

Too lightly. She didn't turn her gravity on. By the look of her, barely any muscle at all, she wasn't in the habit of wearing gravity. She busied herself unhitching the oxen first. The poor animals were spindly, too.

Don't judge, Sass implored herself. She silently pointed toward the stables.

Forb, the husband, paused to collect a computer before hopping to the veranda in two bounding steps. "Don't forget the candles, dear! It'll be dark soon!" he admonished the wife, then turned to Sass.

This particular brand of settler bowed instead of shaking hands. Sass tried her best to mimic the wasted man's mannerism. "Everything is all set for you, Mr. Turner —"

"Forb, please," he interrupted. "We're Cyber-Mennonites. We use no titles."

Good for you. That would explain the conspicuously plain grey clothes flapping from their emaciated forms. She flashed a quick polite smile, and led him to the office.

"I planted the rice for you last week. Couldn't wait." She showed him the field plan on the display screen that formed the desk surface.

"That's rice over here. Soy and wheat are coming along. Kitchen garden, of course."

Forb cozied up to the desk, mouth open, caught between delight and stricken guilt. "I — Thank you! I never expected the fields would come ready planted."

"You can make your own plans between now and harvest. The soy is ready Dawn after next." Ten days from now.

"Sassafras, I'm sorry, but I have no more money to offer you," Forb stammered. "For the seed, the crops already in..."

"No problem," Sass said. "It's yours. All the planting records are on here." She tapped the desktop. "Instructions. Taxes. Harvest pickup. How to contact me with questions."

They bent their heads over the computer together to review the documenation. Forb was content to complete his inspection tour in virtual. The farm featured an extensive array of fixed eyes and drones. Since the cycle would be dark for his first days here, she made sure he knew how to inspect by infrared.

"There are lights on the livestock?" Forb asked in concern.

"I sold my animals," Sass reminded him. "But there you go." She touched a control that resumed the 24-hour diurnal setting for the livestock, regardless of what the moon's sky was doing.

"Thank you," he said, and promptly disabled it again.

Sass sighed. No wonder his livestock looked as dispirited as their owners. "Anything else? Or ready to —"

Chicago bounded into the office. "There's a —!"

"There's a what?" Forb inquired, frowning displeasure at his wife's interruption.

"There's a skyship in the barn," she said, then gulped.

"My new home," Sass agreed, with a creaky smile. "If you agree all is in order, Forb?" she asked hopefully. She brought up the final hand-off forms on the screen.

"More than!" Forb agreed. He hastily thumbed the final payment release. "I can't thank you enough, Sass, for leaving the farm in such wonderful shape! Sure you can't stay for dinner?"

Sass wondered what kind of big deal Cyber-Mennonites made of sunset dinner. "Nope. I'll just get out of your way."

She grabbed her last-minute carton from the kitchen, and set off to meet her future.

The Turners stood in the kitchen garden gaping as she backed the skyship *Thrive* out of the barn. She nodded and waved from the cockpit, and left her prison for the sky.

3

Our records from the stellar explorers are reliable. Likewise reports from the first decade or so of the terraformers. But after that, the terraforming colonies began lying to Earth. They asserted their independence in the face of increasingly desperate demands from the mother world.

"Dammit," Sass muttered, as an official police flitter nestled in for a landing beside her skyship.

A cop could hardly be here for anything except to hassle her. She should know. She'd been a cop most of her life. She'd parked in a dead dry field by a ghost town to relax and watch the best part of sunset alone. One of her favorite things about Mahina — sunset lasted for hours.

She winced as a marshal stepped out of the flitter. "Clay," she acknowledged. "What can I do for Mahina's finest this evening?"

"Sass," he returned. "Got another chair and a beer?"

She sighed and rose, and waved him to take her seat. She trotted up the cargo ramp to fetch another striped-canvas folding chair, and the rest of the 6-pack.

"You look good," Clay said.

She handed him a beer, and erected her new chair one-handed. The social requirements attended to, she retrieved her beer and raised a toast. "TGIS." *Thank God It's Sunset.* Like her, Clay Rocha was one of the few people left on the moon Mahina who remembered the phrase with *Friday.*

"Skoll," he returned, lips pursed in disapproval. "No one says TGIS anymore. No one lives in this town anymore. If you were looking for your fellow rebels. None left."

Petticreek was a rebel stronghold once. She hadn't expected to find old friends. "Looking to enjoy sunset in peace," Sass countered. "You look good, too, Clay."

And he did. Almost any healthy man with proper gravity muscle would look good to her, starved as her eyes were. But Clay worked at it. His chest and shoulders were nicely sculpted, his jaw firm and square, brown hair ruffling in the breeze. It was a long time since she last tripped her parole officer Matt into bed for entertainment. And Matt was a long-limbed skinny settler, like most. Clay's body was powerfully attractive.

His personality was not. Sass firmly squelched the temptation. Clay's body was off limits. As though to add a cherry on top, a wedding ring glinted on his finger in the final red beams of sunlight.

"Married again? How many times is that?" Sass took a swig of beer.

Clay shot her a glower. "Six. We're actually divorced. She got old." He struggled to sit erect, a position the sling chair did not encourage. "So you're out. Congratulations and all that. I'll be watching you like a hawk."

"I have a parole officer," Sass pointed out.

"You've got Matt twisted around your little finger," Clay replied. "What did you do, sleep with him?"

Yes. None of your business. "I've been a model prisoner. I'm reformed."

"Did he brief you on how the moon's changed?" Clay asked, with a nod toward the ghost town downhill. "I understand you're off the nets during confinement."

"Matt took me into town on Dusk sometimes," Sass said. "He granted me net access a couple months ago. To sell the farm, buy the ship. Ease my way back into society. Acclimate."

"He know how old you are?"

She shook her head. "New parole officer every five years. You have crow's feet."

Clay peeled a strip of wrinkles off the eye corner closest to her in demonstration. "Reusable, but they don't last very long. Here, a present. You look like you're 20." He extracted a packet of wrinkles from his jacket pocket and handed them to her.

The cosmetic looked as easy to install as a band-aid. She'd have to play with them later. "Thanks. I do look a bit young for a captain."

"Looking young isn't the problem, though, is it?" Clay murmured. "Inside I'm still burnt out by the decades."

She refused to engage his defeatism. With her new used skyship, she embarked today on a fresh start to rejuvenate her spirit.

They fell silent for a few minutes, to watch the red-hot limb of sun shrink to a point, then wink out below the horizon.

"How many settlers are left, Clay?" she asked. "The nets say a quarter million. Hell, less than that survived the trip from Earth." She jutted her chin toward the ghost town.

"Need to know," Clay replied. "You're out of the loop. Permanently."

"The farm's new owners made sure they had candles ready for 'the dark.'"

There was no 'dark' on the Pono side of Mahina. The moon was tidally locked to face the gas giant planet. From any particular spot, between now and sunrise Pono would pass from half-full to full and then to half-full on the other side. But it never budged in the sky. Back on Earth, the noon sun was half a million times brighter than a full moon. She looked it up once. Here the difference was only about 1,000 to 1 at full gas planet, and 10,000 to 1 for 'the dark days' when the gas giant was half full, right after sunset or before sunrise. Granted, it got darker during the eclipse when Pono snuck between Mahina and the sun. Eclipse light was a special underwater hush sort of deep turquoise. The 'dark' light was extra green. The sunset light was yellow-orange, sunrise tinged with blue.

Human eyes could easily see in any of them clear as day. If those eyes were any good. Like the rest of their health, the Turners' eyes were bad.

Clay scowled at her. "It isn't up to you to solve night vision. Thoughts like those could land you right back on a farm. Maybe you'll get sentenced sky-side next time. Watch the stars through dark of night. Planning a next time so soon, Sass?"

"Hell, no." The rebellion hadn't accomplished a damned thing. Or rather, it had, but Sass was practiced in her contrition.

"What are your goals?" Clay's eyes raked the ship, sizing it up with a frown. "I can't believe you want to live in one of those again."

When they terraformed the moon, their bunks were stacked six high in the hold of a skyship just like *Thrive*. Three people per bunk, shared in shifts. Latrines were out on the raw regolith, the unimproved rock and dust debris of the moon's native grey.

"I get the captain's berth this time. The quarters are nice for a dozen people. Instead of hundreds. And I can pop all over Mahina." After being stuck on an isolated farm for two decades, Sass expected this feature to be orgasmic. Most Mahinans rarely made it to the next town.

Clay's dubious squint suggested he still wouldn't use the word 'nice' to describe her battered ship. "What did you name it?"

"*Thrive.*"

He snorted. "And you're still pretending you've given up the rebellion? *Thrive* isn't even a noun."

Sass shrugged. "I have given up. Been there, done that. Gave it my best shot. I lost. Doesn't mean the cause was wrong. You know I'm right."

He shook his head, lips pursed. "We're law enforcement. It's what we do, law and order. Not terrorist —"

"I wasn't a terrorist, and you know it," Sass snapped. "I had a worthy cause. I fought for it. When the city was willing to negotiate in good faith, I shut down the rebels."

Clay changed the subject. "You'll need a gunner."

She was locked out of the guns, as he well knew. Part of her parole. "Offering me a job as a marshal again? Like you, Clay?"

"Like the city would trust you again. Kendra Oliver sent me here. To inquire your plans. She's annoyed that you bought a skyship. She intended you to stay on the farm. Maybe buy a flitter to get laid on weekends. The skyship makes her nervous."

The evil spider Kendra Oliver was Head of Security for Mahina — Sass's very ex boss. The woman made her skin crawl. A marshal like Clay remained under Kendra's thumb. Once FBI, Clay Rocha was Oliver's favorite of the settler law enforcement top echelon. Kendra considered the ex-beat cop Sass too stupid for the marshal job, probably true and very unkind. That Kendra took an interest in Sass's current doings was bad news.

"And here I was touched that you cared," Sass sniped back. "Plans. There's this guy I hired online. Partner, really. I'm selling him a stake in the ship. We'll try to make a go of it, flying odd jobs. We meet tomorrow. And get started making our first million."

"No one says 'make a million,'" Clay prompted.

Sass winced. How often would she slip like that with her new crew? She'd been alone too much lately.

Clay sat back, as though placated by her mistake. "This I have to see. Sass, what do you know about building a business? Never mind. What's your cover story?"

"Look, Clay, it wasn't my idea to live a lie. What choice do we have?"

Her nemesis looked at her sympathetically. "We face a thousand choices every day. Even if it's only how to lie well." He took another swig of beer.

Sass relented and told him her tentative cover story. The enemy gave her pointers. She didn't offer him a second beer. Within the hour, Marshal Clay Rocha was gone.

She almost regretted that. Would it be so bad to get drunk and reminisce about Earth with Clay? She doubted there were a dozen left who remembered Earth. Maybe take a friendly tumble in bed with a well-knit man instead of a weak and lanky settler, gone long and stringy from the wrong gravity.

No. The damned man still got her hackles up.

4

Mahina was among the least Earth-like of the first Diaspora colony worlds. But its challenges were similar to Ganymede, one of Jupiter's moons in the Earth system. Ganymede's experience gave Mahina's terraformers a leg up. Sadly, no records survive from Ganymede.

"Let me give you the tour!" Sass tried for bouncy enthusiasm. She hadn't expected two of them. Her new business partner Abel Greer arrived at the skyship with a wife in tow.

"Oh, mercy, it's so *b—!*" Jules Greer said, cornflower blue eyes wide as saucers above a bony face splattered with splotchy freckles.

Big, Sass expected she meant. Instead the ship's Earth-normal gravity added to the gawky girl's personal grav generator. Almost two *g*'s slammed her to the cargo bay floor at the top of the ramp.

"Ah, sorry, I should have thought to mention that," Sass apologized. Or someone should have told her, if Jules didn't know any better. Sass's opinion was that her husband was that someone. "I forget sometimes and do it myself." That was a lie.

Stolid Abel offered a hand up to his young wife. He looked 35 years old to Sass, which probably put him around 25. The girl looked more like 15, just past that shooting-up stage. Hopefully she was at least 18. *Don't judge.*

Jules wasn't fazed in the least. *"Woot!* My brother and I did that once! Put on both our generators to see what it felt like. He threw up and passed out! I was fine, though. Til Pa caned us for taking our generators off." Jules grinned ear to ear from her misadventure, displaying pronounced dimples and buck teeth. "Don't you worry, Miz Captain Collier. I'm sure to get space legs! I've always been agile!"

Jules Greer looked agile as a newborn colt. And they were parked in a hay field, not in space. Sass's false smile grew rather fixed. "Abel, you didn't mention..." *A wife.* "Never mind. So this is the cargo bay."

With a solid muscular build almost unknown among settlers, and methodical ways, Abel Greer seemed the antithesis of his wife. His tawny skin and black hair and features spoke of well-mingled Earth ancestry, unlike the pale Sass and Jules. He frowned worriedly around the two-story reclining cylinder of the hold. Partly two-story. A rusty catwalk ran above them to connect the living spaces. The cabin space cut into the hold like a gallery on the port side of the ship.

"This isn't much volume." He squinted at the overhead. "How do we secure cargo?"

Sass shrugged. "In practice, this is all living space and storage. Normally cargo comes in shipping containers. We latch the ship on top of them and take off."

"Oh! And then we have all this room." Abel said, brow lowered as he thought it through. "Wait. Does the gravity extend to the containers below?"

"Nope," Sass confirmed with a grin. "Still have the mass to control, but only the moon's one-sixth g to lift against."

Mahina's gravity was somewhat higher than Earth's moon, but still rounded to one-sixth. Originally the coincidence surprised Sass, but apparently there were other moons of similar size in Earth's system, too. Gravity seemed to favor balls of this diameter.

"Outstanding. Wait — can't we just reverse the gravity?"

"Um, why?" Sass asked.

Abel patiently explained, "If you extend negative gravity to the cargo, you nullify the moon's pull, and only have to overcome inertia. To steer the cargo."

"Oh." That cast a glimmer of insight onto a certain section of the owner's manual, about grav tractors. Sass only skimmed that part on first reading. "I'll send you the manual. But yeah. The ship is space-capable. They said. I haven't tested that part yet. Only space-capable to the orbital, though, really. We'd need an engine upgrade to go anywhere except on a slow ballistic trajectory."

Abel blinked. "A what?"

"It would take years to reach another planet. Unless we upgrade the drive." She hoped to do that someday.

Jules swirled in her cotton calico dress, head back to soak in the grungy ambiance. But apparently she was listening. "How long have you had this ship, Miz Captain Collier?"

"Dawn before last," Sass admitted. Ten days. "I've only flown it three times so far."

Jules spun to a stop, a beatific smile stretching ear to ear to showcase her buck teeth. "Abel, you hear?"

Abel cleared his throat. "That's, um, the day we were wed."

"You've been married a week and a half?" Sass replied in astonishment. Her eyes narrowed. "How old are you, Jules?"

"Fifteen years, ma'am," Jules assured her. "I'm old enough to wed."

"I meant to marry her next year," Abel muttered guiltily. "But her father took away her grav generator when she...reached womanhood. Shot up 10 centimeters between visits. Stretch marks all over."

Jules pecked a kiss on his cheek. She was a couple centimeters taller than him. "I'm powerful glad to have my grav back. And I couldn't ask for a better husband!"

Don't judge, Sass implored herself. "An arranged marriage?"

"Our fathers, yeah," Abel confirmed. "I've known Jules all her life." He smiled warmly at his lanky teen bride. "I'm a lucky man."

Sass was persuaded. However bizarre it felt to her, the couple seemed authentically bonded, and fond of each other.

"Don't worry, Sass," Abel assured her. "Jules is young, but accomplished. Our families have a strong work ethic. She learned her skills and numbers."

Jules gave an exaggerated nod.

"And what is your career, Jules?" Sass asked. She wondered what she might have answered at 15. Certainly not *'I want to be a cop.'* Definitely not *'I want to leave Earth and colonize a moon unfit to live on.'*

Jules grinned and grabbed Abel's arm firmly. "I'm a wife, ma'am! Trained and ready."

Wife. Not a job description Sass expected to budget for.

"She'll be all kinds of help around the ship," Abel promised. "Cleaning, cooking."

"Right." Sass decided it was time to change the subject. "This way to the engine room. It's bright. So we keep dark goggles by the door for everyone on the ship. Even passengers. That's a law."

They affixed eye protection from a rack by the door. Then Sass opened the steel door to her favorite section of the ship.

Jules clapped her hands in delight. "It's like a jungle in here!" She waded in, arm shifting a fall of cucumber vine out of her way.

"If you don't grow crops," Sass explained, "the waste light just turns to waste heat. So why not? Jules, the dwarf fruit trees are to the left. Don't get too close to the 'sun.'"

A six inch red band was painted on the deck, with raised rivets, circling the star drive in the middle. Jules nudged a rivet with her toe. "That's what this is?"

"Right. Inside that line, you need to wear one of these white suits, and the face mask. Even outside the line, you need sunblock to spend much time in here. And never skip the sun goggles. Looking into the engine core is worse than the sun. It'll blind you."

Jules nodded solemn understanding. She resumed studying the magnificent bounty of crops, with a few ornamentals thrown in. "We can't eat all this! May I?"

Sass waved for her to go ahead. "Sorry, I left my picking basket in the galley."

She eyed the cucumber vine warily. Last time she was in here, it wasn't blocking the door, nor bearing fruit. It must have grown a meter since she left the farm.

"Well, there's a little income," Abel said. "Sell the surplus. We don't have an engineer to maintain this, right?"

"They said it was pretty easy," Sass said. "I've got the instructions. And you said you've worked with machines?"

"Commercial extruders," Abel confirmed. "That's the family business."

Sass nodded doubtfully. "I guess I've always programmed my own extruders."

Extrusion was the dominant building technology on Mahina, both foamcrete and plasglass. There was no shortage of wood. Sass's farm buildings were mostly built from that. But carpentry took skill and effort. Extruding a building was simple and cheap. You stapled down a foundation, provided a fairly small pile of raw materials, then let the programmed robot go to work. The resulting structure was inherently insulated, formed mostly of air.

Abel grimaced. "Yeah. Most people do. My sister bought me out of the company. That's most of the money I'm investing."

Sass nodded enlightenment. Her eye caught on a tomato plant. A cucumber growing a meter in a day was extreme. But the tomato adding a half meter was downright disconcerting. "Jules? Maybe this could be one of your jobs. Keep the crops picked. And pruned. I can show you how." She wasn't sure how well the ventilation would work if the plants became overgrown.

"Will do, Miz Captain Collier!"

"Just Sass," Sass invited. "Or captain."

"Yes, ma'am, captain!"

"The bridge?" Abel suggested.

"And the kitchen!" Jules added with enthusiasm.

After depositing their goggles, Sass drew them through the rest of the ship. The auto-doc medical bay was reassuringly thorough, if awfully white and clinical, tucked near the engine room. Eight cabins perched atop the cargo hold. The forward half each sported their own compact washroom facilities, and the four at the back sharing, two cabins per bath. Two of those were equipped with four bunks apiece. The owner's cabin had the largest bed.

"I guess this'll be yours," Sass said brightly. "I'll move my stuff."

"Or we could get a bigger bed for..." Abel opened the door across the way from Sass's new room, the one she intended for him. Some unfortunately placed support beams prevented any wider bed in there. "I see."

Sass shrugged. "The other two upscale cabins I thought we might rent out sometimes. This is fine for me." She hoped she was done spending time alone. Whereas the newlyweds would want plenty of time in their cabin.

The galley, dining area, and lounge were inserted between the upscale and downscale cabins, with a floor laid across the steel grating that formed most of the upper walkways. The bridge in front was a tight fit, with two seats and a map table, and a wraparound window over the control panels. The 'captain's ready room' Sass had already declared 'the office,' as much Abel's as hers.

"And that's the interior," Sass concluded. She gulped. If he backed out —

"We love it!" Jules cried. "Don't we, Abel?"

Abel turned puppy dog eyes at his exuberant baby giraffe of a wife. Sass tamped down a grin. The man was besotted. So was Sass. She hungered to have these young people in her life, with a burning intensity. To them this was fresh and new and full of potential. Life hadn't trained them yet not to get their hopes up before it crushed them like a bug.

"Say yes, Abel," the captain breathed. "I'd show you the business plans. But they're a blank canvas, ours to write together."

With difficulty, he peeled his eyes off his bride and turned back to Sass. "Due diligence. Let's see her fly. And then put together the balance sheets. But so far...yes. If the money is what we said online. We love the skyship."

Jules whooped and threw her arms around him.

Sass's grin of delight escaped. She held out a hand to shake with Abel. And a partnership was born.

The couple's maiden flight around town in *Thrive* was sheer fun. Abel couldn't try out the co-pilot controls because his bouncing wife was on his lap shrieking in glee.

The books were every bit as blank as Sass promised. She had no idea how to run a business. One of her co-convicts set up the accounts for the farm. She didn't dare risk any more capital to finish buying the skyship without a partner. She'd offered him a tenth ownership. Business affairs were up to him. It was an incredible opportunity for such a young man.

His due diligence did turn up a couple minor glitches.

"You didn't buy the business as a going concern? Like, the customers along with the skyship?"

"I don't think he had any customers left," Sass admitted. "He retired."

"And our cash reserves?" the prospective first mate asked. "I've got six months' personal expenses. This is a real stretch for us."

Sass figured in her head. "Personal expenses? I should have a couple years left over."

"The tank is full?"

The ship ran on water and reagents. The dry chemicals were poured into a hopper. But close enough. "Almost full. Should get about 50 more flying hours without a refill. Depending on how heavy, of course."

"That's tight." Abel frowned. "Your reserves are after taxes, right?"

Sass's heart skipped a beat. "Taxes?" *What taxes?*

"The title transfer and registration. Five percent."

Sass pressed her hands against the edge of the work table. She pushed her chair back. She blew out. She considered. The seconds ticked by, while Abel gazed at her in earnest concern.

It took her twenty years farm labor with five strong adults to save up 20% of the price of *Thrive*. Compound interest supplied the rest of her share, from her savings on her previous forty years salary as a marshal. Abel leveraged his entire young life, plus a sister willing to buy him out of his inheritance, to amass 10%.

"That's a problem," Sass allowed.

They had only five cycles to solve that problem — 35 days.

5

The terraformers of Mahina — the moon's founders — built an enclosed city for 30,000. Atmosphere generation was on target to generate a breathable atmosphere within 150 years.

"Soybeans?" Sass repeated, with a marked lack of enthusiasm. She twirled the tail of her straw-colored hair, corralled as usual into a sloppy French braid.

"There's an opportunity," Abel claimed. He opened a scratch worksheet on the table display in the office. "The urbs have a monopoly on transporting crops to the food factory."

By urbs, he meant Mahina's ruling class, the citizens of the moon's largest city of Mahina Actual. The 'Actual' part distinguished the original moon base camp from Mahina Orbital.

"The urbs are the only buyer," Sass pointed out. "They can collect it at your bin. Or they can buy it at the factory. They're still the buyer."

The soy factory crushed the beans and processed them to produce half their food supply — oil, faux meats, livestock feed, protein components of other foods, the works. The urbs had tech that could build nutrients from inorganic components. But soybean plants were more efficient at converting sunlight and soil into organic compounds. Besides, farming gave the settlers something to do.

Abel shook his head, confident of his calculations. "They charge too much."

Under farm arrest, Sass never had the option to transport her own. But some freeholders did it — piled the harvest onto the family truck and carted load after load to the collection silos, to bypass the transport fees.

She was diverted by the cryptic labels on his worksheet, mostly icons and audio buttons. "Could you label those? I can't tell what you've taken into account."

"I can't read and write. I mean, visually," Abel confessed. "It's going to take me a long time to listen to the ship instruction manual."

"Ah." Of course. Children weren't taught to read on Mahina. Why bother when the computers did it for you?

Sass demonstrated how to make the computer transcribe those audio labels and insert readable text next to them, so they could both read the accounts easily. This kept her entirely distracted from the important point.

Abel's math was wrong.

THE FIRST EXPENSE Abel neglected was the boxes. The factory flyers used standard steel shipping containers for this purpose, 2.5 by 2.5 by 6 meters.

A seasoned extruder professional, Abel could build a box of equivalent size and strength, and somewhat less volume, with thick foamcrete.

His sister gave him a pallet of opaque foamcrete and transparent plasglass mix for free. Just add water. They had enough reagent to build a replica of the Taj Mahal or a 20-story skyscraper.

Hardware fittings cost extra, of course.

He built his first container at the standard large size, twice as long at 12 meters. But he wasn't upset when Sass assured him that yes, there was a reason for the 6 meter half size. They couldn't mix beans from different farms, in case the shipment was declined.

Abel gazed at her stricken. "If the factory declines, we need to bring the beans back to the farmer? I guess I need to add that to the contract terms." And most containers would be partly empty.

Sass nodded sadly, and thought about it. "Actually, we should inspect the beans. Not accept them in the first place if they might be rejected. The factory transports bring along a buyer agent from the factory to inspect on pickup."

"I'll look into it," Abel promised. He was the business guy.

"I can finish the container," Sass offered, freeing him to attend to that small thing.

Chopping the long box in half was straightforward enough. Measure carefully, mark the corners, set a device to apply the dissolving agent. For all Sass knew, foamcrete might be a soy product itself. But as she worked, an unease grew that she was forgetting something.

As she kicked the pair of boxes apart, the first obvious thing was that her containers needed doors. And a bulkhead to hold in the beans. Because a standard container door went all the way to the bottom of the box. Well, for today maybe she could just build a solid wall on the thing, with an opening at the top to load beans through.

Load beans...

"Can I share the extruder, captain?" Jules interrupted. "I don't want to get in your way."

"Um, sure," Sass said, losing her train of thought. "What are you making?"

"A vegetable stand! By Dawn, we should have plenty to sell. Peaches and strawberries, too."

Today was golden Glow, the mottled yellow gas giant full and bright above them in the night. Most people had the day off, like Sunday back on Earth. At any rate, the darker half-gas 24-hour periods bracketing Glow were named Saturday and Monday, with Monday the start to a business week that ended at sunset on Dusk. Dawn was the day after Monday, two days from now. Dawn's actual sunrise occurred in the wee hours after midnight, pretty much ignored in favor of sleeping.

"A vegetable stand. What a great idea! Thank you, Jules."

No, a couple days' worth of engine vegetables wouldn't make a dent on the tax problem. But it might cover the hardware expenses. Sass got busy explaining to the extruder how to finish squirting out her door side onto the boxes. Once she got that going, Jules kept them entertained designing her stand, a variation on the basic hollow mushroom floor plan, with a 270-degree counter flange at waist height to showcase the produce. The mushroom top provided shelter and pizazz. A wall for the back third would protect the money. They'd cut a door on that side.

Sass completely lost her train of thought.

Abel came back hangdog. "I found an inspector who's willing to work after hours. But he wants time and a half. And he doesn't bring his soy meter home at night. Renting the tester will cost as much as the guy. I couldn't find any for sale."

"No, you wouldn't," Sass agreed. "There's a meter built in to the grain bin at the farm for moisture levels. Color, texture, insects, mold — you check that by eye. Then the meter applies the soy factory acceptance tests. The urbs don't publish specs for that. They don't want people to cheat the test."

And there was something else... Well, it would come to her later. "Abel, I've got a bad feeling about this."

He stubbornly shook his head. "We have to try it. The first run might not be as profitable as we'd like. But we'll identify the snags and improve."

"Why do you want to do this so much?" Sass asked, dubious.

"We need a bread and butter operation," Abel explained. "Something that might be low margin, but dependable. It pays the bills. Besides, we're committed. I've already scheduled a pickup tomorrow evening, and the inspector. We meet him at the factory at quitting time."

Sass noted that this added a bonus trip to their fuel costs. "So we collect soybeans and hold them til the factory reopens on Dawn?" That was the day after Monday.

"Because they don't accept delivery after hours." Abel sighed. "Of course they don't. Well, maybe when we've got the bugs worked out, they'll trust the inspector we paid so much for, and we can just leave the container..."

Sass and Abel dolefully came to the same conclusion, as they regarded the container. That wouldn't happen anytime soon.

Abel murmured, "The profit margin here might be a little..."

"Little," Sass confirmed. "The vegetable stand is coming out nice, though, huh? Jules is doing a great job."

"Is that what that is?" Abel tilted his head, then frowned. He considered the cargo ramp. "Um, sweetie? That's so clever, and really pretty. But could you pause the extruder a moment? I need to check something."

Yes, in fact the mushroom cap was too tall to fit through the cargo hatch upright, and too wide to roll on its side. Fortunately, the extruder was still working on the counters. Abel narrowed the canopy parameters for ease of rolling, and handed the extruder control back to his wife with an indulgent smile. "This'll be great, Jules! You're so clever."

Jules nodded emphatically, proud of his praise for being a clever and frugal wife. "And your sister gave us a bag of paint mix, too. She's so kind!"

Abel perhaps had a different perspective on his sister's generosity. "Or you could leave it plain."

"The raw foamcrete is kind of mushroom-colored," Sass mused. Indeed, without any pricey additives, the basic foamcrete was a slightly tan shade of light grey. Perhaps that's why an extruder came with a hollow mushroom design pre-loaded into its repertoire. Every house with children seemed to feature toadstool seats. Most were painted with gaudy polka-dots on the cap.

"Trust me!" Jules returned. "Bet I'll surprise you!"

6

Earth's emergency exodus saddled Mahina with a quarter million settlers only 42 years into their 150 year terraforming plan. The atmosphere was not yet breathable.

A conveyor belt. That's what Sass forgot. The first small farmer they visited on Monday didn't own one.

Eventually Sass imagined they'd have all sorts of handy spare equipment lying around *Thrive,* pumps and hoses and widgets. But she didn't have anything that could pinch-hit to scoop soybeans out of a bin and transport them into a shipping container. Well-to-do farmers installed them to hang from the barn roof on travelers, so they could shift the belt to service a number of bins. Factory flyers used a clever folding arm.

Abel returned the farmer's deposit and apologized for the over-sight. He called around the other farmers they hoped to service this evening — approaching sunrise. Neither had a conveyor belt. But a large client for Dawn was equipped and willing to ship his beans early.

"He said they should be dry enough?" Abel told Sass.

Qadir, the lanky rental inspector, chimed in. "What's the name?"

"Essen," Abel supplied.

Qadir pursed his lips and shook his head, but didn't explain. And they flew to Essen's farm.

"They're dry enough!" farmer Essen insisted, when Qadir found his beans barely within tolerance.

Qadir slammed the little testing door shut, and pushed the button to stir the bin, which bounced and rumbled beside them.

"What's the issue?" Abel asked Sass worriedly.

"Above 15% moisture content, soybeans rot in storage." Sass kept her voice low to avoid Essen taking umbrage. "And they're paid by dry weight."

Qadir let off the mixing button. The bin sighed and rustled to rest. He tapped on the digital readout. "Too wet." He opened the access port and sniffed. "If I were you, I'd get these laid out to dry right now."

"I should have gone to bed an hour ago!" Essen hollered at him.

Qadir snorted. "While your beans rot. You keep making the same damned mistake, Essen."

The *Thrive* contingent retreated into the ship, the farmer still hurling imprecations at them. Abel tried calling the farmer he'd lined up for Wednesday, day after tomorrow, and caught her asleep. This time he understood when she groggily explained that her beans weren't dry yet.

Daybreak began to lighten the horizon. Sass hurriedly dropped Qadir off home. Abel paid him a full day's wage plus rental on the meter he never used.

Sass hopped the ship to the factory parking lot nearby, and dropped the cargo ramp as a horizontal shelf. She stepped outside and took a seat, danging her legs a couple meters above the ground, yawning mightily, to watch a bit of the approaching sunrise before bed.

Abel forgot the gravity gradient when he stepped out to join her. His firm stride bounced him off the ramp onto the raw regolith below, unterraformed moon rock. He sheepishly hopped back up and took a seat beside her.

"I could change the terms of service," he suggested. "Require a conveyor belt and dry beans before pickup."

Sass counted their days of effort, and cash outlay on fuel and Qadir, and winced. "Are we losing money if we do the next farmer?"

"About a thousand profit," Abel replied. "After the fuel and inspector. Not very good wages," Abel allowed. "But some."

Sass rose and bopped him on the shoulder.

"Sass? There's a finicky detail to trip us up in every industry, isn't there?" Abel looked up at her sad and vulnerable, reminding her how young he was. This was only his second career.

"Every job I've seen. We'll find better margins somewhere. Sleep well, Abel."

———

"IT'S A PEACH!" Jules explained to a small boy at the mushroom produce counter. "A fruit, sweet and juicy. I have samples, if it's alright with your Pa."

"I'd love a sample," the father agreed, stooped to fit under the mushroom cap awning. Nearly 3 stringy meters tall, clearly he shunned a grav generator for himself, though his boy wore one.

Jules gave them each a tiny sliver of ripe peach, and a bonus sliver of strawberry besides. "If you buy at least ten credits, you can use the slide for free. Peaches are three apiece, strawberries three for two credits."

The slide had some stair bits and parapets mixed in. The route caromed from an empty container set on end, down off the mushroom, and into the taller hay beside the mown market field. Jules played with the extruder during lulls in traffic.

Sass set down a crate of produce and watched her operate. The captain and Abel were stuck in the office studying before their soybean run after supper, trying to find that better opportunity.

"Lordy!' Jules exclaimed, after she settled up with the customer. She poked through the new box, finding ripe little tomatoes and cucumbers aplenty, over a dozen pears, and more lettuce and spinach. "Is this just from today?"

"My plants like that engine room," Sass agreed. "How's business?"

"Booming!" Jules said proudly.

Another couple kids thumped to a landing on the mushroom cap before banking away for the final slide into the hay. The women cringed and laughed.

"We take off in a half hour," Sass warned her. "Need help to close up shop?"

"I'll stay open to sell this!" Jules insisted. "Thank you! Just go when you need to. Don't worry about me!"

Soon they took off to pick up the inspector and his gadget, and found the next farm.

"Perfect as always, Willow," Qadir assured the client, showing her the readout on his soy quality tester. "You sure grow a fine soybean," he crooned.

"Still not looking, Qadir," the fit and forty Willow returned wryly. "Husband just bit the bucket last year. I've barely begun to enjoy life as a widow."

Sass grinned. She recalled a couple inspiring breakups along the way. No one to clean up after was a powerful aphrodisiac.

"Are we ready to load up?" Abel asked eagerly.

Qadir scowled at him for spiking his flirt.

Willow looked puzzled. "Load up now? Deliver tomorrow?" She folded her arms and looked over the extruded containers *Thrive* perched atop, like a mama hen on a clutch of socially awkward eggs, all corners. "How do you ventilate the boxes?" She asked Sass, correctly assessing Abel as clueless. Willow was a bright one, with a firm hand on farm management.

"It's only over—" *Overnight*, Sass began to say. But it was late Dawn, heading into Wednesday. The factory wouldn't open until 0800, twelve hours of sun from now. She sighed.

"I'm up by oh-six," Willow consoled her. "C'mon back then and load up. My beans will be the same, if they stay in the bin."

"Right, oh-six," Sass agreed, and firmly shook the fellow farmer's hand. "Sorry for the hassle, Willow."

"It's all good. Bound to be a few kinks to work out on a new job."

They waved good-bye, and dropped Qadir home.

"Sass," Abel asked, "you did say the factory's cut is 28%, right?"

"Yup, 28% at pickup," Sass confirmed. "What did you say on the contract?"

"A 25% discount on factory pickup charges."

Sass should have known better.

BY THE TIME they made it back, Jules was sold out. She'd made a friend to sit on top of the mushroom shop with, all laughs and smiles.

He was a male friend, compact and well-knit and looking about Abel's age, dressed in fine clothes like an urb. Sass trailed Abel onto the field to help wrangle the mushroom.

"Abel!" Jules called with enthusiasm. She clambered promptly onto the final leg of the slide.

Abel managed barely to reach the bottom of the slide in time to catch her in his arms. He drew her sideways and let her new friend in his fancy pants land on his butt.

"Meet Eli Rasmussen! Eli, this is my handsome husband, Abel Greer. And that's our handsome captain, Sass Collier!"

"Beautiful captain," Abel suggested. "Handsome is for —"

Eli ignored his words and stuck out a hand to shake firmly. "Sir, ma'am, I'd love to see your garden. Jules told me you grew this fine produce in your engine room."

Abel crossed his arms and regarded the dandy. "You don't look like a gardener."

Too right, Sass thought. *He looks like an urb. A dork of an urb, too.* A sizable luggage box waited patiently by the mushroom, which struck her as odd. But she smiled brightly. "I suppose we can give you a tour. We need to pack up first, though."

Through sheer lack of talent, Eli carried a crate of the shop trays and utensils, while Jules steered his baggage into the hold and brought the cash box. Sass and Abel manhandled the mushroom.

They considered recycling the slide.

"But wouldn't it be fun to keep?" Jules urged. "An express route from the catwalk to the hold!"

Sass figured newlywed Abel was incapable of saying no to his teen bride while a perceived rival looked on. "I'll just lock up your cash box for you until after supper, Jules," she offered. She trotted away on that errand. Abel could handle the foamcrete slicing and carry in the slide himself.

He showed off his mastery of power tools by affixing the longer carton-to-mushroom section of the slide to the catwalk. Meanwhile Sass moved the ship, kicked the spare container back into position among the quartet, then grappled on and parked the chicken on its eggs again. So to speak.

Jules drew Eli into the kitchen to help her clean the trays and all the dirty pans she'd left in the sink. After breakfast, she'd baked four fruit cobblers to sell alongside the produce. The galley was still a wreck.

Done moving the ship, Sass leaned on the catwalk rail to watch Abel's progress. The slide in the middle would be kind of handy. The stairs lay at either end of the hold, the forward set more of a steep ladder. But the galley was here in the middle.

Abel kept the railing unaltered. He demonstrated to the captain that it was plenty strong to swing under, to launch into the chute with momentum.

"Jules?" Abel called. "Your slide awaits! Ready for the debut ride?"

"Yay!" Jules yelled. She barreled out of the kitchen at a run, to dive under the railing, arms outstretched to ride belly down, face forward.

Abel's mouth hung open. Eli trotted from behind to reach the railing between the captain and first mate. Fortunately Jules had built a high bank on the sharpest curve, which flipped her over onto her back. She used the second bank to rise and pivot on her butt. Then she was feet forward instead of head first. She still smacked into the raised cargo ramp at full speed at the bottom with a mighty *THUNK*.

"Woot!" Jules cried. "Perfect, honey! Ow. You've got to try it!" She laughed out loud.

"After you," Sass invited Abel. Eli nodded, bemused.

Abel solemnly swung himself under the railing — which was strong enough — and used that momentum to slide halfway to the first bank. Where he came to a stop. He took a few scoots to get moving again. Then he shrugged and hopped off the side, flicking his gravity generator for a placid landing.

"Huh," said Jules, and enveloped him in a hug. "Awesome job on the slide, honey! Just how I wanted!"

Sass turned to Eli. "Getting late. Want that tour of the engine garden?"

"Yes I would," Eli told her, with an emphatic nod. "I should probably protect my good pants."

Sass nodded, and turned for the ladder. But Eli changed his mind and shot the chute, feet first, caroming even better than Jules had, for a resounding *THUNK.*

"Oh, what the hell." Sass stepped back to the kitchen, and hit the slide top going even faster than Jules, taking the ride on her back. Eli had used one half antigrav to counter the ship's field, his best guess at Jules' technique. Sass tried it at 40%, and hit the cargo ramp the fastest yet with a *THUNK.*

She also broke her finger. She surreptitiously tugged it straight before getting up and dusting herself off.

Eli held out a hand to pull her up, with a glance to her broken finger, and a sympathetic smile. He limped himself, but only for a step or two. Of course. His body carried a nanite suite, too, though of a far more recent and legal design.

"I won't tell," he murmured, too low to carry to Abel and Jules. "I really am very excited to see your garden." His eyes were alight.

Dammit. The last thing Sass needed was someone who knew her secret.

7

Earth settlers outnumbered the 'urbs' of Mahina Actual by a factor of eight. The city could not, and would not, accept them. Urbs and settlers got off to a bad start.

"Fabulous," Eli breathed. He stepped backward to better behold the plum tree.

Sass hauled him forward again. That was the second time her guest had stepped into the engine's no-go circle. "You'll get a burn if you..."

She didn't bother to finish the sentence. She wouldn't take a burn from that engine. Probably Eli wouldn't either. Their nanites would repair any damage so fast they'd never notice. She supposed it was possible to commit suicide by plastering herself onto the core. More likely she'd black out from the pain and wake on the floor when the worst was healed, the front half of her clothes burned off. Embarrassing but hardly fatal.

"Of course, thank you," Eli said earnestly.

The settlers suspected, but didn't know for sure that the urbs were self-healing, practically immortal. At first, Sass thought it impossible to keep such a secret. Yet rational people who had a nanite suite

49

wouldn't tell a mortal like Abel and Jules. Which left only lunatics spewing the secrets, advantages, and abuses of the urbs. People with sense didn't believe them.

Sass told her fellow inmates at the farm. They didn't believe her either. Time cured that.

"I see why you put the plants in here," Eli mused. "Obvious, really. But where did you get the fruit trees? And what are you feeding them?"

"I have a fertilizer I tweaked."

"I should mention I'm a botanist," Eli clarified. "Geneticist."

Sass adjusted her vocabulary accordingly. "Standard NPK hydroponic components, my own custom mix. The pH tailored for each species. Plus chicken manure and fish meal. I never quite trust the scientists to add all the trace components, you know? It got too oxygen-rich in my greenhouse, so I added a CO_2 burner, and brought that along. Oxygenate the nutrients. A lot of tweaks, really."

Eli regarded her wide-eyed.

"What?"

"You're very good at this," he mused.

"I've had a very lot of practice," Sass retorted. "Still. This engine light must have some universal magic beanstalk spectrum to spark this kind of growth. I've never seen anything like it."

"How long have they been in here?"

"Just a couple weeks. Or one. Took a while to set up before I left the farm."

"And you didn't get these results before? In a greenhouse?"

"No," Sass replied. "I always thought the plants grew faster at night, under lights. And I kept adjusting the spectrum. But nothing like this."

"And the fruit trees? Where did you get them?" Eli pressed, his voice too soft for the Greers to overhear.

"Here and there," Sass said quellingly.

Eli spun on her decisively. "Captain Collier, Jules tells me you have extra rooms. I would like very much to stay with you. I was looking for, ah, a place to rent. And use of your grow room."

Sass narrowed her eyes at him. "That's odd." Used to be, the urbs stayed in Mahina Actual. Aside from the marshals, they didn't mix. The marshals were settlers who enjoyed city privileges. Would that have changed?

Puzzlement flickered across Eli's brow. "Is it?"

"How much rent?" Abel pounced. He and Jules had hung back, but he happily waded in for a money discussion.

"Whatever is appropriate." Eli scratched his nose bashfully. "I don't have a lot. Would a thousand credits a month do?" Four weeks equaled a month on Mahina — 13 of them to the Earth-length year.

"Yes," Sass and Abel agreed promptly. A thousand credits was the average person's take-home pay for a month.

"Payable in advance?" Abel suggested.

"Yes, of course. Oh, wonderful!"

"Let's have supper and celebrate, then!" Sass herded them out of the engine room. Last to leave, she shot a puzzled last glance around the rampant growth. She wouldn't mind a scientist's opinion on this. And he'd even pay for the privilege. *Silly urb.*

While Jules rustled up a late supper, Sass and Abel showed Eli the six available cabins. A thousand credits grew to seventeen hundred in rent, as Eli decided what he really wanted was the two single-bunk cabins with a shared bath sandwiched between, for a bedroom plus lab suite.

He was overjoyed to hear that they intended to move around, not in the same town from cycle to cycle, or even day to day. Sass and Abel were overjoyed to pocket the rent, and scheming already to rent out more cabins. Jules laid on an excellent quick meal of soy bacon cheeseburgers and potato fries with a salad.

Eli retired to unpack in his quarters. Sass promised to freshen the paint or linens or whatever he needed. She never did get the story of why exactly an urb botanist happened to be in a settler market field with his worldly goods made portable.

She had her secrets. He had his. Her business partner Abel thought her lack of questions was odd, but she was the boss.

Including the new boarder, Jules' take for the day came to over 3,000 credits. So far, Sass and Abel racked up 150 in costs.

AFTER GETTING to bed late on Dawn, they were up by 05:30 to load farmer Willow's soybeans. This was a dusty, itchy affair in the hot Wednesday sun, sweating in goggles and scarves.

Sass was pleased to waste only a few bushels on her learning curve. Less pleased with the two hours it took.

They took off in wilted triumph and landed in the inspection line already formed in the factory parking lot. Qadir cut them a break and carried out his official inspection within the hour.

But there was a hitch again. Of course. The way they normally dumped beans into the elevator was to open the container door, slide up the bulkhead, and let the contents drain from the bottom of the container. Sass had only built a filling aperture, not a pouring one. Unable to rotate the box upside-down without strewing beans everywhere, they'd have to position the container for drainage, then cut a hole. Twice, since they had two boxes from Willow.

Qadir apologetically requested that they wait for lunchtime, instead of tying everyone else up.

By half past one, they'd managed to dump their haul. Jules captured terrific video footage of Sass and Abel looking like fools dangling from ropes to cut a hole in the container. Abel flipped upside down at one point.

At last, they proceeded to the office to settle up. The factory buyer simply pressed a button to transfer the money to Willow's supplier ID.

"Don't I get a receipt?" Abel asked. He hadn't even seen the credit amounts on her terminal.

"Not your beans," the lanky woman replied. "Next!"

Sass yanked Abel's arm before he could argue. "Settle up with Willow instead. Call her."

"But aren't we entitled to —"

"No," Sass stated categorically. As a farmer the past 20 years, she identified with Willow. "Let's get out of here."

By the time Abel finished eating lunch, the farmer had headed into town to celebrate her harvest pay. And not just any podunk market town, either — she planned to party up a storm in Mahina Actual. No, she couldn't access her accounts from the settler arcade. But she should be home by Eclipse. No, she wouldn't send Abel her financial statement. But they were welcome to drop by for a drink.

The torpid heat and sun exposure of late Wednesday — the hottest segment of the week-long true day — combined with frustration and short hours on sleep. Sass and Abel sank into a long nap before dinner and lingered over coffee to chat desultorily with Eli and Jules.

These two were delighted with each other. Eli staked out a 10-degree arc of the star engine's plant zone for his very own. Jules helped there, as well as redecorating Eli's rooms to his pleasure. Apparently she'd plied the extruder to create the wet lab bench of his dreams. They planned to feed and drain it with garden hoses from his bathroom.

Sass was amused. Abel not so much.

At last, Sass banked the ship to park by Willow's fancifully extruded squat tree house just before the sun blinked out.

The mercifully cooling hours of Eclipse were among Sass's favorite of the cycle. Most settlers scurried home before Mahina's brief true night. Sass enjoyed the darkening azure light as a few pale stars slowly appeared against dark indigo velvet. Even after all these years on Mahina, she slept best during Eclipse.

She was glad Abel could walk easily in the creepy submarine gloom. Some settlers were unnerved by the darkness, or malnourished so their eyes went bad.

The two stepped up and knocked on the good solid wood door, made of spruce no doubt. The landscape's aspen trees were no good for lumber. Or much of anything else, so far as Sass could tell, aside from relief from unbroken spruce.

"Hello, hello!" Willow's sunburnt cheeks glowed with radioactive intensity, and she hung onto the door for support. "Come in! Drink before office?"

"Business first," Abel suggested, before Sass could accept.

Willow weaved along the entry way to the core of her tree house. A spiral staircase led to the private stories above, with an express fire-pole down the middle. Beyond lay her office, a generous semicircle of the trunk opening to the left. Shopping bags from her splurge in Mahina Actual still lay in a heap off to the right.

The farmer plonked into her master control chair. "Alrighty. So here's the payout."

She turned the desk screen upside-down from her so all three could look at the document. Abel's eyes lit up at the size of her paycheck. Sass was also impressed. Willow did almost as well as she had on her last soy harvest.

"That's the taxes, and there's the delivery discount, four-eighty credits. I owe you three hundred sixty credits. That was the deal, right?"

"What..." Abel's finger stabbed rudely in the line above, an order of magnitude larger. "I thought we got three quarters of that."

Willow clucked her tongue and chuckled. "*That,* my cutie, is taxes for four months. Ain't nothing to do with delivery. The factory just confiscates it the second I get paid, like wages. This line is the delivery discount. Here you go." She clicked a button and deposited the measly three-sixty credits into *Thrive*'s company bank account. Where it pinged for Abel's attention on its modest contribution.

"Pleasure doing business with you. How about that drink?" Willow lurched toward the spiral stairs.

Abel tried to beg off. But Sass followed up the stairs. "Really kind of you, Willow, to help us work out the kinks. You were our first delivery."

Willow laughed. "And probably last."

"Very likely," Sass agreed. "There's no margin in this, is there?"

"Three trips out to my spread? You're lucky if you break even. And really, I'd hire you again just for giggles."

She lurched to a wood counter between her kitchen and open

living room. These filled the second story of tree trunk. She poured grain alcohol into three chunky crystal glasses, zapped them with an ice wand, and waved to a particolored array of flavorings for her guests to help themselves, tall brilliant vials arranged like a pan flute of test tubes. Willow splashed her own with bourbon flavor, clearly her favorite by the liquid level.

Abel looked dubious. Sass tried 'watermelon.' Nope. That tumbler of alcohol didn't remind her of watermelon in the slightest. But it was strong and sweet and a pretty coral hue.

Willow flopped into a deep couch, and propped her feet on a handy upholstered mushroom — foamcrete below, dark brown with green whorls above, a sophisticated adult version of red polka dots.

Sass selected an armchair nearby and a hard-top orange toadstool for her feet. "Only hire us again for grins and giggles, huh?"

Willow shrugged. "Look, I like you two. But you saved me what, a hundred twenty credits? I blew two hundred celebrating payday. And you spent how much on fuel and that lech Qadir? What's your profit?"

Abel set aside his red-hot cinnamon drink to calculate it out. "Zero. Including the first farmer who didn't have a conveyor belt." In disgust, he took a deep draught of his ruby-red fire drink.

Willow waved that off as inconsequential. "Learning curve."

"Do you get to Mahina Actual often, Willow?" Sass inquired, to socialize before another round of business. No matter how little the farmer missed her late husband, she must get lonely.

"No," Willow replied. "I don't like to risk my truck. It's 50 kilometers to the city. One rock, axle breaks, and I'm in debt again for the damned thing. But a friend borrowed a flier from her delivery gal."

"That's handy," Abel acknowledged.

Enough small talk. "Do you have any other work that would be worth our while?" Sass asked. "Landscaping, maybe?"

"I would fancy a hill." Willow pointed out a window. There loomed the eclipsed dark of the gas giant, outlined by an olive green nimbus. "Right under Pono. That'd be pretty. Got a bid once. Cost like ten thousand. Not that pretty."

"How much would you pay?" Sass followed up.

"Thousand, maybe? Depends on the size of hill I'd get for a thousand. Just the earthmoving, mind. I'd lay my own irrigation grid and plant the trees."

"Right. Maybe add a stream?" Sass suggested.

Willow frowned, perhaps unable to imagine such a thing. "See how I like the hill first."

Sass polished off her watermelon syrup booze in a slug, and thunked the glass down on her toadstool. "Might get back to you on that. Want us to lock up downstairs on our way out? Don't get up."

Willow didn't look capable of getting up. Sass led the way out.

"Do we want to work for her again?" Abel asked. He clung close to Sass, spooked by the dark and trying not to show it. "And can we really build a hill?"

"Need a gunner for that," Sass replied. She hopped up to the cargo ramp and took a seat, feet dangling. "More wages. More fuel."

"You're not a gunner?" Abel asked, claiming a seat beside her more cautiously.

Operating the guns was a parole violation. "Can't. We could hire someone. Maybe they'll want a room." Why had Clay Rocha suggested a gunner, anyway? "How are you coming along reading the manual?"

"About an hour in."

Sass sighed. At spoken speed, the ship's manual could take him a year. If he kept at it. But who would?

"I'll cancel the rest of our pickups in the morning," Abel said, rising cautiously. "If we aren't making money, we're losing it."

"I'll call the guy I bought the ship from. See if he had any clients we might pick up."

Sass stayed out to visit with the stars. A dozen dim ones were visible now.

If there was a legal way to earn enough money with this ship, she didn't see it.

8

Volunteers from near-Earth colonies on the Moon, Mars, and Ganymede formed the Colony Corps. They provided the ships, crews, and expertise for the emergency evacuation of Earth refugees to other star systems. This was a one-way trip.

Kassidy Yang knew how to make an entrance. A camera guy preceded her, a willowy eight-foot settler, walking backwards in his bulging camera goggles, directing a trio of drone outriders to capture other angles.

This commanded the attention of every eye in the grotto restaurant. People craned their necks to see, wondering what was coming.

Then a couple of teen girl bumpkins close by the archway squealed in delight, hands to mouth. They jumped out of their seats in rapture. "Kassidy! Kassidy!" They reached out hoping to touch her.

The star herself loped in grinning. Her face was flawlessly beautiful, of course, a warm blend of old Earth India and Asia with a touch of something angular, maybe from the Middle East or Europe. Huge blue-violet eyes flashed above a full-lipped curving bow of a mouth. A camera dot graced her brow. A mane of glossy black ringlets framed her heart-shaped face, iridescent with rainbows like an oil sheen on a dark puddle. Her lean buffed body, every bit as flawless, moved with an athlete's ease, encased in skin-tight fake leather corset and stretch jeans, likewise oily. She was compact, shorter than Sass, a vibrantly healthy urb without a trace of settler lankiness.

She greeted the two teeny-boppers like long lost sisters, or lovers, rushing to embrace the pair of them. Poses were struck to make sure the cameras got the best angles as she kissed them both, smack on the lips.

By then, other fans rose and surged forward for their turn getting souvenir pictures with the action star. Young or old, male or female, she kissed every one of them on the lips. Half she swung backward over her arm to kiss, men and women alike, Earth-normal shaped urb or attenuated settler.

Sass and Abel rose and stood at their table out of the way to wait. Abel stepped sideways to evade a friendly fern. "I hope she doesn't kiss us like that."

A pet peacock strutted by. The first mate looked uncomfortable with the lush tropical surroundings of the false open-air garden-restaurant. Settlers were barred from most of the city of Mahina Actual. But the shopping plaza lured nearby tourists in to waste their hard-earned money, and granted the illusion of inclusion.

Sass was less impressed by the tourist grotto. As a marshal, she used to keep an apartment inside the city. The scattered potted plants out here were nothing compared to the interior pocket biomes. The air conditioning was subtle. The wait staff was entirely settler. Gravity was turned off. Otherwise visitors who didn't use generators might get hurt, was the argument.

On the other hand, she was tolerably impressed with the video star. Kassidy left each of her fans grinning ear to ear. Now she blew them a final kiss of devotion, and turned to approach her appointment. Sass was relieved to see the camera guy dismissed in her wake.

"Hello, hello!" the star cried, gathering Abel, then Sass, for a smooch. She did not, in fact, kiss them on the lips. But she did smear glossy purple lipstick on their cheeks.

"It's so good to meet you! I feel like I already know you from checking your references. But still. Face to face is so important, to see if we have the right chemistry, don't you think? Sit, sit! My usual, all around, my tab!" That last was directed to an eager lanky waiter, who scampered away, thanking her lucky stars for such a rich lunch table.

Sass bit her lip, hoping the celebrity would honor her request to keep her background information confidential. She needn't have worried. Kassidy Yang was all about public appearance.

"First, thank you so much for coming."

"No trouble," Sass claimed.

Kassidy waved that away. "Time and fuel. I know I killed your day. Be sure to bill me. Say 500 credits for two people for a day? Plus fuel?"

Sass could see Abel's eyes begin to glow with greed. She was pleased the youth hadn't been star-struck by the pretty woman's entrance. But wave enough money under his nose, and he might lose his instinct for self-preservation. He made a happy note on his pocket comm.

Sass had to admit the bit of generosity tilted her own judgment in Kassidy's favor. "Thank you. That's very kind."

"I can't imagine a worse reference for me than Contreras." Kassidy rolled her eyes happily. "What a worrywart. Old and fussy."

Contreras was the skyship's previous owner. Sass called him seeking contracting ideas. "He wasn't quite sure whether to recommend you." Contreras called Kassidy a dangerous lunatic. Also made of credits, catch-phrase music to Sass's ear. "Something about sky-diving?"

Kassidy nodded and leaned forward. "That was the last gig I tried to hire him for. I still haven't found anyone willing. They just don't understand the math. But Sass, I hope you will. May I call you Sass? Captain Collier seems so formal."

She unfolded a screen and spread it in the center of the table. Abel helpfully cleared a flower vase, candle, and salt shaker out of her way. The tech for this flexible display wasn't available for sale to settlers. Abel was falling deeper in love with the client by the moment. Sass attempted to be more critical to compensate.

"It's called a HALO dive," Kassidy explained. "High Altitude, Low Opening —"

"How many sky dives have you done?" Sass interrupted. "I've never heard of anyone skydiving on Mahina."

"No! Exactly," Kassidy agreed. "No one has. That's why it's such an awesome opportunity for my fans. We can work up to it, over a whole month. And every week, a new exciting episode. First parachute. Verify terminal velocity."

"What is 'terminal velocity'?" Abel inquired.

"How fast you're going when you splat on the ground," Sass clarified. "What is terminal velocity here, do you think, Kassidy?"

"About 0.4 of what sky divers experienced back on Earth. That includes the one-sixth g gravity, but only 0.9 atmospheric density. Actual speed depends on how you arrange yourself. Here, I made a table. The slowest — that's what we'd start with — is only 84 kph, for belly-first, arms spread for maximum drag. See it's much safer than it was on Earth."

Eyes round in disbelief, Sass leaned forward to study her tidy little table of speeds at which to hurtle uncontrolled to splat against the moon. Yes, gravity was lower. No, terminal velocity was not survivable. A belly-flop going 84 kph would be quite fatal, even for Sass. Maybe. Damned nanites would reconstruct her, though.

"But you would have a parachute," Sass suggested.

"Absolutely. Oh, of course!" Kassidy laughed. "I'm not insane. I thought the first real dive could be from the top of an ozone spindle. That's a thousand meters."

Sass nodded reluctantly. "My farm was next to an atmosphere factory."

Kassidy pressed her lips in silent sympathy. The turquoise glow of the force field on that side of Sass's farm kept people out for their own health. High ozone levels made you age faster. Smelled funky, too. Generating atmosphere wasn't enough on Mahina. They had to continually build a complex outer skin to hold the air captive. Gravity was too low to hold the gases by itself.

Abel recoiled. "Why was your farm next to an air factory?"

Good question, Sass allowed with a sigh. With so much unclaimed land, vast and useless unimproved tracts between settlements, why develop land that was bad for your health?

"It was cheap," Sass attempted. "And good for the plants. Of course, we were outside the danger radius." *Probably.* "Kassidy, did you allow for how much shallower our atmosphere is than Earth's?"

"Doesn't matter," Kassidy claimed. "As you fall, the atmosphere gets denser, right? And terminal velocity slows." She tapped her grid of numbers. "At the bottom, this is what you've got."

Sass frowned, trying to picture someone slowing as they fell. "You need oxygen at 1,000 meters."

Kassidy tried to wave that concern away. "I'll only be that high for a few seconds."

"For your first sky dive," Sass insisted. "Maximum precautions. Maybe you reach enough air to breathe in a few seconds. Maybe it takes 40 seconds. Maybe you pass out before you can open the parachute. Maybe you rely on gravity generators in the first place. It's not like Mahina supports a parachute industry."

Kassidy sat arrested, then a smile bloomed and slowly took over her face. "That's it. I want to hire you! You're perfect!" She sat back in triumph.

The waiter took this opportunity to slip their lunches onto the table, carefully avoiding the oh-so-pricey large flex-screen. "May I...?"

"Oh, of course! Silly me." Kassidy swooshed her screen off the table and folded it as though wadding a cloth napkin. "My favorite here. Shrimp vinaigrette on avocado. The fresh-fried croutons are divine." She beamed appreciation at the waiter, whose hollow-cheeked face basked in the glow.

Abel, lost in the physics discussion, regarded his plate in consternation.

"You'll love it," Sass promised him. Outside the citadel, there were no avocado trees, and certainly no farm-raised shrimp. "Excuse me, could I possibly have the avocado pits?"

"I — I'll ask," the surprised waiter promised, and scurried away again.

"Is your skyship here?" Kassidy asked Abel. "I'd love to see it."

"Ah, no," Abel replied. His train of thought got derailed by the prospect of eating yellow-green slime. He watched in concern as a dainty forkful approached Kassidy's lips.

"Abel's wife Jules is working a market," Sass said. "We took the shuttle and left the ship with her."

"You have a shuttle," Kassidy breathed in rapture. "Tell me, could I rent the shuttle sometimes?"

"Of course," Abel pounced. The word 'rent' cut straight through his culinary fog. The concept of rent delighted him. That was the sort of 'bread and butter' income he failed so spectacularly to achieve with the soybean transport business. Rent was so much more convenient.

"No," Sass overruled him. "You can hire a shuttle ride, with one of us at the con." Contreras had been very clear on that point. As had Kassidy's arrest record for driving violations. The charming daredevil could not be trusted as a pilot. Ever. "Five hundred a day? Plus fuel."

"Reasonable," Kassidy purred.

"Perhaps you'd like to rent a cabin on board?" Abel suggested.

"What, you live on the skyship?" Kassidy said, entranced and entrancing.

He extolled the virtues of living on *Thrive* and their three-day vocation in hostelry. Meanwhile he'd decided the texture of tiny cultured shrimp was too bizarre. Sass surreptitiously scraped his discard pile of tiny pink-and-white curls onto her plate. She hadn't eaten shrimp in decades. The waiter returned with three avocado pits in a little take-home box. Sass nearly glowed in thanks.

Sass was the older and wiser, skeptical partner. Yeah, a quick glance back over her life history put paid to that theory. Kassidy had them both tied around her pinkie in under twenty minutes.

The video star flitted off to pack, having more or less invited herself to dinner and a few overnights to try out the accommodations. She left the partners to wait for her over coffee.

"She's crazy," Sass murmured, blissful in the fragrant steam. She'd forgotten the rich full-bodied taste of real coffee, unknown outside

Mahina Actual. The clotted cream was thick as butter. She had high hopes for sprouting the avocados.

"She spends money like water," Abel added in rapture. "How much today, 600?" He'd quoted her 100 credits per night for the cabin. Sadly, that would convert to only 1000c if she rented regularly. The extravagant lunch neared another 50c, but didn't help their credit balance.

Sass sighed and clunked her coffee down. "Way to burst my bubble. Jules is going to out-earn us again, isn't she."

Abel nodded sadly. "And as a hotel, our cabins are kind of… shabby. The galley is a horror show if you look too close."

Sass scowled at him. The entire *Thrive* was a dented rust-bucket, true. "*Thrive* has character. Charm. Peaches."

Abel shrugged a fair-enough. For a sky hotel, their fresh produce was excellent. And the plumbing worked mostly.

Kassidy bounded back with a mere 12 cubic meter wardrobe on a grav carrier, a beautifully inlaid fragile piece of wooden furniture. "My closet," she explained winningly. "So much easier than packing!"

Abel gallantly took over steering the massive box through the shopping plaza and into the grassy field of visitor parking. The next lot over was smooth foamcrete, beautifully sculptured, with a two-way moving walkway to the city under a tree-lined sun awning. That lot was urb-only. Fortunately sunset was nearing again, shadows lengthening and the three-plus-day onslaught of sun drawing to an end. The dusty field had emptied some since prime time when they arrived. They were parked on the far end.

"This won't fit in any of the cabins," Abel grumbled to Sass. Kassidy strode in front of them, occasionally breaking into a skip. Judging by how firmly her skips ended, she kept herself in shape by cranking her gravity above Earth normal.

"It's fine," Sass assured her business partner. "We can strap it onto the catwalk dead-end by the ventilation fans. We don't need access to that bit very often."

Sass returned to her thoughts. She'd been free for almost a week now. She hadn't earned much money. But maybe she'd found something she'd yearned for much harder.

She might have friends again. *Thrive* was turning into a home.

They reached the shuttle. No way that closet could cram inside. Sass hopped the flier on top to grapple the box. She banked into the air like a falcon clutching a fresh-caught rat.

Not that her young friends had ever seen a falcon, or a rat.

9

There are tantalizing clues that rogue medical nanite engineers from Ganymede may have experimented on their passengers. The colony at Ganymede itself did not survive.

"Quitting time for sunset!" Kassidy called down, throwing kisses at the crowd.

No sooner had they arrived back at *Thrive,* than she climbed atop the skyship to record the market scene for her fans. Drone-bot cameras zipped into the small throng. A follow-up drone politely accosted market-goers to request permission to use their likeness on Kassidy Yang's livecast.

Sass didn't mind. No one needed an audience while manhandling a 3x2x2 meter box up a rusty metal catwalk ladder. Fortunately Abel thought to swaddle it in shipping quilts before they could scratch the precious woodwork. The audience came automatically with Kassidy. Eli wandered into the kitchen for a snack, and stood mesmerized by the door, staying out of their way.

By now, they'd managed to securely strap the thing in place, yet still provide closet door access. Sass was less confident in the arrangement to hold the cabinet doors shut against shifting contents. Abel was mostly embarrassed to be peeking into a lady's underthings, all too vividly displayed for his imagination.

Damn those nanites. They seemed to believe Sass's peak health involved an exuberant libido. If only they'd included some kind of user manual. But no, the suite injected into her cadre, Clay Rocha included, was a lab rat special, undocumented and proscribed. The Mahina urb doctors were both horrified and fascinated when they noticed. If anyone knew who developed her nanites, they didn't admit it.

"All clear below?" Kassidy boomed from above them. She had some kind of pocket public address system up there.

"She's building up to a finale," Eli commented. He hopped down into the hold to watch. Sass and Abel followed suit.

Jules called up from outside the cargo door. "All clear on the slide!"

A heavy thump hit the top of the ship. Another. A third, after a longer wait. Sass and the guys, just emerging onto the cargo ramp, craned their necks. But the curving top of the ship blocked their view. Then Sass caught a glimpse of Kassidy ridiculously high in the air.

She used her grav generator and *Sass's ship* as a damned trampoline!

An ear-splitting war cry preceded a final, hollow thump as Kassidy hit Jule's children's slide, practically going terminal velocity. Since they'd last been outside, the slide was reconfigured. Instead of gently depositing children into the tall hay, it ended just after the tight curve, an up-sloping launch ramp into the field.

Kassidy thundered around, flipped halfway through, and sailed into the air arms first on a perfect parabolic artillery trajectory. At the last conceivable fraction of a second, she cut in her grav, reversed on antigrav, and flipped in the air, to firmly plant her landing facing the crowd.

She wobbled and had to step one foot backward for balance. The slight stumble made Sass feel better. Slightly better. No, not really, she decided.

But Kassidy swooped her arms wide and took a generous bow to thunderous applause. Well, as thunderous as maybe forty late shoppers in a trampled field could manage.

The starlet followed up with one more wave. "Be sure to watch my highlight recap on Glow. Where you're the star! Tell all your friends!" She pointed to onlookers in turn, possibly catching every one of them on her way back to the mushroom stand. She paused along the way for a couple more posed selfies with fans.

"I'll kill her," Sass mentioned to the guys flanking her.

"Do you think she actually harmed the ship? Just jumping?" Abel wondered.

Eli took another sip of his drink. "You could charge extra rent. Use of the ship in broadcasts. Wear and tear."

Abel and Sass turned pursed lips on him.

He shrugged non-apology. "You seem hungry for credits." He turned and escaped inside, before anyone could recruit him to help pack away the mushroom and slide for the night.

Eli paid rent. He didn't work as crew.

"Fair," Sass grumbled. She and Abel strode down the ramp to grab the mushroom stand. Kassidy helped Jules carry the accoutrements that weren't nailed down to roll inside the thing.

Sass and Abel were back in the hold sidling the market stand into its storage spot when another voice boomed.

"Collier! Captain Sassafras Collier! Get out here, you felon!"

"Who's asking?" Jules called back. She and Kassidy still stood on the ramp, paused to chat with one of Kassidy's fans in the apricot light of impending sunset.

"Lucas Massey," the belligerent voice replied. "Him she's cheating out of his inheritance. That effing ship!"

"No," Sass breathed. "No, no, no..." She handed off a strap to Abel to escape their task.

Of course an intrigued Eli popped his head out from his cabin above.

"This ship belongs to Captain Collier," Jules returned. "And my husband, Abel Greer. They own it outright. You have no claim. Move on before I call the sheriff."

Dammit! Sass was still clambering over a segment of slide. Finally she burst out onto the ramp.

"I do have an effing claim!" Massey hollered. "I claim that old bitch stole my inheritance! Who are you?"

"I'm that old bitch, um, her daughter," Sass said. "Also named Sass Collier. There are no liens on this ship. My mother inherited everything from your dad, Lucas."

"She lied to you! Shit. You could be that whore's twin."

Sass scowled at him. "Jules, Kassidy, go inside."

The young women responded by leaning together, all eyes, and whispering. Kassidy's lanky middle-aged fan, standing waist-high by the ramp, peered between their legs.

"Kassidy, you damned well better not be recording," Sass hissed at her.

The gorgeous starlet held up a control dongle to eye level. Grinning, she pantomimed the exaggerated press of a button, followed by a twisting key on her lips.

Right. Sass turned back to Lucas Massey, son of a dead lover. The ill-favored brat was 15, last she saw him. He couldn't be more than 40 now. But he looked old, stretched over eight feet by lack of gravity, then bowed nearly double, his skeleton weak. Discolored patches on cheeks and brow spoke of skin cancers from not wearing sunscreen on the bright days. Missing and rotten teeth and shabby clothes completed a thoroughly decrepit appearance.

Sass replied, "No crime to take after your mother." Though it wouldn't have harmed Lucas to look more like his dad. He was a hunk in his day, Drake Massey.

"So get the bitch out here."

"I am Captain Collier," Sass clarified. "Mom is dead."

"Dead? Since last sunset? Your *mom* took possession of this ship a few cycles ago," Massey said. "Your *mom* left the penal farm one cycle ago at sunset. You saying she died between then and now? Cuz funny thing is, the picture on the bill of sale looks just like you."

Great, the brat did his homework. Sass bit her lip. She never was much good at lying on her feet.

"You ain't the mom! You're the same Sass Collier that stole my dad!" Massey accused, pointing a finger at her with his whole body. "Except you're all young and trim! Like an urb, never stretched!"

Sass didn't have a good lie for that. "I was an urb once," she conceded. *Never!* she screamed within. "But I joined the revolt for real. With your dad." She swallowed. "He loved you, Lucas. But you never came to visit. Not once."

"Mom wouldn't let me," Lucas claimed.

"Maybe at first," Sass allowed. "Drake died eight years ago of old age. Where were you?"

Lucas licked his lip. "I was a feckless youth."

Sass huffed a laugh. "And now you're a useless old man. Look how you've grown." The yutz spat on her last time they met. The feeling was mutual.

"You tricked him into leaving everything to you!" Lucas yelled.

Sass shook her head. "Drake disowned you. In his will. Left you and your brother a single credit each. The court already paid you. Need another credit? I might have a coin somewhere. But you won't get another from me. He loved you. He risked everything to make a better world for his kids. And you turned your back on him."

"You turned him against us!"

"No. I didn't." Well, against Lucas's mother perhaps. Sass maintained the sons might be salvageable once they escaped the harpy's clutches. But Drake wrote to them, every year. Letters returned, delivery refused. Drake last spotted this sorry excuse for a man 20 years ago, in the bleachers at their trial. The trial staged for public consumption, anyway. The real one was secret, the proceedings sealed.

She was glad Drake never saw the man his son had become. "Go away, Lucas."

"You haven't heard the last of me! My claim is good."

Sass turned on her heel and headed into the cargo hold. She gave a quick press to the close-ramp button, just enough to jerk Kassidy and Jules into motion. Jules forgot about the ship's gravity threshold again, but fortunately Kassidy caught her arm before she slammed to the deck.

Once they were in, Sass held the button unnecessarily until the hatch was fully sealed. Then she turned without a word and trotted up the catwalk, to the bridge, and flew them out of here. She'd could park somewhere friendlier for sunset. Someplace empty.

She wasted fuel to fly to the edge of the Grand Rift, an original feature of the moon that escaped visible terraforming. Created by tectonics rather than water, it wasn't glorious like the Grand Canyon back on Earth. And it was only a single side of a canyon. But its striated rock cliff face bore bands of rusty red, sandy tan, and lichen green. Sass remembered just the spot to park. The slow lowering sun blazed nearly perpendicular to the rock. The cliff glowed its colors, rising above dusty gray regolith stained gold. The settlers agreed from the start that this natural wonder should remain in its native moon-rock state. The caustic onslaught of oxygen only made the colors prettier with the passing years.

Sass wanted to stay in the bridge and hide until dark fell. But old habits died hard. Sunset must be toasted. To absent friends, rest in peace.

"You deserved better, Drake," she murmured. She rose to find a beer and face the music.

She found the others already spilled out onto the gravelly regolith, admiring the view. Kassidy had bounded atop a boulder a hundred yards away, but bounced back to join them when she saw Sass emerge.

Sass plonked down a 6-pack of beer and sat on the ramp. Eli stepped up with a nod. He claimed a beer and a perch beside her. He brought a handful of throwing rocks, and deposited them in a little pile between them to share. The other three slowly gathered at the base of the ramp, Abel's arms crossed.

"You have questions?" Sass invited without welcome. She took a swig of her beer and skipped a stone. Good idea — skipping stones blew off some steam and soothed her.

By tacit agreement, Abel had the greatest right. "How much risk is he to the company? His lawsuit. If your inheritance is overturned, can he take the skyship?"

Sass blinked in surprise, then pulled out her pocket comms tablet, the ubiquitous digital assistant. She talked her way through the calculations as she performed them.

"The most he could possibly claim is one fifth of the sale price of the farm. That's 37,000 credits. The ship cost 2.2 million. So that's less than two percent of my share of *Thrive*, and doesn't touch your share. Worst that could happen is that I pay him off over time. If he tried to put a lien on the ship, they'd laugh him out of court.

"Thing is," she continued, "Lucas disowned his dad. Drake tried to reconcile. But Lucas spat on us. I'd fight him in court because what he's doing is wrong. But it wouldn't get that far. I inherited the farm free and clear. OK?"

Abel had his own tablet out, his expression crestfallen. "I only own 8.5% of the ship, not 10%."

Sass cocked her head to the side. *Because that's what matters here?* "I rounded up. I wanted a 10% partner. I interviewed seven people. You're the one I want. The rest were sketchy."

"Sketchy?"

"I didn't trust them. You're young, earnest. Have business experience. I trust you. But I wasn't so honest in return. And I apologize for that, Abel. But if I told you I was a felon just finishing my sentence, I didn't think you'd give me a chance. Your family would have told you to steer clear. And I proved them right. Still. I wanted you. I hope you'll accept the compliment, and the apology."

Abel waved that away in irritation. "Accepted. It's my extra one and half percent of the company I take issue with."

Sass's eyes lit. She scrambled up and held out a hand to shake with him. "You're worth it, partner."

"But I haven't been," Abel argued, accepting the handshake but stubbornly holding to the numbers.

Sass shook her head and sat back to her beer. "How was your take today, Jules?"

"Made 1750 credits, captain!" Jules announced, straightening with pride. "That's a third more than Dawn. Dusk is great for sales. Payday, you know. And Abel and I are thinking up new tricks. Should bring in over 5,000 a week soon. Abel taught me everything I know about business." She beamed encouragement at him. "And your garden is a fantastic producer!"

Sass nodded, smiling, and met Abel's eye. "Our contract says you're 10% owner. Your marriage says that Jules owns whatever you do. I got two partners for the price of one. Not open to renegotiate at this time."

When the captain put it that way, Abel couldn't help but give his teen bride a hug, and drop the argument.

"Kassidy?" Sass invited.

"I'd love a tour of the ship, captain," the vid star replied.

"You don't have an issue with…news?"

"I researched your background before I took our appointment. I know who you are. I'm dying to see this ship garden. Did your farm earn that much?"

Sass laughed out loud. "Don't make me do math again. That's Abel's job. At a guess? No. We sold the damn grain and beans. We ate the good stuff, or gave it away to charity. Abel, put that thing away. It doesn't matter." He'd stood earnestly ready to run the numbers for her.

"I have a question," Jules volunteered. "Were you involved in the Petticreek Massacre?" Big eyes gazed up from the base of the ramp, hoping it wasn't so.

The Massacre killed over a hundred urbs, and several thousand settlers, totally outgunned. Sass nodded slowly. "I was. We were. We tried to stop it. Landau was out of control. That was a fight the rebels couldn't win. The five of us — the 'Petticreek Five' — weren't there for the massacre. We turned ourselves in the day after. Betrayed Landau."

Sass selected another stone from Eli's pile and skipped it across the scree. Even fist-sized rocks cast wriggly black bars of shadow across the ground now, as the sun started to dip below the close horizon. If she let her eyes out of focus, she could almost imagine it as open water, riffled in a breeze. Mahina sported no open water. The dessicated air would suck it dry. Even the forests and grasslands relied on a buried network of irrigation pipes.

Betraying Landau and the Revolt was the bitterest thing she'd ever done.

"You did the right thing, Sass," Eli said beside her. He quietly addressed the others. "I've read up on the Petticreek Five. In return for turning in Landau and the Revolt, Sass and her partners won concessions. Each settler is entitled to the first two babies free of charge. Every child on Mahina now gets a grav generator by right. No cost. The protein stocks for your kitchen printers are enriched with trace nutrients, Jules. To keep settlers from going blind. Help brain development, so they don't grow up stupid. If they eat right and use their generators, they can grow strong like Abel." He winced a little at the gawky Jules. "You need to use that grav. And eat the factory protein, some every meal."

Jules nodded firmly. The damage was done for her, by going off grav at the exact wrong time, just as she shot up with puberty. She'd remain a few centimeters taller than she should have been. But if she used the appliance conscientiously to age 18, the bone attenuation shouldn't grow any worse. Her precipitous marriage brought that lesson home for her.

Happily the teenager was in love with a good man, so it worked out.

Before the Revolt, settlers had to scrimp and save to pay for the grav generators. Buying a child was ruinously expensive. The urbs claimed they weren't sure why babies couldn't carry to term outside the creches at Mahina Actual. But a baby born naturally on Mahina was a rarity, and cruelly malformed. Providing the children with grav generators was an expense the settlers too often skipped. Still skipped by religious loons like the Turners who bought Sass's farm. Their thin and friable skeletons were just the most visible symptom. The brain damage was as severe as fetal alcohol syndrome. And their hearts were weak. They died young and stupid.

But Sass tried. The urbs granted the main concessions the Five sought in the Revolt. In return they gave up Landau and the rebel HQ. And Sass betrayed everybody except the four sentenced to the farm with her.

Emotion made her voice husky, and water stood in her eyes. "Thank you, Eli."

"Thank you," he replied softly.

"Not all urbs are like that," Kassidy said. "The ones who made you fight so hard for so little."

Sass nodded and shot her a grateful smile. "So how old are you, Kassidy? Did you know me at the time?"

The starlet grinned. "Nope. I'm twenty-three. Younger than Abel."

Sass should have known. Kassidy's kind of whole-hearted exuberance didn't last, no matter how long her looks survived.

"Forty-two," Eli offered. Jules and Abel's eyes widened. "But I was too busy studying at the time to pay attention. Not a good excuse. Sorry." He scratched his ear sheepishly, and selected another rock to skip.

Sass absolved him. "Fat lot you could have done about it."

"And that," he agreed. "We needed the Revolt. I wish we hadn't, but there it is."

Sass touched his hand in gratitude, and grabbed herself another rock to hurl skipping across the ground. "I got a nice farm out of it. That and the magic of compound interest bought us a ship. Jules, when Abel explains compound interest to you? Listen carefully."

Of course, currently she watched her savings evaporate like water on hot regolith.

No one asked how old she was. Maybe Kassidy and Eli already knew.

She forgot all about her avocado pits. After supper, giving Kassidy a tour, she found them soaking. Eli had taken care of them for her. He placed them in his own segment of the engine room so as not to disturb Sass's hardworking plantings.

The captain choked up to see that. She really liked her young shipmates.

10

The settlers of Mahina originated in the Adirondacks Mountains in Earth's North American continent. The region was flooded with refugees from the drowned coast.

After Kassidy's triumphant dive from the atmosphere spire, at her request they headed for the bar in Newer York.

Sass hadn't visited the town in decades. She didn't know how many decades. The place wasn't that memorable. The market parking field was next to the school playground. The school itself was a sober brick-like edifice, instead of the more whimsical ones that tried to entice children to attend. Judging from the accretion of farm-scales visible from the air, the town probably hosted around 10,000 people, about average.

Or 10,000 at its peak, at least. Most places had lost more population than they gained since their founding. Even if Newer York specialized in livestock, too many fields grew hay. When a farm fell out of use, the neighbors planted it in hay for safekeeping, ready for a new farmer, should one happen along. The price per proven hectare was set, regardless of demand.

It wasn't easy for Sass to locate a buyer for her oversize spread.

Fortunately Forb Turner planned to found his own little town, revolving around his sect of Cyber-Mennonites. Cousins were en route, at horse-drawn wagon speed across the trackless moon dust. The isolation, and unusually generous water availability from the atmo plant, were selling points. Forb didn't worry about the ozone levels as much as he should have.

The five of them strolled down the middle of the grassy Main Street, attempting to admire the usual shop fronts — sheriff's office, bank, food store, consumer goods, hardware, church.

Abel studied the concrete-textured boxy molding around windows and door in distaste. An industrious someone had etched fake joints on the building surfaces to mimic a texture of stone blocks. Possibly as a nod to the old New York, the town architecture maximized square corners in its raw mushroom-colored foamcrete.

The bar was the final building on the block-long Main Street, the opposite end from the school. In keeping with the older New York theme, the entrance featured a brass and glass revolving door, flanked by potted young spruce trees. The window advised BAR in pink glow tubes. A billowing cloud of vaper fog encased a trio of workmen on an extruded faux stone bench outside.

Abel paused at the door, perplexed. Sass slipped in first to demonstrate how to operate the thing. She stopped within to gaze around, as the others negotiated the unfamiliar door. Eli flanked her first. Jules and Kassidy took several spins in the door. Abel dutifully stuck with his wife in play.

The place was nearly empty, at what should be a peak hour on Glow. The bar featured pool table and darts, as well as ping pong and foosball and air hockey, plus a music keyboard and karaoke rig. The sparse patrons ignored all that, hunkered down over drinks and low-voiced conversation.

Sass sighed, and led the way to the bar. An eight-foot stooped barman eyed them warily, polishing a glass. Several of the bright rainbow pan flutes of flavorings like farmer Willow's stood arrayed on the bar for patrons who wished to flavor their own grain alcohol.

"Pitcher of beer please?" Sass requested. "Five mugs. We'll try your local if you have any."

"Two," the barman replied. "Light or dark." He spat into the sink.

"Is either of them real beer?" Sass inquired. Sometimes they served beer syrup and carbonated water.

"Real beer concentrate."

By then Abel and the door spinners caught up. "Let's go with a round of flutes and a pitcher of lager," he decided. Most of the bar patrons nursed amber beers.

The barman sluggishly complied. "What's a bunch of urbs doing here?"

"My wife and I aren't urbs," Abel replied. "Neither is the captain. I'm from Palm Springs. My lovely bride hails from down south."

"Captain?" the barman inquired. He ruled out Eli and Kassidy, to scrutinize Sass. "Of what?"

"Abel and I own the skyship parked in the field," Sass replied. "Eli and Kassidy here are our guests. Clients. Know of anyone with work for a skyship?"

"Work? Plenty. Can pay for it? No." He flicked a resentful glance at the urbs. *Only an urb could afford that.*

Kassidy interjected brightly, "Mind if we use the toys, sir?"

"What they're here for." The barman poured a cup of brown goop into a clear pitcher and gunned carbonated water into it with a hose. An ice wand served as a swizzle stick. Empty mugs and tumblers of everclear he arrayed on a tray. He totaled the order and displayed the price on the bar surface. "Prefer you pay now. Only regulars run a tab."

Sass wordlessly transferred the funds, with an insultingly low tip. They all helped carry, and Sass led the way to a table amidst the games. She offered a greeting to the one occupied table in the play zone. "Hope you don't mind if we make some noise!"

The hen club quartet hastily rose and retreated to the far side of the bar.

"How about karaoke to warm up the room?" Kassidy suggested.

"From a cold start?" Sass judged the hoodoo too strong. The zombies would not rouse. "Maybe ping pong and work our way up."

Kassidy laughed and claimed a paddle. She bent to a competitive stance, challenging Sass with flashing eyes.

Sass tried a swig of the beer first. She nodded and set that aside. Yup, beer flavored sweet soda, with notional alcohol. She grabbed the other paddle and squared off.

Kassidy didn't even know how to serve. She merely tossed the ping-pong ball underhanded toward Sass. But she was having a blast, high on life. As the only one of the group who knew how to play, Sass was hard-pressed to herd the randomly flying ball back across the net. She recruited Eli to assist on her side. He used his hands to swat at the ball if it might otherwise hit him. Abel joined Kassidy. They kept Jules busy retrieving lost balls. The table came with a half dozen. Kassidy kept them all in play.

"What, are you trying to hit everyone in here?" one man demanded. He walked over and returned a ball to the hopper.

Yes. "No!" Kassidy laughed. "I'm really just that bad! Kassidy Yang. How you doing?" She transferred her paddle to her left, and stuck out a hand to shake.

"Hunter Burke," he replied. "Good to meet you."

He perched on an empty table with his beer, to settle in and watch. Unlike most here, Hunter Burke looked like he'd worn his gravity properly as a youth. His build was Earth-normal, and nicely muscled. Regular features and a firm jaw made him handsome, and he knew it. Sass judged him in his late twenties, not a bad match for Kassidy.

She wouldn't mind him herself, come to that. *Damn those nanites.* They arrested her appearance right about 25 by her Earth standards, more like 20 to Mahina eyes, with a libido set to maximum.

"Hang on," Hunter said. "Kassidy Yang? The vid star?"

"I am!" Kassidy exulted. She explained her triumph of the day, leaping from the top of the ozone spire. She popped a ball into another innocent patron's beer while she spoke. The woman chose to be aggravated rather than amused.

"I spotted Newer York from above," Kassidy prattled on, oblivious. "So when it came time to celebrate, I chose you!"

Maybe a half dozen bar denizens paid grudging attention by now. Sass wryly thought the town had captured more of the old New York character than they knew. Not that she remembered the old city first hand. The coast was drowned north to Poughkeepsie by the time she could remember, the Hudson too broad to see across. She was near Kassidy's age when she escaped into the Adirondacks before the stampede.

Sass shook off the flashback. "You play, Hunter Burke? I'd kinda like a real game. Maybe you could join Kassidy over there. Steer a ball my way once in a while."

He grinned and supplanted Abel, who was only too happy to reclaim his drink. Eli tactfully bowed out and challenged Kassidy to a game of darts. Abel soon drifted into conversation with his own kind, successful businessmen in town.

Hunter proved capable of hitting the ball direct to Sass.

Sass hadn't expected the switch, after she'd gone out of her way to feed Hunter to Kassidy. Her eyes and grin flashed a little more. Her hips swung. She indulged in a pirouette after slamming the ball back at him. He did his best to reciprocate.

Soon, he lay his paddle down and conceded defeat. He was good, but no match for Sass. "Have a drink with me. No, don't finish that one. All the alcohol's wafted off by now."

Sass conceded he was right. She let him fetch her a fresh glass of everclear. She colored it with the bourbon and scotch flavored flutes, half and half until bourbon colored at least. Unfortunately the flavors were sweetened. The net result reminded her vaguely of flat rum and Coke. *Good enough.* She downed it.

"Want to see my etchings, Hunter Burke?"

He laughed. "No. I'd sure like to see the inside of a skyship, though."

"Could do. Abel! Hunter's walking me home."

"Aw, captain!" Jules cried. "Stay! The party's just getting lively!"

Indeed it was. If Eli thought he had a shot at Kassidy tonight, Sass suspected he was sadly mistaken. She headed out, dangling Hunter's hand over her butt. They squeezed through the revolving door together, and chattered their way back to the ship.

Her following tour of the ship was cursory. "Cargo ramp. Toys in the hold. My cabin's this way."

"Yes, ma'am!"

She grabbed cups and a real bottle of whiskey from the kitchen as they passed. "A shame they don't serve the good stuff in the bar." She drew him into her room and took a seat on the bed to pull off her boots.

He poured them quick splashes of whiskey and handed her one. He raised his in toast. "To Sass Collier of the Petticreek Five."

"Aw hell." Sass downed the whiskey in a single gulp. "I won't even get laid out of this, will I."

Hunter laughed. "Could do. Did I ruin the mood?"

"I'd rather get laid than toast my mother."

"You're the one and only Sass Collier. And you're older than my grandma. Lucas Massey is a bad weasel to cross. The rebellion is still alive, Sass."

Sass pursed her lips. "More interested in sex than your sales pitch. Such a shame. Good looking. Great ping pong. Then you had to talk politics."

"Alright then. Sex first it is." He pinned her shoulders to the bed.

A frolicsome time later, Sass lay draped across the bed belly-down, feet up on the bulkhead, arms crossed and head dangling off the side, luxuriating in a gifted amateur back rub.

"Can I talk about the rebellion yet?" Hunter asked.

"No. Never. I did what I could."

"You have a skyship now. That makes things possible."

"Not exactly a stealth getaway vehicle. How many skyships you think there are on this moon?"

"Five," Hunter replied. He leaned down to tickle her ear with his whisper. "And you're dying to hear what the op is."

"No. I'm not. I'm dying to make a go of my new skyship. A new life. If Lucas is talking, maybe he mentioned I just got out of prison. Ever since Petticreek. I am reformed."

"I don't believe that."

"Believe it, baby butt. A grav generator for every child. The right nutrients in the food. You've got a chance now. That's all I asked."

"And how's that working?" Hunter demanded.

"You tell me. I've been under farm arrest for 20 years." Too late, Sass realized that conceded him the initiative. "You look alright."

"Yeah, I look alright. Because my dad worked for the city. Collaborator. So I grew up strong as an urb, almost like a real Earther. And came home to Newer York to visit my friends. While they all grew wasted."

"Didn't use their generators," Sass attempted.

"They did use grav," Hunter countered. "They ate the damned protein. And they breathed the air." His pummeling of her back grew a bit too animated.

Sass stilled under his hands. "You're saying we didn't get it right."

"I'm saying the settlers are still wasting away. Out of the men and women in that bar, Sass, how many looked alright to you?"

Sass shook her head. "Doesn't prove anything. They were over 20. And even if they weren't. Hell, look at my friend Jules. She ate right. She wore her grav religiously. Then daddy took it away right when she had a growth spurt, and boom. She shot up in weeks. Bones weakened for life. Bastard probably thought he was doing right by his daughter, too. Helped her fit in. Sure, fit in with the sickly."

"It's got to be more than that," Hunter insisted. "And the urbs know how to prevent it."

"It doesn't got to be more than that," Sass countered. "The simplest explanation is often the truth." She levered upright and yanked the blanket around her chest and cross-legged lap. "Hunter, I finally got my freedom back. I want that. I tried. And I don't know you from Adam. Time to go."

"Sass —"

"Thanks for the sex. It was great." She snapped his pants at him, and started skinning into her own jeans to escort him out.

"Just let me tell you about —"

"Put those pants on, or I trot you onto the field naked." To underscore her point, she pulled a knife from under the mattress. "Get dressed. And get out."

Hunter chose to comply in silence, since she playfully mock-stabbed the knife at him each time he tried to speak. Their clothing restored, she twisted his wrist behind him in an arm-lock to march him down through the hold and out the ramp. She remotely lowered that by voice command to open by the time they reached it.

She freed his arm at the base of the ramp. "Thanks for the fun time, Hunter. See you around."

"When you change your mind, contact me," he returned. "Or even if you want to use me for my body again, old lady."

She snorted a laugh. "I suppose a good-bye kiss couldn't hurt." She gave him a thorough one, then stabbed a finger in his sternum to push him away. "But I'm done with rebellion."

"We'll see."

"Captain!" Jules called out waving. "Have you two been talking on the ramp all this time? How nice!"

The crew headed back from the bar. Eli appeared to be steering Abel. Kassidy was draped on Jules. Abel's young bride was only allowed one beer. Which left the fifteen-year-old the only sober member of *Thrive.*

"We're not done, Sass," Hunter promised. He strode away under the full gas light of Glow.

11

Many interstellar armed services claim descent from the Colony Corps.
They delivered settlers to ten worlds scattered across six star systems.

Kassidy rapped on the office door after breakfast. "Got a minute?"

Sass raised her head from the accounts and smiled welcome. "For our best customer? Always!"

Abel attempted a wan smile as well. His hangover was monumental. Though the context had changed, Monday still felt like Monday. Somehow the half-gas gloom of Saturday was fun to begin the weekend. The same dim light two days later made a depressing start for the work week.

Kassidy bounced in to perch on a cabinet bolted to the steel bulkhead. *Thrive's* office was a bit snug. "Just had to tell you. The skydiving response has been phenomenal! The first finished episode aired while we were at the bar last night. That was the intro, an hour of our initial tests. Verify terminal velocity, jump from 100 meters, equipment and stuff. And a tour of *Thrive* — yay, crew!" She laughed and clapped.

"But now my live subscribers are through the roof! Abel, you underestimated your cut yesterday."

Abel frowned. "Why subscribe after the jump? They already missed it."

"It's called live, but they can rewind for 36 hours. Yesterday evening they saw the opening episode. Now everybody's talking about skydiving at work. I bet I'll get a spike of new livecast subscribers at lunch and evening today."

Mahina sported no time zones. Lunch and zero hour — 'midnight' for a new 'day' — were synchronized moon-wide. People even knocked off early for sunset where the celestial event ran early. Of course, sunrise happened on Dusk instead of Dawn for the nightsiders, whose half of the moon faced away from the gas giant.

Sass pursed her lips and considered the stunt woman's third eye camera, right where Hindus dabbed the red spot. "Kassidy, you're not broadcasting now, are you? From my office?"

"Don't worry. I have an offline-for-business placard showing now. I always tell you when I'm recording."

Sass's eyes narrowed on a twinge of misgiving.

But Kassidy burbled onward. "Most subscribers don't have time to watch live. But my fans leave comments with timestamps for the best scenes. My editor and I love it! We always start with the fan comments when we put together our weekly episodes."

"So yesterday's dive from the spire will broadcast next Glow?" Abel asked. "For non-subscribers."

"Glow after next," Kassidy replied. "We're trying to build, spin it out over four or five weeks. But that's not what I wanted to talk to you about. I'm getting requests like you wouldn't believe! 'How can I do this?' 'How much does it cost?' 'Does *Thrive* take passengers?' 'Can I come along and watch you jump?'"

"Oh, no," Sass murmured, seeing where this was headed.

"I want to run a contest for my fans! Lucky winners get to come watch the event live! Of course, we'd pick them up, wherever they are, and drop them back. Hm. That might get tedious. Maybe five fans? Can I, can I, please?"

"A raffle," Abel suggested. "*Thrive* gets half the proceeds?"

Kassidy snapped her fingers in delight. "There you go! Multiple raffles! Jump with Kassidy from 50 meters! See the second-to-last show live! Join us for the finale 3,000 meter jump!"

Sass reached over to tap on Abel's comms tablet. "Legal check, Mr. Business Guy. Can we carry passengers?"

"Oh," Abel said, making a note of it. "And we'd better address the pressure issues first. Did we check whether we need a permit to carry Kassidy and Eli?"

"I checked," Sass replied. "They qualify as crew. They live and work here."

"It'll be so worth it," Kassidy urged. "If we offered today, jumps from 50 meters? Just name the town. You'd be turning people away. And passengers could be a huge business opportunity for you. Here we're close to Mahina Actual. Most towns, though, they never visit the city. Sometimes you see someone put together a tour truck. But it's a miserable long drive across rocky dust. Dodging boulders and crater walls. Even nearby, there's them that has, and them that don't. A rich farmer or a shopkeeper has a truck. Ordinary people? If they can't walk, they don't go."

"I wonder how much they'd pay, though," Abel wondered, already jotting notes.

Kassidy shrugged. "Not just Mahina Actual, either. What about a night-side tour? You could even offer a tour to the orbital! I'd be your first passenger! Except I get it free, included in my rent." She grinned. "Well, no, because I'd be recording like crazy."

Sass gazed at her admiringly. "You really love your work, Kassidy."

"Oh, it's not work," the young woman replied. "I'm on a mission. My fans get a chance to really live through my shows. Adventure! Adrenaline! And not in virtual either, some dumb fantasy world. Real life! Real excitement! On Mahina!"

Sass sat back entranced. "That's exactly what you're doing, isn't it?"

Kassidy sobered for a moment. "It's not enough to survive, Sass. People need dreams."

Her celebrity face returned as she hopped off the cabinet. "Get me the numbers, Abel. I can deliver paying tourists. Oh! Schedule. This week, we need to scout locations for the next two jumps. I'm thinking one is star side, so two days scouting? And I need to go home to the city for a couple days."

"How about now? I can drop you there," Sass offered. "I have appointments from lunch onward."

Kassidy nodded happily and left to pack.

"What appointments?" Abel inquired.

"Personal, Abel. I should be back by 14:00. We can work on the pressure seals."

They put their heads together to think through what they'd need in place to accept passengers.

SASS DONNED a pair of dark goggles and slipped into the engine room. She held her breath a second, checking for Jules or Eli. But she was alone with the star drive and the plants. She breathed deep relief of the moist rich air.

A couple weeks ago she felt she was dying of loneliness on the farm. But she got used to it. Nothing surprising had happened on that farm in years, only what she herself planned and instigated. Now busy young people burst out doing random things.

Well, there were only four of them, and Eli was in his forties. Still. She didn't control what happened around here.

And she loved that. Still, she was off balance. And it'd been an annoying Monday. Taking passengers required more investment up front. So far nothing paid a return on the right order of magnitude to cover that looming tax bill. This damn skyship was a money pit. She bought it hoping to uplift the settlers. In time, she'd save up enough money to upgrade it for space travel, beyond the orbital, and open trade with other worlds.

Yeah, so far she was headed for blowing all her cash reserves to pay the title transfer taxes. The lawyer this afternoon assured her there were plenty more taxes where those came from. And her two best-paying clients so far were urbs, not settlers. Eli wasn't even very lucrative. Jules earned more with the produce stand.

Sass firmly told her panicky visions of financial ruin to shut up and give it a rest. The lawyer was confident he could quash Lucas Massey's nuisance suit, at least, trying to claim a share of *Thrive* from his dead father.

Someone had rearranged a few of her tomatoes. She took a moment to figure out what she was seeing. Three tomato plants had moved onto a large oval dais on the floor. This oblong was bisected on its longer diameter by a wall that reached 4 meters high. Her tomato cages were tacked to this new wall as high as they reached, only 2 meters. Above that, she'd let the plants flop down to the floor. But now the vines were untangled, expertly pruned, and neatly trussed to an array of eye bolts running up the platform's center wall. The whole plant stand was extruded from foamcrete, of course.

Eli. With Jules assisting.

Sass placed her tomatoes as close to the drive light as they wanted. She told the ship to turn the engine down before bed to give the plants some dark. Tomatoes and peppers needed dark to thrive, and the crew didn't need the engine blazing while they slept just to keep the systems running. The ship was ready to move in 20 minutes from a warm start. That was faster than Sass got herself moving in the morning. The schedule ran on automatic.

She stepped around the back side of the wall. This was outfitted with shelves, each angled downward to a lip, running all the way up. Without her exuberant vines in the way, she could see nutrient drip pipes. So far they were only hooked up to a waist-height shelf, empty, and the tomato tubs on the other side.

It's a lazy Susan, she finally realized. The platform could be rotated to turn the tomatoes away from the engine, to give whatever was on the backside a chance to face the blazing light of the star engine in the middle of the chamber. A tentative nudge with a toe confirmed that the platform was locked against rotation at present.

That's good. Asking permission would have been better. She considered the fruit trees. Perhaps she could arrange a blackout curtain. Although she did rotate them a quarter turn when she remembered. A lazy Susan would help there, too.

Busy with Kassidy and Abel, Sass hadn't paid much attention to quiet, mild-mannered Eli. She wandered over to his assigned corner. Here he'd constructed wire racks, only up to her shoulder height so far. But the tilted shelves latched onto steel uprights bolted to the overhead.

That's one pressure leak accounted for. She made a note of it. At least bolt holes in her airtight engine room were easy to seal. Compared to all the replacement gaskets she needed to print, based on her afternoon spent policing the airlocks with Abel. The seals didn't matter in normal atmospheric operations. The outer hull was airtight. The skyship couldn't have passed inspection otherwise. But to open a door at 3,000 meters for Kassidy to jump out, Sass needed all compartments airtight.

To reach the orbital. To reach another world... She snorted. They'd need to make a profit first. They were in no danger of that. Maybe they could get by with only sealing the small airlock, and wait on the huge cargo ramp gaskets, suffering old age and dry rot beyond hope of repair.

Those were the ones that stranded her in the airlock yesterday.

No, the cargo ramp couldn't wait. That could lose pressure for the hold, and leave them all trapped in their cabins.

She irritably made another note to store a pressure suit in her cabin. Then she corrected that to the bridge. As captain, her ship wasn't going anywhere without her on the bridge until — *hah!* — they could leave Mahina orbit. That would take a drive upgrade, not just a few gaskets.

But what was Eli growing? She picked up a standard seedling six pack, each cell with an infant tomato plant poking up its skinny blades of starter leaves.

Strange. There being exactly two varieties of tomato to choose from on Mahina, cherry and mid-size, she expected identical seedlings. But these were three different sizes, each with its own neatly labeled tag. The planting date was 12 days ago, the day after Eli took up residence. The tag also bore a variety name, *Cherokee Purple, Roma,* and *Brandywine,* two of each.

That entire shelf was the same, 6-packs of those three unfamiliar varieties. The next shelf bore pepper seedlings. Mahina supplied only one variety, a green bell pepper. As a cop in the Adirondacks, Sass never had time for gardening. But she remembered *Jalapeño.* Like the tomatoes, each 6-pack held two each of three varieties. Another shelf held baby cabbages, green, red, and Chinese. The next shelf bore 40 single pots, planted a couple days later with nothing sprouted as yet, labeled *Macintosh Apple* and *Bartlett Pear.* She certainly remembered those from Earth.

"Time we had a chat, Eli," Sass murmured. She brought a 6-pack of baby cabbages along.

12

_____

The Aloha system hosted three receiving colonies: Denali, Mahina, and
Sagamore. The five other solar systems of the Diaspora housed only one or
two colonies.

"Sass! Any requests for dinner?" Jules interrupted her on the way to Eli's cabins, sticking her head out the galley door.

"How about a romantic dinner for just you and Abel? Eli and I can fend for ourselves."

Jules beamed in surprised pleasure. "Thank you, captain!"

Sass nodded with a smile. She rapped on Eli's workshop door, then barged in without waiting for a response. Eli hastily finished draping a cover on one of his foamcrete workbenches. Not a gifted sneak, Sass felt.

She plonked the baby cabbages on his desk and took a seat on the only available high stool. She smiled, and pointed out his desk chair, inviting him to sit.

"Eli. I was just in the grow room. I see you've been busy. I've been so distracted with Kassidy, I haven't paid you enough attention."

Eli flinched, as he obediently took his chair. "Oh, I don't need any attention."

"Where did you get the seeds?" Sass asked.

"Here and there —"

"The truth, Eli." From the expression on his face, Sass could see he was evolving more lies. She chose to try a different tack. "How is it that you happened to find my ship? To ask for lodging. Rather unusual, isn't it? A scientist needs extensive equipment. Colleagues to talk to. Weird supplies." She glanced pointedly at the draped bench. "You didn't find us by accident."

Eli swallowed. "I'd been hunting for lodging and greenhouse space outside the city. I passed through that town a while back. Made some contacts. When Jules set up shop and sold such unusual produce, one of them called me. Got a friend to fly me out to see for myself. And found Jules completely delightful." He attempted a smile, in a wincing, hopeful sort of way.

"Out," Sass echoed. "From Mahina Actual."

Eli licked a lip. "Yeah."

"Would it be safe to presume that whatever you're doing, is not welcome in the city?"

Eli pursed his lips and looked away guiltily.

"I'm not sure if you caught this part the other day, Eli. But I'm on parole. If I do illegal stuff, I lose my freedom and my skyship. Who knows if I'd get a farm again. I got lenience in exchange for turning in Landau. If I screw up again, they might sentence me to the phosphate mines."

Eli gulped.

"So I need to know. What kind of illegal is what you're doing?"

Eli shook his head. "Given your legal situation, you're better off not knowing."

"My last career before prison was marshal, Eli," Sass countered. "If I told a marshal I didn't know you were doing something illegal? On my ship, in my own grow room? She'd never believe me."

She could just picture the scowl on Clay Rocha's face. *Even you can't be that stupid, Sass Collier.* To which she feared her defense was, *My idiocy is boundless.*

She sighed. "You're growing plants that aren't approved for field use on a controlled terraformed moon. That's why my peach tree and strawberries and all are confined to greenhouse life." Never mind that she thought the rule was absurd. But Mahina Actual controlled the genome of Mahina. Along with everything else.

"It doesn't have to be that way," Eli replied softly. "There is no reason for Mahina to have such a limited biota. Especially not for our food supply. Mahina Actual enjoys ten times the food diversity."

"Grown indoors or in controlled fields," Sass replied. "Eli, I have some experience with *plants*."

"What if I told you that limited biodiversity is contributes to failure to thrive in the settlers?"

"That I could believe," Sass allowed. "But does it add up? Humans lived in extremely limited conditions even back on Earth, Eli. Submarines. Space stations. Sailing ships. Bunkers. Deserts."

He shook his head. "Not for their whole lives. Sailing ships and deserts don't count. Those are natural worlds. Those would be fine. Children born and raised on a submarine or a space station would not be fine. Even in the mega-cities on Earth, or packed refugee camps, people changed. Started to lose the desire to reproduce. Increased aggression, addiction, suicide. Cities countered that tendency with parks and trees, and richly varied foods. Here, what do we have? Painted foamcrete? Hedgerows of aspen and spruce?"

"Granted you're preaching to the choir, Eli," Sass allowed. "But surely there's a reason the terraformers limited the plant life." She couldn't recall offhand what the justification was.

Eli shook his head. "Control. Sass, they never wanted the settlers."

She snorted. "Tell me something new."

He met her eye. "They still don't want the settlers."

"Eli, you can't believe that. That Mahina Actual is deliberately trying to kill us off."

"They have your genome. You're female. They would have harvested your eggs. Actual people are extraneous and unnecessary. Often uncooperative."

Sass stared at him. "Look, Eli. I'm no fan of Kendra Oliver and her goon club. And yes, obviously, they never wanted us settlers. But you go too far."

"Fine, don't believe me. But to answer your question, the seeds came from a gene fab. I have it right here." He undraped the section of workbench.

In ultra slow motion, Sass stepped off her high stool and approached the device, a utilitarian grey steel box that could fit snugly inside a briefcase.

Eli pressed a button, and a section of its cover lifted gently. Inside was a tray with 20 shallow slots like finger depressions in cream-colored plastic, forming a 4 x 5 array. Each held a drop-sized bit of yellow.

"What am I looking at?"

Eli handed her a magnifying glass. "Japanese cucumber embryos. The green light indicator says they're ready."

Sass bent closer to study the little specks of life through the lens. They did indeed look like cucumber seed leaves. "Ready for what?"

"Packaging," Eli said. He carefully extracted two embryos, then closed the lid and pressed another button. "You can plant them directly. That's what I did with the seedlings in the greenhouse. I'll plant these two. Or you can coat them to create seeds for storage. You don't have room for twenty cucumber vines right now."

He lovingly transferred the two tiny plants into holes in starter pots, and watered them. He set the baby cabbages next to them under a tabletop light. "They'll germinate faster without the seed coating."

Sass frowned. "This can make any kind of seed? From a... genome? That's the genetic data, right?"

Eli nodded, but clarified, "It can make any kind of embryo. Not just seeds. I only have the packaging worked out for seeds, though. Mammals, for instance, would need to be transfered to a placenta, in vitro or in vivo. Likewise a chicken egg. I don't have a machine to build the rest of the egg around the embryo, yolk and white, membrane and shell."

The indicator light soon blinked from yellow to green again. He popped the top to display 18 neon pink cucumber seeds, a familiar flat pointed oval about a centimeter long. Normally they were off-white, but Sass recognized the shape. Now that she thought about it, a cucumber seed was simply a cucumber embryo with a tough skin coat for protection.

"Hot pink," Sass commented at random. She was still thinking.

Eli grimaced. "I have five different coating colors — Look, that's not important."

"No," Sass agreed. "This is a genome factory. And you stole it from the labs in Mahina Actual."

"I did not *steal* it," Eli objected. "I invented it. A portable field system for printing plant life. Any plant life. Not just crop seeds. In fact, that seed coating is only good for some species. Most you're better off planting the embryo. Like a peach seed or avocado. Their pits form a very complicated seed coating." He frowned in vexation.

He resumed his seat at the desk. "Sass, I thought you'd appreciate what I'm doing. You want the settlers to thrive, don't you? You even named the ship that — *Thrive*. I'm not saying my little seeds can solve everything. But they can help enrich this world. It's such a damned desert out here."

"Twenty seeds at a time," Sass mused. "That's not much."

"Actually twenty copies of the same seed," Eli admitted. "Genetically they're clones. I can only print a single genome at a time. But I didn't add the Mahina sequence that prevents reproduction. These plants can multiply by their own seed, recombined by breeding."

Sass didn't know what to say. "That's magical, Eli. That's brilliant."

His sad face, with a few false starts, struggled into a grateful smile. "Thank you, Sass. That means so much to me."

Sass meant to follow up with, *But this is completely illegal and I can't have it on my ship.* But she couldn't say it. Kassidy with her ridiculous sky dives. Jules with her farm stand mushroom, introducing the masses to her peaches and strawberries and carefully fed hothouse tomatoes. And now Eli with his Johnny Appleseed quest. They were exactly who she wanted on *Thrive*.

She sighed. "We'll get caught."

Eli's face grew obstinate. "Let them. They'd make themselves ludicrous. To the urbs, Sass, not just settlers. In the city, we've used this technology all along."

"Alright."

"Really?" Eli leapt up and threw his arms around her in a hug. When she didn't reciprocate, he awkwardly shuffled back. "Sorry. It's just, this means so much to me, Sass. Someone who understands."

"Yeah, but paws off," Sass returned. "I'm playing captain now. What did you tell them, by the way? Scientists don't usually go walkies from the lab."

Mahina Actual wasn't that large a city, maybe 30,000. Their scientist density was high, founded as terraforming headquarters for the moon world. Still, scientists reported to lab bosses and supervisors. A hierarchy jealously battled for funding and equipment. Sass would expect one of their finite number to be missed.

"I developed a drinking problem," Eli explained. "Over a failed romance. Left the city to get my act together."

"Sorry to hear that."

"It's a cover story, Sass," Eli retorted. "I made it up."

"Ah." On the whole...Sass wanted to try the cucumbers. She couldn't even remember how purple cabbage tasted different from green, let alone Chinese. She looked forward to tasting them again, seeing their different colors and textures. The uniform rows of crops on Mahina always struck her as oddly sad.

She rapped the table and rose decisively. "This is making me hungry. Let's go scrounge some dinner."

"Sass..." Eli said. "You know, I could use more reagents."

"More what?"

"Um, bio goop. To make embryos out of."

"Don't push your luck, Eli. I could still kick you out on your ass."

"Yes, captain." Eli fell in meekly to follow her to the galley. Judging by shrieks and giggles up the companionway, Jules and Abel were happily occupied.

13

The settler selection process on Earth varied between nations. In most cases, the powerful and the military claimed priority, plus dependents. The Adirondacks pickup was by lottery, by profession.

Three days later on Thursday, Sass set *Thrive* gently in a flat valley between the great stepped pyramids of the phospho-gypsum stacks. The 50-meter pyramids measured kilometers across at the base, piles of the dross from Phosphate Mine 3 on Mahina's dark side.

Happily for their bank balance, *Thrive's* shuttle didn't have the range to reach the dark side of the world in a reasonable amount of time. Kassidy paid for the whole ship for this jaunt, for the day.

Phosphate Mine 3 included both mine and company town. The population came to just over 4,000 miners and management and family, Mahina's largest settlement facing away from the gas giant Pono. The only other jobs here were service industries like bars and food, subordinate to the primary mission of keeping the mines productive. Phosphate fertilizers supplied the foundation of Mahina's agriculture.

Kassidy leaned forward between Sass and Abel's seats on the bridge, craning her neck to see the top of the pyramid. Compared to the Grand Rift, the gypsum stacks were grey, squat, and ugly. The bare minimum of navigation hazard lights adorned the tops. Painfully bright flood lights marked the corners. Other than that, the trash heaps were mostly visible as giant black holes against the sea of bright stars above the horizon.

Kassidy breathed enraptured, "These pyramids are the largest man-made structures on Mahina."

She'd won permission from Sass to record and broadcast live from the bridge for this trip. Sass let her make the most of the view without comment. Most of the flight in, there was precious little to see. The star side of Mahina didn't much bother with outdoor lighting. People stayed inside through the bitterly cold dark days, especially Wednesday and Thursday, local weekend. Lunch might be synchronized moon-wide, but weekend on the flipsides of the globe coincided with the dark half of their cycle.

This was not inspired by sympathy for the miners, Sass thought sourly. Machinery got crotchety in the cold. Most of her compatriots in the rebellion ended up in the phosphate mines, while Sass's Petticreek Five retired to build a pleasant farm alongside an air cracking plant.

"Any thoughts, Sass?" Kassidy invited. "For my viewers?"

Sass considered how to speak her thoughts without sounding rebellious, despite the memory of men and women she imagined died here fast. "It's tempting to climb the pyramids, isn't it?"

"Absolutely! Maybe this is where I should skydive, onto the top of a pyramid. They're already lit as a target."

Sass shook her head. "They're poisonous. Radioactive. Uranium, cadmium, other dangerous impurities are mingled into the phosphate ore. As they degrade, they kick out radon gas. Causes cancer. In daylight, you'd see that the pyramid walls are sealed with foamcrete on this side, facing the landing pad. Still. We walk fast from here into town, and wear pressure suits."

Kassidy was taken aback. "Surely if it was that dangerous, they wouldn't have put the parking lot here."

"Everyone wears a pressure suit outside," Sass clarified. "Sunny day or cold dark. Probably says so on that sign over there."

They peered through the window, but the sign was too far away, and directly under a blinding floodlight. Kassidy plucked a drone camera out of the air and used its zoom optics. "Huh. You're right. Shouldn't they put that sign where people can read it?"

"They don't get many visitors," Abel offered. "When I called to ask for a tour, they put me on hold half an hour while they found someone to say no. There are no public tours. The plant manager invited us to lunch, though. Said his family loves your show."

"Awesome! What's his name?"

"Atlas Pratt."

The name sounded familiar, but Sass couldn't place it.

Kassidy grinned to her drone, now freed to fly again for her closeup convenience. "Great job, Abel! And thank you so much, Atlas Pratt and family, for inviting us into your home! That means so much to me! And right now, I am psyched to get out and see your town and mine!" She laughed. "I mean, your mine and your town. You knew what I meant. Let's get those suits on!"

Kassidy continued, "Cameras off. Truly, Abel, great job landing us a home visit." She reached around his seat to give him a half-hug from behind. "They really wear pressure suits all the time?"

"Outdoors, yeah," Sass agreed. "The dust is radioactive and gets into everything. And at this point of the cycle," she checked her instrument panel, "it's minus thirty Celsius. Great view of the stars, though. Once we're past the floodlights."

Within 10 minutes, the three of them crammed into the two-person airlock in their suits, and cycled it. Kassidy wore the same form-fitting sleek outfit she used to jump beside the ozone spire at the atmosphere factory. Sass and Abel wore bulkier high visibility red work gear, neatly labeled Collier and Greer.

Sass tried not to dwell on what a hassle it would be to get rid of the dust. They charged Kassidy enough to cover the effort. Jules and her mushroom produce stand they'd left at a town 120 km from

Mahina Actual. Eli stayed with her for moral support, since her husband was hours away in case of emergency.

To Sass's consternation, Eli was also selling baby greens. Edible produce a mere two cycles from planting was uncanny. Even Jules knew that. Hopefully she'd keep the intriguing tidbit out of her sales spiel.

Sass put the skyship's farm business out of mind, as they hopped onto the crushed grey regolith and locked up.

"Do plants not grow here?" Kassidy asked, as they began trudging toward town.

"Plants grow better with artificial light for the dark cycle," Sass confirmed. "Mostly they use greenhouses for table vegetables. Bulk food comes from Pono-side."

"I didn't see any greenhouses flying in. That would be pretty."

"They're shuttered so they don't waste light in the dark cycle."

A little farther along, Abel halted to throw his head back and look up. Sass and Kassidy followed suit. There was still a little light pollution from the slag heaps and the beckoning town entrance ahead of them. But the lights were directional and scattered little. The stars looked far brighter and closer than they had at 1,000 meters under full gas on Kassidy's ozone spire jump.

Sass turned slowly, looking for familiar constellations. She drank in the starlight after so long without it. She could count on one hand the times she'd visited Mahina's dark side. The stars were none too visible from Earth, either, among the desperately packed refugee camps of the Adirondacks. One of Mahina's fellow moons gleamed as a tiny blue crescent, far smaller than the Moon seen from Earth.

"I think the moon is Gola," Sass murmured, pointing. Mahina was the innermost of Pono's three largest moons. "That's a rare sight, even dark side." The moon didn't orbit Mahina, after all. They circled the gas giant Pono, and spent most of their time far away. Someone had explained to her once that Gola and Sagamore never appeared in Mahina's sky at the same time. If Gola was near, Sagamore lay far behind Pono.

Abel stood still staring above, a stranger to the stars. Occasional meteorites flared and streaked, burning out on entry to Mahina's atmosphere.

Kassidy copied Sass's approach more exuberantly, spinning under the stars, head thrown back until she stumbled from dizziness, laughing out loud. Panting, gloves on scuba-suited knees, she asked, "Is Earth up there?"

Sass shook her head slightly. "I don't know. That splotchy lighter band is the Milky Way. Our galaxy. But I don't know where Earth's star would be."

"Is it a cloud? The Milky Way?" Kassidy had never seen a real cloud. Mahina occasionally formed a few ripples of condensate, high in the sky. But no fluffy clouds, no rain.

"No. Millions, maybe billions of stars. Or there may be other cloud-like things mixed in, I don't know. Mostly stars, I think."

"The other stars, outside that silvery spill, they're farther away?"

Sass shrugged in her suit, then realized Kassidy wouldn't see the gesture. "I'm sorry, Kassidy. I'm not sure. Maybe some are closer. Others are galaxies, not stars. Much farther away. The faint band crossing the Milky Way is the outer rings of Pono. The same highway Mahina travels along. So some lights are stars, some are galaxies, others nearby rocks and dust. Different distances."

"Millions and billions," Kassidy repeated. "Looking up, I feel like I'm falling into infinity. Alright, that's my sound-bite and I'm sticking with it. It's cold out here, folks. Let's head inside."

They stumbled along the a raised foamcrete walkway. This provided a smooth surface above the rocky dusty regolith. Their eyes drifted back to the stars half the time.

The dark town loomed like a single vast warehouse. A line of lights marched above three doors, two generously human-sized, plus the huge hangar-like doors of a cargo lock. The rightmost door was labeled 'In' with an up arrow in a green ring. A no-go slashed red circle warned them off the 'Out' door.

The doors weren't airlocks, just dust mitigation measures. Abel hauled open the heavy entry for them, and they stepped inside. As soon as the door closed behind them in the entry vestibule, heavy-duty blowers blasted them, and suction vacuumed away the dust. Then a green light beckoned them to enter the next industrially tarnished room, a larger space with locker-room style benches. Signs on the wall reminded miners to rack their suits for cleaning to the right. There were no facilities for guests, but a rack on the other side was labeled 'Temporary.' The door forward advised 'No pressure suits beyond this point.' As usual, each sign included fairly articulate cartoons. Most Mahinans couldn't read, relying on ubiquitous software to do it for them.

In case one still couldn't figure it out, there was a button on the wall labeled with a question mark. Perhaps out of habit, Abel punched the button. A recording read out the signs, with elaborations simple enough for a six-year-old to follow. An indicator light lit next to each sign in turn, though one of the lights was burnt out. The recorded voice advised them that they were on camera — Kassidy located it and waved — and that touching a pressure suit other than your own was against the rules.

"I'd prefer a locker," Abel grumbled, but started peeling out of his suit obediently enough. Sass and Kassidy stripped their gear as well. Thinking Abel made a good point, Sass draped her ugly overalls to hide Kassidy's scuba chic.

At last free to explore the town, they stepped hopefully out to the end of a broad corridor, into another world.

14

Regardless of the selection system, settlers included a high proportion of doctors, farmers, fighters, and police. Maintaining order among the colonists was crucial.

Inside Phosphate Mine 3, the walls, ceiling, and floor bore the mushroom shade of unimproved foamcrete, grimy from hands. Dim lighting strips tacked along the ceiling were a familiar product supplied on industrial spools. They followed the hallway into town. Occasional doors to either side fed into other corridors of doors, apparently serving small residential apartments, with stairs to more apartments on the upper levels.

They overtook a shambling handful of men and women, lanky and hunched.

"Hi!" Kassidy cried, with a wave and a broad grin. "We're visiting. Where's some fun in town?"

Her smile grew fixed as the locals struggled to respond. Most grew agitated and grunted or waved their hands. One tried to catch the shiny camera drone drifting alongside Kassidy.

An older woman, maybe a gray-haired 30, appeared to be the mental giant of the group. "Pachinko is fun. Now we go play pachinko." Several of the others cheered or clumsily clapped their hands.

Kassidy nodded. "I hope you have a good time playing pachinko today."

And the group from *Thrive* passed to continue on their way. Green fronds and brighter lights beckoned ahead.

"Why would you keep the mentally handicapped at a mine?" Kassidy asked the other two, disturbed by the interchange. "That doesn't seem safe."

Before Sass could respond, Abel did. "In my town, the slow children were sent away. Kids said they were sent to the dark side. That's what happened if you didn't do your homework and learn to read."

Sass shot him a sharp glance. Had he worried about that as a child? With his thorough stodgy temperament and reliance on software readers? That he might be sent away for being slow?

She replied gently, "Abel, those stories were true. There aren't facilities in the Pono-side towns for people like this. If a family can't handle their own, they hand them over to the authorities. They're sent somewhere like here."

While everyone continues the lifestyles that create far too many defectives. By now, there were no genetic defectives on Mahina. All children were gene-crafted in the city on some device like Eli's. Infants were nurtured there and delivered to their parents at age one, provided the parents still appeared competent to rear a baby at that point, two years after applying for a child.

Those fragile-limbed vacant people had been perfect one-year-olds. When Sass was imprisoned, the intellectual failure rate by age 20 was around 15%. What degree of deformation counted as physical failure was a matter of opinion.

Only settlers landed here in the phosphate mines. Urb children grew up safe and well, to enjoy perfect youthful health to age 80.

"You're getting angry, Sass," Kassidy warned. "I'm sorry I asked. Here we are!"

The corridor opened to a broad indoor plaza. A high vaulted ceiling looked like it pressed up through the mostly flat top of the town-warehouse. A busy pachinko parlor, replete with plinks and whizzes, flashing lights and giggles, occupied an open storefront to the right.

They hastily turned left. The center was basically an indoor park, with potted palmettos individually lit among whimsical foamcrete benches and climb-on sculptures. The collection at hand formed a miniature golf course. Tall and shambling people, dressed in grey coveralls, played in slow motion. Others sat and stared vacantly, often with walkers or canes resting beside them.

Sass doubted any of them were over age 30. *Don't think about it,* she implored herself, blowing out. *Maybe bringing Kassidy dark-side was a bad idea.*

But her exuberant young starlet spied an ice-cream shop, and made a beeline for it. Kassidy delighted in the vanilla-chocolate-strawberry triple swirl soft-serve. The cones were free, one per customer.

Sass was confident that the 'ice cream' had no cream in it, and amounted to a convenient way to sneak the addled townsfolk their vitamins. The shop sign advised they were open from 0900-1600 Wednesday and Thursday. Closed on workdays. She lingered at a toddler parked in a stroller nearby. His blank incurious face was tinged blue.

"Found you!" cried a man, hurrying toward them on the promenade. In this land of the post-human, to Sass's eyes he looked like a throwback to Earth. Older middle-aged, thinning grey hair, with coarsening features and a paunch belly which strained the buttons on a khaki business shirt, he appeared neither urb nor settler. He waved and smiled at townsfolk in the park, and beamed at the visitors.

"Atlas Pratt?" Abel asked when the man came into range. He thrust his hand out for a manly shake, and introduced himself and the women. Pratt's name and 'General Manager' were supplied on the man's shirt. Not that Abel could read.

"Welcome, welcome!" Pratt boomed happily. "I see you've found the ice cream. And Nico. How are you this fine day, little man?" He bent down and shook hands with the baby as well. "Where's your dad, I wonder?" He rose and peered around.

Sass felt gratified that the general manager also had a problem with this seemingly abandoned blue infant. But no, a teenage girl as lanky as the rest loped toward them, obviously off-gravity.

"Mr. Pratt, sir!" she said, bobbing her head. "I'm playing golf. Nico is watching!" She beamed, expecting praise.

The mine boss supplied the praise in full measure, then inquired, "And is Nico getting to the doctor every day?"

The girl, Pamela, nodded exaggeratedly. "Doctor says he's good today! His dad is working. So I took him. I like working for Mr. Copeland! He's smart."

"I'm so glad. Enjoy your weekend, Pamela. And you too, Nico."

With that, Pamela skipped back to her golf game, not too far away.

Atlas Pratt turned back to his guests. "Nico is the son of my newest foreman. His wife went a little crazy one evening at his prior mine. Decided the city delivered the wrong infant. She hid Nico out in the mine after bed, no protection. Poor little guy hasn't been the same since. Copeland transferred here for the baby's sake, away from the mom. Guess he's supervising weekend maintenance this cycle. Anyway! Welcome!"

He turned toward the far end of the town-building from where they entered. The *Thrive* trio fell in behind him. "I hope you don't mind. I invited some of my crew to join us for lunch. Big fans of your show, Ms. Yang!"

"And your family, sir?" Abel asked. "You said you watched Kassidy's show with them."

"We do! Remotely," Pratt clarified. "My ex-wife and daughter and I. We get together by video every Glow. Watch your show and visit. They live in Mahina Actual. My wife divorced me when I was sentenced."

"You're an inmate," Sass gathered.

"Yes. You don't remember me, do you. Well, they deactivated the nanites." Pratt looked a bit hurt, though, as he rubbed his jaw, sagging with the years.

Sass studied his face more carefully. "The inside man at Mahina Actual? I knew there was one, but never knew who. I asked the rebels not to tell me anything too sensitive. Because of my position as a marshal. Just as well, since I turned on them."

"One of the inside men," Pratt agreed. "There was another, deeper cover. He's still in place for all I know."

Sass stopped walking. "Would you prefer I leave, sir? You could visit with Abel and Kassidy without me."

Abel. Sass shot a glance at him, wondering what he made of Pratt's comment about nanites. Her partner's habitual thoughtful frown yielded no clues.

"Not at all! Please stay," Pratt insisted. "No, Sass, I wasn't accusing you of turning me in. My ex-wife did that after the Massacre. You had an apartment around the corner from us, is all."

"Oh." Sass did remember that, vaguely. She hadn't spent much time at her place in the city. "Your daughter had red hair?"

He nodded, beaming. A warm and smiley sort of man, Atlas Pratt. "Still does. Gorgeous color."

"You didn't do mines in the city, did you?"

"No," Atlas agreed. "Chief medical administrator. Over the research and treatment staff both. Not a doctor myself. Just a manager. And here's my place. Quite a bit larger than average. Rank hath its privileges."

By now they'd turned off the main thoroughfare past the vaulted atrium into a quiet cross-corridor, clean and hushed. Pratt opened a door much like the others.

He ushered them into a generous open living room, airy urb-style replete with plants. The dining table stood heavily laden with a salad-based luncheon. Beyond that, an entire window-wall over-looked the town's interior greenhouses. A conversational grouping took center stage, with a twist. One couch and arm chair were sized for Earth-normal people, the remainder for long-limbed settlers. Pratt's furniture included several ceiling-mounted swings, their seats at Sass's shoulder level. These were already claimed, a favorite perch among his half-dozen low-gravity friends.

Everyone took to their feet to welcome the visitors. They remarked on Kassidy's latest weekly shows, and how they loved *Thrive*. Pratt's introductions made clear that these were foremen and managers, the staff he worked with closely. The men and women were certainly a brighter bunch than they'd met so far.

As the group drifted toward the salad spread, Sass sidled up to Pratt. She murmured quietly, "Were they exiled with you? These foremen?"

"No. They died years ago. The ones sentenced with you?"

"The same." They shared a sad smile of understanding.

The two separated to enjoy the company of the young people they found themselves among now. Sass tried not to dwell on the probable contaminants in the salad. They wouldn't do her and Kassidy any harm. Abel ate clean food at home on *Thrive*. The four Earth-normal sized people sat on normal chairs. The others half-sat on high stools and picked up their plates from the table to eat. Each happily hammed it up as the drone camera zoomed in for a closeup.

The miners laughingly confirmed that the last place Kassidy should jump was onto the gypsum stacks. Not healthy, that. One suggested a handsome crater about 20 klicks northeast. He'd seen it from the air visiting another mine.

The cheerful lunch came to a close. Atlas took the visitors onward to view the actual mine through a window-wall at the far end of town from the parking lot. He recommended they admire it from a distance. There was little to see on the weekend. Between walking and decontamination, it would take a few hours to explore it. The gaping black down-ramp was large enough for *Thrive* to roll in.

"Probably not that interesting to you," the manager concluded sadly. "But it's important. Everyone eating on Mahina, relies on us." He beamed for the drone. "I'm proud of our contribution."

Kassidy teared up, and threw her arms around him. "Thank you so much for all you do, Atlas. For Mahina, and for these unfortunate people."

"Well," he said, his own eyes brimming and voice husky, "I hope they don't see themselves that way. They're happy and normal. But thank you." He met Sass's eye. "Never give up. Rebellion wasn't the answer. But something."

"Something," Sass agreed. She shook his hand firmly, and they took their leave.

On the trip back to Pono-side, Sass found the crater they recommended. She landed in the middle. With no light pollution whatsoever, they stepped out in their suits and drank their fill of the stunningly crisp stars and splotchy Milky Way crossed by Pono's bright rings, and Mahina's perpetual meteor shower. The star-side sky was gorgeous, awe-inspiring.

And Sass felt like a complete and utter cad. She'd taken the easy way out of the rebellion. Meanwhile Atlas Pratt went to the mines. He tirelessly strove to lead and protect the afflicted for 20 years.

How did she ever think she could escape the cause? She'd won concessions from the city, sure. But they weren't enough. Her people still failed to thrive.

15

Mahina was not the worst of the Diaspora colonies. It was one of the most successful. However its human failure to thrive rate was high.

Meanwhile, in an ugly little ville called Poldark, Jules and Eli broiled under the Thursday sun. They hoped for some shopper traffic once school let out. As lunch recess came and went an hour ago, they had a couple hours to kill.

Thursday was not a market day in Poldark, population 3,000 according to the sign. Abel set them up at the hay lot terminus of Main Street. The school lay at the far end, two blocks away, extruded to look like a lumpy castle. The playground equipment featured a shallow dry moat with fake stone bridges on the front side, in addition to the main entrance drawbridge and portcullis. Jules spotted about five children playing during recess. Maybe they had a better playground out back.

It was the school castle that lured them into thinking Poldark was a nice settlement. Along with the leafy greens, their opinion had wilted since then.

Since the mild lunch rush of perhaps six customers, they'd had nothing to do but sit and chat. Eli read most of the time. He used his eyes instead of his ears for this, which Jules found a bit creepy. But she supposed brainy urbs were different from normal folk.

She leapt to her feet eagerly as a trio of shambling men headed their way down Main. "Eli! Fetch me the greens from the cooler?"

Eli set aside his reader and walked to the short container parked next to the mushroom. Rather than set out all their wares at once, they stored most of their stock in there. Besides, the sturdy box supported a longer play slide than mushroom alone.

"Hello, gentlemen!" Jules called sunnily. "Care for some fruit? I've also some fine baked goods. Delicious fresh greens. If you're a farmer, I have transplants for some unusual vegetables. What can I offer you this fine day?"

The men, with dirty looks at each other, strode up and glared at the offerings arrayed on the mushroom flange counter.

"This here's a farming town, chickie," the first man growled at her. "What are we needing any of this scheiss for, huh?"

Jules licked her lip, intimidated. She plucked up a peach. "D-do you grow peaches, sir? Fine and sweet as can be. It's a fruit! Just three credits apiece."

"Wha-at?" another jeered nasally. "Price of four beers!"

The third concurred. "What kind of idiot would spend three credits on a fruit? Peach? Never heard of that."

"Fuzzy, too," added the first tormentor. "That some kind of mold?"

Jules swallowed and returned the peach to its display plate. She looked to Eli in entreaty, now emerging from the shipping container with a tray of red and green lettuce.

"Their greens is defective, too," commented the second. "That ain't green. It's purple."

Eli tried a smile. "Right you are, sir! I can see you're a man of intelligence and wit." He set the tray on the counter. He broke off a red leaf and tore it in three. "I want to give you each a taste of this."

The three men accepted the purple leaves dubiously, and chewed. Idiot 2 swallowed first. "Tastes like lettuce. I don't like vegetables."

Eli sighed.

"You look like an urb," Idiot 1 observed. "Puny. You and the missus fancy folk from the city?"

"Oh, we're not married," Jules said. When their appraising eyes shifted back to her, she hastily flashed her wedding ring to amend this. "I mean, I'm married. But not to him. Eli's a friend. He works with my husband."

"Yeah? So where's your husband?"

"He flew night-side today!" Jules shared proudly. The girl was still amazed she'd married someone so worldly and exciting. Romping with Abel sure beat hell out of sharing a bed with her younger brother, too.

"You trying to make fun of us?" the spokesman demanded. "Like we should be sent star-side cuz we're failures?"

Jules recoiled, too intimidated to even deny she meant any such thing.

The guy wheeled on Eli, nearly a meter shorter than him. Though at least Eli could stand up straight. "That your work, *urb*? Cull failures and throw them to the dark?"

"I'm a botanist," Eli replied, arms crossed. "A scientist. I work with plants. Like the red lettuce."

"Well that's effing useless!"

"Yeah, rego stupid!"

"That's purple, not red."

Eli retorted snootily, "If you don't want to buy something, please leave so you're not driving away other customers."

"What customers?"

Eli scowled. "Before we call the sheriff."

"I *is* the sheriff, fool," the first guy clarified, getting into Eli's face. "And I think you's selling dangerous food...stuff. And that slide? A child could get hurt!"

———

Benjy Acosta switched into his light portable virtual reality headset as the slavering purple ogre hollered at him to get out of the house.

Dad was like that, and ever so much easier to take when dressed in a frilly pink-and-lace pinafore. A brief flash of raw Poldark slipped in between headsets, though. The real dad was 2.5 meters tall, though much hunched, because the screwup didn't wear his grav generator right as a kid.

Not a mistake Benjy would make. *Nothing* could inspire him to turn out like dear old Dad. Safely restored to VR, he enabled his lecture filter. This recorded a couple seconds and then squealed it at a high-pitched over-speed. He smiled pleasantly at the ogre and headed out the side door onto Cross Street, the second of Poldark's two brief streets, for a grand total of four paved blocks. The farm access roads were simply crushed regolith between hedgerows of spruce and aspen. VR made it all look far more appealing.

He turned onto Main and glanced both ways. He checked for mobs, not traffic. Poldark banned vehicles from the foamcrete-paved downtown. Benjy's reality overlay usually provided a few level-appropriate monsters to fight here on Main. Dad the dentist was especially aggravated to see his compact and useless 20-year-old son battling invisible monsters in front of his storefront clinic.

But there was a new twist today. A giant mushroom had sprouted at the vacant lot end of Main Street. Giant rats appeared to be intimidating a beautiful elf and chubby dwarf. He'd never seen this quest before. *Awesome!*

Ignoring the small dinosaur who'd instantiated to play, and vaulting the virtual fences in his path, Benjy ran toward the mushroom, yelling out, *"Ooh-la-la-la! Yip-yip-yi!"*

Droopy rat 1 wheeled toward him. "Benjy Acosta, shut up, you rego fool!" he piped in quick falsetto.

Benjy hastily disabled his zip-squeal anti-lecture feature.

"Howdy, sheriff!" Benjy replied. To be on the safe side, he pulled his VR goggles onto his forehead. To his delight, the gaudy mushroom didn't vanish. The two strangers looked even more interesting IRL — in real life. The purple lettuce inspired him to double-check that his VR was off. "Awesome!"

"A customer —" Jules adjusted her nervous voice down an

octave. This concerned Benjy briefly, but she resumed at a normal pitch. "Welcome, sir! What can I offer you today? Perhaps you have a sweet tooth? I have strawberry coffee cake, with real strawberries!"

Benjy blinked. Maybe he should lay off the VR a couple more hours a day, like the old man was always saying.

"I'll try anything once," he replied. That was the right policy for inexplicable offers from friendly girls he hadn't known his entire life. He avoided the girls in Poldark. The vicious backstabbing gaggle of dimwits vied to marry the 'doctor's son' for his imagined wealth. "But what's that?" He pointed.

"A delicious real strawberry! Three for two credits!" Jules supplied, trying to smile at Benjy despite a nervous glance toward the sheriff. One of his goons had taken over the quest to physically intimidate Eli, leaning his face well inside the scientist's personal boundary.

"Colter," Benjy addressed him, "are you trying to kiss the city dude? I didn't know you ran that way, big guy."

"Why you —!" Goon 2, Colter, spun around and launched a slow haymaker Benjy's way.

Benjy stepped back. His assailant's momentum caused him to spin around harmlessly. "Don't worry about them," Benjy told the fascinating stranger girl. "I'll protect you from the lawman."

"My hero!" Jules replied, grinning at him.

Benjy frowned and shook his head a little. Yeah, wow, reality was a little intense today. Then he closed his mouth and recalled the conversation. "I would absolutely love a — Wait, did you say two credits? Ma'am, your prices are a little steep for Poldark."

"Right? I was telling her!" complained the sheriff. "These city...drifters!"

"Drifters?" Benjy asked. "Did you meant grifters, sheriff? Con artists."

"Yeah, grifters! They's selling crazy scheiss at ridiculous prices! Look at that — purple lettuce!"

Benjy obligingly peered at the purple lettuce in delight.

The sheriff continued, "Urbs spit on folk like us! They was talking all threatening-like about star-side, too."

"I think your groceries look magical," Benjy assured Jules with puppy-dog eyes. He should know. He spent much of his life surrounded by magic in VR to escape Poldark. "The sheriff has a point about your prices, though." He rapped on the mushroom with his knuckles. "Don't go anywhere. I'll be back in a jiff with my money."

"Oh," Jules said, despondent. That left her and Eli facing off against the irate idiots again.

Benjy winked at her. "Don't worry. All bark, no bite." He clapped a hand on the sheriff's shoulder. "Right, sheriff? No worries. I'll wrestle these city snifters for you. They're sneaky brainy sorts. Don't let 'em confuse you!"

Benjy ran off up the street to grab his credit tab from home. No loping in that boy's stride — he pounded the pavement hard at over a gravity while out for his exercise break.

"Who's confused?" the sheriff called after him. "I ain't confused!"

However he had lost his train of thought. He stood with lips pursed, scowling after the uppity dentist's boy. The college kid had a point. If there was brainpower to contend with, the town's sole educated family were likely best equipped to deal with it.

The sheriff returned his glower to Eli and Jules. "We'll all just wait here for him to come back."

"OK," Jules agreed.

Eli nodded and slipped back into the mushroom, closing the back gate. He took up his reader again and read...*silently*. No earphones or anything.

"What is he doing?" the sheriff demanded.

Jules leaned forward across the counter to whisper. "Reading. By sight."

Truly unnerved now, the sheriff gathered his sidekicks and withdrew twenty paces to keep an eye on the interlopers from a safe distance.

Benjy ran back with hard footfalls, his lanky father the dentist pacing him with long floating Mahina-gravity lopes.

"Doctor Acosta!" The sheriff waylaid the older man to address his concerns with the official village brain.

Benjy hit the side of the mushroom running, hard enough to rock it off its ground staples. He apologetically righted it and tamped down the stakes. "Sorry about that. Credit tab. I want one of everything. I'll pay half what you're asking. Dad, you want one of everything, too?"

"Absolutely!" Dr. Acosta agreed. "We'll test it for you, sheriff. You don't need to stay. I'll contact you if anything dangerous is happening. Count on us."

As the sheriff departed grumbling, the lanky dentist joined them at the mushroom flange, rolling his eyes. "Apologies for the welcome committee. Sheriff's an idiot. But so is everyone else in town."

He paused and noted the empty parking field. "How did you get here? With a giant mushroom and a...big box? Is that a slide?" He chuckled. Dr. Acosta wasn't a bad sort. Despite being a purple ogre in pink pinafore in his son's eyes.

Eli explained the missing skyship *Thrive* while Jules collected one of everything for two.

Dr. Acosta sobered and coughed. "You really take people star-side?"

"Just the one person so far," Eli replied, at a loss. "Our friend Kassidy Yang plans to do a sky-dive. She lives with us on *Thrive*."

"*Really?!?*" Father and son said simultaneously. "Wow, oh, wow..." They said that in chorus, too.

The dentist cleared his throat and gathered back his dignity. "So you don't take defectives away to work the phosphate mines."

"We don't," Eli agreed hastily.

"Dad," Benjy said dismissively. "That just a story they tell idiots in school to make them do homework. And this is the peach? It's fuzzy!" He laughed out loud, petting the peach. "And look, it's got a crack like a —" His father elbowed him in the head. "It's very pretty. And fun to pet. What's your name?"

"Jules Greer." She splayed her fingers to better display her wedding ring. "I'm married to the first mate of *Thrive*. And this is our boarder, Eli Rasmussen. He's a doctor, like you, Dr. Acosta."

"Actually I'm a botanist," Eli explained to the dentist apologetically.

The elder Acosta nodded understanding. "How'd you make the lettuce purple?"

"Our captain grew that," Eli admitted, a little vexed. "I should ask her. I crafted these transplants, though. This one is a purple cabbage."

Jules had interpreted 'one of everything' as the edibles. "Would you like transplants, too? Tomatoes, cabbages —"

"Yes, I see the labels," Dr. Acosta interrupted her. "Sure. Yes, I would."

"Dad, we don't have a soil garden," Benjy pointed out.

"Eileen has a garden. She'd love to grow them for me."

"Eileen is a harridan, Dad. She wants to trip you into bed."

"Did you say 'boarder?'" the dentist inquired. "You pay rent, to live with," he waved his hand to encompass the mushroom experience, "all this, and travel around?"

"Yes," Eli agreed. "It's wonderful."

"How much does that cost?"

"I pay for two cabins," Eli said. "I think Kassidy pays 1,000 for a single cabin with a private bath."

"Oh," the dentist said sadly. Way out of his price range.

Benjy joked, "What are you thinking, Dad, a traveling dentist act? Van's not good enough for you anymore? Spread your wings?"

"I was thinking what fun it would be if you went away for college," Dr. Acosta grumbled. "Learn from a scientist who can make purple cabbage. Travel the world."

Benjy suggested, "Get rid of me so you can shack up with Eileen."

"That too."

Jules followed this solemnly. "We have less fancy cabins. Bunk beds and a shared bathroom."

"I have my own room, thanks," Benjy replied.

"Two hundred a month," Dr. Acosta offered. "And the scientist, you know, talks to the kid sometimes. Encourage Benjy's studies."

Eli agreed, "I could help with his homework."

"Dad?"

"Two fifty," Jules countered.

"Sold. Son, go pack."

"I don't believe this."

The dentist slapped his son's hand away from his plate. "Eat your peach on the way. You know, Jules, he's also a gunner. The one bright spot of him living in VR all the time. He can run any gun simulator. Any chance he could earn his keep?"

"Dad? You can't sell me to a skyship!"

"I'm not selling you. Pay attention. I'm paying them to take you away. Go pack. You'll have the time of your life. You'll see. Go forth, do great things. Talk to intelligent people. Find a life out there. Call home sometimes. I'll miss you after a year or two."

Benjy stood staring at his father in disbelief, fuzzy peach in hand. Remembering this fact, he took a deep bite. The peach was delicious, and so different from the same old apples. "Well, alright. I will then!"

"Good. Now do I pay first month's rent to you, Jules?"

Benjy stalked off to pack his VR gear, clothes, and sundries. "You're still paying my college tuition!" he yelled back at his father.

"Yes, yes, through the nose," Dr. Acosta agreed with a sigh. "So hard to launch a child in life. Sometimes you need to supply a boot to his rear. You know?"

"Absolutely, Dr. Acosta," Jules agreed. "Your total comes to two hundred and ninety-four credits today."

"Of course it does," the dentist replied sourly. "Worth every cent, though. Especially purple cabbages. Eileen will like that."

16

Why Mahina was so peaceful is unclear. One theory holds that splitting the settlers into very small towns, too far apart to walk between, with little transportation, made revolt difficult to mobilize.

"Poldark is the worst market town ever," Jules reported sadly, once Abel caught her up in a hug. "Didn't even clear 500 credits today. Still have half the baked goods left over. But I found a new renter! Abel, meet Benjy Acosta!"

Benjy's head in its VR gear continued bouncing to his own sound-track. His arms, bearing a filigree of sensors like silver lace gloves to the elbows, flew around him as he pivoted from the waist, fending off attackers visible only to himself.

"He's a gunner," Jules added helpfully. "Only I'm not sure he's ever fired a gun. Just the sims. But I got 250 credits rent for a bunk!"

"Captain, please report to the mushroom," Abel requested over his intercom. "We have a situation."

"He's a college student," Eli offered helpfully. "Very...bright."

Abel pursed his lips and let that pass without comment. Sass and Kassidy were already heading down the ramp. He prudently drew the captain out of earshot of his wife to explain the situation.

Kassidy amused herself by inserting her hand in the way of Benjy's air-swipes. After he accidentally hit her twice, he yanked up his goggles to complain at the interference. And he froze, eyes wide. "Kassidy Yang! My Dad and I — I mean, I'm a huge fan! Wow, wow, wow…"

Sass watched in amusement, listening to Abel with half an ear. "So you want me to tell your wife she screwed up, so you don't have to?"

"Yes. That."

"No." Sass strode over to confront Benjy, perched on his sizable grav-trunk of necessities. She sized up his muscular compact physique, so at odds with the mine they'd just left. Kassidy yielded to the captain, grinning.

"Sass Collier, *Thrive's* captain. You're a college student, Benjy Acosta?"

"I am, yes, ma'am," Benjy replied, his eyes still star-stuck on Kassidy.

Sass snapped her fingers in his line of sight to command his attention on her. "Mahina University distance education?"

"You know of some other college on this moon?" he quipped, then noted Sass's pressed lips and straightened his posture. "Yes, ma'am, Mahina U. Science and tech. Haven't made up my mind on a specialty yet. Sophomore year."

"So you can read, write, do calculus, study, get phenomenal grades, and still waste your time in VR? And have great muscle tone to boot?"

"Uh, thank you. I think. Yes. Ma'am." Benjy thought that covered all necessary replies.

"Benjy, tell me. Why aren't you suffering from failure to thrive?"

Benjy screwed up his face sideways in puzzlement. "Huh?"

"He's immersed in an enriched environment," Eli postulated.

"He's shooting for his dreams, grasping for the brass ring," Kassidy suggested.

"His dad's really smart, too," Jules offered. "Though his dad's, um, tall."

"He's a VR deadbeat," Abel pointed out. The first mate was having trouble getting past this prejudice. "And for two-fifty, he gets a bunk room that sleeps four and a bathroom for eight to himself."

"Well, he'll share if we get other..." Sass trailed off. "Gunner, huh? Think you can build a hill?"

"Sure! I mean, I've never touched a real gun. But Dad offered to buy me these gloves if I got certified. Blew out the scoreboard! Hills up, hills down, invading armadas destroyed, whatever."

Benjy craned his neck to look around the posse staring down on him like a lab rat on a dissection tray. He peered around them to consider *Thrive*. "PO-3 skyship, Pono Orbital model 3. Sweet ride! Quad AX52-B guns, NQ8's on the bow chasers. Grav grapples probably max out at minus one g. Quarter g for something really massive. Sure, I could build a hill with that."

"It's been used to build hills before," Sass confirmed. "*Thrive* built ridges around my farm. That's how I met the prior owner."

"Cool. I had a question, captain. Does this room include board?"

"No. But labor does." Sass figured it was only fair to throw a bone to Abel. Making the kid work for his feed should soothe the first mate's ire.

Benjy sighed and glanced back down the block toward his dad's dentist office. "Awesome. Where's my bunk?"

"After you load the shop into the hold," Sass said. "Abel can show you how it goes. Do that and we'll feed you dinner and breakfast."

Abel snatched the VR gear off Benjy's head. "And no VR while you're working."

While loading the produce stand into the hold, Benjy learned that whistling, kick-boxing, flipping the bird, trying out the slide, and spinning the mushroom stand upside-down like a top, were also prohibited while working. Most of that he invented expressly to yank Abel's chain. He succeeded.

"Honey," Jules called down to her red-faced husband, "why don't you come up for dinner? Benjy can finish up. Benjy, I printed prime rib for your first night. We can eat just as soon as everything is put away and the ramp's closed."

Benjy completed his tasks rapid-fire, and hopped up to the catwalk on antigrav before a fuming Abel could finish trudging up the stairs.

"I adore prime rib," Benjy assured Jules.

He was better-looking than Abel, with tawny skin, regular features and sunlit hazel eyes. His light brown hair was freshly edged and clipped short. His build was ripped with muscle from gravity training. He was smarter than Abel, who could never have applied to Mahina U because he couldn't sight-read, nor write without computer dictation. And Benjy was closer to Jules in age, too.

Abel loathed the kid at first sight, and his feelings spiraled downward.

As the first mate dragged into the kitchen, Sass added fuel to the fire. "Abel, tomorrow Benjy and I are building a hill. Unless you need Abel to run errands for you, Kassidy?"

FOR THEIR PRACTICE run at hill-building, Sass selected a stretch of regolith near the dark verge, where the bottom edge of the gas giant Pono lurked a few degrees below the horizon. Unlike most of Mahina, the winds were strong here, only calming for a few hours at local sunrise or sunset before switching direction. She landed *Thrive* with the bow pointed directly at the strangely squat Pono, engorged by optical illusion.

Sunset came early at this spot. This was inconvenient, it being Dusk today. But it wasn't worth the fuel to fly any farther. They'd burn through credits enough rearranging the surface of the moon.

"I want a windbreak ridge with a dip to frame the gas giant," Sass explained her artistic vision.

"And not block the sun?" Benjy inquired, trying to wrap his head around the assignment.

Sass was a cop, not a mathematician. She steepled her fingers at a low angle, then waved an arm to suggest the sun crossed the sky, then shrugged helplessly. "It won't block the sun. Much. More with trees. But that would be nice."

"OK, but Pono is there." Benjy pointed straight ahead. "Dark-side is that way." He pointed left, perpendicular to the gas giant. "You want to angle the ridge to split the difference? But there won't be a saddle for Pono. Unless you want a long ridge that wraps around."

Sass pursed her lips. "Um, maybe just a windbreak for today?"

"How long a windbreak?"

"Do we need to know that ahead of time? I mean, couldn't we just start, and stop when the sun goes down?"

Benjy gazed back at her bemused. "No. Maybe I need to explain how this works. Could we use the office table?"

Once they'd retired to the next room, he flipped on his VR goggles and jacked into the display that filled the desk surface. He set a blank gray background on his image to represent the regolith, then drew a purple line. "Let's say this is the ridge line you want. At basic low grade, this is the footprint." A rounded magenta outline ballooned out from the peak trace.

"That's 150 meters," he continued. "Now to build up, I need to cut downward. So this ridge is surrounded by valley. That's where I cut the wedges that we stack for the ridge." A red trace ballooned out from the previous magenta balloon line.

"Now that would leave a cliff on the other side of your valley. Which would crumble. So instead we make a gentle valley." Yet a third orange line ballooned out from the second.

"So now we're about half a kilometer out from your ridge line," he concluded. "The overall footprint is a kilometer wide. Unless I cut somewhere else and dump it here. But that would cost more fuel."

He ceased speaking. Sass stared at this diagram, frowning. "Your point?"

Benjy sighed. "Say that ridge line is a kilometer long." He adjusted its length to match. "That means we need to cut and rearrange nearly two square klicks of regolith. The program estimates an hour per wedge. Here's the wire frame."

A new nest of fine green and yellow traces appeared to show the wedge collection. Benjy rolled the wire frame a little so they weren't looking straight down on the project, and tweaked the ridge for its silhouette to taper off more pleasingly, steeper at one end, with a mild asymmetric saddle. He also bent the ridge slightly for aesthetics.

Benjy paused and frowned. "No, our guns and grav are more powerful than that." He tweaked the simulation parameters so the rat's nest of guy lines simplified. "So that's 40 wedges to cut and move and position."

"Got it," Sass said slowly. "How many for a simple hump on the regolith to start?"

Benjy saved his ridge and started a new design. "This one is only 12 wedges. But no one's paying us, right? So we could build half the hill for practice, and leave the edges here to crumble. If someone wants to come along and finish it later, then we gave them a head start."

"Does your program also estimate the fuel cost of this?"

"I don't know what parameters to give it," Benjy admitted. "Maybe we learn those from the first wedge? The program default says 80 credits per wedge. Give or take."

"No wonder these things are so expensive," Sass murmured.

"I'm confused, Sass. Didn't you say you hired this ship to cut a couple ridges around your farm? Didn't that cost like tens of thousands?"

Sass scratched her eyebrow. "We didn't pay for it. The farm was adjacent to an atmosphere plant. Now that I look at this, they built the ridge to edge the air factory, and my farm was in the cut valley, and the lower ridge was the other side of the valley."

"That makes sense. Sweet, that you got a valley for free."

"Yeah. Could we make this hill...lower?"

Benjy tweaked the simulator for another five minutes. "That's about the cheapest hill you're going to get."

Sass frowned at him. "That's the same number of wedges."

Benjy shrugged. "But each one is smaller. Lower fuel cost."

They decided to cut two wedges, then pause to revisit the plan with a better idea of the time and fuel costs.

17

Gravity generators were a key enabling technology for the Diaspora.

Benjy dried sweaty hands on his pants. The vertical cuts were easy on his end, though Sass found the precision piloting a bit nerve-wracking. Now it was time for the low-flying angled cuts and Benjy's turn to be anxious.

He blew out sharply, and stretched his fingers one last time. "Ready."

Sass started them forward at dead slow, barely 2 meters above the plain, requiring her to keep a sharp eye out for boulders. "Begin cutting in 5, 4, 3 —"

"Sass? Abel returning," came the first mate's voice over the intercom.

Sass dropped her head and shook it, sighing. "Sorry, Benjy, coming back around to start over. Hey, Abel, welcome back. Kassidy with you?"

"She stayed in the city. Can I approach? Or are you firing the guns?"

"Firing. Hang back a few klicks. Sorry. And Benjy — 5, 4, 3, 2, 1, fire."

Using the port side emplacement, Benjy fired the pair of heavy duty plasma guns downward but mostly sideways at a gentle angle, keeping the power level dead on the midpoint. "Slower, Sass," he requested. "Better."

A shriek echoed up the hold, followed by, *"Stop!"* Then Eli apparently remembered the intercom. His repeated shriek of *"STOP!"* came deafening over the speakers.

"Cut, Benjy," Sass agreed. "We'd better see what he wants. Abel, you can come in now."

Benjy obediently cut power to the guns. "But how are we going to —"

Eli burst through the bridge door, dark goggles pushed onto his forehead, white eye sockets surrounded by a nasty red sunburn. "The plants!" he puffed, out of breath from running up the ladder. "The engine!" *Pant, pant.*

"Oh hell!" Sass rose at a run. As soon as she was past the foamcrete statuary clutter in the hold, she hopped the railing down from the catwalk, goosing just a moment of antigrav to break her fall. She hit the ground running, and hauled open the door to the engine room, traversing the length of the ship in a couple seconds — her best time yet.

The smell of scorched leaves assailed her the moment the door was open. Terrified, she waded in. The cucumber leaves by the door suffered definite sun scald, but the damage hadn't gone too far. Belatedly, she reached back for a pair of goggles, heart still pounding, and settled in to inspect the damage.

"Sass? Abel," came over her intercom. "You stopped. Something wrong?"

"Nothing fatal. Sorry, clear to dock, Abel."

Benjy and Eli caught up to her a quarter of the way around her circuit of the engine room. Not having received the full tour yet, Benjy prudently donned goggles and hung on the doorway in fascination, while Eli barged in.

"What did you do?" he asked. "It was fine in here, and suddenly it was like the engine went nova. Ten times as bright. Hot, too!"

"Yeah…" Sass agreed. She turned and gave him a hug. "I'm so glad you were in here to save them. And that you're OK! And Benjy, that you didn't want to use full power. I forgot about this."

"Forgot about what?" Eli said, picking up some lettuce seedlings. They were done for. He set them back on a higher shelf.

"The engine kicked up few notches to power the main plasma guns," Sass explained. "Were you in here long? Benjy, did you use different guns for the vertical cuts?"

"Not long," Eli replied.

"Same guns," Benjy answered. "Low power though — level 1 for verticals, 5 for the almost-horizontals. They need to cut through half a klick of stone."

"Could we use lower power and go slower?"

"That's what I was doing," Benjy agreed. "I was nervous. We don't know yet whether 5 is enough." The engine offered his choice of 10 power levels to feed the guns.

"Oh." Sass continued drifting around the room, evaluating her plants.

"Ew!" Jules announced from the door, donning goggles and holding her nose. She'd flown in with Abel, from shuttling Kassidy to the city. "What caught fire?"

"Our crops," Eli explained. "The damage isn't…so bad." He transferred a whole flat, 48 seedlings, to his reject shelf.

"Yeah, most of my plants will make it," Sass confirmed. "Computer, set temperature to 16 Celsius in the engine room. Shut that door, will you?" The blowers came on obligingly.

"Sweet!" Benjy said. "You have cabin coolers?" Air conditioning was a rare treat among settlers. He sidestepped out of the way as Abel finally joined them, having squared away the shuttle in its parking nook along the hull.

Jules happily explained to Benjy how to access the environmental controls for his bunk room, half again the size of Sass's cabin. So was his enormous bathroom.

Sass finished examining her prize peach tree, which seemed

unharmed. She perched on the ladder to consult her tablet. She studied the overhead. "Computer, open moon roof."

A section of hull obligingly slid open above them. A clear bronze sky, dimming for sunset, stretched above them.

"Why do they call it a moon roof?" Jules wondered. The moon was underfoot. The gas giant was likewise invisible, squatting on the horizon somewhere ahead, not above them.

"English is from Earth," Benjy theorized. "Earth was a planet. Their moon traveled across the sky. Their sun, too. Maybe sun roof meant protection from the sun?"

Sass's estimation of Benjy's IQ rose another notch. Other than that, she ignored them. "Computer, vent engine waste light and heat through the moon roof." The engine dimmed significantly, especially toward the bottom of its column. She turned away and looked around the darkened compartment. She flipped up her goggles, and nodded in satisfaction.

"Computer, add to gun ready procedure. Query, *'Did you water the plants?'* End query."

"Noted."

"Computer, add to-do list, space-ready. Item, move the plants. Item, dolly for the plants."

"Noted. Captain, the air conditioning —"

"Computer, keep the air conditioning on in here. Adjust strength as needed."

"Noted."

Sass sighed. "Alright, let's try this again. Eli, you stay in here by the hatch, on the intercom. Benjy, if Eli yells stop, you stop. Don't wait for me to agree. And let's take it from the top."

"Um, Sass?" Benjy hazarded. "How are we going to resume a 6-degree angle cut?"

"Roughly," Sass replied, "I imagine."

They finally finished their first slanting transverse cut. The grav tractors tried to dislodge the giant cheese-wedge of crumbly regolith, cauterized by plasma seal along the bottom and vertical edges. The interrupted cut was just far enough off true that it wouldn't lift.

Eli reported all was still well with the plants. The waste light venting worked fine. "Can I go now?"

"Not just yet," Sass told him. "We haven't lifted a slice of moon yet."

"Ah," Eli replied sadly. "Can I water the plants?"

"At your own risk," Sass advised.

She and Benjy needed two more passes at the interrupted section, and added a bit of wiggling, before the tractor could finally work the slice free from its bed. Sass brought them up 2 meters, 10 meters, then all the way clear of the new hole in the moon. In ultra-slow motion, below walking speed, Sass guided the ship and its phenomenally massive load toward the spot and orientation on the wire frame where this particular puzzle piece fit in the plan.

Benjy monitored their trajectory on the plot, as Sass continually corrected back and forth just a little. "Maybe next time, it's worth laying in an auto-pilot path," he offered.

"Needed to get it out of the ground first," Sass countered. "But you're —"

Just 40 meters shy of the intended destination for the wedge, it broke into two pieces, one of which fell to the ground and shattered back into regolith.

Sass paused the ship, hovering. "Now what do we do?"

"That's one way to make an even smaller hill," Benjy suggested. "Pick up chunks of ground and drop them on the same spot, one by one."

"And if we were under contract to build the hill as specified?"

"We have to build the hill the client paid for, huh?"

"Or we don't get paid," Sass confirmed. "Life as a grown up is a little different from VR that way."

"Right," Benjy acknowledged. "Let's put this piece down where it goes, then revise the plan."

"OK." Sass completed the fidgety business of getting the giant chunk of rock at the exact spot it belonged, and slowly let it down. Finally the moon bore its weight again. Grav tractors off.

Sass's shirt was drenched with sweat, a drop standing on her nose.

GINGER BOOTH

After so long pussy-footing around, she yanked the throttle back left to spiral upward at twice her usual speed, then banked a sharp right into an abrupt landing just outside the wedge hole. She almost wished she could feel the gees of the turn, but the ship's internal gravity could compensate for far more than that.

"Um, Sass, I'm sorry —" Benjy began.

Sass cut him off. "You have nothing to be sorry for. Benjy, this is what happens when theory meets reality. That's why we're rearranging the regolith for practice. You did great. For a first time? This was amazing. Lunch break?"

"Hell, yeah! Sass? Thanks."

She squeezed his shoulder, slipping between their seats to exit the bridge.

After lunch, they got the chance to explore more nifty features of *Thrive*.

While they retired to the office to revise the hill plan, Eli and Jules stepped out to play on the broken rock. Some people just have a knack. Eli accidentally slid into a crevice. Jules managed to hop safely away from the crumbing edge he rode down. But the unstable scree continued to pour onto Eli, burying him up to the waist. He took some nasty hits from rocks to his arms and head as well.

Along with the moon roof, *Thrive* offered a trapdoor hatch in the cargo hold floor. A winch and cables on the ceiling enabled the skyship to pull a load up through the hole. VR goggles firmly in place for computer-annotated vision, Benjy rode down to Eli on the cargo hook, while Sass drove and Abel managed the winch.

Another first time, this operation was none too smooth, either. Benjy had a hell of a time figuring out how to pull the man out of the debris without inflicting more damage. But within the hour, Eli was resting comfortably in the auto-doc, not far from his plants.

"He'll be stuck in there a week," Benjy quipped.

"I heal fast," Eli corrected him with a yawn.

On the way back to the drawing board, Benjy was uncharacteristically subdued, thoughtful. "Sass, it's true, isn't it? Urbs are self-healing. Eli didn't need that auto-doc. Did he?"

"I'm sure it's helping."

"You have it, too?" he asked. "Whatever it is? That's why you look so young?"

"Not the same as Eli's," Sass conceded. "I have an earlier, experimental version." *Without the safeguards and limits.* "Can't speak for Kassidy."

Eli would enjoy superb health until he was about 80. Then his nanites would suddenly cut out. He would age rapidly, his face visibly melting year to year, probably to die around age 90. That was the plan, anyway. Eli's nanite suite was only developed 50 years ago. The first cohorts using that technology hadn't reached the expiration date yet.

Sass's nanites had no such limits. If they were somehow deactivated tomorrow — and last she checked, they didn't know how to do that — she would resume the human aging process from a perfectly healthy 25-year-old body. *Maybe.* The doctor had confided that it was possible her nanites had adjusted her cells at the genetic level to such a degree that she'd never age, even without them. She might only lose the astonishing rapid healing.

She didn't mention this to Benjy.

He quipped, "Is this like, 'I'd tell you, but then I'd have to kill you'?"

"No. Just personal. And kind of loaded. Back to work, gun-boy."

18

The most crucial enabling technology, of course, was the star drive.

Sass stopped the ship suddenly, dangling the second-to-last slice of regolith.

Benjy worriedly checked the wedge. "Sudden moves are bad for structural integrity."

Sass waved that away. These final wedges they just smashed to smithereens to fill in the core of the hill anyway. The carefully shaped sides were already laid.

"Water," she said.

"Jules," Benjy said over the intercom, "please bring the captain a glass of —"

"Jules, belay that," Sass overrode him. "No, Benjy. Over there, where we just pulled out this block. Ground water."

Benjy studied the dim field, eyes on the wrong direction. By now it was Saturday, under the light of the half gas giant. To Abel's great disgust, Sass and Benjy decided over sunset drinks yesterday evening to complete the pointless hill in downtown nowhere. With each slice, they were still learning, and gaining mastery of the process. Sass's point was that without a complete hill under her belt, she didn't feel prepared to take a contract, even at a steep discount where they'd lose money. Most landscaping jobs involved neighbors. Accidentally loosing a chunk of regolith on a third party's home or fields had the sort of consequences that risked bankruptcy, or negligent homicide.

Abel countered that they were already losing money on this practice project. He lost the argument, and ended up flying a shuttle errand before lunch to fetch Sass another 600 credits of fuel. This was an expensive pointless hill in the middle of nowhere.

Abel was even less pleased when Sass suggested they put it on the map as Mount Benjy.

Benjy himself favored the name Practice Hill, wanting to reserve Mount Benjy for a future masterpiece. They all got a good laugh out of that. Except for Abel, who now stewed in the office over make-work while the other two had their fun.

Sass tapped Benjy's shoulder and pointed him in the right direction. "See the dark seepage?"

"Wow," Benjy agreed equably. "We could call it Water Hill."

Sass grinned. "You don't get it. That, my young friend, is 12 grand you're looking at. Finder's fee for the water. Add to that land claim rights around it."

Boggled, Benjy looked back at the black seepage in the scree. "Cool! Um, Sass?"

"We need to put this rock down, don't we?" They chuckled.

Sass slowly got the mass moving again toward the central volcano-like funnel of their mound.

Benjy returned to plying his simulators to perfect its alignment. Once they were above the crest-to-be, he instructed, "Rotate 127 degrees. Forward 12 meters. Perfect. And 300 meters up."

"On station," Sass reported at the top. The air was noticeably thinner here, but not to an uncomfortable degree.

"Tip it now," Benjy said. "Plasma corner down 3 degrees. Perfect. Ready."

They both adjusted their views to enjoy the show. "And splash!" Sass announced, releasing the grav tractors.

A half kilometer sliver of regolith fell to shatter into the hole below, with a mighty bellow of dust like a small volcano erupting. They both laughed out loud.

"That never gets old!" Benjy said.

Still chuckling, Sass lowered *Thrive* to collect final measurements as the dust settled.

Benjy frowned over his simulation, fidgeting with parameters. Finally he shook his head. "Let's just go with the plan as-is, captain. Last slice! Or break first to tell Abel about that water thing?"

Sass grinned and hit the intercom. "Abel? Please report to the bridge."

The first mate was indeed much happier on his way out. This cash-sink practice hill would make a generous profit on the water. He could stake that claim right now.

Another forty-five minutes — they were getting faster — and the final chunk of regolith shattered to smithereens over the crest of Practice Hill.

"All hands, this is your captain," Sass hailed them over the intercom. "Please look out the port side of the vehicle — that's left when you're facing the bow — to behold Practice Hill and its surrounding moat, in their finished glory!"

She steered *Thrive* in a promenade around the hill itself, then backed off for another circuit down the center of the surrounding new-cut valley. Abel and Jules stepped in to watch over their shoulders. Eli offered congratulations from his cabin, having elected to graduate from the auto-doc at bedtime.

Benjy pulled off his VR visor and tossed it aside. For the first time since childhood, his real life was ever so much cooler. His game standings were falling, and he couldn't care less.

Practice Hill was a lumpy mound, gently sloped. Several key structural wedges sloughed sideways during the bombardment from above, which added a pleasing asymmetry.

"Grind some soil on it. Lay a watering mesh. Plant some trees. And that will make a downright handsome hill," Sass said in deep satisfaction. "Those jagged edges on the valley floor I'd smooth out with the soil grinders. I'd plant the crest in hay for a lookout point.

The sunset view would be glorious. Put the house right about there for wind abatement."

"That's what happens next?" Benjy asked. "On a real hill? Wow." As the gunner, his job ended with the regolith cuts. "So does *Thrive* offer full service, ma'am? Or just the land shaping?"

"Just this," Sass confirmed. "Grinding soil and laying water are a farmer's stock in trade. And Practice Hill comes complete with a water source."

Abel asked Sass to take a closeup loop around the dark water seepage, which continued to spread.

"Well done, captain," he said in awe. He offered a hand to shake with Benjy as well.

"Alright!" Sass said, turning *Thrive* to set down just outside the new valley. She parked so the half gas giant hung to the right of the gas-lit hill. A breeze was picking up now as star-side heated into day, though not as strong as the gale-force winds in the opposite direction during Pono-side day. This was the side of Practice Hill to live on. If anyone ever did.

Sass returned *Thrive* to operational rest settings, complete with closing the moon-roof and returning the engine to quiet plant nurture. "And that's a wrap. Abel, did you submit our water claim?"

"I did indeed. We are asked to stay in place. They're sending someone out. That might be them now." He indicated a moving blip on the proximity plot.

Sass stood and stretched. "I need a quick shower before meeting the authorities. Benjy, you've earned your meals for the month. Next job, you earn wages. For now, you're off duty. I'd like you to think about something, though."

"What's that?"

"Between the cutting valleys and the hill, this thing is bigger than a standard farm. A farmer can't afford to ruin all her fertile fields."

"Oh."

She clapped him on the shoulder. "Tomorrow let's do some research. How to build smaller hills. I pay you 10 credits an hour for that, though — 12 when you operate the guns."

The wages Sass quoted were skilled and super-skilled rates for Mahina. A dump like Poldark offered Benjy few opportunities to earn even an unskilled 5 credits per hour for a measly handful of hours a week. His father the dentist probably couldn't average 10 credits an hour. Two days of hilariously fun work probably would have sufficed. But that offer put it over the top. Benjy's loyalty to Sass now approached hero worship.

She felt much the same about him. It was possible to thrive here, even without the nanites. Benjy was proof.

———————

SASS PLOPPED into her sling-back lawn chair, another waiting empty beside her. Clay Rocha called ahead. Sass told the others to let her handle this guest solo. He landed in the distance to inspect the water seepage for a while, giving Sass time to ready herself for company.

Now his two-person flitter, a third the size of *Thrive's* shuttle, banked in smoothly, and settled a dozen meters from Sass. A few moments later Clay emerged.

"Evening, Clay!" Sass greeted him. "You do that so smooth, barely kick up the dust. Can I offer you fresh fruit and coffee?" She indicated the tray table between the lawn chairs.

"Don't mind if I do," Clay agreed, and sank into the seat. "These chairs are hard to climb out of."

Sass nodded. "The intent is to leach away all ambition. Inspire a nap."

"Mission accomplished then." He popped a slice of peach into his mouth and savored it. "This is downright civilized. For the middle of nowhere."

"Beats hell out of the first time," Sass quipped.

The immediate flashback made her regret saying it. The relentless anxiety of inadequate atmosphere. Too few personal grav generators to go around. A few pressurized geodesic domes, but only for the technicians manning the equipment inside. The rest of them hotbunked on the skyship, racks stacked 6 high in the hold. Working 14 hour shifts on the regolith in breathing gear.

And two cops to manage the conflicts.

Clay grimaced at her for reminding him. That phase ended half a century ago.

She swallowed and changed the subject. "Your rank seems awfully high to inspect a water claim, Clay. No offense."

"None taken. But that's a good water source. And a fine hill. Your first?"

"Yeah. Out here practicing with my new gunner. Promising kid. Strong, compact, Mahina U student. Found him in a crappy town named Poldark."

"I know Poldark," Clay confirmed grimly. "Not a thriving place. The castle veneer on the school shows a little spirit, though."

"That was this kid Benjy and his father," Sass said. Jules teased the story out of Benjy over sunset drinks last night. "Benjy was terminally bored with that school and everyone in it. Too bright. His dad decided it was a teachable moment. That you can reframe the problem, think outside the box. As a hobby, they got busy with an extruder, built a castle exterior for the dull pillbox school. Family hobby. Took a couple years."

Clay digested that a moment. "He's thriving. Smart dad."

Sass nodded. "Benjy claims the man acted in sheer self defense. His mom died when he was little. The usual, failure to thrive, cancer. The dad was stuck with a hyper kid, spewing questions a mile a minute, in a town where nothing ever happened. Just stupid people scraping by. The dad's a dentist. He needed that kid in school."

"Benjy ought to appreciate that dad."

"Benjy's twenty. There's time for gratitude later. For now, he's away from home for the first time. Easier to push away if he resents the parent."

"Glad my youngest is past that point," Clay acknowledged. "This Benjy bears watching. Is that why you took him?"

Sass shrugged innocence. "Still just trying to make a profit with this skyship. The last owner did landscaping. He was the only settler who offered the service. Seems like a promising line of business. Didn't you suggest it, too? I needed a gunner?"

"Yeah, and — Never mind." He settled back with his coffee. At a gentle interrogative noise from Sass, he finished the thought. "Your skyship is space capable. Can't go up there without guns. That's all."

The moons were only the largest chunks in the ring orbiting the gas giant Pono. Local space required both pilot and gunner to navigate through the mixed debris field. Also the primary reason to break atmosphere was to mine some asteroids. Or go somewhere else.

"Hear anything from the other settlements?" Sass fished.

"You know I haven't," Clay growled. The two were deeper in the know than other settlers, even better briefed than most of the urbs. Or at least Sass was in the know when she was a marshal, before her banishment to the farm. The powers that be in the city blocked communication with the two other settled worlds of the system.

"I wonder if they're even alive," Sass murmured.

"You should ask your boarders," Clay hinted. "Rasmussen and Yang."

Sass was annoyed but unsurprised that Clay knew who lived on her ship. "Care to give me a preview?"

"No, I'll leave that to them. I wouldn't mind hearing the answer, though, if you find out anything."

Sass sighed. "Why are you here, Clay?"

"Dispensing a little justice. Kendra Oliver would stiff you on the water find. I'm witness that it's a first-rate claim." He pulled out his tablet and performed some calculations. "I authorize release of the 12k finder's fee."

Sass's comm pinged to announce the deposit to her accounts. She'd expected that payout to take months through a stonewalling bureaucracy. "Thank you very much!"

"You should consult with an attorney. This place is so isolated, I imagine an atmo spire will be your best offer. But I might like the opportunity to counter-offer, if I may. Assuming you don't plan to farm this yourself."

"No, sir. I've had enough farming for now." Sass frowned at the horizon. "Why would you make an offer?"

Clay was silent for a minute. Sass waited him out.

"You've dredged up a lot of memories, Sass. Things I thought I'd put away for good. Like your little visit the other day to Atlas Pratt, missionary to the failed and forgotten. This little group of proteges you're collecting intrigues me. Especially Kassidy Yang. She's got the ear of the people. Kendra Oliver called me on the carpet twice since your release."

"Unpleasant," Sass acknowledged. Oliver was dictator in chief of Mahina Actual. In practice she was absolute despot of their whole world. "But hardly my fault. And not illegal."

"No," Clay breathed softly. "But it opens new opportunities. Be careful, Sass."

"For the record, Clay, I am not trying to overthrow the city. Tried that once. Realized it was a mistake. The urbs aren't the problem. Failure to thrive is the problem. We need the urbs as allies. Not enemies."

"Any insights on that?"

"No offense, Clay, but if you're talking to Kendra Oliver, I've said more than I should. I'm not breaking the law." She struggled to clamber out of the sling chair. "I'll certainly give you a ring once I see the offer from the hydrologist. How many years do you think that'll take?"

"Within the week, actually," Clay replied, accepting a hand up. "Told him I was interested in buying. There hasn't been a new surface water find in decades. It's a big deal."

"Thank you for advancing me the money," Sass said. "Big of you."

"You're welcome. Sass, you need to be careful not to incite rebellion with Kassidy Yang's broadcasts. Her livecast from the phosphate mine was taken the wrong way in high places." He blew out. "Sure you don't want this farm? You need to keep a low profile. You chose an awfully conspicuous client."

"We need the money. Kassidy is a blast. Anything else?" Sass started folding the chairs as a hint that this interview was over.

"Guess not," Clay returned. He returned to his flitter and took to the sky.

Once he was out of sight, Sass reopened her chair and sat to contemplate his visit. She collapsed the other chair to the ground to discourage company.

What the hell just happened?

Was Clay trying to protect her? And if so, from what? Maybe it would have been smarter to ask her old colleague why he was being so nice to her today.

19

The core of the star drive was a fusion reactor, capable of generating prodigious power from water and a few reagents. This basic level of the device powered homes, industry, and through grav generators enabled air travel, even into orbit.

"Rocha!" Kendra Oliver barked, as she barged into Clay Rocha's suite in the city. "Why didn't you report in?"

She kicked at a knee-high baby goat, placidly munching in his living room. Clay left his doors open for the animals to wander in from the botanical garden and petting zoo. In distaste, Kendra stepped carefully along the foamcrete walkway that wended through his living room, instead of the living grass carpet. The critters did leave their little piles. Drat the man.

She reached the doorway of his bedroom, and leaned against the entrance arch, admiring Clay's sculpted backside in the nude.

Clay remained in his bathing grotto, facing away into the waterfall, until he was certain he could keep his face in the game. Kendra was annoyed today. She wouldn't be in the mood to strip and pounce on him for sex during his shower. Probably.

He allowed himself one invisible sigh, then turned. "Kendra! I didn't hear you come in." That was a lie.

He tuned down the waterfall to plash along its rocks as a bedside fountain, and grabbed a towel off the plants that lined its pebble-tiled basin. He shot her a crooked smile that did not reach his eyes.

"Turn that thing off," Kendra growled. "The dripping makes me need to pee." She crossed to his bed and sat, crossing elegant long legs in turn to toss off black stiletto heels. The bedroom at least had a hard tile floor as a livestock deterrent. Though she noted in irritation that the ceiling was presently missing. Half the room was lit by a three-quarter Pono and the remainder in shadow. "Unless that's a game you'd care to try. Shall I piss on you?"

"Perhaps another of your playmates for that." The last thing Clay wanted was sex with Kendra this evening. His nanites had other ideas, damn them. He wondered if Sass had such trouble managing her appetites.

No, he knew she did. Not that her libido was any of his concern.

He crossed quickly to his wardrobe behind a bank of ferns and exotic flowers to pull on some clothes before Kendra could take any more of hers off.

"What do you need, Kendra?"

"I ordered you to investigate Kassidy Yang," Kendra reminded him. "And then you hared off across the regolith to witness a water claim."

"Yes, the claim was valid. We'll have to see what the hydrologist says. But quite the occasion. The first new surface water find in decades, isn't it?"

"Funny, I don't follow the hydrology news," Kendra growled. "Why do you?"

"Water is important. We could thicken the atmosphere with another spire. Someone told me that. I forget who."

"Kassidy Yang." Kendra nearly spat the name. She didn't give a damn about tossing the yokels another atmo spire.

Clay pulled on bluejeans and a yellow-and-white striped rugby shirt. Kendra hated it when he dressed down, and seemed most aroused by his FBI-style dark tailored suits. Hence his choice of extra-casual wear. "I believe Yang was in the city today, Kendra. I flew out to the verge, as you noted."

"Why are you playing dumb? And dressed like a rego fool, too."

"No progress to report, Chief," Clay replied coldly. He remained standing, with crossed arms.

Chief of Security was Kendra's official title. As such, a marshal like Clay reported to her. Marshals were the top law enforcement with worldwide authority, unlike a sheriff constrained to a single town. Her interpretation of what counted as security was exceedingly broad. Everyone answered to Kendra one way or another. The lucky ones didn't know it.

The baby goat tried to wander into the bedroom and slipped on the tile. Kendra plucked up one of her stilettos to aim at it.

Clay hastened to pick up the goat and carry it outside before Kendra could hit it. He paused to give the animal a treat on the way, to make sure she'd be eager to come again, despite the mean lady. He closed his glass-paned French doors on the gardens. The entire back wall was windows in one form or another, to invite his privileged lush view into his home.

"Why must you let the zoo in?" Kendra demanded, having trailed him into his living room.

Clay perched on a couch back in front of the floor-to-ceiling windows, in full view of the many citizens strolling through the park. "Good company. They surprise me. Don't you get tired of everything being under control? Predictable?"

"Is that why you liked raising your own brats?" Kendra picked up a childish paper-mâché creature from a display shelf. She deliberately tossed it to the floor and stomped on it.

Clay stared at the crushed gift, and time stopped. Hunter made that dog for him as a Father's Day gift when he was six. He and his mother lived here with Clay full-time then. The boy called it a corgi, though it barely looked like a dog. Clay used to read with him every night. His favorite book was on dog breeds. The gene-crafters miserly supplied Mahina with only one canine variety, a little black mop. City ordinance permitted only four of the beasts, kept here in the botanical gardens with the goats. No private pet ownership. Essentially because Kendra Oliver hated animals and children. Hunter would have loved his own dog.

Kendra was saying something. Clay wasn't listening.

"Get out," he interrupted her. His eyes raised to meet hers in fury. "Never enter my apartment again. Bitch."

"What did you say to me!"

Clay rose decisively. "Get out. And stay out. Permanently. I'm finished with your sexual harassment."

"How dare you!"

Clay grabbed her elbow and dragged her to the solid front door by the kitchen. That let out on the street instead of the zoo. "We're done. Bye, sweetie. Bitch."

He shoved her out in her stocking feet and slammed the door behind her. He blocked it shut with his shoulder while he reprogrammed the locks to keep her out.

She continued hammering and yelling at him. "You answer to me, Rocha! I am the law on this moon! You won't get away with this!"

"I obey lawful orders," Clay returned. "Sex is optional. I'm sure you'll find someone else for your dirty work. Kassidy Yang is perfectly legal."

There, the door was reprogrammed. Kendra could easily get someone else to override the controls, but she was too lazy to learn the skill herself. The old harpy's muscle tone was cosmetic only, maintained by nanites rather than sweat. He let her hammer and screech.

Heart still pounding, Clay sank to a seat at the kitchen table. *What have I done?*

Hunter wouldn't give a damn about the papier mâché corgi. He disowned his father years ago. He bore his mother's maiden name now, Burke. He was a rebel leader — maybe *the* rebel leader for all Clay knew. As their deepest mole, Clay operated through dead drops. He couldn't leak what he didn't know, and in his risky position, it was paramount that no one expose him. Not even Sassafras Collier or Atlas Pratt knew that Clay was their inside man.

Though Clay certainly knew about them. He covered their asses often enough. He sighed anew. A shame Atlas's wife proved untrustworthy. Yang's broadcast was a shock, to see the warm-hearted administrator still striving for his ideals, but grown old.

Sass he felt less guilty about. Her prison sentence was self-inflicted.

But maybe I could tell Hunter. He deserves to know his father backs his cause. That I'm proud of him.

The pounding finally ceased as Kendra left to ruin someone else's evening. He should toss her stilettos into the zoo for the goats to chew on. Once upon a time, she scared him, and her mother before her. He got over that decades ago. Even this charade, kicking her out and refusing sex with her, was a reprise performance, overdue. He staged a blowup once a year or so. It turned her on, kept her pliant when they had the inevitable makeup sex.

Hm. Maybe it was more like five years since the last time he'd blown up at her. Getting to be like an old married couple. The thought made his stomach churn. *Whore for the resistance, more like.*

Clay picked up the flattened corgi and studied the damage. *Maybe I could just ask Hunter how to fix the dog.* Not that the grown man would know any better than his father did. But at least he would know the keepsake mattered to Clay. And how much he hated Kendra Oliver. That much he could admit, to open a crack of dialogue between them again. The father needn't expose himself all at once. He didn't deserve the absolution of the confessional.

Benjy, Clay recalled, blowing through taut lips as he pulled himself together. He meant to follow up on this Benjy. He didn't have a profile yet on Sass' latest acquisition. She'd certainly been busy gathering oddballs. He shook his head. As usual with her, no rhyme or reason, no carefully laid plan — just collect people she liked, and hope for the best.

No, he was a gunner. She needed a gunner. *Poldark. Dentist.*

In a matter of minutes, Clay located the medical and scholastic evaluation for one Benjy Acosta from his college application. The boy was built from sperm and egg, not genome data, though here in the city of course. They'd run only basic disease marker tests on the baby, not the full genome. But Mahina University had a tissue sample. Clay ordered a full gene sequence, marked the request urgent and sensitive, and told them to hold for pickup.

That much was easy, and should be ready by Dawn, two days hence. How to get the data analyzed in any meaningful way would be trickier. Clay didn't trust the medical researchers in the city. He wasn't even sure what they did for a living anymore. They'd had over a century to study failure to thrive. So far as he could tell, the scientists couldn't be bothered about the syndrome since Atlas left.

No, that wasn't fair. They'd find it an interesting and challenging problem. Kendra must have axed their funding. The only nanite developers left were willing to block treatment for the settlers, as Kendra insisted. Mahina's advanced nanite suites were custom-tailored in the lab for a single person.

Unlike the nanites that flowed through Sass and Clay's veins alike, making the pair a strange sort of technological brother and sister.

Clay's face hardened, remembering the very different treatment he and Sass received on a muddy field in the Adirondacks before embarkation. One giant syringe held a single diabolical cocktail. A familiar cold rage burned in Clay's chest at the recall.

Ten cops. Only six survived the injection. Would any of them have volunteered for a chance at immortality? Knowing it came with a 40% chance of immediate and agonizing death? Not even immortality. Clay and Sass were the last ones standing.

He wondered if she knew the others were dead.

The nanites they received were miniature factories. The rest of their nanite suites were constructed after injection, by the first ones. The techs here couldn't reverse engineer the original cocktail. The marshals' full-custom nanites, the ones that still coursed through their blood, hailed from a distinct engineering lineage than the technology's progression on this moon. Mahina Actual didn't understand them.

No one knew who injected them, with what.

Clay shook off the memory. Seeing Sass again brought up too many things best left in the past. The immediate point was that Mahina Actual was a small town. Its brainpower supply was sorely limited. Hell, that was true of the whole moon. With barely 150,000 left, Mahina's whole population amounted to an abandoned rural county back on Earth. They might have an expert who could figure out why Benjy was different, why he thrived when almost everyone else languished without customized nanites.

Clay filtered through the other current students at Mahina U, and added one more genome to his sequencing request. That was it. The university had only four settlers, from bachelor's degree candidates to post-docs. Genome data was already available on two of them.

Well, maybe the data could show something, maybe it couldn't. What little biographical data the university records held, he transfered to his computer, too.

Nature, nurture, genetics — something made those four children thrive. They needed to know what. Sass had good instincts.

That attended to, Clay picked up the broken paper-mâché corgi. And he called his ex-wife, Rosario Burke. They divorced after 10 years, per Clay's standard contract with women, no hard feelings. They were practically strangers now.

Rosario answered promptly, on visual. Her hair was pure white and wispy, her face netted with wrinkles and pocked with skin cancer sores. The crucial UV sunblock wore thin on a hot day. Sun damage compounded over the years. Her eyes were clouded with cataracts. She wore an oxygen cannula taped to her nose. She might not make it to age 50.

She still flashed him a saucy smile when she recognized his face.

"Rosario. I need to bury the hatchet with Hunter."

"About time!"

"Past time," he agreed. "Where can I catch him by surprise? Preferably not doing something illegal."

Rosario laughed.

20

It's a shame that the star drive wasn't invented even a few decades earlier. The fatal damage to Earth's atmosphere was avoidable.

"Sure is awesome to have a scientist aboard," Sass said, squeezing Eli's shoulder and beaming at him. "Pump's all set. We're filling the tanks now."

She settled beside him, arms propped on the catwalk railing. Today was Glow, the following day, dedicated to goofing off and hobby projects throughout the Pono-facing towns of Mahina. Below in the hold, Benjy was teaching Jules to handle a sword in VR.

Less inclined to silly pursuits, Sass and Abel decided that they owned a well, and knew how to use it. Water wasn't especially expensive, but *Thrive's* tanks were prodigious. Besides, it was a fun family project. Eli provided the chemical analysis. Benjy drilled the well hole. And Sass and Abel rigged pipes and pumps. All by the romantic idiocy-inducing light of the full planet squatting on the horizon, next to handsome Practice Hill.

The gas giant looked enormous so close to the horizon. Sass had forgotten that effect from full moons on Earth. Granted, it was windy outside.

They now had their very own filling station. Eli assured them the water quality was within parameters for the skyship's environmental systems. They could even fill a pool and swim in it if they wanted, provided they didn't drink too much. Jules talked about making a water slide. But the nocturnal chill and wind dissuaded them. Maybe when they came back on a sun-up day.

Eli nodded thoughtfully beside Sass, and gazed down at the playful youngsters of the crew with a slight frown.

"Hey, Eli?" Sass said. "Yesterday, the marshal seemed to think you might know something about the rest of the system. Off Mahina. Do you?"

Eli's eyebrows rose, and he shook his head. "No one does. Well, outside Kendra Oliver's team. That woman is a control freak."

"Huh. Why?" Sass's brow crumpled. "I mean, I understand that Kendra feels she needs iron control over what happens here. We settlers outnumber her colony. We were forced on the urbs against her will. She holds a grudge. She won't risk letting us gain the upper hand."

Eli glanced at her. "Surely Kendra isn't that old?"

"No," Sass conceded. "She was a child. Her mother had the reins then. Died of the cancers in her 50's. But Kendra took over her mother's torch, and her attitudes. My point was, I get the control freak part. But why block news from off-moon?"

Two other colonies shared this solar system, another moon and a planet in the Goldilocks zone. Plus the orbital station and whatever other space- or asteroid-based installations there might be. Sass arrived here over 65 years ago. But that was all she knew of the Aloha system beyond Mahina.

Eli canted his head. "She's ferociously protective. Any news would come through the orbital. That's our interface. But she's used it as a dumping ground. Scientists who won't toe the line here get exiled to the orbital. My thesis advisor is up there. Maybe that's what your marshal meant."

"What did he do? Your thesis advisor."

Eli sighed. "He recommended we radically expand the number of plant species across Mahina. Enrich the lives of settlers, yes. But also there's a danger inherent in monocultures. Mahina assumes that our crops have no natural enemies. We're completely quarantined. But evolution marches on. There's no shortage of bacteria or algae. Humans carry an enormous suite of microbes in the digestive tract. The current biota is livable, but brittle. And so very poor. Outside the city, settlers live in a desert bleaker than any on Earth. Too few species."

"Kendra exiled him for saying that?"

"When he started to sway people against her, yes. He argued that her role was to keep order, not the terraforming mission. She shouldn't have any say on Mahina's biota."

"Scientific infighting then."

"Basically," Eli agreed.

"You haven't heard from him since?"

Eli remained silent a suspiciously long time. "Three years ago. He inspired me to proceed with my seed fabricator. Better than nothing."

"Huh," Sass acknowledged, not buying it. "Why?"

"Never mind. Sass, I meant to tell you," Eli said grimacing. "I'm having trouble with my Earth seeds. They don't grow as fast as yours. You know your theory, that there's a 'magic beanstalk spectrum' in your star drive? You might be on to something. Only backwards. The magic spectrum might be in the plants, not the drive."

"The plants are optimized for that wavelength?"

Eli winced. "Spectrum. White light comprises most wavelengths."

"Eli? Sue me for talkin' sloppy. You know what I meant."

"Right. I'm making a hash of this. I want to investigate. But I need instruments I don't have here. And I need to work here, outside Mahina Actual."

"Because Kendra Oliver punishes people who study questions she doesn't want answered."

"Exactly."

Sass glanced down at Jules and Benjy, happily smiting invisible foes. Looked like a good workout. "Like failure to thrive?"

"Maybe," Eli conceded.

"Tell me, Eli. Can your research prevent failure to thrive?"

"By itself, no. It can help. Unless..." His face looked briefly distracted by a new stray idea. "Well, I could look into that too, a bit."

"Why do you know that?" Sass demanded. "That more species diversity can't prevent failure syndrome?"

"It's not enough by itself, Sass. Look, someone like Benjy has spent his entire life bucking the trend. While everyone around him, including his parents, succumbed to some degree. A rich life, full of different species and challenges and threats, can nurture the clear intent to never, ever let up. To always be disciplined. Never slack off on the grav, eat right, get enough exercise. When the oxygen sensor beeps in the night, immediately rise and get into an oxygen mask, and keep it on. Sleep in a room surrounded by plants, so the damned thing doesn't keep waking you up. Or sleep with an oxygen cannula on your face."

One of the luxurious things about living on *Thrive* was that the ship minded the air quality for them, and automatically corrected issues. The atmosphere was usually fairly good these days, especially in a town surrounded by trees and fields. Sass noted most people didn't even carry emergency air. They just tolerated mild hypoxia. On a continual basis, brain damage accrued.

Eli glanced around and lowered his voice. "And even with all that, Benjy was simply born smarter than most. Jules or Abel could do the same right things — Abel probably did. But he wasn't cut out to become a Benjy. Jules and Abel aren't stupid. Far from it. Neither are you. You're a different kind of smart."

"So you're saying we have all the right ingredients, but not the right humans to take advantage of them?" Sass frowned and shook her head. "I believed that, Eli. I really did. When I turned over Landau for the grav generators and the improved food supply. Keep the babies in the city for a whole year. Give every settler the first two children for free. Those were big concessions."

Eli waved a hand. "But it's not enough. Something still isn't right. We can't add a grav-plated life for every settler, Sass. Inside a sealed paradise like Mahina Actual. Because this moon doesn't have the resources. We don't even have the resources to build ships to go get the resources. That's why the settlers live in such sorry conditions. But you know what? Since I've been with you, I think it really sucks to live in that city anyway."

Sass snorted. "City. It's a small town, chock full of petty people. Pretending to be on their best behavior. Except their top pastimes are gossip and backstabbing."

Eli nodded emphatically. "I'm happier here. And Sass? Without their nanites, I doubt the urbs would thrive inside the city either. If that's thriving. They live under Kendra." He mock-shuddered.

"Not my kind of life," Sass agreed. "So what did you need from me?"

"Just a few things. Reagents. More parts to build multiple seed fabs. Gene splicer and centrifuge. An in vitro rig to birth some animals."

"Sure, I have some in my footlocker. You're welcome to borrow them. Eli? Why are you asking me?"

"I want to liberate this from the city."

"You're out of your mind," Sass snapped. "Steal equipment from Mahina Actual?"

Her raised voice caused Abel to stick his head out of the office, then saunter over to join them.

"I'll pay you," Eli said, earnestly appealing to Abel. "I don't have a lot of money. But I could get you into the fruit tree nursery."

"A fruit tree?" Sass replied indignantly. "You want to rob Mahina Actual and you'll pay us with a nice fruit tree?"

Abel pointed out, "No, he wants us to steal the fruit tree, too."

"Hundreds of them," Eli protested. "Bertram, my mentor, grew them to distribute to every town. Kendra said it sent the wrong signal, rewarded settlers. They're just growing in an automated warehouse now. We can take as many as fit in the hold. Please?"

"I prefer cash in advance," Abel noted, arms crossed.

Sass grumbled, "I prefer not getting arrested."

"What if I get you a nanite synthesizer?" Eli pleaded. "Just think about it."

"Eli?" Sass replied. "Think about paring down your ask. To something doable. And a little closer to legal. OK?"

Eli slunk away toward his cabins.

"Did he really suggest we steal hundreds of *trees* from Mahina Actual?" Abel mused. "Trying to picture this."

"You missed the part that would get us jailed for life," Sass said. "Stealing a nanite synthesizer."

"What's that?"

Sass knew she should answer with something vague. But her eye fell on Jules and Benjy below. "It's what makes the urbs immune to failure to thrive syndrome. Their most carefully controlled tech."

She'd said too much. She stole a guarded glance at her partner's stolid, calculating face, checking for impact. Maybe it would bounce off.

"That would tend to solve our financial problems." Abel considered a moment more, as his face hardened. "Permanently."

Ah. He had understood. "That's flat-out war, Abel. And we don't know how to use it."

"So we kidnap a technician, too. Though if Eli wants to steal this thing, he must know how to use it."

Sass turned her gaze down the catwalk where Eli had disappeared into his cabin. "Abel, even in the rebellion, we never dared steal a nanite synthesizer."

Sass tried to remember why that was. The obvious was that the city would never rest until they got it back, with reprisals. The settlers could lose even the concessions they'd won. Or worse. Mahina Actual controlled the atmosphere spires, and the gun-bearing skyships, save this one.

Atlas Pratt flashed to mind. Maybe they did intend to steal a nanite fabricator, and simply didn't tell Sass. She never knew about Atlas. She couldn't spill what she didn't know. Ruefully, she noted that she spilled whatever she did know all too readily. Like now. She wasn't cut out for conspiracy.

Abel caught her eye, muscles around his mouth rigid. "So we look into it. Maybe you dealt with the wrong people. Rebels, idealists.

What the job needs is a competent crime syndicate. Marshal Sassafras Collier. I'm guessing you know where to find the kind of criminal who can do business."

"Oh, good," Sass breathed. "A crime of the century heist, and *my skyship* visits Mahina Actual that day. And get in bed with a mob boss. While I'm on parole for rebellion. When did you turn into a rebel, Abel?"

"The instant I learned this tech exists. Sass, the mystery is how you ever believed for an instant you'd let the rebellion go."

"Well, I had 20 years practice pretending." She leaned on the railing again to muse. "Multiple stages. It's...possible." Actually, now that she permitted herself to think the unthinkable, pieces started to swim into place. A cop understood all too well how to accomplish a crime the smart way.

"We'd need *Thrive* for the trees," Abel said practically.

Sass snickered. "We could skip the trees."

Abel shook his head, still furious. "We take our trees."

"Agreed. Just not the same week. How are we doing on taxes?"

Abel shrugged. "Past the halfway point. Both on money and time limit. Still need over 50,000 credits. Only two cycles left to come up with it."

Sass checked their balance on her tablet. "No. We've got 85 grand. We only need 110."

"Need to pay taxes on the income we use to pay taxes," Abel clarified sourly.

"Dammit. Did you call Willow? To book a hill?"

Abel nodded. "Says she was drunk. She doesn't want to buy a hill. I put out a classified ad, offering the service." He sighed mightily. "At least we made a profit on the water bounty."

"And we're all practiced up on the guns," Sass growled and rubbed her forehead. "I'll call Willow. We might need to do it at cost plus labor."

This is what she should be worrying about — how to pay her taxes. Get her business off the ground. Scrupulously honor her parole. Build a new life, leave the past behind. *Again.* Dammit, if she got caught ripping off proscribed technology from Mahina Actual, she could lose *Thrive,* and so would Abel and Jules. She doubted she'd get as cushy a jail term the second time, either. She swallowed and licked her lips.

"Sass?" Abel prodded. "We're doing this. Stealing the stuff from the city."

"Too risky, Abel. Too crazy." Sass felt as though something quailed within her to say it — a chunk of her soul perhaps, hardening and shriveling within.

"My dad says the old get risk-averse. Because he screwed up so many times along the way and promised, 'I won't do that again!' Now he's afraid of his own supper. Lets my sister make the business decisions. Because Dad can't make up his mind. He didn't get wiser. He got hidebound. You think he's right? You're older than my dad, right?"

Sass scowled at him. "Yes, I'm older than your dad. But I'm not old. Abel, we could lose *Thrive.* Everything you've got."

Abel shook his head in firm denial. "Everything I've got is Jules. We keep her out of this. She's too young. The rest of us do it because it's right. Right?"

Just to imagine agreeing with him was enough to unclench Sass's shoulders and fists. That shuddering compacted lump of soul unfurled in her gut. She blew out a sigh of relief and began to nod. "Right. I knew I picked the right partner." She tugged his sleeve to reel him in for a handshake and half-hug.

"Damn straight. And Sass? You're getting younger every day."

"Wise ass." She snuffed amusement. He was right.

21

The base version of the 'star drive' was insufficient to power a true interstellar starship. 'Star' referred to fusion, the process that powers a sun.

Abel completed a perfect landing in the Newer York parking lot the next evening, and shut *Thrive's* systems back to domicile mode.

His piloting skills were getting pretty good. Sass, supervising from the copilot seat, thought she might let him drive the bus solo soon. She was about to pay him the compliment.

He opened his mouth first. "So. We're here for you to...*date*... Hunter Burke again."

"I suppose it's a date," Sass allowed. "I called first. Abel, I'm not dating the guy. I'm shacking up with him. I meet him. I bring him back. We have sex. We negotiate. In the morning, Jules opens her farm stand. Clear?"

Abel glowered. "Because he's in the resistance."

"That and he's a good lay. Abel? I'm not married. I can have sex with whoever I want. Surely you did before you married Jules?"

"I married a virgin!"

"Well, she's only fifteen."

"I was a virgin too. I didn't ask Jules if she was. No, I'm sure it was the first time for both of us."

Sass chuckled, then took in his hurt face. She attempted contrition. "That must have been...awkward. And um, very sweet."

"I studied up first!" he protested. "Just because I can't sight-read doesn't mean I'm an idiot. I picked out the best instructional videos, for us to watch together on our wedding night."

Sass clapped a hand over her mouth, trying to be tactful. It didn't work. She squeaked laughter, tears brimming from her eyes. "Here, darling. I have a porn selection to start off our wedding night!"

A vein throbbed on Abel's beet-red face. "They were very helpful!"

With difficulty, Sass brought her chuckling back under control. "That's... thoughtful of you, Abel. Sorry. I learned the sweaty groping amateur in the dark way, in a tent full of mildew."

"Mildew?"

"Never mind. Do you and Jules want to walk to the bar with me?"

"No!"

"Fine. You're just cranky because we're doing Willow's hill for time and fuel."

Sass was pretty sore about that lousy deal, too. But they needed a real hill and a good reference. And Willow drove a hard bargain. They'd just come from her place. They'd spent most of the day planning the operation and ironing out the contract.

Turned out Willow really did want a sizable hill. She needn't sacrifice any of her fields for it, either. She had several abandoned farms next door which she'd been gradually assimilating into her own. There would be no adjacent valley — Sass and Benjy would cut unincorporated wasteland a few kilometers away. They found an awkward daisy-chain of abandoned fields from the outskirts of town to the target field, to lower the risk of dropping debris. All Willow needed was permission from the town, and then to seal off the soon-to-be-buried irrigation netting. She should be ready for them next week.

"That pisses me off, too," Abel allowed. "But I just — I don't know, Sass. I feel like I ought to be protecting you."

"Are you experienced with criminals?"

"Only on legal contracts. Criminals hire extruder services too. They pay cash."

Sass's eyebrows rose. "Good to know. But not my point. Can you shoot a gun?"

"No."

"Any good at hand-to-hand fighting? Knives?"

"No!"

"Good thing I can protect myself then." She grinned at him. "Do me a favor, Abel. Don't scowl at guys I bring home. Especially Hunter. You're not my dad."

"But does he mean something to you?"

"He's a friend, Abel. I'm allowed to make friends off-ship, aren't I? Isn't that better than me shacking up with Eli, or Benjy?"

"God, yes. But this is a sensitive business contact! You're using him as a liaison to the resistance!"

"Yeah, and I think being *friends* will help with that. Not my first rodeo, Abel. Hunter and I are already that kind of buddies. Backsliding would be unfriendly."

Abel scowled. "We're going to have to do a lot worse than this to carry off this plan, aren't we?"

Sass gave him a half-hug from behind. "Yes. But this isn't a sacrifice. I'm just having fun. Quit worrying. That's an order from your captain."

———————

SASS LIT CANDLES around her cabin, for a golden dancing ambiance that rendered the corrosion on the bulkheads as interesting texture. She should get around to painting. When she moved into *Thrive*, she painted the captain's cabin — now Abel and Jules'.

Hunter poured. She accepted a glass of whiskey from him as she settled beside him on the narrow bed. She should get bolsters, too, so she could lean back and still have her knees bend off the bed. For now the two perched leaning forward, feet on the floor.

"You seem pensive," she fished, when he made no move to put an arm around her. Everybody was moody today. Willow. Abel. Benjy was skittish about bidding a real hill, as well. Now Hunter.

"Yeah. My dad showed up to make peace with me today. Told me some surprises." Hunter rotated his glass a few times in his fingers, then took a sip. "He's not who I thought he was."

"Disconcerting," Sass acknowledged. "Is he better or worse?"

Hunter chuckled softly. "Much better. I mean, I'm still not going to change my name back to his, but. See, he's a marshal. I thought he was a patsy for Kendra Oliver. It's more complicated."

"Marshal which?" Sass growled.

"Clay Rocha."

Sass thunked her glass on the nightstand and shifted a half meter from Hunter on the bed.

He laughed. "Had a run-in with my dad, did you?"

"We have history," Sass allowed. "Hunter, I hope you didn't promise him updates on the resistance. Clay is law and order to the bone."

"He didn't ask. And that's what I thought about him. But it's more complicated. He's trying to work inside the system to accomplish the same stuff as the resistance. He's still sore about the Petticreek disaster. He'd won an agreement from the urbs to build settler kindergartens. Like mini-cities. Grav plating. Gardens and a zoo. Kids could live there to age 15. Who knows, maybe I would have lived in one after my parents split."

Sass guessed, "But then Petticreek, and the urbs reneged."

"Any conflict strengthens Kendra's position. Us settlers need to be kept down. But Dad claims most urbs don't buy it anymore. Younger ones, like Kassidy and your other boarder. They don't remember Mahina before settlers. The older ones are fearful. But all they really care about is not losing their city. They'd be happy enough helping the settlers build their own. Speed up the terraforming."

"Those would be good things," Sass allowed. "But the urbs always renege."

"Hasn't been tested for twenty years."

"Not true. Example. There's an automated warehouse in Mahina Actual with hundreds of young fruit trees. To distribute to the settlers. Never happened. Hunter, we pay taxes to the city. For what? They haven't built a new atmo plant in decades. The protein factories pay for themselves. The phosphate mines are convict labor."

Hunter shook his head. "Preaching to the choir, Sass. I don't doubt the resistance. Just wonder if Dad has a point. If we could manage a peaceful renegotiation."

"Between who and whom?" Sass countered. "Settler relations for the urbs is controlled by Kendra Oliver. Until the city changes that, there's no bargaining partner of good faith on the urb side. And on the settler side — who?"

Hunter shot her a crooked smile. "You betrayed the last rebel leader. You'll understand if the new one doesn't want to know you."

"Point taken. He's probably the wrong contact for what I need, anyway."

"What's that?"

Sass hunched forward, elbows on her knees, and caught his eye. "I need a better class of criminal. Organized. Businessman with a network. The type interested in profit, not mayhem, who can handle something serious." Actually, that described Landau pretty well, the leader executed after Petticreek. *Damn Landau anyway.*

Hunter stilled. "For?"

"I have a highly sensitive bit of business. I'm not ready to talk about that yet. But it could mean a breakthrough for settlers against failure to thrive. I'd like to start with a relationship. Feel each other out. Offer skyship services. I don't know, maybe deliver real beer kegs or something. Someone makes decent booze on this moon."

"Dad would be very interested in that breakthrough," Hunter mused.

Sass shook her head firmly. "Not Clay. Laws will be broken. Urb laws."

"Might know a guy," Hunter allowed. "I'll ask. Get back to you."

Sass didn't get to shack up that night. The thought that Hunter was Clay's baby boy was a major turnoff.

———

"DON'T TALK," Sass murmured, in last minute instruction to Benjy and Abel flanking her. With that, she strode to the door guards who stood sizing them up from the end of a back alley. Schuyler was the second largest town on Mahina, a scruffy industrial and distribution hub. This alley was deep in the bowels of its warehouse district a couple hours before Eclipse, a few days later.

"Here to see Josiah," she announced. "We have an appointment at nineteen hundred."

"Names?"

"No," Sass replied with a hard smirk.

The guard shrugged. He snapped their portrait with his comm and sent it ahead for confirmation. "Leave your weapons here."

Abel and Benjy handed over tasers. Sass held up open hands. For her, even owning a weapon was a parole violation, let alone using one. Abel felt the need to supply some for *Thrive* if they were dealing with criminals. Sass happily helped him select them, and approved the expense. But she herself could only bear arms on her ship, in defense of her people or property. In theory.

The second guard who frisked her got overly personal in his grop-ing. She grabbed his crotch for a firm squeeze in return. Sass quite enjoyed the staring contest that followed. "Bet you'll blink first."

He blinked immediately from the suggestion. "Bitch." He shoved her to proceed inside. "See you on your way out."

"Look forward to it," Sass assured him.

"Why —" Benjy attempted when they were inside in the dingy corridor.

Sass cut him off. "You don't talk here. Remember? Save questions for home."

A dozen strides brought them to another doorway bracketed by lanky goons. These looked dim enough to start drooling any minute, but more attentive ones stood behind the guy seated at the desk. All of them carried hard-core flechette pistols. Sass wasn't surprised. Go into the lion's den, and the lion has the upper hand.

The mob boss leaned back. Around two meters tall, his frame was only a touch stretched by low gravity, sheathed with mature muscle. Sass guessed him in his forties. His face was coarsened and lined by sun exposure. Force of personality and cold calculating eyes made that craggy face intimidating. He left his desk display showing profiles of the three visitors before him with their snapshot from the front door.

There was a single hard-back chair in front of his desk. He didn't invite anyone to sit in it.

"Josiah," he named himself. "To what do I owe the pleasure?"

Sass strode forward and tapped her own face on the desk. "Sass." She waved fingers at the other bios rather than supply redundant introductions. "Captain of the skyship *Thrive*. Thank you for meeting us. We'd like to offer our services. Develop a business relationship."

"Cut the crap," Josiah broke in.

22

Intra-system spaceship guns of the period defended the craft from rocks and debris, not other spaceships. It was centuries before the first space combat, though at least one ship was accidentally destroyed by friendly fire along the way.

The mob boss Josiah glared at Sass across his desk. "Do I look like I need a skyship? Hello, we're in Schuyler. Distribution hub for this whole rego moon. I got transport."

"*Thrive* also has guns. We do landscaping —"

"Yeah, we subscribe to Kassidy Yang's feed." Without leaning forward, just extending his long arm, Josiah tapped up Kassidy's profile to squeeze beside Benjy's on the desk surface. "Quite the high profile traveling circus you're running, Sass. I trust it's occurred to you that I don't livecast my business dealings. Yang is not a feature."

Sass shrugged one shoulder. "I find her convenient cover, actually. We have an excuse to go strange places. The phosphate mines. Mahina Actual. Orbital."

Josiah's eyes narrowed in calculation. "To do what?"

"The hope is to build a relationship first. Trust is earned. Perhaps a landscaping project —"

"Sure, build a public park," Josiah quipped. "I'm noted for my philanthropic works. Not. Look, Hunter claimed you had merchandise to bring to market that required business organization of my caliber. Skip ahead to that part."

Sass allowed that it was time to give him a teaser. "What if I had something that made a real difference against failure to thrive? Miracle level. What if that something would give Kendra Oliver conniptions?"

"Conniptions," Josiah repeated. But he was hooked. In feigned disinterest, he threw up his arms in a stretch, and cracked his back. "Always happy to make Oliver's day, of course. One of my points of convergence with the resistance."

"Convergence," Sass echoed in appreciation. "A question, if I may. You are not, in fact, a leader of the resistance, are you?"

"Hunter mentioned your past history," Josiah acknowledged. "Though I wonder if he knows how old you really are?"

"A lady never tells."

"Hm. What you're suggesting is a product of universal demand, and near-infinite value. That part I like. But the opposition's resolve to shut us down might also approach infinite. Do I have this right?"

"That's about the size of it."

"Alright. I think I understand the need then. Trust is earned. As it happens, I have two associates currently interred at Phosphate Mine 3. One appeared on Yang's show. I'd like them back."

No wonder he'd agreed to the meet, Sass thought, as Josiah blanked his desk and tapped up two other bios.

Abel leaned closer, and craned his neck in an attempt to look right-side up without crowding the mob boss's personal space. He tapped the face on his left.

Sass nodded to him. "We had lunch with that one. Warwick." She didn't recall the name, but read it upside-down easily enough. "Friend of Atlas Pratt, the general manager. Foreman, right?"

"I don't care what he does at PM3," Josiah returned. "Smart guy though. This other one, Copeland, recently transferred in from another mine. Looks like he acquired a wife and baby along the way."

Skyship Thrive

This triggered Sass's memory. She hovered her hand over the desk display. "May I? I want to check the baby."

Josiah scowled. "Why? Go ahead."

Sass sidled around the other end of the desk, to read sideways if not right-side-up, and tapped the baby's name, Nico Copeland. His mugshot wasn't particularly familiar — babies looked a lot alike — but his medical history confirmed her suspicion. "We met the baby. Sad story. Copeland was on duty that day. The wife is a definite ex. She's not at PM3."

"Small world. Not interested in sob stories," Josiah said. "But Copeland might not leave without his brat."

"The baby's at PM3 with Copeland," Sass confirmed. "So you want three extracted? Two foremen and a baby. We could do that."

Abel made a gargled noise, but kept his mouth shut as Sass shot him a sharp look.

"Say twenty grand for a jailbreak?" Sass offered.

Josiah's arms fell to his desk with a thump as he hunkered forward to haggle. Sass retreated to the far side to square off against him.

"The payment was goodwill, and trust earned," Josiah countered.

"That's your offer? A warm fuzzy?" Sass replied with a sniff. "I offer you a jailbreak on the far side of the moon, at significant risk to my company. And I get paid in well wishes and dirty diapers?"

Josiah bridled. "Three grand."

Sass planted her hands on the desk edge and leaned toward him. "Eighteen."

"Fifteen. And that kid better come with clean diapers."

The two locked eyes in a contest of wills. Sass broke first into a grin. "That's affirm on the clean diapers. Half in advance."

Josiah let a brief smile escape, then sobered up. He wiped the bios from the desk and brought up a list of accounts to peruse. "I don't suppose your guns are any use for cutting hay."

"There are cheaper ways to cut hay," Sass replied. "You're looking for a shell company to pay us from? Any transport company would do. Or something that needs water. We own a private well."

171

"Do you?" Josiah's eyebrows rose. He selected a company to pay them with. "An intriguing assortment of completely random services you offer, Sass. You might want to focus your business model."

"We're just getting started," Sass returned defensively. "Casting around for our market."

Josiah shot her a crooked smirk. "Let's add forty cubic meters of water to that down payment. A tanker truck worth. One grand. That's eight and a half grand to start."

"The water is presently un-metered," Sass said. "I have no staff there. Though there's a hydrologist from the city poking around my claim. He needs to be avoided. Just started today. Not sure how long he'll be there. Probably go home by sunset. Maybe every night."

She meant night in the after-hours sense. It was two days until dark arrived after sunset.

Josiah paused thoughtfully. "I could handle those complications for you. Staff to meter water. Leave pesky management details to us. Pay you royalties."

"Tempting," Sass returned. "And exactly the sort of services I was hoping your organization might handle. But the hydrologist is there to evolve an offer, I hope. I already have a promise of a counter-offer. You could bring a third offer to the table. Though I must confess, I have a bias toward the urb offer if he makes one."

"Why?"

"That would be for another atmo spire. The urbs haven't built a new atmosphere factory in three decades. Air is good. I like breathing."

Josiah nodded, brows raised again. "Point. We'll leave it at forty cubic meters for now. Honor system. Location?"

Sass had turned her comm off for the meeting, but Abel's played a *ka-chink* on receipt of the cash deposit. He verified the amount, then set his tablet to display the coordinates of their water pump at Practice Hill, with a snapshot of the rudimentary facilities. A pipe stuck out of the ground, with a hose coiled next to it. The dusty gray bulk of the hill loomed beyond in the half-gas murk of Monday.

Josiah honestly chuckled at the view as he transcribed the coordinates. "I like you. You're quirky, and your business sense is ludicrous. But I like you. When do I get my people back?"

"Next week." Sass rapped on his desk. "I'm pretty happy with this transaction too. Let us build trust." She offered her hand.

"By all means," Josiah agreed, and rose to return a firm handshake. "You'll show yourselves out."

By his tamped smile, Sass suspected that Josiah watched their entrance and anticipated a show. That door guard had time by now to stew on her crotch grab and get teased about it by his partner. She returned his smile sunnily, and led the way out.

As she reached the door, the mob boss added, "Two successful deals should buy enough *trust* to hear more about this miracle, Sass."

The captain paused in her stride, but left it with a nod, and continued out. In the hallway, she murmured to her partners, "We can't start a fight. But if that guard grabs me, he's the one who ends on the ground. Right?"

"Damn straight," Abel concurred.

"Um," Benjy said. "They're armed."

Sass smothered a laugh. "You haven't fought outside of virtual, have you?"

Benjy admitted, "Not with anyone...strong."

"It'll be fun," Sass assured him. "Hi, boys!" she belted out to the guards as they reached them. "Weapons, please."

She ducked under the left-hand guard's expected swing, then came up on a quick burst of two anti-gravities to bowl him over. Abel simply crowded the right-hand guy with his shoulder, causing him to step backwards off their little shaded portico. No one stood around in the direct ultraviolet of Mahina's Wednesday sun if they could avoid it.

"Benjy, pick up our weapons, please," Sass told the cowering youth between them. "Have a lovely Eclipse, gentlemen."

"Why, you —!" The offended guard lunged for her legs.

Sass lightly hopped over him and hung there in mid-air. He swiped at her ineffectually, as she bobbed just a few centimeters out of reach. "You should really pack a better grav generator."

"And learn how to use it," Abel concurred, settling his taser back on his belt. He stepped down from the portico with a polite nod to the other guard, who had no beef with them, and simply enjoyed the ruckus.

Benjy scurried behind Abel, quick to keep the slightly older and larger man between him and the armed guards.

The aggrieved guard let off his impotent arm-swiping and reached for his flechette gun.

Sass dropped down and kicked his hand away from the gun before he could draw it. "You're less amusing," she barked at him. "I had business with the boss. Successful business. Back off!"

"She's right," the man's partner volunteered with a grin. "She keeps getting the better of you, idiot." This comment served to redden the goon's face a shade darker.

"Yeah! Back off!" Benjy attempted, stepping forward for the first time, fists presented before his face.

The furious guard rammed one straight punch through both of his fists, causing Benjy to punch himself in the nose. Sass shook her head and pulled the boy behind her for safe-keeping. Abel passed him even farther back.

"Try it again," Sass invited the goon, beckoning with her fingers. She side-stepped, nice and springy. "Remember all this got started because you mauled me. Nobody feels me up without permission, perv. Like a rutting pig. Oink."

With that, he lost his common sense and lunged at her as though to grab her in a bear hug. Sass goosed her anti-grav, vaulted over his head, then came straight down on his upper back at double g, slamming him back to the ground.

She stood on his back a couple seconds, still at 2 g. "Tap out."

"No!"

"Tap out and I'll show you how I did it."

"To hell with you, whore!"

Sass shrugged to the other guard. "Any suggestions?"

"I can stand on him while you leave."

"Thank you. Pleasure doing business." Sass bowed, then hopped off as goon 2 stepped onto the man's gun hand. "Til next time."

As they walked off up the alley, Benjy sped up as though he'd break into a sprint to flee. Abel clamped a hand on his shoulder and pulled him back to walk between them. "We need to teach this kid how to fight."

Sass grinned. "Running is for losers, Benjy. Never run from a predator."

"I didn't realize you were that good, Sass," Abel said thoughtfully.

"Cops and robbers," Sass returned. "Same kind, same game. It takes two to tango."

"What kind of business is Josiah in?" Benjy asked.

"The usual," Sass said lightly. "Drugs, booze, gambling, prostitution. I imagine he has a quirky sideline or two. But those bring in the big cash."

"It's a parole violation for you to be here," Abel muttered. They'd had words about the wisdom of Sass coming along for this outing.

"It won't be the last," she replied. "But could you have done that without me? Even with me coaching in your ear?"

After a few more paces, Abel conceded, "Probably not."

23

The interstellar star drive was a stunning breakthrough, allowing travel between star systems in a mere three subjective years for those on board, most of it spent accelerating and decelerating to a warp point.

"Sass?" Kassidy sauntered into her own cabin. The captain was trespassing, kneeling on the stunt woman's bed.

Sass pivoted and sat abruptly on the cheerful gaudy bedspread. "Welcome home! Everything go OK in the city?"

"Yeah?" Kassidy replied, brows furrowed in question.

"We were thinking you could use new cabinets." Sass waved a hand to encompass the bulkheads. "So your belongings could fit in here. Instead of your wardrobe blocking the mechanicals. I'm measuring."

Kassidy chuckled in relief. "Sure. Sorry about clogging up the catwalk. We could put it in the hold for now."

Sass shook her head. "Not an issue. We don't really care about your closet."

Kassidy dropped her business bag in a corner, and swung a leg over a chair back to perch on it backwards. Sass's thigh muscles hurt just watching that effortless high kick. Kassidy was limber as a ferret. "Sass, I'm not following."

"We have a spot of...liberation we'd like your help with. Basically a trip into Mahina Actual, to swap out your wardrobe. And Eli's. So we'd make you a new set of cabinets for your cabin here. Carry them in, repack, come back out. Easy."

Kassidy nodded, amused. "And by liberation you mean smuggling?"

"Exactly. Just some science stuff for Eli. Abel and Benjy will go with you to handle the heavy lifting."

"But not you?"

"I would draw Security's attention like a lightning rod," Sass confessed. "They probably wouldn't let me through the door."

Kassidy laughed. "Whereas I'm a show biz ditz. Kendra Oliver would roll her eyes at me refreshing my wardrobe. Got it. Sure. Sounds fun. But please don't hang a cabinet over my pillow. That's claustrophobic. Maybe under the bed?"

The two women got busy with the laser measuring meter. They fed the dimensions into a 3D simulation of the room, so they could try different layouts. By raising the bed to waist height, with storage underneath, and building up cabinets and vanity on the short wall, they could manage to shoe-horn quite a lot of storage into the modest cubic. The bed itself was already on a spring system to stow against the bulkhead. They could shift that higher. The largest new cabinets would be easy for Kassidy to swap out for repacking. Or at least no harder than her giant inlaid wardrobe, and considerably more modular and scuff-proof.

Sass considered the final plan. Abel would hate it. The standard-sized kitchen cabinet doors and hardware would run them a few hundred credits. "Maybe Eli will pay for it."

"Upgrade the cabinets and I'll pay for it," Kassidy said. She took the tablet back from Sass and leafed through the available cabinet doors. "These!" She handed Sass back her choice of brilliant bitter-sweet orange in fiberglass instead of the cheap spruce. "That'll brighten the place up!"

"Or make it claustrophobic," Sass murmured. "And cost ten times as much. How about we buy the cheap white and a can of paint? Paint them one at a time and stop when the walls start to close in. These others would look better in the kitchen."

"Anything would look better than your kitchen."

"True," Sass allowed with a sigh. "Kassidy, are you planning to stay with us after your sky jumps? I thought you were only with us for a month or so."

"I'm having a blast." Kassidy flopped down on her bed. She twisted her legs into a yoga pretzel pose, propped up on her side for conversation. "I love your ship. I love the company. I love traveling. We'll think of more stunts!"

"Fantastic! We aim to please. If we keep you on long term, maybe we can afford to decorate the kitchen."

Kassidy nodded, grinning. "I'm not buying you a new kitchen."

"Worth a try. Say, Kassidy, I had a question. Marshal Rocha said you might know something about what's happening off Mahina? In the other colonies."

Kassidy frowned. "Friend of yours? Clay Rocha?"

"I wouldn't call him a friend exactly. Colleague. Worked together for years. I was a marshal before my farm stint."

"Ah. Yes. Um, my dad was exiled. When I was seven. Dad was a nanite engineer. Collaborated with a geneticist. They were an item. Lovers. I don't know how much that had to do with it. But Mom accused them of reckless research, got them exiled. He was on the orbital for a while. We'd talk by video. Then Sagamore recruited them. The other moon was willing to permit their research."

"You were close to your dad," Sass hazarded.

"Not anymore." Kassidy winced a half-smile. "Anyway, that's an issue between dear Dr. Paripati and me. My mom. I stayed in the creche and avoided her for the most part. Neither of them raised me."

Sass could see that. The celebrity was a black hole for attention. Mahina Actual's creche facilities were convenient and extensive, with excellent child care staff. Kassidy was hardly the only kid who lived there full-time, and dreaded parental visits from preoccupied science types unused to children.

"What was your dad's research?"

Kassidy pursed her lips. "I'd rather not say. Not that I understand it too well. I never wanted anything to do with engineering and medicine."

Of course not, Sass reasoned. Those pursuits stole the girl's parents from her.

"Sagamore, huh? Have you heard from him since?" Sass had never seen Sagamore, the outer colony moon of Pono, nor the colonized planet, Denali, closer to the sun.

"Yeah, now and then we catch up with a video call. I wish I could send him my shows, but comms feed through Kendra Oliver's office. She won't allow it. Dad mentioned his research once when I was thirteen or so. Tried to share his love of his subject." Kassidy rolled her eyes. "Oliver went ballistic. He wasn't allowed to speak to me again for years. And never about that. He can't discuss Sagamore, either. I can't talk about how Mahina changed. Five minute limit. Most of it wasted on time lag."

"I'm sorry," Sass murmured. "So you can't tell me much about Sagamore?"

"Let's see. They're stuck in domes. Building an atmosphere for warmth and protection from meteorites. But not to live in. Their week is too long — the sun cycle. Nights are way below freezing and last too long. Agriculture only possible indoors under lights."

"Do you know what happened to the settlers there?"

Kassidy quirked an apologetic half smile. "Sorry. We don't talk politics."

"Do you know anything about Denali?"

"Last we talked, he said now I'm grown, he might look into transferring. Population growing. They have almost Earth-normal gravity to work with. Hot Goldilocks planet, oceans and land and alien life. Agriculture in domes only. Earth plants can't compete, and we can't eat the native stuff. Aggressive biosphere.

"It's only cool enough to live at the poles. The planet's tilted like

Earth. A bit more tilted actually. Summer daytime for months, then winter dark for months. Already has an atmosphere we can't breathe. So they're stuck in domes there, too. Volcanoes ring the first colony. Sounds pretty. I'd like to see it. The air isn't caustic or anything. You can go out for a walk with a face mask and a gun."

"A gun?" Sass echoed.

"Very aggressive biosphere," Kassidy reiterated. "I don't know about the settlers there. Only the first wave terraforming colonists, like the urbs here. My folk. Mahina doesn't look like much. But I think we got the prize world in this system. I'm biased, of course." She grinned.

Sass echoed her grin faintly. Landscape trees, farms — breathing was good. Mahina had come a long way. "From the Rockies," she murmured thoughtfully. "The Denali refugees. If there's water, they probably liked it there fine. No harder to dome in than here."

Kassidy narrowed her eyes. "From the what?"

"Another part of Earth," Sass replied. "Dry mountains. Settlers on Mahina came from sopping wet mountains. Everyone in this system came from the same continent on Earth, different locations."

"Just how old are you, Sass? No one remembers Earth anymore. They threw a big funeral for the last Earth-born founder when I was a kid. She left Earth a couple decades earlier than the settlers. But still."

"If I tell you, will you tell me what your dad did? To get exiled?"

Kassidy pursed her lips and considered. "I'd rather not. Besides, I think I already know. Marshal. Earth-born. Proscribed nanites. You must be nearly 100. You don't look any older than me until you put your wrinkles on in the morning. Wow, Sass. That must be...odd."

"It is that," Sass breathed.

"They stopped transmitting, you know," Kassidy said softly. "Earth. The same year the last founder died. Did they tell you?"

"No." The news hit Sass like a body blow.

"They might not be dead," Kassidy offered gently. "Just lost power to the transmitter or something."

Sass nodded and rose to leave as though sleepwalking. "Excuse me."

She retired to her cabin and cried until no more tears came.

Clay was right. Kassidy bore news from beyond Mahina. Sass supposed it didn't matter. It didn't change anything, that Earth was dead, or offline. That colonies survived on Sagamore and Denali, forever encased in domes. The bottom line was unchanged. This dull little ball of regolith with its gas-giant sky was as good as they'd get.

Humans needed to make Mahina work.

Sass's last nagging concern for what Kendra Oliver might do to her shrank to a pinprick and popped. Screw Kendra if she couldn't take a joke.

24

Pre-Diaspora interstellar exploration stayed within a 12 light year radius of Earth. Although the subjective time to travel was always three years, the elapsed objective time was roughly equal to the number of light years the ship traversed under warp.

The next phase of Sass and Abel's plan was the actual heist. Benjy helped Jules set up shop in the Mahina Actual visitor lot to serve the sunset rush.

Sunset was official end-of-week party time moon-wide. The annex, the urb shopping mall open to settlers, saw their biggest traffic of the week. The parking lot was filling fast. *Thrive* only managed to snag its two great spots, close to the entrance, because they were reserved for oversized vehicles and deliveries.

Jules quailed behind the mushroom flange counter. "You expect me to get in trouble?" She hadn't bargained on that.

Abel leaned in for a kiss. "You're not doing anything wrong, baby. If security says you're not allowed to sell here, just apologize and pack up."

"Try to keep them talking," Sass added. "Ask questions. Offer treats. Suggest the authorities should talk to your husband, or your captain. Stuff like that."

"They won't put me in jail?" Jules had been most disconcerted by Kassidy's video of the convicts at PM3. Baby Nico Copeland especially worried her. She gulped.

Abel squeezed his wife's hand. "Won't come to that. And if it did, I'd come get you out right away. Promise. Love you! Be good!"

Sass said bracingly, "Time to go." She wouldn't go with them. As an ex-convict, they probably wouldn't let her in. If they did, they'd watch her every move. Sass wouldn't put it past Kendra Oliver to stage fake charges just to arrest her again.

Benjy, with Kassidy, Eli, and Abel, joined the throng surging into the mall. Three of them dragged grav-carriers behind them. Abel's carrier was amply laden with Kassidy's huge inlaid wooden closet, stuffed with most of her wardrobe. Kassidy drew along a few of her new empty replacement cabinets, custom built to fit under her bed, instead of blocking the environmental fans compartment on the catwalk. The heirloom-quality armoire would not be returning to *Thrive.* Benjy steered a third carrier, bearing the single largest of her new cabinets, a smaller closet with a one meter square footprint, over two meters tall.

They passed through the mall, packed with settlers dressed in their best. To most settlers, the potted palmettos and peacocks looked like paradise. The ubiquitous particolored everclear flavor flutes were marketed as posh.

Eli led the way past the low-rent food court to a door marked 'NO ENTRY.' A slashed red circle subtitled for the illiterate. The armed guards rendered both redundant.

Eli and Kassidy presented their faces to a machine for verification as urb citizens. The scientist gestured disdainfully to the *Thrive* crew. "Day laborers. We need their help with the luggage." Eli did the talking. In the urb hierarchy, young Kassidy might be popular, but Eli's scientific credentials carried weight.

The female cop scanned the cabinetry for weapons, and opened a few doors to peek in. All seemed in order. "Anything you carry out needs to be inspected," she reminded them.

"Of course," Eli replied, acting bored and altogether too important to be pestered by door security. They passed on through the doors.

Next came the utilitarian front vestibule, a mushroom colored grubby corridor safe for glimpsing by the customers at the cheap food court. They turned a corner to the inner door, and pressed a button. A camera swiveled above. The guards they'd just parted from buzzed them through the next lock.

Only there did they enter the true city of Mahina Actual. They stepped through a force field into full Earth gravity. They breathed deep of moist rich air, pure and fragrant with the scent of a million blossoms.

"Whoa," Benjy murmured, as they passed the threshold.

Abel gazed around beside him, eyes wide. Like most, they thought they'd seen the city. They'd been to the mall. They'd eaten the burgers and fries at the food court. As Kassidy's guest, Abel ate once in the fancy restaurant. Benjy had visited the special-events atrium where they welcomed distance education students to Mahina University. Among settlers, these young men were upper crust.

But they'd never entered the real city.

A hummingbird paused a fraction of a second, as though to look them over. "Is that a drone?" Benjy asked, breathless.

Kassidy explained, "That's a bird. The drones are solid color. Silver for security. Blue for sanitation. And they don't have wings. This way."

Benjy spun to look for 'wings.' On a hummingbird, wings flapped so fast as to be nothing but a blur. Abel grabbed his shirt to draw him along.

"The air feels heavy," Benjy said wonderingly. "Am I having trouble breathing?"

"Just richer than you're used to," Eli replied. "Humid. There's water in the air."

"It's cool in here." Out in the mall, the air was warm, but a welcome break from the late afternoon heat of Dusk. Past the force field, the temperature dropped another few degrees. A few citizens, visible a hundred meters further down the broad plaza, wore riotous colors sarong-style over a lot of bare skin. Joggers and bicyclists and fitness walkers wove through.

Benjy looked up through the branches of fruit-bearing trees. Brilliant light cables snaked through the tree limbs. Glowing turquoise threads of a force field were all that seemed to lay between him and the deepening olive sky above. Pono hung half-full in the sky behind him. The floor beneath was tiled in slip-proof shades of terra cotta, tiled in graceful patterns that flowed upward into curbs around the tree trunks. Harmonious planters and sculptures and benches lay scattered throughout.

"Wait til he sees the botanical gardens," Eli murmured to Kassidy.

She grinned. "Save it for the way out. Abel, we're this way."

They split off on a cross-corridor by a sidewalk restaurant. Robots readied tables for the sunset rush. Though he hailed from the wealthiest family in Poldark, Benjy had never owned a robot. He'd been impressed as hell with Kassidy's camera drones. Yet the urbs wasted robots on setting the table?

Eli continued along the plaza, Benjy following slack-jawed on sensory overload, gazing all around. When he stared at the invariably young and healthy compact people, they generally scowled at him and scurried away.

The scientist turned them onto a cross-corridor, bearing people in white lab coats coming the opposite direction.

"Is that a uniform?" Benjy asked. "The white coat?"

Eli didn't answer until they reached the next gap in pedestrian traffic. "Don't ask questions in public. Hold up."

Benjy obediently stopped. Eli pulled a matching white lab coat out of the closet, complete with dangly breast badges. He shrugged it on before continuing.

By this point the corridor had grown more utilitarian. Planters still lined the way under wall-mounted spotlights. Pedestrians stepped over more robots starting to clean the plain tiled floor. This went on for another several hundred meters, past occasional locked industrial-size double doors as traffic dwindled.

Some doors bore coded labels like 'H2O-306' and 'ATM-315.' Benjy theorized that meant they were on corridor 3. The letters probably indicated departments. Other doors seemed to be utility rooms or cross-corridors.

"Eli Rasmussen!" a man barked out. He bore down upon them with purpose. His bearing said 'senior,' though his body looked the same age as Eli and Abel. The man's plump baby face made him appear younger than Benjy. "At first I thought you'd come to your senses and returned to the city! But that's a settler, isn't it?"

It? Benjy bridled.

"Dr. Conroy," Eli acknowledged, cringing. "No, I'm here to check on a few long-term experiments. Keeping a hand in. My intern, Benjy." He gulped.

Conroy barely glanced at Benjy. "A man of your seniority. What would Bertram think of you now, hm?"

"I don't know, sir. I wish he were here to ask."

Conroy scowled. "Rasmussen, he isn't here because he broke the law!"

"No, sir," Eli said, finally meeting Conroy's eye. "There is no law against what Bertram did. Kendra Oliver didn't agree with it. That's not the same thing."

Conroy blanched. "Very unwise, Rasmussen. *Most* unwise." He turned and stalked away after the other scientists fleeing to happy hour.

"You stood up to him," Benjy murmured, astonished. "Good for you."

Eli attempted a wan smile, and gave it up. "Thank you. Bad timing, though."

"Who's the blowhard?"

"Director of terraforming. Lead scientist here."

"Ah." Not a good person to cross then, Benjy deduced.

At last, still fifty meters shy of the corridor's end, Eli applied his badge to door 'BOT-387.' Dim lighting automatically arose along the

GINGER BOOTH

walls as they entered a group lab area, low-walled office cubicles surrounded by smaller labs and offices.

Eli ordered Benjy to park his closet next to a door. He swiped his card and presented his eyeball for scanning. The door unlocked, and Eli breathed deep in relief.

He called Kassidy with a simple, "We're here."

Benjy hadn't realized until now that Eli wasn't sure his credentials were still valid. He debated sending Abel a quick warning text. But Sass was concerned about the extent of communications in this plan already.

Eli pulled a box out of the closet, and passed a handheld electronic tool to Benjy. "Do your thing. That machine is Sass's prize." He pointed out a blinking flat box device about 75 cm tall. "I'll make sure we're alone. Listen for voices or footsteps. When in doubt, act stupid."

"Can do," Benjy assured him as the scientist furtively scurried away. Benjy firmly resolved that whatever happened here, he didn't plan to look as guilty as Eli.

He applied his inventory management tool to the nanite synthesizer Eli had indicated. He located its transmitting sticker. No sooner found, than peeled off and applied to the underside of the counter below. Now inventory would show this thing right here, regardless of where they took it. Another pass assured the youth that was the only transmitter on the box.

To be on the safe side, it would be better if something drew about the same amount of power from this spot. Fortunately this room appeared to be unused at present, and collecting castoffs. Benjy rummaged and found a similar sized box with a handy 'RECYCLE' sticker. That also had an inventory tracker.

Benjy grinned and transferred the recycling sticker onto the nanite synthesizer. He considered transferring the tracker sticker as well, but decided all trackers should stay in this room. He turned to unplug the prize synthesizer.

He froze as he heard voices. Eli was talking to a woman. He couldn't make out words. But it sounded like social banter, the woman friendly, Eli kind of defensive. This was not unusual for Eli.

Sass had warned Benjy that Eli was being overly optimistic about time. So far, Benjy believed her more than the botanist. It took them a quarter hour just to walk across town. So he turned back to his work.

The synthesizer was cabled to a computer on the right, another flat boxlike device on the left. In reservation, Benjy turned on the computer. The display defaulted to a screen that operated the nanite synthesizer. He poked through its help tree to find troubleshooting. He was rewarded with a schematic of the four part system - synthesizer, computer, sequencer, and centrifuge — everything sitting between the computer and the sink. In addition, operating two of the devices required particular reagents. Benjy had no idea whether Eli had — or planned to steal — the needed supplies. And for the moment, he couldn't ask. *Dammit, Eli!*

Benjy took careful note of what stuff to collect before powering down the equipment. The monitor and input board, at least, were generic. He could leave those behind. More stickers were shuffled. A careful peek into the lab bullpen, and muffled voices, reassured him that no one was in view. He shifted the wardrobe to block the door. He started filling it, with far more equipment than they'd planned. Cheery green 'RECYCLE' stickers weren't going to get this equipment past inspection.

But that wasn't the plan. Heist today, transport later, was the plan for the nanite synthesizer. They just needed to cart all this crap, rendered untraceable, to Kassidy's place. Getting it out of the city would take a number of trips. For today's goals, if stuff was piled teetering on top as they wended through the halls, that made them conspicuous. But not illegal.

Benjy artfully staged the counter to look reminiscent of its original state. He got half of it assembled, then dismantled it again because the dust patterns betrayed the wrong equipment. Apparently the bots didn't clean very well inside locked labs. He wiped the counter down with his shirt-tail and started over. Nothing else in this small room looked remotely like a centrifuge to replace the one he was liberating. He gave up and stuck a box of castoff lab beakers in that spot.

Reagents... Logically, all the stuff fed into this equipment should be stored in this room. He wished he'd researched what these things looked like before he'd disabled the computer. Instead he systematically rummaged through a couple cabinets checking labels. Then he realized that was exactly what his inventory tracking device was made for.

He plugged in the first reagent name, and *bingo!* That stuff turned out to sit on the bottom shelf of the first cabinet. He'd missed it, a fine gray powder in a square plastic jug, about 4 liters.

Then he tried to pick it up. The damned stuff was the approximate density of gold. Another ten minutes down as he figured out how to use his personal grav generator to shift a 75-kilo jar into the cabinet.

"Eli, why are you still chatting up an old girlfriend?" he muttered to himself. At least their voices had migrated out to the corridor by now.

Another 2-liter jug of pink liquid — no heavier than water, thank you. Plus three jugs of blue because there seemed to be a lot more of them. And two little cartons not much bigger than his fist joined the collection. The last supply item had him sorely puzzled until he realized it was the faintly opalescent salt-like substance stored loose in something like a plasglass ten-pound flour bin.

Upon opening, its dust induced a reflex sneeze so strong it wracked Benjy's entire body. His sneeze blew a small cloud of caustic dust out of the bin before its lid snapped shut.

"What was that?" came a female voice, much clearer than a moment ago.

25

The last technological breakthrough to power the Diaspora was medical nanites.

Abel's first stop was Kassidy's place, to drop off the cabinetry. Then they'd proceed to their main project for the evening.

Getting there was easy. She lived only a block off the main drag, a few minutes walk from the fast food court where they entered the city.

Her cross-corridor was styled something like the buildings of Newer York, but in fake brownstone. The city's true ceiling was a transparent dome superstructure high above. Mahina Actual was formed of giant warehouses with geodesic plasglass roofs. Roof supports were styled as lamp posts in this sector. The minor block wasn't as charming a garden as the first plaza. But its sidewalks were pleasantly tree-lined, and not with spruce or aspen. Bicycles and other transport traversed a lower lane between the pedestrian curbs. Blooming flower boxes hung from windows and sat on front stoops.

"Low status housing," Kassidy explained apologetically. "The best apartments are in the biomes. But assignment is by seniority. Old people get the lakefront and the zoo. Places with a good view."

"I see," Abel replied. He didn't really, but Abel had a thing against looking stupid. His mother warned him that by not asking when he didn't know, he made his fear a reality. He still didn't like to ask.

Abel coaxed the jumbo wardrobe up the building's front faux-stone steps. The grav-carrier knew how to climb. Getting it through the doorway was trickier, since it wouldn't fit upright. Kassidy went ahead to dump her stuff, then returned to help him maneuver through the tight squeeze. Navigating the stairway up to Kassidy's second floor apartment was easier.

The building only held three apartments, two on top and one on the ground floor. Aside from being immaculately clean, the hallway didn't look much different from those in the familiar blocky buildings back home in Palm Springs, a modest town devoid of both palms and springs.

Inside, Kassidy's apartment seemed opulent to him. To Abel's discomfort, it was loft-style, a single room encompassing bedroom as well as dining table, kitchen, work zone, and sitting area. Kassidy was a tornado-grade slob in the bedroom quadrant, a chaotic clutter of unmade bed, discarded clothes, and unfamiliar objects. She pointed out a slightly clearer corner where she wanted to return the giant wardrobe.

Abel toed clothes out of the way and jimmied the ungainly box back into position. "I'll let you repack in private," he muttered, uneasily eyeing a statue of an elephant-headed man copulating with a naked dancer.

Kassidy laughed. "You're almost as big a prude as my downstairs neighbor. Settler posers. Ever hear of Reverend Ellsworth? His wife and kids."

Abel paused, stunned. "My mother follows Reverend Ellsworth. Whole family really." The preacher Ellsworth with his strong message urging morality, monogamy, and sobriety was one of the most influential voices on Mahina. His following beat even Kassidy's, since he appealed to the less adventurous.

Ellsworth was a settler, not an urb. Or so he claimed.

Kassidy nodded, nose already in her closet, selecting outfits and tossing them to form a new pile on the floor. "He's a fraud. Fully backed by Mahina Actual. In payment for his propaganda, his wife and kids live here in the city. Except the wife believes his patter. Always a disapproving word for me. Don't be surprised if she bangs on the door. She doesn't like it when men visit me."

"Reverend Ellsworth is a collaborator?"

Kassidy shot him a glance. "No, Abel. I'm a collaborator. When she worked as a marshal, Sass was a collaborator. Ellsworth is a fraud." She started adding whimsical underwear to her pile. "'Collaborate' is not a swear word, you know. This world could do with more cooperation."

Abel hurriedly retreated into the living room area rather than observe Kassidy's flying bras. He wondered how much of his straight-laced family values came from Reverend Ellsworth. Did it matter if a fake did the teaching, if it struck home as true?

He pursed his lips. It mattered that his mom donated money to his ministry.

"Why would the urbs sponsor a preacher?" he demanded in vexation.

"To encourage settlers to be tax-paying, law-abiding, and boring," Kassidy ventured. "Obey authority. Don't make demands. Just my opinion, Abel." Surprisingly, she packed the clothes from the floor into the new cabinets rapidly and very neatly.

Abel privately pledged to have a talk with his mom. Jules, too. Her family were also faithful followers of the Reverend. Ellsworth was part of what they had in common.

"There," Kassidy announced. "I'm all set. Let's go. I can show you a couple biomes along the way. Eli won't be finished as quick as we are. We might have an hour to kill. Or three."

"Probably three," Abel conceded. Eli was smart, and his heart was in the right place. But science did not reward the quick and flexible. Bit of a plodder. Abel rather liked that about him. "Hopefully Benjy will kick him along. Hey, Kassidy? What's a biome?" The fact he didn't even know Ellsworth was a fraud inspired Abel past his usual no-questions reticence. Mom was right. Not asking when he didn't know just made him an idiot.

Kassidy flounced into a maroon plastic leather armchair, one of two next to a matching love seat. "Mahina Actual is the terraforming headquarters for the moon, right?"

Abel nodded. He didn't ordinarily think of it that way, but OK.

"So our main industries are scientific research. Especially, how to make Mahina more like Earth. We have data for all the species of Earth. We can regenerate them anytime. But they're not like sofas or potted plants. You can't just plonk them in and expect them to thrive. Each big species depends on smaller ones, and on each other. For instance, the trees. They're big and flashy. We can see them. But they rely on the soil below, which is chock-full of microorganisms. The animals need the trees. All of them rely on Earth-normal gravity. A biome is the whole assemblage.

"Anyway, the city has labs, and factories, and storage districts. And living quarters and social spaces, of course. But it also holds living zoos of different biomes. Forest. Lake. Desert. Savanna — that's grassland. Ocean, but that's low priority. We use the ocean tank as a swimming pool. Tropical and subtropical versions of forest and grass-land. The closest biome to here is temperate forest — trees that can handle a freeze. Point is, much of the city is a living science lab. You'll see."

She hopped up and retrieved her grav carrier. Abel's waited ready to hand, flipped to vertical while empty. They'd need those.

Thrive's industrial-size carriers sported a new feature for this adventure. The gurney-sized pallet platforms were hollow, and scan-proof. Sass procured them in Schuyler via her new mob relationship. A quick call to Josiah was all it took to connect to the right seller. After Abel and Kassidy finished their own project, Eli's first load of ill-gotten gains would leave the city tucked into the grav carriers themselves, while security inspected the load on top. A scan of the pallet would show nothing but the inner metal cage that extended the grav field.

But first they went tree-shopping.

Kassidy led an amazed Abel through the promised stand of temperate forest and a stretch of subtropical savanna. The forest was an immersive experience, with birds and squirrels and chipmunks. Mixed leafy and needle trees crowded so close together, with such a rich understory in the dusk, that for a few minutes Abel could see nothing but forest. The large savanna was less engaging. More open, similar in size to a few farm fields, it was ringed with other biomes and apartment buildings. The only wildlife Abel saw there was some insects and a lizard.

Soon they reached the city's exterior wall, and followed it along a dry path beside a putrid-smelling marsh with gnarly shrubs not much taller than Abel. Some creature splashed in the channels but he couldn't spot it.

"Mangrove. I wish they'd drain that and start over," Kassidy groused. "The door we're looking for should be coming up...there."

They paused before an industrial double door with windows. Another warehouse building stood a stone's throw away, with a broad raised foamcrete walkway between, flanked by moon rubble. Kassidy contacted Eli, and he buzzed them through.

Stepping outside into his native Mahina, Abel was startled by the smell. The dry ozone-laden air seared sinuses which had opened in the moist city. He smelled metals he'd never noticed before. The low-angled setting sun was blocked between the tall buildings, leaving this short passage in a greenish murk of shadow and the odd feeling that the light was the wrong color. Strange. The light and moisture had seemed welcoming and inviting when he entered the city. Now he was back to normal, yet it felt harsh and wrong.

They scurried across the gap, and Eli buzzed them through again.

Abel's sinuses loved the change, as he breathed deep of moist living greenhouse. Row after row of saplings stretched out before him, each in its own foamcrete pot. Their heights ranged between 1 and 3 meters, in many shapes. The light was consistent with outdoors here, unaided by light pipes over the trees. The temperature matched the outdoors too, he realized. He looked up. The warehouse was open-air, with no dome roof or forcefield above. Yet the air smelled infinitely better inside its walls than outside. Strange.

"How's Eli coming along?" he asked.

Kassidy replied, "Didn't say. Sounded a little harried, so I left him to it."

"OK. You pick a tree." He fixed one of Kassidy's third-eye cameras to his brow, and contacted Sass. "We're in."

Watching via the camera, she talked him through finding the security arrangements, in a booth not far from the door. Abel pulled on work gloves and operated the monitor as directed, acting as her eyes and hands, but not brain. Sass didn't want him to use voice controls and leave a voice print. He couldn't read the screens she navigated him through.

"Good," Sass said. "The sensors are all motion-activated. We'll change that to sampling." She told him how to wipe the security records of the past half hour, then reprogram the camera regimen. Her new schedule would enable the motion sensors for one hour a day, at oh-five hundred. If this were a part of the city anyone cared about, she explained, it wouldn't be this easy. But watching trees grow was hardly a security priority.

"You're all set," Sass said. "How's it going?"

"We're good," Abel reported. "Don't know about Eli. This place is strange."

"It is that," Sass agreed. "Enjoy it, but stay on task, alright? Be safe."

"Will do. Oh, hey, Sass, did you —?" He meant to ask her advice on tree selection, but she'd already disconnected. He shrugged and exited the security booth.

"What did you pick?" he asked Kassidy. She struggled to carry a nearly 2-meter tree toward the grav carriers. He almost waded in to take the pot from her, but from past experience, she was stronger than he was. She adored effort. So he settled for flipping a grav carrier pallet down to horizontal and positioning it at the ready. The pallets were a bit too wide to traverse the tree aisle.

"Olive!" she reported proudly. "It's not very big. Should we take two? Maybe olive and grapefruit?"

"I've never tasted an olive or a grapefruit," Abel confessed. "They're food, right?" She plonked the tree onto the pallet before him, a spindly looking thing with its trunk heavily trussed to a support stake. Each branch bore a dispirited spray of small waxy yellow-green leaves, and a few small berries. "Not very productive."

"It's just a baby," Kassidy defended. "The grapefruit is flowering. And it looks prettier."

They waded back into the aisle together to pick out a taller grapefruit tree, which looked overdue for a bigger pot. Eli called while they carried it out of the aisle together. Kassidy waited until they got the pot onto the pallet before she answered her comm.

"Benjy what?" she demanded, gazing at Abel stricken. "Be right there."

26

Medical nanites were developed in parallel with the Diaspora. These were vital to compensate for the human environmental shortfalls.

B enjy would have worried about being discovered a lot more, if his hand weren't dripping blood from his sneeze. His nose burned in a way that inspired him to sneeze not at all. Instead of laying low, he lurched for the sink and turned on the water full blast to wash that evil crap off, including his hands and eyes and everything else not protected by his work overalls.

"Not to worry, Jez," Eli said on the far side of the wardrobe. "Student intern. I should let you go. Get back to supervising him before he breaks something. So good to catch up!" Meanwhile he jimmied the wardrobe around.

Benjy couldn't care less. *What is this crap? Am I going to lose my eyes?*

"Benjy, sorry I got held — What are you doing?" Eli inquired.

"Stuff, from the bin. It burns!"

Eli cautiously peeked into the bin at arm's length. He closed it to read the label. "Jesus. Be right back."

"Eli? *Eli!*" Benjy yelled after him. "That was not helpful! Bastard."

Eli didn't stop. The door to corridor 3 closed behind him.

Water still ran pink from Benjy's nose. He tried snorting clean water in and blowing out alternating nostrils. The burning was less, but damn it hurt. One of his eyes and both hands were burning, too. Red streaks darted up his forearms as though blood poisoning crept toward his heart from an infection. His heart was pounding a mile a minute and his breath came in ragged gasps. He was pretty sure that part was panic, though.

The door opened again and Eli returned with something like a white briefcase with a red cross on it. "Just one more moment, Benjy. Right with you..." He sat to the closest computer out in the bullpen and appeared to be checking something.

"Doctor!" Benjy demanded.

"No," Eli said. "We can't risk it, unless... No. Thank God. Yes, we can handle this ourselves."

"Sass!" Benjy demanded.

"No, really! I've got this," Eli insisted, jotting down a couple more notes on his pocket tab. "Unless... Hm." He resumed tapping.

"Your bedside manner sucks regolith," Benjy assured him. "I wanna talk to Sass. I don't trust you."

"Just — wait." Eli finally grabbed the briefcase and came to him. Casting around wildly, he couldn't find what he was looking for, and slammed on all the lights instead. This being a plant lab, the maneuver conjured lamps of an intensity approaching the Wednesday evening noon sun. They ducked while he hastily dialed it back a bit.

Benjy's eyes now added swimming red and green blotches to his symptom list. "Rego fool!"

Eli ignored that. He peeled Benjy's eyelids back with his thumbs and studied them. "Good, that's a little...not too..." He squirted a few drops into each eye. "Oh, you'd better keep your eyes closed. Those drops will dilate your..." He didn't finish that sentence either, opting instead to pry Benjy's head back to get light into his fiery nostrils.

Benjy kicked him in the shin. "How about I sit first?"

"Sorry." Eli pulled over a rolling lab stool. He realized that didn't help and traded it for a desk chair with a helpful back from the cubicles. He peered into Benjy's nostrils, looking worried. When the scientist thoughtfully stepped back from that, Benjy presented his red-streaked forearms. "Ah...histamine..." Eli selected a hypodermic from the first aid kit and pressed it to Benjy's arm.

"What was that?" Benjy asked.

"A powerful antihistamine. To see how much of this red is damage, versus —"

Benjy zonked out, sound asleep before the sentence ended.

That's when Eli called Kassidy for help.

AFTER SHE FINISHED HELPING Abel disable the tree room security, Sass called her old foe, Marshal Clay Rocha. "Hi! I'm in the parking lot at Mahina Actual. Wondered if you'd care to share a sunset drink. I got the hydrologist's report today."

"Good timing," Clay replied. "I'm flying in now. I see *Thrive*. Meet you there."

With a twinge of misgiving, Sass scurried out to wait by the mushroom stand, in case Clay thought there was a rule against it. Sass didn't know of any.

Jules reported that business was slow to nonexistent. People passed her by, intent on grabbing a burger and fries at the fast food court.

"Are those good?" Jules asked forlornly.

"Yeah. Not as good as yours. It's more the illusion of the urb experience."

"Illusion?"

"The tourist mall isn't much like the inside of the city," Sass clarified. "Urbs don't go there."

Clay was now hopping a steel fence between his deluxe parking lot and the gravel one they stood in. A quick flick of gravity made steel fence-hopping a trivial matter, despite his habitual FBI-style suit. The FBI had changed names by the time Sass left Earth, and

'Federal' referred to a different government altogether. But a cop like Sass still called Clay's type the Feds.

Jules hailed another potential customer, ending the conversation.

Sass strode forward to shake hands with Clay. "Jules is one of my crew," she said by way of explanation. "I have some crops growing in the engine room. She makes extra pocket money by selling it. Brings in a surprising amount. Care for a drink in the mall?"

With his usual cool professionalism, Clay studied the mushroom stand. "You've never shown me your ship."

"Alright." Sass managed to hold her wince until she turned her back on him. She waved at Jules, but was ignored. The teen was happily enlarging an order for an eager customer.

Sass brought Clay in via the smaller lock, since the ramp was closed to discourage nosy tourists. "The hold is huge without sleeping racks," she said, waving an arm around the cavernous space.

Clay looked bemused by the slide. "I figured the crops would be in here."

"Engine room," Sass said. She dutifully showed him the garden and med-bay, and headed up the main stairs.

"Years," Clay murmured. "And I never saw the upstairs. Or the engine room, for that matter."

Sass reflected that they'd seen the med bay often enough during those early years. She should reminisce, get him talking. Instead she said, "I hope you don't mind, but I don't feel right showing you anyone else's cabin. This one's unused."

She opened the door to the empty bunk room at the back. The group bath passed through to Benjy's. The young slob had left both doors open and a damp towel on the floor.

But Clay left it at his automatically thorough observation from the bathroom door. "Might have been fun from these racks."

"I came upstairs once back then," Sass replied. "These cabins were used for storage, not bunks. The crew was packed into the captain's quarters. Which I can't show you, because I gave it to the first mate and his wife. That was her at the produce stand." Sass drew him along to peer into the kitchen zone, the office, and the bridge.

"And my cabin. Abel and Jules' is bigger, but hey, the whole ship is mine."

Clay smiled politely, and strode into her cabin to claim a seat on the bed.

"I thought we'd have drinks in the kitchen," Sass objected. "Or outdoors. I usually toast sunset out under the sky."

"If you want," Clay agreed. But he studied the room from the vantage of her bed first. "I guess you're busy repairing the rest of the ship."

Sass frowned defensively. "I painted the captain's quarters first. Yeah, I need to get around to this. I don't spend much time in here. Except to sleep."

"Hm." Clay rose and glanced into the bathroom. That part she'd painted, because the rust level was off-putting. It looked like mold. Mahina was too dry for mold. The refugee tents back in the Adirondacks left her with a phobia, though.

"This is pretty civilized," Clay conceded. "Alright, I'll stop being nosy." He shot her a quick apologetic smile.

They decamped to the kitchen. Sass shifted the wall display to show the best available angle on the progressing sunset, from the cockpit cameras over the back of the parking lot. She stood staring at it. "No. Mind sitting up top?" She grabbed a six pack of beer and the ice wand.

"Up top," Clay echoed, not understanding the suggestion.

Sass strode out to the catwalk and jumped a few times until she caught a rope dangling from the overhead. "Computer, open mid cargo top hatch." She stumbled a bit on that designation, not sure what this particular lock was called. But the ship got the gist and unlocked the hatch for her. The rickety ladder responded to a yank on the rope, dropping to meet the catwalk. "Excuse me, Clay. Normally we just jump onto the roof." She handed him the ice wand to carry, and started clambering up, angling over the hold.

"Of course," Clay acknowledged. "Because who wants to behave like an adult."

"Up yours, Rocha. Coming or not?" Privately she quite enjoyed watching him climb the rusty rungs below her. He hastily tucked the ends of his fancy tie into a pocket, and stepped ever-so-gingerly to keep the rust off his fine suit and shiny shoes.

Sass's work overalls didn't occasion that kind of fuss. She did pause to look over the seals on the hatch, though. The inner lock gaskets had been replaced. The outer hatched could use the same. She sighed. Always something. She popped her head out and set the beer down to the side before crawling the rest of the way onto the ship top. She turned and offered Clay a hand so that his suit needn't suffer.

"So do we stand or," Clay began, then took in the view. An array of spongy exercise mats lay inexplicably on top of the ship. "Because…?"

"Because my crew are slobs who forgot to put them away?" Sass now required Kassidy to haul wrestling mats up here before using *Thrive* as a trampoline. She strode to the mats and gave them a flick to dislodge the dust. "There. Fairly clean." She plonked down on a corner, leaving plenty of room for Clay to sit.

"Charming." Clay elegantly levered himself down to sit, then contemplated the reddish state of his hands. "Screw it. We haven't fought a match in years. Shall we?"

"Not a bad idea. After beer and business." She opened her beer and shoved the ice wand into it for a quick zap. She offered it to him.

"You can keep that one," Clay said. He applied the wand to the side of his bottle the correct way, on a lower, slower setting to cool the liquid without ice crystals. Sass's short cut marred the beer flavor and carbonation.

And Clay did like to do things correctly. *Don't argue with him,* Sass reminded herself. "To sunset."

"To sunset," he agreed. They clinked bottles, then saluted the half-Pono and the hot pink beady eye of the sun. The orb should sink below the horizon within the hour. "Hydrologist."

"Right. I now have two offers on my water well. The hydrologist wants to place the property 'in reserve' for an atmo spire."

"And not build one? Damn them to hell."

Sass raised both eyebrows. "My sentiments exactly. Another entrepreneur is interested in operating a water station."

Clay curled a lip dubiously. "Waste. So you're asking if I had another proposal?"

"If you do, I'd love to hear it. There's enough water to support two atmo spires and a thriving town."

"Thriving is in short supply. To thriving." Clay saluted with his bottle and drank again.

"You don't happen to have money for an atmo spire, do you?"

"That would take more than money. Give me a week or two to think about it."

Clay was businesslike and efficient, traits Sass found convenient for the purpose of getting rid of him quickly. But today she needed to keep him talking. Possibly for hours. "Could do," she allowed. "Though I need to pay taxes in ten days. They call it title and registration."

"You should appeal that," Clay advised. "That sale was a settler to settler transaction. No jurisdiction to pay taxes to. Of course, unless you want the ship impounded, you have to pay the taxes on time. While you appeal."

"And the date of appeal will never come," Sass said. That was the usual system. "What do they do with these taxes, anyway?"

"In theory? Fund atmo spires. And infrastructure." He eyed her through his beer glass. "Your act of contrition is wearing thin."

"You never believed it anyway. I think I did, though." At a gentle noise from Clay, she expanded on that. "When I left the farm. Can you believe I changed all the sheets for them? Left the place so clean and tidy for Cyber-Mennonites. Sold all my livestock, so they wouldn't be grav tortured." Sass frowned, groping for what she was trying to say. "I don't want armed overthrow of the city, Clay. I never did want war. But I can't let it go."

"You and Kendra are the same, you know," Clay said.

Sass shot him a glare. Dragging this conversation out for ten minutes could be hard, let alone hours. She had a plan for that. The plan was escaping her at the moment.

"I didn't mean it as an insult, Sass," Clay said softly. "I meant you're both ferocious protecting your own. If you could see that urbs and settlers are both your own, we might get somewhere. We need the scientists."

"We need the scientists working on the settlers' problem," Sass argued. "And I am not Kendra Oliver."

Clay sighed. "No. She's a devious bitch. You're too direct and simple to get things done. How did you live to our age, and still see everything so black and white? Everything went gray for me a long time ago."

Oh, yeah. Here was the thread Sass meant to tug on. Shared history.

"You were the idealist, Clay. Much more than me. High-falutin' professional values, fancy education. I was an ignorant cop from the DP camps." Displaced persons, climate migrants, were DPs in the official jargon. "Keep the refugees from killing each other over scraps. Those gardens in the city, they're a fantasy. They don't remind me of Earth. Not the Earth I knew."

Her Earth was ugly and muddy and mean. By the end there was hardly a day of good weather. Most days the storms were too strong for a tent. Yet moldering tents were all the shelter most people had.

Clay surprised her. "I saw a botanical garden once on Earth. Pennsylvania somewhere. Not tended like the one here. Overgrown with poison ivy. Birds, squirrels, the standard local critters. It was spring, trees in bloom. Daffodils, tulips. The sun broke through for a few minutes. Beautiful."

The guarded flood-gates opened. They reminisced as the alien sun sank below the horizon. They even laughed over the stupid stunts the settlers pulled while they worked from a skyship like this one. That gig was far more up Sass's alley than Clay's. She always saw it in his pained expression. Some yutz without a grammar-school education would explain why exactly he'd killed his bunk-mate. Or shattered a highly calibrated, priceless piece of equipment by digging a latrine with it. Sass could laugh with the idiots. Clay longed for some white collar crime. Or even someone to play chess with him, or hold an intelligent conversation. Yet the urbs treated him as just as unwashed and ignorant as the rest. The Ganymede crew held themselves aloof from both.

After a bit, Sass went down to grab another six pack. They'd both ignored their comms, which hummed repeatedly. She stole the chance to read her messages.

"Oh, hell."

Clay must have done the same. He called down from the hatch. "Sass? Eli Rasmussen and Kassidy Yang. What are they doing in the city?"

"Just grabbing odds and ends. I'll be right up."

"They brought two crew members along to collect odds and ends?"

"Eli planned to get me a tree. As a gift. Needed help with the tree and some furniture. And I wanted to see you!"

"Maybe I should go deal with this," Clay said slowly.

"No, you're off duty! And you were going to tell me about that genetics thing. What was that thing?" She grabbed the beer and hurried onto the ladder to block him from coming down. Not that he couldn't just hop down a few stories onto the parking lot. But he wouldn't, because it was rude. She hoped.

"There we go," Sass announced with a grin after he gave her a hand up from the ladder. She opened a beer and thrust it at him. More distraction was in order. "Why did we never get together, Clay?" Bad timing. No, that wasn't sexy at all.

"Get together for what?"

"Sex. Your nanites. My nanites. Don't tell me you aren't horny all the time."

Clay pursed his lips in a frown, then took a swig of warm beer. He grimaced and crouched down by the mats to grab the ice wand again. "We're colleagues, Sass. You're one of the guys."

"You sleep with Kendra," Sass accused. *Wait. That's not what I meant to say.*

Clay's warm complexion grayed and he dropped his eyes. "You knew about that?"

"Yeah. So don't get holier-than-thou on me, Clay."

"You don't understand," Clay murmured.

"What's to understand? The nanites make us horny as hell." In vexation, Sass pulled the ice wand out of his hand. "I find the woman repulsive. The nanites still think you should screw like a bunny."

Clay met her eye again, honestly puzzled. "That's not —" He stood and abruptly kissed her. "There. Better?"

Sass reflected that she got a sexier kiss from Kassidy Yang the day they met. And she wasn't into women. "Huh. Why doesn't that work between us?"

Clay rubbed his forehead as though soothing an incipient headache. "Because that's how I meant it?" He grasped her forearm lightly. "Sass. You're the closest thing I've had to a partner since the Adirondacks. But you blindsided me on the rebellion. I blindsided you on Kendra and...didn't tell you other things. Because you can't keep a secret."

"You're saying we're not attracted to each other because we kept secrets? I'm pretty sure my nanites don't care about that, Clay. They just want sex."

Surprised, he laughed out loud. "Oh God, Sass. Stay this shallow forever, won't you?"

"And now you call me stupid again. OK, that's a definite turn-off. Sit. Drink your beer. Swine."

Chuckling, he did so.

Good, that bought her another few minutes. Hopefully she could spin this out long enough for the crew inside the city to get their act together.

27

Each colony advanced its own strain of nanite technology in isolation. Communication between colonies was difficult or non-existent.

"Why did you knock him out?" Kassidy cried, trying to rouse Benjy.

"I was trying to stop a histamine reaction," Eli whined. "Here. See? No red stripes. There were red stripes running up his arms."

"You're a menace," Kassidy snapped at him. "Pack your stuff. We need to go, and get Benjy into the med bay."

"I'll help," growled Abel, inserting himself bodily between Eli and Kassidy in the cramped side lab. "What else do you need? Pronto."

"I — Dammit." Eli ran his hands through his hair frantically. "I don't know what any of this stuff is that Benjy collected. I told him to grab the — this one." He rapped one of the flat equipment cases. Kassidy wasn't on the need-to-know list about the nanite synthesizer. Her mother was highly placed in the Mahina Actual medical hierarchy. Sass figured it was best to leave the stunt woman out of the loop as long as possible. "Can you wake him?"

"Not with a first aid kit!" Kassidy retorted.

"Never mind," Abel cut in. "What else do you need, Eli?"

The scientist pulled out his pocket computer. "This way."

"Did you jigger the security cameras?" Abel queried, trailing him with an empty grav carrier. They'd left the trees out in the corridor.

"First thing when we got here," Eli confirmed. "In here." He started pulling jugs and boxes and bags of supplies out of a cabinet. Abel stowed them in the pallet's hidden compartment.

"He already took a centrifuge," Eli muttered, thinking out loud. "Is that a... Yes, that's a gene sequencer. Then I need a splicer." His eyes cast around wildly, to settle on another side lab across the way. "There. Meet me back at Benjy. Start transferring things."

Abel quickly returned to the cabinet Benjy had stowed stolen equipment and supplies in. The pallets couldn't hold everything, and Sass was particularly emphatic that the nanite synthesizer must not leave the city today. Nothing exited the city that couldn't be explained by Eli's research alone. They could extract the nanite synthesizer on a far less dramatic exit, just Kassidy swapping out her wardrobe as she did every week.

Abel reserved one pallet for electronics to be determined, and efficiently transferred reagents into all other available hidden cubic. He had no idea which grey electronic box was the nanite synthesizer. He couldn't even ask in front of Kassidy.

"He's coming around," she said, bending over Benjy. She gave him an enthusiastic kiss on the lips, adding a glossy purple accent to his scarlet nose and bloody eyes. "How you feeling, handsome?"

Benjy puckered his mouth, blew out his cheeks, then vomited in Kassidy's general direction. Fortunately, the stunt woman was agile, and the stream only hit the floor.

"No offense," Benjy muttered. He started to wipe his mouth on his sleeve but didn't trust it.

"I'll just go find a cleaning bot," Kassidy said breezily, and headed out.

With her out of the way, Abel seized the opportunity to whisper in Benjy's ear. "Which equipment leaves today?"

"Do I look like I care?"

Abel took the kid's upper arm in a vice grip. "You'd better."

"Fine." He quickly identified the items he'd amassed in the cabinet. "Still need the dust from hell, stored in that bin. Make Eli do it. After I'm out of the room. Can I have a drink of water?"

Abel released his arm. "Feel free." He turned back to stowing chemicals.

"Would it kill you to be decent to me?" Benjy demanded.

"You look closer to dying than me," Abel observed. "Figure out your cover story, genius."

Eli arrived to thrust another lab case into Abel's hands. "Pack this, it's a priority." He hurried back out.

"Don't pack that," Benjy overruled him. "Still has a tracker attached. Here. Bring me the tool, too — that one." Grumbling under his breath all the while, he swapped stickers and rendered the gene splicer safe to hide. Kassidy returned with a captured cleaning bot. Benjy made her drop the tracker label into the box of reject glassware.

"Eli, we're running out of space," Abel growled with the botanist's next deposit.

"Dust from hell," Benjy reminded him.

"Yeah, fine," Abel acknowledged. "And Benjy says you need to collect some of the stuff that attacked him."

"That... Hm," Eli said. "One more box first. We can store the rest at Kassidy's." He disappeared again to rifle other lab rooms.

"Whatever did this to Benjy," Kassidy asserted, "does not enter my apartment. What is this crap, anyway?"

"Don't know," Benjy grumbled. "We need it for...one of those." He waved vaguely.

Distrustful, Kassidy plucked up the inventory tool, and swiped the poisonous bin. She froze. "What the hell are you stealing? No. No, I won't be a part of this!"

"You already are," Abel growled at her, and snatched the tool back.

"Abel, you do not have anyone qualified to use this!" Kassidy returned. "What, you think Eli can design nanites? All scientists are alike? He does plants! Nanites are a medical engineering specialty. I should know, my dad —"

"Not your problem," Abel cut her off. "And you're not going to turn us in. Because we're business partners. You've enabled us every step of the way."

"Hah! Not for this! They'll be lenient because —" She swallowed. She didn't have enough leverage. They might go easier on her for turning in the others. But like Sass twenty years ago, Kassidy would still be punished. "Dammit!"

"You're going to turn a blind eye," Abel ordered. "We get out of here safe. Then we hash it out. You, me, and Sass. For now, though, boy wonder already made our getaway harder. You figure that out."

Abel turned his back on her, and swapped out one of Eli's precious cases for the nanite synthesizer. Kassidy didn't know which steel box was which.

Eli returned with another cardboard box of electronic guts and gurgling bottles, and a full-body hazmat suit with visor and gauntlets. He handed off the supplies to Abel to stow, "Top priority!" Then he stepped carefully over the busy vomit bot, and started donning the hazmat suit.

Benjy lurched to his feet to clutch Kassidy's arm, swaying. "Out. Get me out of here."

"God, Eli," Kassidy said, hugging Benjy upright. "You're burning all your bridges. You'll never be able to come back from this. Don't do it."

"Already done," Eli replied, snapping his face visor closed. He reached to flick a switch and turn on a fan, then lowered the retractable fume hood over the salt bin that Benjy hadn't noticed. Not that Benjy would have understood what it was. "Evacuate the room, please."

"Go, go, go," Benjy urged.

"Going," Abel acknowledged. He thrust the first grav carrier and cabinet out of the way. He pulled the door shut behind them as soon as Kassidy and Benjy were through. Then he pushed another pallet to Kassidy with his boot, the one he'd swapped the nanite synthesizer into. "Load this one with the trees. And the kid." He shifted the cabinet onto the filled second pallet, and started to fill the core of the final empty.

Benjy had noticed Abel's swap. He couldn't argue with that. Clearly they couldn't leave the prize instrument with Kassidy. He desperately wanted to know why she drew the line. But Abel was right — not here, not now.

Besides, he couldn't even walk, and his bloody eyes burned. Kassidy propped him in a desk chair, and used his foot to hold open the corridor door, while she re-loaded the trees.

"Here we are," Eli said proudly, emerging with a steel vacuum jar of the caustic crystals. His face mask was off. His gauntlets and hazmat suit remained.

"Seal that in something," Abel demanded. "And put that gear away." He ducked back into the lab to retrieve their inventory management handheld, and shoved it into his pocket.

"But it's already sealed," Eli pointed out.

Able pursed his lips.

"I could double-seal it," Eli allowed. He tried to hand the canister to Abel while he stripped off the suit. Abel wouldn't touch it, so he set it on the floor with a sigh. "I do know what I'm doing, Abel."

"Huh. Hurry up." Abel shot a quick update to Sass, *Starting out.*

"Company coming," Kassidy hissed through the door crack. She opened the door wider, and hauled Benjy's dead weight through. She pulled the door closed, with the two of them stuck outside.

Set to rest, Benjy had dozed off on the antihistamines again. But the abrupt transition into a fireman's carry, and view of Kassidy's rump closeup and upside-down, half-roused him. "Wha—?"

"Sh," Kassidy crooned. "You had too much to drink for sunset, my young friend. Hi!" She greeted the approaching white jacketed scientists with a disarming grin. "Glad it's sunset."

The scientists paused to chat affably. They looked like an attractive man and woman, also in their twenties. But unlike Benjy, Kassidy understood their badges. She put their ages around 50 and 65, probably the head of a lab and her top acolyte. Fortunately this lab was not theirs. After a few social noises, and Kassidy's promise to say hi to her mother for them, they passed on toward the end of the corridor, to enter the final lab on the left.

"Phew," Kassidy whispered.

28

On overpopulated Earth, nanites for life extension were absolutely proscribed. But in the colonies, unassisted life expectancy could easily fall to the 30's, or even 20's.

Inside the lab, Eli's steps slowed as he put away the hazmat gear, and donned his white lab coat again. He gazed around, and retraced his steps to every room he'd visited, or stolen from.

Finished packing, Abel sat on a pallet and watched. After a couple minutes of the scientist moodily drifting from room to room, the first mate sighed and rose to join him.

"All signs of theft covered?" Abel inquired dubiously.

"Well..."

"It's not possible to cover this theft, is it?" Abel pressed.

"Not entirely. No. No, I won't be coming back." Eli unconsciously stroked his lab coat.

"Then we're leaving. Now," Abel insisted. "Eli, this is not a decision point. This is an action point. Move."

"Over twenty years of my life —" Eli was feeling the enormity of his defection, and it paralyzed him. *Never again?* His mentor Dr.

Bertram would be proud of him. *Really?* Bertram was gone. This was Eli's own life he was throwing away.

"Tell me over a drink later," Abel commanded. "Move." *Terrific.* They were behind urb enemy lines. Both his renegade urbs were suffering cold feet. And Benjy was out of commission, draped groggily between tree pots.

With Abel propelling Eli's reluctant steps, they and their grav pallets rejoined Kassidy and Benjy in the corridor.

"Wait," Kassidy said, as the door closed. "Where's the cleaning bot?"

"We left it cleaning," Eli replied.

"Go get it," Kassidy insisted. "It's got Benjy's vomit in it."

With a sigh, Eli went back to retrieve the bot.

Abel set a brisk pace up the long hallway. They still had to visit Kassidy's place again before they could get out of here. The storage cabinet couldn't pass security inspection. Abel would love nothing better than to dispatch one of his urbs on that errand to speed things up. But he was the one supplying the resolve. They had to stick together.

During sunset happy hour, there was little traffic at first. Scientists they passed barely raised an eyebrow at this group intent on their business. Kassidy directed them to a back way to her block instead of emerging onto the downtown plaza again, crowded with party-goers and joggers. She released the cleaning bot to head that way, though. They made it another block, fairy lights twinkling from the trees as the city dimmed.

A petite woman emerged from a cross-street, fists on hips that glittered with a gold-embellished purple sari. "Kassidy!" she barked.

"Mom," Kassidy breathed. The corners of her mouth and eyes drooped in dismay.

"What in heavens are you doing?" the mom demanded, still barreling down upon them.

"Keep moving," Abel insisted.

"I can't," Kassidy hissed back to him. "Just business, Mom. I'd like you to meet my friends from the skyship. Eli Rasmussen, Abel Greer, and Benjy. Gang, this is my mother, Dr. Paripati, Director of Endocrinology."

Eli looked suitably impressed, and nodded respect. The title flew past Abel and Benjy without making much impression.

Dr. Paripati pointed a bony be-ringed finger of accusation at Benjy. "What's wrong with him? He needs medical attention. Wait. These are settlers!"

"Yes, ma'am," Abel interjected. "I need to get my crewman back to the ship and into the med bay. You'll excuse us." He tugged Kassidy's elbow.

"I am speaking to my daughter!" the director spat at him. "Kassidy, explain!"

Kassidy shrugged and spread her hands helplessly. Assured and charismatic in every other setting, her self-confidence fled under the hawk nose and beady eyes of this dragon lady.

"And not very respectfully," Abel countered. He threw an arm around Kassidy's shoulders and stiffly hugged her to him. "I don't think you should speak to my lover that way, ma'am."

Kassidy emitted a faint squeal of suppressed surprise, but he'd managed to engage her dramatic flair and sense of humor. She plastered her body against Abel's side and stroked his chest. She gave her mom a sharp bratty nod that said, *Yeah, so there!*

"Come along, darling," Abel demanded.

"You have not heard the last of this, young lady!" Dr. Paripati vowed. "In fact! Security! I require a team at my location immediately."

"What have you done?" Kassidy breathed. "Mom, I will never forgive you for this!"

"Let's go, *darling,*" Abel insisted, grabbing his grav carrier and ramming hers.

Kassidy's mother waved an airy hand. "It won't make any difference!" she called to their backs. The *Thrive* group were already racing to Kassidy's place.

"Eli!" Abel barked. "Wait outside." Kassidy continued into the apartment building without stopping, Abel hot on her heels.

"But — Right." Eli considered for a moment, then bent solicitously over Benjy, who hissed at him. "Shut up and act grateful, kid. Security will be on us before Abel's back."

This seemed likely. No sooner did Abel and Kassidy cross the threshold than the downstairs apartment door banged open, and two children squirted out. One of the lanky brats jumped onto Abel's grav carrier, quickly followed by his little sister. Their settler battle-ax of a mother stood fists on hips, much like Dr. Paripati had.

"What is the meaning of this, Kassidy?" the tele-reverend's wife Mrs. Ellsworth demanded. "Running in and out with men! I am raising small children here, and you act like a hussy!"

Kassidy pinched the bridge of her nose.

But Abel was only too happy to cross the bogus Reverend's wife. He shoved Kassidy to keep moving. Then he reached over and grabbed the brats by their collars and bodily deposited them back on the floor. They squealed outraged protest and fled to hide behind their mother's hips and glare back, making rude faces. Abel barreled up the stairs.

"How dare you touch my children!" Mrs. Ellsworth called after him.

"Control your spoiled brats, madame."

"You can't speak to me that way! Do you know who I am?"

"Yes, I believe I do," Abel returned. "And I shall be telling a great many people about you and the Reverend's cozy deal in the city. Kassidy, could we mention your *neighbor* on your show? I'm sure other settlers would be most interested."

Mrs. Ellsworth briefly gaped like a fish, then slammed herself behind her door.

Kassidy was already in her apartment. Abel scurried to catch up. In nothing flat, they staged Eli's cabinet of botany supplies, and loaded Kassidy's new clothes cabinets. Abel led the way back down to the street.

Security had already arrived with a smug Dr. Paripati. "The settler boy. He's ill. Take him to medical immediately."

"There's no need for that," Eli insisted. "We have medical facilities just outside. Closer than medical."

Paripati insisted, "I am a medical doctor. You are a washout. What is your field again?"

"Botany," Eli growled.

"Yes, well," Paripati said with a sniff. "Guards, Kendra Oliver will meet us in medical when she's available. Bring both of the settlers. And the botanist."

Eli folded his arms over his chest and narrowed his eyes at the guards. "Exactly what crime do you think you're arresting me for, hm?"

"You have nothing on either of us!" Kassidy chorused. "And you have nothing on these settlers, either!"

"They're helping us move some things out to their skyship," Eli explained. "Nothing more. Thank you, gentlemen, but your assistance is not required."

Paripati reasserted her key points. "Kendra Oliver. In medical."

"Is this how you handled Daddy?" Kassidy demanded of her mom. "When you had him exiled? Guards, this is a cat fight, not a security concern!" To illustrate, she leapt over a grav carrier and shoved her mother by the shoulders.

A guard reluctantly grabbed her and got kicked in the shins for his trouble. With a helpful assist from Eli, he did manage to secure Kassidy's arms behind her back. But the athlete used their anchor as leverage and launched a roundhouse kick at her mom's gut. Paripati dodged.

"She called Oliver," the guard apologetically explained to Eli — Tamber, by his name tag. "We don't have a choice. Ms. Yang, there aren't any charges against you yet. Cooperate, please?"

Kassidy spat at her mother. "Fine! Bitch. Keep her away from me!"

"Uh, yes. Dr. Paripati, perhaps you should go on ahead," Tamber the cop suggested.

"That is my daughter!" Paripati insisted.

"I caught that part, ma'am," the cop agreed blandly.

"Hmph!" The doctor stalked off imperiously.

The guards gave her a block head start before they reopened negotiations with their charges. "Your only way out is through medical. You need to talk to Oliver. Or they won't let you through the gates. I'm sorry, Dr. Rasmussen, Ms. Yang. Come along quietly, please?"

"Very well," Eli replied while Kassidy was still evolving a caustic enough reply. "But my young intern does not, in fact, need medical attention. We have given him first aid. We have perfectly adequate facilities on our skyship."

"I caught that part, sir," Tamber agreed blandly.

Abel shot an update to Sass. Then he led the way following Paripati to medical, steering his grav carrier full of hidden damning goods to meet Mahina's head of security. This trip was not going well.

"WHAT THE HELL is she doing here!" Nearly an hour later, Kendra Oliver sauntered into Benjy's alcove in medical. Ignoring everyone else present, her eyes landed furiously on Sass.

Clay commented mildly, "Security took custody of her crewman. Sass wants him back. She's here under my supervision, of course."

Sass nodded, face carefully cold. "Mahina Actual has no right to hold Benjy against his will."

Kendra crooked a lip. "He appears unconscious."

"Medical treatment was inflicted against his will," the marshal Clay informed her. "The only criminal act in evidence."

Tamber the cop was still stuck there. He clarified deferentially, "There was a mild domestic disturbance before you arrived. Sir."

Clay shrugged. "I don't appreciate Dr. Paripati disrupting my sunset because of a spat with her daughter. She's caused a lot of fuss and bother over a simple trip into the city to collect some belongings."

"Trees," Kendra observed, visibly annoyed that Clay defied her. The grav carriers and trees were parked in the hospital corridor, a traffic impediment to all.

"A gift," Sass explained. "From our friend Dr. Eli Rasmussen." She indicated the botanist with a flourish of the hand.

And what is stowed in the pallet beneath those trees? Sass's heart pounded and palms sweat. But she needed to appear cool and arrogant here. If Kendra opened that pallet, with a word she could impound *Thrive* and imprison Sass and her crew.

Eli nodded, aloof. "We have several thousand trees sitting in a warehouse, doing no one any good. They need field-testing. A long-term research study."

"I trust you have clearance for this project?" Kendra demanded.

"Not yet," Eli allowed. "I require initial tests to draft the proposal. The trees are an abandoned experiment of Dr. Bertram."

"Seems reasonable," Clay said. He glanced to Tamber for agreement. The cop prudently elected instead to glance into the hallway, keeping an eye out for Dr. Paripati. The current truce granted this room to Kassidy, and her mother stayed out of it.

Clay continued, "Kendra, security insisted that we wait for you. But on my authority as marshal, I'm ready to escort these settlers out of the city. The urbs are his concern." He nodded respect to Tamber.

"No charges against Dr. Rasmussen and Ms. Yang," the cop supplied.

Kendra glared at Clay, and strode to the console by Benjy's bed. She tapped around his medical status, then poked into his personal files.

"He hasn't been charged with anything, Kendra," Clay pointed out.

"True, ma'am," Tamber corroborated. "The boy hasn't done anything except ask to go home."

Kendra demanded, "What was he doing handling these toxins?"

Eli shrugged, arms folded in mild arrogance. "Intern curiosity. He opened the wrong bin. I can't be expected to babysit every moment. But no harm done to the lab." He successfully exuded a reassuring attitude — to Kendra — of not giving a damn whether the dumb settler lived or died.

"Intern." Kendra rapped the counter in irritation. "It says here he's a Mahina University student. A settler. Rare and precious. I think we should protect him from harm and unsavory companions. Give him a dorm room, keep him here in the city. We'll make the offer when he wakes."

Sass bridled in fury. Steal her Benjy? "How dare you! He's my crewman! I demand he be released immediately!"

Score, Kendra's cruel smile exulted. She'd found Sass's pain point.

Clay kept his cool. "A hostage, Kendra? Because?"

"I don't trust her," Kendra spat at Sass. "She's up to something. A proven traitor."

The two women glared into each other's eyes.

Clay sighed. "I will relay your offer to the student tomorrow." Kendra tried to interrupt, but he continued speaking right over her. "Tonight, I escort them back to their ship. You have no grounds to hold this boy against his will. You go too far, Kendra."

"You'll pay for this, Clay," she hissed.

"I usually do," he agreed acidly. "Kendra, have a lovely evening. Guardsman, I'll take it from here. You can go."

Tamber split immediately, before Kendra could contradict Clay.

Kendra wheeled on Sass. "You haven't heard the last of this, Collier! You're a fuck-up and a traitor. To settler and urb alike. You were a sorry excuse for a marshal, and you're a failure in business now. Which surprises no one. I will find out what you're up to. I will take that skyship from you. And this time, no mercy. I'll see you rot in the mines!"

With that, Kendra stalked out, her stilettos clicking furiously.

"Thank you, Clay," Sass breathed. Her face burned from Kendra's insults, which struck all too close to home. And worst of all, Sass's pathetic role in this heist. Her people risked everything. While her own heroic role was what? She dragged Clay in to hide behind.

"Whatever is in those pallets, don't let me find out about it," Clay gritted back, eyes flashing rage at her.

29

With the Diaspora from Earth, advances in technology appeared to stop dead for several centuries. This characterization is unfair.

"Stow the grav carriers before you bring in the mushroom," Sass directed Abel back in *Thrive's* hold. "Leave the trees for Eli."

She itched to join Kassidy and Eli in the med bay to assure herself that her Benjy was OK in the auto-doc. But Clay was still with her. Sass borrowed a wheelchair from medical to cart the youngster here. Clay insisted on coming along to retrieve it. "I could have returned the chair to the door," she griped again.

"We're not done," Clay growled. "In private. Now."

"Clay, I appreciate your help but —"

"Now," he repeated.

Sass reluctantly led him to her cabin, grabbing some more beer along the way.

"You appreciate my help," Clay echoed. "Like hell. You used me."

"A little," Sass conceded, taking a cross-legged seat on the bed. "In case something went wrong."

He remained standing, in a cold stance he'd taken to chew her out all too many times over the decades. "I'm not yours to use."

"Oh, lighten up, Clay. It's a marshal's job to mediate between urbs and settlers. All I did was ensure we got you between us and Kendra. I didn't want to take a chance on whoever was on call. And we had stuff to discuss. Have a beer."

"I've had enough beer." He unclenched enough to take a seat, though. "I deserve to know what your team was doing in there."

Sass shrugged. "I agree you deserve to. We helped Eli liberate a few things to continue his plant research. His career got torpedoed when Kendra exiled his mentor. He escaped the city to continue his life work. Which happens to be terraforming this moon. Plant side."

"Which the city is equipped to do. And your tugboat of a skyship is not."

"Don't insult my ship. OK, I get that you're annoyed. But do you see this landscape changing, Clay? More atmo spires going online? Fertile green spreading across the regolith? One guy. Trying to buck an inept system, by doing his job. I tried to help. Sue me."

Clay pursed his lips and studied her. "That's not the whole truth."

"It's close enough." And time to change the subject. "Oh, hey, you never told me about the genomes thing before my crew outing went pear-shaped."

Earlier, to Sass's surprise, once they set aside their usual prohibition against discussing Earth, their trip to Mahina, and decades of shared history, the conversation came alive. They talked freely about the forbidden until they were both laughing out loud with the relief of the confessional. Current day issues took a dim back seat to their wide-ranging reminiscence. No sex, but they had a great practice bout fighting on the mats.

She regretted using him this evening. Otherwise they might have finally buried the hatchet.

"Genomes," Clay agreed. "You got me thinking. I sequenced your boy Benjy. Plus three other settler students I found at Mahina U. The school has tissue samples."

"A complete invasion of privacy." Sass was neither surprised nor bothered. Her objection was purely for form's sake. Mahina Security and its marshals violated privacy all the time. "Wait, there are four settlers in Benjy's class?"

"No. One's a grad student, another fourth year, plus one other second year in Benjy's class. That one's a girl. They offered her a place in the dorms."

"Got it. Go on."

"Well, mostly they're their parents' children."

Sass blinked parsing that sentence. Then her eyebrows rose.

Clay nodded. "Yeah, there's another gene sequence spliced in. Several, really, spread across different chromosomes. Identical between the first two. A couple revisions in the younger pair."

Ridiculous, Sass thought. Benjy wasn't her kid. But she was outraged all over again that someone would screw with her Benjy. With an effort, she got hold of her rage. *He's not my Benjy.*

Sass blew through pursed lips. "What does it do? This gene sequence."

Clay shrugged one shoulder. "Who would I ask?"

"Leave the data with me?" Sass wheedled. "And the inserted bits they identified. I might ask a couple people."

Clay considered that for a moment. "Give you the results of my illegal violation of their privacy. Hm."

"Clay, whatever that experiment was?" Sass argued. "And it sure sounds like they deliberately experimented on human babies. It was successful. Benjy is a wild success. That's wildly interesting. To us settlers. Is it so interesting to the urbs? I don't know. Did you run a literature search?"

The urb scientists still went through the motions of publishing peer-reviewed research 'papers.' No one printed them, merely read them electronically. In most cases, the reviewing peers comprised the world's sum total audience. But funding, promotions, even choice housing assignments relied heavily on these reports. The publish or perish imperative was alive and well on Mahina.

"Couldn't find anything. There's a lot I don't know," Clay replied judiciously. "For instance, how many fetuses got this genetic insert. If it was even applied at conception. Though I did check Hunter's genome, my son. Out of paranoia. He doesn't have it. Urb students don't have it. But Sass, we don't know how many lanky normals are out there with the same gene splice. Or worse, the failed experiments. We have a small sample of successes. Four. No idea what they were trying to accomplish. Or who. Or why."

"I think you just argued my case for me," Sass pointed out.

"No offense, old pal. But I'm the one who ordered the data. You have a track record with keeping secrets. Not your strong suit."

Sass felt her face warming just a little. But she forced herself to hold his eye resolutely. "You wouldn't tell me if you didn't want a second opinion. I'm not a geneticist. So I'd have to reveal it to someone. Same goes for you." She paused to let him reflect on that. "So give."

"You could give me a name. Who you plan to ask."

"Contra-indicated," Sass said regretfully. This was common enough, to refuse to identify informants. She meant to ask Atlas Pratt for a lead. She did not choose to direct Clay's attention thataway at this time.

He rose from the bed. "Still thinking. I don't have it on me. Want to visit my place? They've got fireflies in the botanical gardens now. I don't know what else since you last saw it. A lot, in twenty years."

Sass nearly refused on automatic. But the memory of July fireflies arrested her. "You would do that? Bring me into the city again? Kendra will be livid."

"In my custody. You're never more than a meter from me. But yeah. Why not."

Sass's eyes narrowed. "Kendra Oliver is why not." She rose abruptly herself.

Clay pressed his lips together in fury. "I'm not her slave. She just thinks I am."

"Aha. You're using me to rub her face in it. Maybe include a twenty minute dalliance in the bedroom with the curtains drawn. While we talk instead of satisfy the damned nanites."

"Consider it payback. You used me. I use you."

"Fair," Sass said. "I'd like to see fireflies again. Assuming you can keep me out of Kendra's clutches. Thank you."

"Sass, you could not possibly hate Kendra Oliver as much as I do."

"Sure." Her sarcasm was clear. "To know Kendra is to hate her."

Clay scrubbed his forehead with his fingers. "Fine. Let's go."

On the way out, everyone seemed safely behind closed doors as they passed through, except for Abel and Jules still stowing the mushroom stand.

Clay paused at the trees standing in her hold. He studied their ID tags, but 'scrubber olive' and 'scrubber grapefruit' failed to enlighten him. He broke off a tiny olive fruit and bit into it.

"Pfaw!" He immediately spit the olive out into his hand, with a face that had sucked far worse than a lemon. "Tastes like iron."

"Huh. Not ripe."

After that was clear sailing back into the city. In the gardens, Sass stood mesmerized as the fireflies danced. She wrestled a baby goat on Clay's living room lawn. They laughed and talked til midnight. They did dally in the bedroom for half an hour.

And he escorted her out by the food court with the data for another clue.

Sass reveled in the feeling of victory. They'd accomplished a heist of the most jealously guarded scientific equipment on Mahina! And maybe, just maybe, she'd made a friend again of Clay Rocha, the only one on this moon who shared her long history and mysterious nanites.

She was on cloud nine until she got home and peered into the auto-doc. Benjy's blood-filled eyes blinked out at her morosely.

With Clay by her side all evening, no one had a chance to explain to her exactly what happened to the kid. "I don't want to know til morning," she decided. "You need anything?"

"I'm good," Benjy whimpered.

"Good." She kissed the crown of his head and headed upstairs to the bridge. Lest a certain someone in the city decide to try something while brooding into the wee hours, Sass shifted *Thrive* to a safer parking spot outside Newer York. Kendra's reach was long, but she wouldn't strike on a whim deep into settler territory.

———

LATE TO BED in the silent skyship, parked by a somnolent town, Sass drifted off the second her head hit the pillow.

After a few hours dead to the world, her deep slumbering mind rose to shallower shoals of dreams, to process the enormity of the day behind her. First on the subconscious agenda was the day she met Clay. The day they became something other than human.

Sass raced in memory through a ragged tent city of climate refugees. Cold rain driven on a vicious wind slashed at her from a blackened sky of towering thunderheads. She tripped over corpses in the mud that grasped for her ankles. She ran through flapping laundry which stood no hope of drying. She dodged guns and sticks, and body slams from broken men. The stench of human waste, offal, and the bloated dead assaulted her nostrils despite her perpetual face mask. Earth's air alone wouldn't suffice anymore, too high in toxins, too low in oxygen as the plant biomes failed. Mold and mildew, perpetually oozing from the filthy tents, lodged in her lungs. Her breath rattled with exertion as though from walking pneumonia. She ran hopelessly, searching everywhere, desperately seeking her son Paul.

The clouds lightened to merely gray overhead, sprinkling no more than a gentle drizzle. Her panicked run settled to a jog, then a calm walk. The rows of tents turned orderly, almost fresh and white. The denizens looked healthier and hopeful, reputable people, though tense and worried.

Blue sky broke through over a grassy rise, an empty dry spot among the miserable teeming crowds. Atop the hill, a skyship beckoned to the chosen few called to this meeting.

Sass took her place and hung her head, humiliated by her muddy pants legs, her heavy sodden anorak dragging her shoulders down in a hunch. Officers from the ship stood before them in bright blue hazmat suits, anonymous behind mirrored face plates.

The ten colonists were called here because they were cops, the blue ones explained. The colony navy would handle the ships. The police on their team, and others, would keep order among their fellow refugees, act as intermediaries to implement orders from the starship crew.

In dream time, their anonymous orders took but an eye blink to convey. Sass focused on her fellow cops instead. Most looked little better than she did, hard-bitten veterans of the DP camps and their endless litany of food theft, domestic abuse, and drug deals gone fatal. The only other woman looked twice Sass's age, worn and harsh, with a hacking cough.

Clay stood out, a gorgeous erect man around forty. He wore an impeccable dark gray business suit. His mud-free leather shoes shone with polish as though he'd just stepped from a meeting on Wall Street, long since drowned and gone. Neither tough-as-nails climate refugee, nor good Samaritan navy from Ganymede, Special Agent Clay Rocha stood alone.

Clay studied each of them in turn, solemn and aloof, arms crossed, with a faintly superior frown. He stared at Sass the longest, eyes ranging from head to mud-booted foot as his lips pursed. A furrow deepened between his brows.

Blue hazmat suits were supplanted by orange, and a ring of Army MP's encircled them. In words long forgotten, Clay furiously demanded the meaning of this. On the group's behalf, he refused to cooperate.

The MP's grabbed him first, held him pinned. A slim orange one approached him with a huge stainless steel syringe. The contents looked like mercury, unlike any intravenous drug Sass had ever seen. The technician bared Clay's arm and swabbed it, then injected him with a tenth of the syringe.

Even after all these years, Sass's subconscious still fixated irate on that detail. The cop Sass Collier spent years fighting shared needles between addicts, especially by her only child. Yet her fellow cops were injected from that same damned syringe, without so much as an alcohol wipe on the needle between stabs.

The MP's released the furious Clay, who resumed his place in line next to Sass. Her turn next. Clay only hissed between clenched teeth at the jab. Sass screamed as the silver fire entered her bloodstream, burned its way up her arm. She panted in ragged gasps as it reached her lungs, then her heart. Clay collapsed to his knees to her left. The other woman cop, to her right, screeched even louder than Sass, but the sound strangled off abruptly. She fell to the ground clutching her heart, her back arced into convulsions. Her feet and arms hammered the ground.

The orange-suited one held up a placating hand. "Reactions vary. To be expected. Next."

Clay listed, then toppled to his side. Sass landed on her knees beside him. The older woman stopped convulsing, her protuberant eyes locked in a dead stare at the clouds above. Sass thought to reach out a hand to close her eyelids, but instead fell onto her hands, bracketing Clay's fancy clean pants legs. She vomited on his shiny shoes before her elbows buckled and she fell the rest of the way.

The next cop died faster, obviously in agony. Sass watched, mouth open, unable to move, her cheek on Clay's thigh, her view 90 degrees off kilter.

She blacked out thinking how angry the superior, educated FBI type would be that she fell sick on his pretty clothes.

30

Research on Earth stopped dead due to brain drain toward the colonies and more urgent concerns. Terraforming and nanite technology continued to develop. But each isolated colony needed to reinvent the wheel, with a painfully small pool of genius to draw from.

Sass woke sweating, her heart pounding at reliving that day in her dreams. She pulled herself out of the bedding, mopped herself with her damp pajamas and discarded them. She considered fresh pajamas, but opted for jeans and a sweatshirt instead. She needed to walk off the dream.

She supposed she shouldn't be surprised her mind rehashed that day again, though the nightmare hadn't recurred in years. She and Clay had dredged up old memories during their long sunset talk. He probably paid tonight with his own insomnia.

Sass wasn't the sort to believe misery loved company. She silently wished Clay good luck with it. She wandered onto the catwalk, hopped nimbly down into the hold, and let herself out by the small side door into the moonlit parking field.

Gaslight, she corrected herself. She walked on the moon. The half-full orb was the gas giant. She adjusted her gravity to 1.2 g's and strode firmly to walk laps around the lot, as she continued arguing with the dream, reconciling phantoms with reality.

The embarkation camp wasn't bad like the tired DP camps. The colonists weren't there long enough, and no more than 20,000 at a time. She wasn't searching for Paul. Her son died the year before, taken by the flu. That year wasn't an especially dangerous strain except when stacked on pre-existing walking pneumonia and drug addiction, with no medical help to be found.

But the emotional content of the prelude was sound. Her years as a DP camp cop in the Adirondacks. Searching time and again for Paul, drugged and sick and in danger. Trying to help the young adult get clean and sober, among desperate tent cities where 'clean' was an impossibility, and no future was available. She still reeled from Paul's death at the time.

They hadn't lived in the tent cities, though. No cop dared enter there alone. She had a nice little house in town. Even searching for Paul, her partner Beth would have been at her side, and another pair of cops never more than a hundred meters away as backup.

Good cop, bad cop. Cops worked in pairs. Beth died too, though, in a scuffle with some black market vitamin sellers. Sass had another partner toward the end. Only for a few months. She couldn't remember his name or face. Why get close? She knew she was leaving.

In the field in Newer York, she broke into a lumbering jog.

Sass won the lottery for colonists. Only the cream of the Adirondacks refugees qualified for colonization. They claimed selection was random among the qualified. No one believed that, least of all Sass. They needed cops to keep order. She was invited to the meeting with Clay in the same letter that provided her embarkation report date in the first wave.

First responders, medical experience, soldiers, community organizers — Ganymede front-loaded that first wave of colonists with the staff they needed. Their tiny navy could only crew the starship, not manage refugees who outnumbered the spacemen by fifty to one.

The settlers saw only their own doctors on the voyage. Sass and

Clay tried to investigate, what had been done to them. But the crew insisted they had no idea who injected them with what. At first. Later the chief medical officer admitted they'd been injected with nanites, after it became obvious that they were self-healing and impervious to accidents that would kill a normal human. But the woman refused to answer further questions on the matter.

Sass slowed her jog to a walk, and dialed her gravity back to a normal one g. Had Clay really disliked her from the day they met? Studied her like a particularly noxious species of bug?

Two women. One died. Four of the ten died from the same damned injection which made the rest practically immortal. There were other teams of cops assigned to other groups of refugees. They died as readily as any other settler.

Huh. One of Clay's first decisions was to separate the women and children from the men in the colony ship hold. That cut sex crimes and harassment and domestic violence to a bare minimum. He was their boss, of course, of the six who survived the nanites. Him with his fancy master's degree and Quantico training, in a whole different league from DP camp beat cops. Clay's right hand man handled the men. His left hand was Sass, to manage the women and children. She allowed a smattering of single dads to stick with their children so long as they behaved.

Was Clay thinking that even then? On first meeting? Sass wouldn't put it past him. Clay was a thinker.

She'd barely finished the 8th grade herself. She enlisted with the army at 14, promised a high school degree along the way. That promise wasn't kept. But she learned a lot, ate well, kept in great shape and out of trouble. As an orphan in the refugee tent cities, her teen years wouldn't have fared nearly so well. After a 6-year hitch, it wasn't hard to land a good job as a cop. She was luckier than most, well trained and better educated.

But Clay with his university degrees was as alien as the Ganymede crew, and later the Mahina urbs.

They didn't dislike each other at first sight. They just weren't sure what to make of each other. And suffering bizarre physical symptoms, all of them bad, they spent a hideous couple days recovering from that nanite shot. He growled a lot. So did she. But he was in charge through his splitting migraine and wobbly knees.

And he was a good boss. Cool, professional, detached. A thinker. A good co-worker, too, later, when they were marshals side by side. Their skills complemented each other. Good cop, bad cop. In the long decades since that day, Sass had to concede she'd screwed Clay over at least as many times as he'd done to her. She expected that kind of give and take with a partner.

She lay in the hay grass to gaze up at the dull green sky. But the grass itched. Playing with her gravity generator, she hopped on top of *Thrive* and lay down on the workout mats instead. She chuckled softly at how the ship's field extended so that wind never blew stuff off as they flew. *Nifty, nifty skyship,* she encouraged, patting the hull fondly.

She met her first skyship the day she met Clay. She even went inside, though she slipped in and out of consciousness during that part.

Her heart and belly still fluttered, despite her exercise. The nightmare wasn't to blame, she conceded.

Who was she to fix Mahina's failure to thrive? Who was she to even think she could try?

She had a few clues and a lame-ass plan. She was an ex-con now. Kendra would love to correct her status back to convict. When she threatened to take Benjy hostage, Sass would have tossed it all to get him back, sacrificed anything, even the skyship.

Benjy isn't Paul.

She shrugged off the thought in irritation. Of course Benjy wasn't Paul. Nothing like Paul. Paul was a sweet kid once, too sweet for the world he was born into, not nearly the scrapper his mom was. So he grew escapist.

Well OK, in that way, Benjy was like Paul, with his childish VR habit. But Sass was curing him of the VR. She and Abel and Eli kept his days hopping, and the kid was disciplined about his schoolwork. That's when Paul started down the wrong path. He graduated 8th grade, to nothing. No more school, no work, no prospects. The Army offered early entry to orphans, not kids from good homes, whose parents could guide and provide for them.

Peace, Sass, she chided herself. *You did the best you could. So did Paul.*

Go for it, Mom, Paul whispered from her heart. *Somebody has to.*

My main qualification is to be a pain in the ass, Sass argued.

Well, better that than a nice old lady who provided clean sheets to the new buyers, and dusted. Sass would never be an old lady, despite the passing years.

She'd rather not pass those endless years in a phosphate mine.

She'd rather see a thriving Mahina after she'd broken her back and nails carving the regolith into farmland, and building atmo spires. Granted she was usually the one breaking up the fights and taking names. She was on the same team, doing her part.

Gut check. Mahina's progress had halted. That was not OK with her. Yeah, she dared. This plan was going forward. Who was she to do it? A pissed-off mom, an ex-cop, a small business owner.

She was someone who dared to rock the boat.

It would have to do.

"KASSIDY, GOT A MINUTE?" Sass asked, spotting the celebrity emerge from her cabin down the companionway the next morning. Mid-morning by the clock — today was the half-gas dim of Saturday.

"Only if it comes with breakfast," Kassidy replied. "Rough night."

They met at the kitchen and companionably assembled Jules' good protein flapjacks, fruit, and coffee. Sass nurtured her mug until the younger woman got some blood sugar humming. Then she opened with, "Abel briefed me on your run-in with your mother yesterday. Do you mind if I ask some questions?"

Kassidy's habitual fey grin was missing this morning. "Alright. Record off."

Sass's eyes widened. She hadn't realized Kassidy was livecasting. "Thank you. You mentioned your dad? Exile?"

Kassidy nodded glumly. "When I was seven. Dad and his geneticist girlfriend. Mom got them exiled for reckless research."

"Abel told me you were opposed to liberating a piece of equipment." Abel mentioned the nanite synthesizer, but Sass thought it better to keep the question open-ended.

Kassidy turned her coffee mug around a few times. "I don't think you understand what nanites can and can't do. Sass, if nanites could make us thrive outside the city, a lot more urbs would escape Kendra and the directors. That's what Dad was trying to do. Part of it. They also experimented on settler children, editing their genomes. That was pretty despicable." She swallowed.

"Did he succeed?"

"I don't know."

"Do you know how many children were modified?"

"That was mostly his girlfriend. Maybe a dozen. They'd be adults now. I don't know if anyone is tracking them, with Dad and Genna gone."

"Their academic names? I'd like to look up their research papers."

"Michael Yang. Genevieve Carruthers. But their papers are sealed."

Sass made a note of the names anyway. She didn't recall them. But they hid their research. The blowup and exile came after she was isolated at the farm. "How old was your dad, Kassidy? Any chance he was designing nanites at the time the settlers came?"

"No. Sixty, maybe. He was born after the settlers arrived. Genna is twenty years younger."

Sass tamped a grin. "Which pissed off your mother no end."

"I bet. No, I was maybe three when my parents split. Not that it made much difference to me. I had fun with Dad, visiting every playground in the city. I endured a weekly lecture with meal from Mom. Still do. I really don't like the woman."

"I'm sorry. Getting back to the nanite synthesizer. We're just wondering if we have a problem. Are you opposed to...?"

Kassidy chewed a thoughtful bite of flapjacks, and washed it down with some coffee. "I wouldn't turn you in. Unless you hurt people and didn't care. But that's not you, Sass. You care. It's just a harder problem than you think. The equipment is only part of it. The nanites that keep urbs young and healthy so long — they're not enough to thrive outside the city. Or so they claim."

"Your dad would know."

"He would. Whether he'd tell you, I couldn't say."

Sass reflected that the sort of man who would edit settler infant genomes was bound to be ethically challenged, whether he loved his daughter or not. "You said he might have moved on to Denali. How badly would you like to see Denali? *Thrive* could reach there with an engine upgrade."

"You're serious?" Kassidy chuckled. "Sass, you need a richer client than me to reach Denali."

"Can't blame me for trying," Sass quipped. "Are we alright, Kassidy? You won't turn us in?"

Kassidy's flashed her celebrity-grade warm grin. "We're good."

But you're not in on the planning sessions, Sass concluded. She rose with matching grin and gave the stunt woman a hug. "I knew we could count on you."

"Four more days to my sky-side night dive! Can you stand it?"

"You've got Jules and Abel scurrying around like chickens with their heads cut off!"

Kassidy's brow crumpled and she cocked her head. "Does that really happen?"

"Only for a few seconds," Sass assured her. She rapped the table and took her leave.

———

WITH ABEL AND ELI — not Kassidy and Jules — Sass squeezed into the med-bay with Benjy to take stock and plan the tricky next four days.

She and Benjy had a real hill to build. *Thrive* needed readying for passengers. Abel and Jules were on schedule with those preparations. The remaining stolen goods waited to be smuggled out of Mahina Actual.

The next smuggling trip would be without Benjy or Abel, just ferrying things stashed in Kassidy's apartment. Sass vetoed another crew incursion so soon. Kendra was no doubt kicking herself today, spinning plans about what she should have done to hold Benjy hostage. Sass didn't dare tempt her.

Eli's investigations would yield no conclusions before Kassidy's dive on Wednesday. The 'scrubber' trees would bear only poisonous fruit. He was bemused that the stunt woman chose trees developed to remove toxins from air and soil, when so many good fruit and nut trees were available. He'd forgotten about the scrubbers.

Eli would have preferred they wait on his experiments, and possibly decide to alter their prison break plans. But they were already committed to Kassidy's schedule, and Josiah the mob boss.

Sass shared with them Clay's unsettling news of alterations to Benjy's genome, and all the other settler students at Mahina U. Benjy took the news quietly, but in a different way than she expected. He feared the university accepted him because he was a human guinea pig, not for his qualifications. The captain assured him that the university saw the same thing she did — he was a smart kid, in a world where smart kids were rare.

He didn't know the other settler students, only that there were some.

Eli couldn't add much insight on a human genetic question. He did plants.

Sass was beginning to recall why she had trouble keeping secrets. She wished she dared to keep a spreadsheet to track who she could tell what.

31

Earth's population exploded from 1 billion to 9 billion in a mere 250 years,
to fuel stunning technological advances. With only the Diaspora colonies
remaining, humanity abruptly dropped to about 2 million and falling —
split between 10 colonies.

The day for Kassidy's big dive on the dark side arrived, a 2000
meter drop onto regolith. They selected Wednesday as the
star-siders' analogue to Glow, a day to relax.

Abel was only grudgingly satisfied with their 12 grand take on
raffle ticket sales for spectators on this jaunt. Expenses ate part of
that. They needed to provide safe seating and view screen and lanky-
length pressure suits for their lottery winners. Kassidy wished to
spare no expense to ensure their guests had the time of their lives.

Abel noted that *Thrive* cleared 30k from the atmo spire stunt.
They had precious few days left to amass taxes. They might come up
short.

Sass wasn't concerned. She could cover a shortfall of a few thousand from her savings. "Relax, Abel. Enjoy the circus."

"Not my circus, not my monkeys," Abel muttered, eyeing the
passengers. He'd picked up the charming Earth phrase from his part-

ner. He'd been stuck flying the shuttle all over Mahina early this morning, picking up the 'winners.' He used the term advisedly. "Idiots."

Sass grinned. She'd wisely stuck to driving the ship to the dark side of the moon, and left the hosting duties to Kassidy and the Greers. Eli and Benjy took refuge in their cabins. Kassidy retired to her cabin as well for the final hour pre-jump to dress and psych herself up. By now, even their experienced public handler Jules looked a little frayed. But now they were holding station for the jump. Time to begin the pageant.

Sass waved for Jules to take a break. She strode to stand before the guest trio, two men and a woman, each a dispirited-looking failure to thrive. Their ages appeared to Sass to range from 40 to 90, which probably made them 20 to 50.

"Hello, hello! I'm captain of *Thrive,* Sass Collier. That was me over the intercom." She casually pointed to the speakers bracketing the cargo ramp. Their upholstered bench faced thataway, complete with pointless and pricey seat belts. "I hope you're enjoying your trip so far?"

Sass paused to invite a response, beaming a warm smile. The woman stared at her blankly, mouth open and tongue lolling. The elderly man to her right peered around Sass searching for the speakers.

The youngest, on the other end, nodded. "Good food. Liked the... orange thing."

"Peaches. Glad you enjoyed that! Did Jules give you a tour of our garden?" Sass accidentally pointed again.

The old guy very slowly rotated his head on his neck to the new bearing. The woman's tongue was unchanged. Perhaps she slept with her eyes open. Perhaps no one could tell.

"The drive room," the youngest offered. "With the crops. That was cool. Goggles."

Sass nodded encouragement. "What's your name?"

"Troy," he replied.

They both looked to the other two and waited a few seconds.

Troy gave up. "They're Annika and Finbar. Um, Annika is her. He's Finbar."

Splendid, Sass thought, consciously forcing her smile. And it fell to her to supervise these three onto the ramp. *Scratch the word 'fell.' Maybe Abel could...?* No, Abel was driving.

"Benjy report to the hold," she murmured to her intercom. She inadvertently blared her surreptitious aside through the speakers behind her.

"So is everyone excited to watch from the ramp? Or would you rather stay inside and watch on the big screen? Annika? Finbar?"

Apparently Annika was paying attention after all. She scowled. "I won! I'm going outside to walk the stars! Can watch the screen at home."

Finbar had thrown up a stick-thin arm to cower behind at the onslaught from the speakers. At least his ears were good. He lowered the arm slowly as he thought it through. "Is it safe? Out there in the sky?"

"Absolutely safe," Sass assured him. "Only Kassidy jumps into the sky. The rest of us stand on the ramp to watch. It's a bit windy out there. But we'll be in pressure suits." She made the mistake of pointing again. Half a second later, Benjy landed with a thump a few feet from her, having taken a running jump to sail over their heads.

Finbar froze like frightened prey from the onslaught of overstimulation.

"We'll be tied to safety lines the entire time," Sass concluded. "I'd like to introduce my assistant, Benjy Acosta. Benjy, this is Troy, Annika, and Finbar."

"Hi." Benjy sketched a smiling wave. The auto-doc did good work. All the blood was cleared from his eyes already. In a quiet aside, he murmured, "Sass, I'm not going out there, am I?"

Sass's gunner was fearless in virtual. When faced with certain things in real life, he proved surprisingly skittish. Sass had asked Eli what was wrong with him. Eli pointed out no one could pay *him* enough to walk the gangplank at 2000 meters. The kid was simply too smart for that stuff. Physical courage was for the lower IQ's, who lacked imagination and common sense. Sass hit him. Only on the arm, but hard enough to hurt.

Sass smiled at Benjy now. "No, I asked you down to help me get our guests into their pressure suits. You'd better suit up, too. In fact, let's all watch Benjy put on his p-suit first!"

"I better be getting paid for this," Benjy muttered, as he leafed through the rack to find his suit.

"Bring mine, too," Sass replied. She nearly added *please*, but she was trying to cure herself of the habit. A proper captain should give orders, not beg.

Benjy dumped his own armful of suit to the deck beside her, and went back for hers.

"Actually, Benjy, bring theirs, too. Let's unbuckle and spread out on the bench."

"No seat belt?" Finbar asked, alarmed.

"We're not moving right now," Sass assured him. Realizing that statement required a logical leap, she clarified, "It's safe. Here, I'll do it for you."

Frozen, Finbar allowed Sass to unbuckle him. Annika slapped her hand away. Troy unbuckled the moment Sass mentioned it in the first place, and retreated as far from Annika as the dimensions of the bench allowed. Sass turned back to help Finbar shift farther down. He'd forgotten that part. No doubt he did fine with routine in normal life.

"Do you farm, Finbar?"

"I had a farm when I was stronger. Daughter has that now," the elderly man replied. "Now I teach reading."

Benjy dumped a suit beside them with a startling clatter. The kid arrested the rolling helmet with an agile foot and passed it soccer-style within Finbar's reach.

Sass prudently decided to ignore Benjy's hospitality style. He was the last one who needed tutoring today. She doubted that Finbar could sight-read. She ordered herself not to dwell on what an illiterate 'reading' teacher taught children. "Ah, a teacher! How nice. And you, Annika?"

Annika's tongue was lolling again.

"I'm a farm laborer," Troy volunteered, with a mortified glance at Kassidy's camera drone hovering above and behind Sass. "Odd jobs."

"He lost his farm," Annika said suddenly, and cackled. "Couldn't pay the taxes! Got a baby to support, too. Troy is dumb." Abel collected Annika first this morning, which explained much about his outlook today. He'd vanished into the bridge, the door thoroughly sealed behind him, no doubt.

"I don't find you dumb at all, Troy," Sass assured him. "And you won a contest. Maybe things are looking up for you!"

Troy looked as though he sincerely doubted that. He stood to claim his pressure suit helmet from Benjy before the chump could dump it to the floor.

Learning is happening here! Sass encouraged herself. "So let's go over the parts of a pressure suit while Benjy catches up." Taking far longer than Sass had imagined, she introduced her charges to all the working parts of the pressure suit.

Finbar interrupted Sass during her explanation of the helmet and intercom rules. "I'll just sit here."

Jules swooped in obligingly. "There won't be any air here in the hold. Would you like to sit here in a pressure suit? Or sit with me and watch from the kitchen?"

Finbar stared up at her mouth open, looking confused.

"Kitchen, I think," Sass decided. "Thanks, Jules. Annika, Troy, are you still joining us on the ramp?"

"Yes," Troy said grimly, clutching his helmet and swallowing hard.

"I told you," Annika reminded the captain.

"Right. So let's put just our helmets on our heads, and practice our intercom skills! Benjy, us too."

Yeah, that went well. Troy and Benjy didn't miss a beat. Sass needed to threaten Annika. Anyone who couldn't master the intercom had to watch from the kitchen. Annika responded better to threats than courtesy. *Good to know.*

Benjy hammed it up worthy of a male stripper as he donned his suit. Annika and Jules enjoyed the un-stripper act almost as much as

Sass did. Shame the kid was so young. Sass renewed her resolve not to screw with crew. Inconvenient as that policy might be.

For her turn, she tried to outdo him. But she had the two guests donning their suits along with her. Her attempts to inject a little levity fell to lie on the deck like dead cats.

Not that any of them had ever seen a cat.

Eventually Sass completed the pressure checks on Annika's suit, and grinned at her. "And we are ready!"

"And don't you look fabulous!" Kassidy cried from the balcony catwalk above, already cased in her skin-tight black suit. She threw her arms wide and turned for her camera drones to show off her outfit. For camera visibility in the dark, Kassidy's fashion stylist in the city added suggestive asymmetric sprays of light tubes to decorate the original unrelieved black. Silvery pulses traveled along them.

Sass found the whorls at hip and butt and bust particularly fetching. Maybe someday when she was a rich captain, she too could buy a sexy pressure suit. She led the cargo hold in applause at the stunt woman's grinning entrance.

Kassidy had not only seen a cat but shared its sinuous knack for landing on her feet. She hopped lithely onto the catwalk rail and jumped up in the low grav, for a whooping midair somersault on the way down. She landed in a lunge, and rolled a wave down and up her spine in a deep bow. A drone zoomed in for a closeup.

"Don't try that at home, kids," she confided with a wink, and blew an intimate kiss to the drone. "I've practiced. A lot."

Kassidy hopped up from her bow and joined them, to ooh and ah over Troy and Annika in their pressure suits. She left a purple lipstick smear on their face plates, and gave them a firm full-body hug. She squeezed Troy's butt a little. She and Annika shared a few hip swings. Then she planted hands on the bench to either side of Finbar's knees and playfully walked them closer until she finished with a thorough smack on the lips, and a whisper for his ear only.

Yes, the old man could still blush.

Kassidy placed a playful gloved finger on his nose and wiggled it.

"Finbar! Time for you to slip into the kitchen with Jules." Her rotating shoulders and uncoiling hips supplied the sexual innuendo.

Jules' hand up was merely friendly. She didn't need to tell Finbar to adjust his grav generator to climb the stairs. The whole ship sported Mahina-normal gravity today for the comfort and safety of their guests. Still, stairs were easier at half that.

"Alright, the rest of us are going out the cargo ramp, right?" Kassidy asked.

"Except me," Benjy inserted hastily.

Kassidy planted a lip smear on his faceplate, too.

Sass offered, "But Benjy will be suited up, and clamped on, and right by the door to help out as needed. Right, Benjy?"

"On this side of the lock?"

"We're evacuating the hold," Sass said, giving his arm a bracing squeeze. "Don't worry. Worst that can happen is that you stand here and haul on a line."

Kassidy shook her head at him grinning. "If heroics are called for, you'll be right at the edge, ready to leap overboard to save someone!"

"Kassidy, don't give the lad ideas," Sass growled. She glanced in disquiet to Troy and Annika. "Intercom check! Right?"

Troy agreed properly. Annika's mouth gaped inside her suit, but she knew how to scream for help if she needed it.

Close enough. "*Thrive* crew! Pressure check."

Sass sealed her own helmet and gloves while the crew accounted for all pressurized compartments, including Jules and Finbar in the galley. Benjy sealed up Kassidy, and they passed with positive pressure seals. Sass double-checked the guests. Then she cabled them up with D-rings latched to either side of the cargo ramp. Benjy demonstrated by walking across the hold just how far their leashes extended.

Sass couldn't think of anything else. "*Thrive* is ready, Ms. Yang. Are you?"

"Captain Collier, I was born ready! Abel! Evacuate the hold!" Kassidy pumped both fists.

"Do it, Abel," Sass confirmed. He wouldn't take orders from

Kassidy. With a couple button presses, she brought the hold lights down to the barest glimmer.

For fun, Kassidy held up a finger 'one,' then spun for 'two,' and kept it up until Abel confirmed over the intercom, "Atmosphere secured. Captain, hold is at external pressure. Ready."

"Opening cargo ramp. Troy, Annika, stay put." Sass punched the hatch buttons. Benjy clutched a wall bar beside her for dear life. She patted his shoulder, and braced her feet for the wind.

Then she was looking straight into the unblinking stars as the ramp dropped away before her. Her mouth likely hung open like Annika's, gazing into solar systems and galaxies seemingly just beyond finger's reach, embedded in deepest black. As planned, they faced directly into the moiré swirls of the Milky Way. Her arm drifted up to touch as though of its own volition.

"God that's pretty," she breathed. No moon. No planet. No artificial light pollution of any kind.

32

Even original Earth plants drew toxins from the air. The terraformers exaggerated those abilities in crafting Earth transplants. Adding breathable gases to form an atmosphere was all well and good. But unwanted trace components always leached into the mix, whether in free atmosphere or enclosed domes.

K assidy boldly strode out the ramp while it was still lowering, to deliver her monologue of first impressions. She didn't have much trouble with the wind. The air speed was high, but there were precious few molecules of the stuff at this altitude. Hurricane winds were weak as a kitten.

"...Seeing this in real life is stunning. Seriously, folks. This view, clear into the soul of infinity. It literally takes my breath away..."

Sass hastily double-checked that the ramp would fall only to horizontal. Then she turned to Troy and Annika, holding a vertical gloved finger to her face plate to remind them not to speak during Kassidy's intro.

She needn't have bothered. The two gazed into the starry abyss with wide stunned eyes.

Sass encouraged first Troy, then Annika forward. She let go but still held her hands out, in case either wished to grasp on again.

Kassidy was right at the edge now, looking down, braced in a slight lunge, one foot behind her. "Yikes, that's a long way down. I can't even see my target circle. Abel, are you sure we're over the beacons?"

"Absolutely."

"Wow. I'm jumping into a crater 3 klicks across. The beacons below form a circle 200 meters across, set by my awesome, *awesome* friends we met at Phosphate Mine 3. They're down below to watch..."

Sass and the guests stepped carefully forward, in the foot-dragging gait they favored to avoid bounding from the floor in low g. Sass pointed to the red line she'd painted on the ramp. Regardless of what the stunt woman did, the others would advance past that line only on knees or bellies. Sass drew ahead, and dropped to hands and knees well shy of the line. Troy and Annika immediately followed suit.

"...You guys look cowardly!" Kassidy twitted them as drones dove at them for closeups. She threw her arms out as though to embrace the whole black vast universe, and laughed out loud.

"Ignore her," Sass instructed. "Stay safe."

Kassidy recorded their voices on separate sound tracks for her later mixing convenience. She could hear them all, though. "Come, come! Troy, Annika, Sass, join me! You'll miss my jump from back there."

Sass grasped the edge first, and peeked over to the moon below. She expected pitch black. Instead the craters and regolith gleamed ever so slightly in the starlight. From this vantage, Mahina looked exactly what it was, the dark side of the moon, little different from the one above Sass as a child, lifeless and cold. Her eyes were better than Kassidy's, for she could just make out the faint fiery dot of the beacon circle below them.

But the view that grabbed hold and wouldn't release her lay ahead and above, with absolutely nothing between her and the grey splash of the Milky Way. Kassidy continued her soliloquy. Troy jostled Sass's leg creeping up beside her. The captain never lost track of the players on this high stage. But her eyes were all for the sky.

"...Say a few words? Troy, you first," Kassidy invited.

"Wow, wow, wow."

Kassidy pealed with laughter. "Annika?"

"My effing God. He's right here."

"God?" Kassidy asked.

"Yeah."

"Yeah," Kassidy agreed with satisfaction. "Sass?"

"It's funny. I feel so small, awed by the majesty. Yet its like something inside me is growing big enough to embrace it. I've never seen anything so beautiful. Yet so cold."

"Beautifully said, Sass. No colors of life, only a divine glory and indifference. Alright. Anyone want to add to their sound-bite before I jump? You don't need to. You were fantastic! I couldn't have asked for better companions on this dive. I thank God to have you watching beside me. You too back there, Benjy!"

Abel commented from the bridge, "Atlas Pratt just called. You're 30 minutes late. It's damned cold for them standing on the regolith, Yang. So jump already."

Kassidy laughed out loud and rephrased for her fans. "OK! Here goes! Can you stand it, girls and boys? I'm backing up for a running jump. And a one, and a two, and —" She screamed defiance and leapt high into the galaxy. She jack-knifed elegantly right in front of them, and unfolded into a dive, pointed hands first before her. Within seconds she vanished out of view.

And soundlessly, Troy unclamped his D-ring, rose to his knees, and toppled down after her, arms and legs windmilling for the traction and purchase they could not find.

"Benjy!" Sass barked. "Yank Annika in *now!*" She was already moving. She stood, unclamped her own D-ring, and dove straight down.

"Ohmygod, ohmygod!" Benjy shrieked, his voice breaking upward. "Abel, Sass jumped after Troy!"

"Get me inside!" Annika screamed at the same time.

"Silence on the intercom!" Abel barked. "Benjy, report!"

"S-securing passenger," Benjy stammered. "In, she's in!"

"Close the ramp. Pull the lines in before it shuts. We're moving before you're done."

Sass wished him luck with that. With her overboard, the ship was Abel's, so she barely listened. She tuned out Kassidy's voice as well, and switched on every light on her own helmet. Carefully, she increased her gravity to fall faster. She needed to catch up with Troy to save him. Without getting killed herself. Without overshooting. In a completely novel and death-defying situation. On the plus side, Sassafras Collier's grav generator had practically been a prosthetic limb for over six decades. Finesse long since turned to muscle memory and reflex. This task was not impossible.

Merely damned unlikely.

Her biggest challenge was that she couldn't see Troy, tiny and dark, falling before her into darkness. She had only seconds to find him. Urgently she wobbled her head around — there! She'd seen a glint of the high-visibility orange of Troy's floppy pressure suit. She backtracked and sent the light beam across him twice more before she narrowed in.

She goosed her gravity again to gain on him. Eased off. Flew past him a few meters out of arm's reach. Above was better, so she could see. She tweaked her gravity again to close the vertical distance, and tried swimming motions to adjust their horizontal distance. Troy was still windmilling in panic, though. That didn't seem to affect his direction.

Sail to the wind? Sass thought, grasping for ideas. She had precious few seconds to work with, but she didn't need to shift very far horizontally. She turned her back to the wind. She closed on him vertically with her grav adjustments. But the wind couldn't push her fast enough.

Flare! Standard suit equipment included a little cold flare gun. Dual-duty, it made the shooter extra visible, and provided a little push in the opposite direction. No sooner thought than drawn and shot, exactly away from Troy's center of mass. And her spin to shoot carried her back around to a mid-air collision with Troy.

Got you!

Or rather he got her, grabbing her around the helmet as she seized his waist. She couldn't see anything, and the ground would be coming up —

That was dumb. Now that she had him, she could just stop falling. As a panicked Troy continued practically trying to unscrew her helmet, she locked one arm through his belt, then jiggered her grav one-handed until they *stopped falling.* Actually, maybe she went up a little.

Sass paused for a couple deep breaths to calm down. Floating in mid-air like this, they were in no immediate danger. Troy was saved. *Cool.*

"Troy, it's Sass. Can you hear me? You need to let go of my helmet now. I've got you. You're safe. Stop grabbing my head. Troy I need you, um...turn to your right. Can you do that?"

It didn't matter what he did, so long as he let go of her head. But Sass knew enough to tell panicked types to do something specific. Commands to *not-do* were a lost cause.

Alas, Troy was too far gone to listen or obey.

Or we could do this the hard way... Sass clicked her helmet release, and slipped down Troy's body. He still clutched the helmet, but her head was free.

The downside of that maneuver was that Sass lost her oxygen, warmth, light, and comms. Her nanites would ensure none of that was fatal. She'd black out soon, though, because they were still a lot higher than she expected. A full lungful of frigid air wasn't helping.

She shifted Troy's body perpendicular to her own and clamped him there between her thigh and her one arm through his belt. Then she goosed her gravity to half Earth normal to speed their way down to thicker air, ears and nose and lips burning with the cold. She squeezed her eyes nearly shut to peer through her eyelashes before her eyes froze.

Yes! She spotted the rapidly-approaching beacon circle, and started cutting her gravity to come in for a landing. *Halves, halves, halves...* Done. She floated the last few meters like a feather. The second her foot touched Mahina's moon dust, she automatically snapped the grav generator back to default — Earth-normal — and Troy dumped to her feet in a plume of dust.

She planted a boot on his shoulder to pry her helmet loose. She popped it back on her head and re-sealed it as fast as possible. A mob of people were fast-loping toward them, sailing through the air in meter-long low-gravity bounds, Kassidy's macabre light-skeleton suit among them. The fiery red beacons surrounding them added a touch of Halloween pagan sacrifice.

Deprived of his security huggable, Troy rolled over and tried to crawl away. Sass sat on his butt to make him stay put until she could deal with him. The *itch* of the nanites repairing her frostbitten face was maddening, especially on her eyeballs and ears. She wished to yank her helmet off again to scratch. But the nanites were fast — she knew the sensation would be over in seconds. Instead she hurriedly cut her lamps so the reception committee wouldn't see her face inside. She touched her warm sealed helmet to her knees in order to hide a few moments longer.

"Abel? Sass. Troy and I landed safe. Out."

"Thank God, Sass! That was a miracle!"

"No, just damned unlikely," Sass muttered, off-mike. She wished, for the millionth time, that her nanites came with user-directed controls. *Cut the adrenaline, please. Heart rate down. I have oxygen, enough with the shuddering gasps.* But no, her body on nanites responded to mental commands pretty much the way it had when she was human — slowly.

I'm still human. I think. Troy is too. Sort of. Homo sapiens Mahina.

Well, great, I saved the innocent.

Sass had to concede Eli's point on different kinds of smart. Jumping off *Thrive* after Troy made no sense at all. A first responder like Sass clearly wanted to be a hero more than she wanted to live. Not that the dive would have killed her, with the nanites. But she hadn't stopped to think. She just jumped.

Meanwhile, Troy had pretty much torched the plan for today. She intended to oh-so-subtly make off with Atlas Pratt and two of his top foremen, to run her bootleg nanite operation. Because no one would be minding the miners during this circus. Or noticing her and the lottery winners. Nor Atlas Pratt. *Dammit.*

Someone — presumably Kassidy — hugged her shoulders while her head was still down. "Sass? Are you alright? Abel's bringing *Thrive* around. We'll have you in the med bay in a few minutes."

The itching had stopped. Sass worked her face, wriggling her nose and everything else. *Yeah. Dead skin sloughing off in sheets.* She sighed resignation and brought her head up to face the music. "I'm fine, Kassidy. Really."

Judging by Kassidy's recoil of horror, she didn't look fine. "Um…"

"Get us some privacy. We board *Thrive* first, alone. OK?"

Kassidy recalled her ground reception committee ringing them, and nodded. She rose and scooted everyone back and away behind Sass, to give her some space. One man ignored her directions and detached from the group, to kneel beside Sass and Troy. *Pratt A, GM PM3*, advised his name tag.

Sass wondered what use it was to label suits where no one could read.

Atlas touched his helmet to hers to talk one-on-one, off the comms. "I'll help you carry him in. Are you both OK?"

"Bet I look like hell," Sass said. "I think we're fine. Physically. But mentally? Troy here jumped from 2,000 meters without grav control." Troy wore a grav controller. But it was set to default, tucked neatly inside his pressure suit where he couldn't reach it.

"Suicide," Atlas concluded.

"Suicide," Sass agreed.

"Let's ask him why in private. Are we —?"

"Good to go," Sass confirmed.

33

The most vexing medical challenge for the colonists was radiation damage.

"Why did you do it, Troy?" Sass asked, hanging over him on the med-bay table. She and Atlas strapped the jumper down for safekeeping after they unpeeled him from his pressure suit.

Sass left Kassidy and Jules and the rest to deal with the hospitality problem — lottery winners Annika and Finbar, plus a couple dozen well-wishers from Phosphate Mine 3 who drove out to plant the beacons and watch the stunt. And if Josiah handled his end of the job, the foreman Copeland and his baby Nico should be transferring over from the transport.

Sass shut the med-bay hatch against those complications. Atlas helped her peel away the dead skin from her brief bout of frostbite. By now, her face looked fairly normal. She had a bad case of dandruff, mostly managed with a stiff brushing and a quick French braid.

Atlas plied a medical multi-meter on Troy, and minded the screen. At Sass's glance of inquiry, he shook his head. Nothing in the man's vitals or blood work explained his sudden bout of insanity. The auto-doc equipment was designed for laymen.

Literate laymen, anyway. An emergency patient could die waiting while someone operated the system by voice interface.

"Money," Troy breathed. He turned his face away as tears began to leak down his cheeks. "Two thousand credits for my wife and baby if I did this. They promised."

Sass urged softly, "Who promised?"

"Urb goon. I didn't believe him at first. But there's this complicated...escrow...thing. I die, the money is Carmine's. I can't make that kind of money. Not anymore. Never. No matter what I do."

Sass pressed his arm. "Shh, Troy. It's alright. Why did they want you to do this?"

"Kendra Oliver. That her name? Top bitch in the city? She wants to shut you down. An excuse to take away your skyship. It was an attack against you." Troy broke down sobbing. "I don't know whether to thank you or damn you for saving my sorry ass. I can't even kill myself right."

Atlas applied a sedative hypo to Troy's neck. "He should still be able to talk," he murmured to Sass. "We're recording." Atlas applied a tissue to mop Troy's eyes and blow his nose. Troy took a few shuddering breaths, and relaxed back into his pillow, though a few tears still flowed.

Sass glanced up at the camera mounted on the overhead, then back to the matter at hand. "No one blames you for anything, Troy. It's going to be alright. Carmine, that's your wife?"

"Yeah."

"We'll call her in a few minutes. I'll let you talk with her, OK?"

"God, she was watching the live feed," Troy said, brow crumpling.

"Sh. Troy, do you have a name for the urb goon?"

"S-Seth. I think. Have a card in my wallet."

Sass fished it out. "Seth Gruman? Mahina Security."

"That's him. My cash card is in there, too. Deposit two days ago, fifty credits. The down payment."

Sass couldn't help it. "That's pretty trusting, Troy. She pays you fifty credits, and you trust her to deposit two thousand once you're dead?"

Troy's eyes looked stricken. "You don't think she would have done it?"

"No," Sass replied. "If I know Kendra, she'd reverse the fifty credits without a trace. Here, show me."

She handed him the cash card and her tablet. He used it to pull up his credit balance. The measly fifty from Mahina Security was already in process of being refunded even now, the largest deposit amongst the wreckage of the man's finances. He'd be docked with overdraft fines when the reversal completed. Sass saved a snapshot of all that, and an official balance report, and showed them to Atlas.

Great, they now had three witnesses that this deposit took place — two rebel convicts and a gullible attempted suicide. Who'd believe them?

"Clay Rocha," Atlas murmured. "Send the med bay video and the bank evidence to Clay."

Sass shook her head in doubt. "Clay answers to Kendra."

"Really?" Atlas countered. "The Clay I knew wouldn't destroy evidence. Or lie. Or be an accessory to a crime. He's worked for Kendra even longer than you did, Sass. Clay knows what she is."

His comments brought her up short. She couldn't argue with that. She also couldn't involve the marshal in their other plans for the day.

That said, they were on the far side of the world, at frigid celestial midnight — by the 7-day sky, not the 24-hour clock. Clay could hardly order them to remain in place while he hopscotched his little flitter here to investigate. The entire event was not only captured on video, but livecast. Outside any sheriff's jurisdiction, a near-fatal con job committed against a settler by an urb, the crime was a matter for a marshal. Right up Clay's alley.

Sass nodded decisively and initiated dictation. Clay would receive a transcript, and the audio. "Clay, Sass. We've had an attempted homicide slash suicide event here. We're 20 kilometers northeast of Phosphate Mine 3 in the Pikachu Crater."

She explained the scenario, and the livecasting wrinkle. She attached unadulterated raw med bay footage from the moment they entered, and her copied reports from the bank. Quick videos of Atlas

Pratt, herself, and Troy attested that this was a true account of what happened.

"Don't meet us here," Sass concluded, appending to the original dictation. "Everyone's leaving. We'll be Pono-side tomorrow." She didn't specify precisely which 'we' she was referring to. With that, she sent off the statement and evidence.

She squeezed Troy's shoulder. "I don't know that any justice can come from this, Troy. But if it's possible, Clay Rocha is the man to get it for you. You rest here. We'll have you back home to Carmine soon. Ready to call her now?"

Troy's face crumpled again. Without the sedative, his emotions would have flailed completely out of control.

"I'll talk to her first," Sass soothed him.

With his help, she made the call and briefed the wife in front of the husband, while Atlas held his hand. Sass assured herself that Carmine wouldn't add any unfortunate recriminations. Some people reacted stupidly to bad news, in Sass's prodigious experience, and jumped to blame the victim. Fortunately Carmine wasn't that way. Sass handed her comm to Troy for a brief and reassuring exchange.

While she was busy, Atlas entertained himself studying the medical bay facilities. "Sass? We brought Nico Copeland along as you asked. The baby who got left in the mine. If he's inside now, I'd like to try him in the auto-doc. I hope you don't mind, Troy."

Troy shook his head vehemently. "I seen him on Kassidy's show. If I'm in the way, just say the word. Did somebody carry him inside his pressure suit all this time?"

Atlas turned and beamed at him. "You're a clever one, aren't you, Troy? No, Nico's dad drove our transport. We have a special outdoor baby carriage for walks, all toasty and safe."

"I'll go find Mr. Copeland," Sass offered, and slipped out.

In the cargo hold, the party was happily watching Kassidy's show as recorded by her drones, after having participated live. The couple dozen PM3 miners mingled with the skyship crew and lottery winners. Purple lipstick smudges spoke of Kassidy's progress working the room. No doubt she'd kiss everyone at least once.

A box-like springy baby wagon parked by the cargo lock. The miners' helmets lay jumbled in a pile alongside, the top halves of their pressure suits flapping loose from their belts. Jules kept the party well-lubricated with hot tea, fresh-baked fruit cobbler, and real beer from a pony keg. Judging by the chill, Benjy and Abel had simply opened the cargo ramp to invite the miners in. The Pikachu Crater dust carried few problematic contaminants. *Thrive* still struggled to restore the chilly space to a more comfortable temperature.

Sass spotted the baby, hanging at the back of the crowd in the arms of a tattooed muscular man only slightly lanky. He stood talking with a man significantly taller but stooped. She strode up and introduced herself. The friend proved to be her other quarry for Josiah, the foreman named Warwick.

"Fantastic ship, Captain!" Copeland said earnestly. "God, I'd love a tour. Was only ever in the hold, coming sky-side."

"Don't let him take anything apart," Warwick warned Sass. "Engineer. Wants to take everything apart. But you don't always know how to put it together again right, do you?" He mock-slapped the younger Copeland up the head lightly. "I'm just kidding, Captain. Copeland here is the best maintenance engineer I ever seen."

"Mahina University?" Sass asked, surprised.

"No, ma'am," Copeland assured her. "My uncle taught me before he passed on. Then I studied on my own. Never had time to finish high school. No Mahina U knocking at my door."

The convicts laughed together.

"And hello again, Nico." Sass bent to gently take his pudgy hand with those adorable miniature fingers.

Nico barely registered she was there. He hung facing the crowd from a baby carrier on his dad's chest, leaving the man's hands free for beer. The child's dull eyes gazed at nothing in particular, his poor lips still tinged with blue.

Copeland sighed. "He's not too with it, ma'am."

"I understand. Atlas wants to try the auto-doc. Would you mind?"

The foreman's eyes widened. "Absolutely! You got an auto-doc? Wow…"

Within ten minutes, the baby was plugged in, and out like a light.

"Damn," said Copeland, peering into the window. "His face is turning pink. Like normal. You a doc, sir?"

Atlas shook his head. "No. Well, technically yes. I have an M.D. Everyone in MA-Med has one. Mahina Actual Medical division. But I always wanted to go into administration." He noted the blank expression on the foreman's face, and clarified. "I was trained as a doctor. But I didn't continue on to practice medicine. I know how to work the machine, though. This is a top of the line auto-doc, Sass."

"Needed to be," Sass replied. She perched on a stainless steel counter in the cramped space, leaving the floor free for Copeland and Atlas to move around. "These old skyships housed the terraformers who worked outdoors before Mahina had a base atmosphere. Asteroid miners, too. Whole lot of injuries."

"And toxins," Atlas added. "Copeland? See here. The red bars show your son's toxin profile when he entered the auto-doc. And the green bars, see how they're starting to fall from the red levels? That's his progress."

"This thing can detox him? Like all the way?" Copeland looked to Sass for confirmation.

She shrugged. Her nanites handled such things. She'd seen near miracles from auto-docs in her first decades here, on settlers after pressure accidents. But she couldn't share her adventures as an adult half a century ago.

Atlas observed no such limitations. "All the way. This style of auto-doc is stocked with 'scrubbers.' A kind of simple nanite that cleans oxidation products and toxins out of the body. Like rust. Too much oxygen, too little, weird gases, all the trace poisons. Scrubbers remove the problem compounds, repair any cellular damage. They don't make auto-docs like this anymore. Fair warning — the baby's diaper will be a fright after this."

Copeland chuckled. "Nothing new."

"Nanites?" Sass asked. "This thing makes nanites?" She had a nanite fabricator all along and didn't know it?

"Scrubber nanites," Atlas confirmed. "Not the genetically-tailored ones."

Sass understood he meant the nanites that made the urbs self-healing and ageless for decades. But the comment flew safely past Troy and Copeland without comprehension, as Atlas intended.

"Why don't they make them like this anymore?" she asked. "Seems useful."

"Useful!" Atlas huffed a sad laugh. "Politics. It's a shame we can't leave the baby in here longer. Could you possibly stay at PM3 overnight?"

"Atlas, we need to talk. Mind if we use my office? Copeland, don't worry. If the auto-doc beeps, press this intercom button and call for help in the med bay." Sass gave Troy a reassuring smile on the way out as well.

34

Most moon or planetary colonies began by building an orbital as home base of operations.

The main thing preventing a prison break from Phosphate Mine 3 was the impossibility of keeping it secret for long. Vast stretches of hostile regolith prevented escape on the ground. Skyships and ore freighters had no trouble, but they weren't exactly stealthy. Security knew who visited the mines and when.

"Atlas, I want to take you Pono-side," Sass announced once they were settled in her office. "Warwick and Copeland, too. And Nico, of course." She licked her lip. "I couldn't give you advance warning. I'd like to hide your escape as long as possible. You're not due back at work for two days."

Atlas shrugged. "I'd be missed immediately. It's not as though I hide in my room on weekends. But why would you kidnap me? And Sass, it would be kidnapping. I'm needed here."

"We have another job for you." She settled in, arms folded before her on her desk, and told him her plan to begin synthesizing nanites for settlers, with Josiah handling the business end, and Atlas as medical director.

263

Atlas listened politely, eyes alight and searching her face kindly.

Sass finished and sucked in her lower lip. "I probably haven't considered everything yet —"

"You certainly haven't," Atlas agreed.

"But that's what I need you for, Atlas," Sass continued. "This is a medical operation. I need you to tell me how to make it work."

"Where to begin," Atlas mused. "Sass, the chances that the synthesizer you stole can cure failure to thrive... Let's back up. You understand that Mahina can't make the kind of nanites that you and Clay Rocha have, right? We don't understand that technology."

"You know about our nanites?"

"Of course. Sass, I ran MA-Med for over a decade. I'm sure we're both frustrated with their lack of progress. But they do study the problem. My point is, we have different nanite capabilities, not nearly as advanced as yours. I don't know what kind of nanite synthesizer you liberated —"

"It was tied to a genome sequencer."

Atlas dismissed that with a toss of the head. "Sass, it was in a botany lab. Chances are it's useless on vertebrates. But who knows, maybe it can build arbitrary custom nanites. Leave that aside for the moment. There is a chance that Nico can be healed because his poisoning was fairly brief and not too long ago. There is no chance — none — that you can reverse skeletal lankiness. Mental damage, incurred and compounded over decades? Probably not. Though I have wanted to try scrubbers for brain plaque."

"Why didn't you?"

Atlas sighed. "Politics. Blocked by Kendra Oliver's faction. The rebellion. Not ready yet, we needed more data...the usual excuses."

Sass frowned. "Atlas, clarify this for me. Scrubbers can do miracles. Let's say I don't care about self-healing or looking like a 25-year-old for decades. What else do the genetically tailored nanites buy you?"

"Quite a lot," he replied. "Self-healing isn't an optional cherry on top, as it turns out. Our primary cause of mortality here is radiation damage. The atmosphere is too thin. We've disturbed radioactive compounds in the regolith. Earth's crust had geological ages of weathering for the half-lives. Um. You understand radioactive half-lives? Never mind. The point is that our environment is rich in radiation that damages our DNA. In eggs — that's why our children are conceived from shielded eggs. But also in our working cells. That looks like rapid aging, hair loss, wrinkles. Continual inflammation and auto-immune disorders, arthritis, heart disease. And cancers.

"Point is, what the genetically tailored nanites do. They have a reference plan of healthy DNA. They scoot around identifying cells that are too badly damaged — by their molecular products. And either repair them or mark them for the immune system to destroy. Mostly the latter. We have designs for seven different models of these things. That's probably enough detail for the moment."

"OK. I think I see. So scrubbers can clean out toxins. But they can't fix radiation damage. Or any damage really. Only the custom nanites, and they have a limited range of things they can fix."

"Right," Atlas confirmed.

"I'm still not clear why you think my proposal is wrong. No, let's put it this way. What would you do instead, Atlas?"

"Thank you. Here's what I proposed. Clay Rocha backed the plan as well.

"We wanted to build satellite creches outside Mahina Actual, to raise settler children. Earth-normal gravity, botanical garden, animals, school. Distributed centers so parents could visit regularly. We'd also use the facilities for medical treatment. Inject scrubber nanites, if nothing else. An auto-doc like yours could work miracles.

"But my main goal was to bring the medical research programs out of Mahina Actual. Engage with the settlers directly."

"But Kendra blocked it," Sass said.

Atlas rocked his head so-so. "Kendra sentenced me sky-side, and put someone else in charge of MA-Med. The creches were 'postponed' because it 'sent the wrong message' to 'reward' the settlers for the rebellion. And they'd already made the concessions you won. So they would wait and evaluate results. Cost concerns. Who gets what, when there isn't enough for everyone. You know how easy it is to justify doing nothing."

"So come Pono-side and tell us how to do it," Sass said. "Atlas, no one settler-side has your expertise." Sass raised her hand to forestall his objections. "Maybe only for a week. Or a month, or a year. Just try. I have more clues."

"You have clues," Atlas echoed sadly.

"Good clues!" Sass objected. "Other experiments that were showing signs of success, abandoned. At least one other scientist willing to work outside Actual. Copeland, Warwick, for whatever they're good for."

"They're quite good," Atlas allowed.

"Adulterated genomes of four settler students at Mahina U. One of them is on my crew. You'll meet him — Benjy. The same genetic sequences were installed in each of them, that didn't come from their parents."

"Really?" Atlas frowned thoughtfully. "That is interesting."

"You heard Troy in there, Atlas. He saw baby Nico on Kassidy's broadcast. What if we have Kassidy show what a difference our auto-doc made to Nico? Don't you think more people in MA-Med would like to be a hero? Escape the petty infighting?"

"They'd love to." Atlas pursed his lips and considered for a few moments.

"Atlas, you're a fantastic administrator. I'm sure you already trained subordinates to step up and run PM3. Using Troy as a cover story, we can even leave here above board, at first. Just say that I kept Nico in the auto-doc and brought him Pono-side for treatment. I brought witnesses to Troy's attempted suicide. You're all my guests, housed on *Thrive* because Kendra is dangerous. Copeland and Warwick will escape. You can, too, if you choose.

"But come with us now. Figure out for me whether any of these clues and machines amount to anything. Whether Josiah — Copeland's boss — could build a viable business to cure people from the settler side, since Mahina Actual won't help us."

"Alright. I'm curious. I'd like to take the time to look over your 'clues.' I suppose I don't even need a promise from you to bring me back when I want, do I?"

"Thank you."

"Give me that genome data?"

Sass unlocked a drawer and fished it out to hand over. "I'll introduce you to Eli. You're welcome to any data we have. Look over the equipment. My house is yours. But please don't leave *Thrive* without talking to me first. For your safety and ours."

"Agreed."

THE REST OF THE 'PRISON BREAK' was easy. Another pair of miners volunteered to drive their tank-like transport, while the rest remained on board for a ride home on *Thrive*.

When they reached PM3, Sass didn't let Atlas out. But Warwick went in to pack some things for him and spin excuses to Pratt's second in command. Once Warwick returned, Sass turned the skyship back for the long ride to Troy's town.

Jules took point on keeping their guests comfortable. She let Abel get some sleep before he had to ferry Annika and Finbar home.

And at Sass's instigation, Kassidy brought her livecast into the med bay to interview Atlas and Copeland about the baby, with especial attention to Atlas's explanation of how the auto-doc was removing environmental toxins. The celebrity drones zoomed in for a closeup of Copeland, eyes brimming with tears unshed, wishing all settlers had access to this technology. To see his listless blue baby turning pink and healthy again before his eyes was a miracle.

Then, still broadcasting live, Kassidy turned to interview Troy about why he jumped. Atlas helped hammer home the salient points about how Kendra Oliver, Mahina Actual Chief of Security, tried to buy his suicide as an excuse to wrest *Thrive* from Sassafras Collier, a hero of the rebellion.

No one had called Sass a hero at the time. Despite the life-extending concessions she won from the urbs, the Petticreek Five were resoundingly condemned as traitors by both sides. But that was twenty years ago, and tempers were high.

Today, Atlas laid the heroism claim on thick. Kassidy made sure it stuck.

Sass fully expected this livecast to be shut down the moment Kendra caught wind of it. But at the time, Kendra Oliver was held incommunicado in her own jail cells while Clay Rocha took statements from anyone implicated in Troy's suicide attempt, from Seth Gruman on up, with especial attention to Kendra's second in command, Guy Fairweather. Clay deputized the security guard Tamber to help, fresh from the memory of Kendra's abuse of power with a settler named Benjy in medical. As a marshal with moon-wide scope, Clay had authority to commandeer assistance from law enforcement, within reason. Tamber recruited other security guards similarly dubious about Kendra's sense of fair play. They managed the jail block for Clay, evicting Kendra's regulars.

Before long, the mainstream news was promulgating clips from Kassidy's livecast and 'shocking allegations' about Kendra Oliver. Baby Nico Copeland got plenty of coverage as well, on urb and settler broadcasts alike. Shots from Kassidy and Sass's starlit sky dives added extra drama.

Kassidy's agent in Mahina Actual made sure the starlet received royalties for these clips. Per their agreement, *Thrive* received a cut of all proceeds.

The cop Tamber reluctantly interrupted Clay Rocha from Fairweather's interrogation to update him on the news. Newer York, Schuyler, Poldark, and Mahina Actual itself were among the cities seeing 'spontaneous' demonstrations in the streets demanding Kendra's head for this.

'Spontaneous' sounded like his son Hunter's doing, to the marshal.

"Let them be heard," was Clay Rocha's verdict. "Keeping the peace is a local matter. We leave that to the sheriffs and MA security. Not you and your team, Tamber. You're with me tonight. Keep up the good work."

Tamber was amused, and grateful not to be on the plaza. Urb citizens were hurling things at the cops. Before long, he imagined the mayor would start issuing psychotic demands, with his top security chiefs locked up.

Clay paused to shoot Sass an update before he returned to his interrogations. "Well done. Bring your witnesses Pono-side, I hope?"

"Absolutely," Sass purred from the bridge of *Thrive*. "Is it too much to hope we can topple Kendra this time?"

"Probably," Clay growled. "But keep a happy thought."

"OK if we drop off Kassidy's other two guests? They weren't involved."

"You can even give the jumper back to his wife," Clay confirmed. "Keep the PM3 staff on board, please. Talk to you tomorrow."

As she drove onward into the gathering grey verge of the bright side, Sass indulged in a fantasy of the triumphant overthrow of Kendra Oliver, with cheering in the streets. Mahina Actual opened wide for urb and settler alike. Little mini-cities with fireflies sprouting up across the moon, amid groves of scrubber trees.

"It could happen," she whispered, alone on the bridge.

But she didn't believe it.

35

Mahina devised unusual 'scrubber' nanites to clean environmental toxins from the human body. They even created scrubber landscape trees. Although there is some question whether the trees relied on nanites or biological processes.

Sass yawned mightily and considered the pulsing red button on her bridge communications console labeled 'Incoming.' That one hadn't lit before. She pulled out her comm to double-check, but she hadn't received any more messages from Clay Rocha. One from Abel said he'd dropped off Annika and hoped to arrive in Schuyler around 08:00, an hour from now.

With a fatalistic shrug, she pressed the 'Incoming' button.

An unfamiliar male voice emitted from a scratchy old speaker overhead. "Skyship *Thrive,* Mahina Security. You are ordered to redirect immediately to Mahina Actual. Acknowledge. Over."

Sass paused to consider. *Thrive* dropped off Finbar around 02:00 hours. From there, Abel set off in the shuttle to get rid of Annika. In the quiet of a sleeping ship, flying through the underwater green-dark of Eclipse, Sass's eyes were drifting closed, so she snatched a few hours' nap before continuing onward to deliver the near-suicidal

Troy to his home, a small town 50 kilometers from Schuyler. They didn't feel a ride with Abel and Annika would improve his state of mind. She was about to take care of that delivery now.

"Mahina Security, this is Captain Sass Collier of *Thrive*. My plans today do not include Mahina Actual. With whom am I speaking? Over."

"Captain Collier, Mahina Security. That was an order. Over."

"I am still trying to ascertain who you are, and why you think you have authority to give me that order. I'd like to speak to Marshal Clay Rocha. Over."

"He is not available."

"Then wake him up and have him call me," Sass suggested. "*Thrive* is a settler vessel. Mahina Security has no authority over me except via marshal. I am happy to speak with Marshal Rocha. Over."

A beep informed her that it was time to take over the automated controls to land in Troy's hamlet. She punched a button to acknowledge, and found the market field by eye in the hot noon sunshine of early Thursday. Pono hung in the sky to her left, an enormous dim disk showing a bright sliver along one edge. She banked around to come in for a landing.

"*Thrive,* you are disobeying a direct order!"

"Whoever you are, buzz off, I'm busy. *Thrive* out." Sass stabbed the *Incoming* button again to terminate the conversation. She called Carmine instead, Troy's wife, then woke Kassidy to say good-bye to her guest.

Once on the ground, the two women met Carmine and her baby girl at the base of the ramp. They escorted her to wake her husband in the med bay. Copeland was in there as well, having fallen asleep on his arms, half-draped on the auto-doc in case baby Nico woke.

Sass ignored the occasional thrum of her incoming messages during the mutual expressions of baby esteem. She liked Copeland, just a touch lanky and sharp as a tack. His manners were a bit rough around the edges, as one might expect of prison mine foreman with mob roots. But his gruff heart was in the right place.

Kassidy was able to offer something more concrete than well

wishes. Troy was famous this morning. Several people had posted job offers to him on the livecast feed. Carmine promised to follow up, so the humiliated Troy needn't to muster the self-esteem to face job hunting today.

All in all, Sass was quite satisfied as they waved Troy and family good-bye from the foot of the ramp. Things were looking up for the suicide she'd saved. "We done good, Kassidy." They traded a high-five and a brief hug, then headed back into the hold's cavernous welcome shade. Sass punched the button to retract the ramp.

"Your tablet keeps going off," Kassidy remarked as it thrummed again. "Anything wrong?"

"Yeah, don't worry about it." Sass brought it out to look. "Or... Huh." Nearly twenty messages queued while she ignored them. Kassidy draped herself to read over Sass's shoulder as she sifted through message headers, careful not to acknowledge receipt of anything quite yet. A series from Mahina Security, of mounting shrill-ness. One from her lawyer. More from security, with one from Abel mixed in. Nothing from Clay, but one from her probation officer Matt.

"Make us breakfast?" Sass asked. "I'll be right up." She waited until Kassidy was on her way to read Matt's transcript. The guy was voice-only literate.

> Sass, you need to cooperate with Mahina Security, or they'll nail you on a parole violation.

The lawyer essentially agreed with Matt, and reminded her of the court case pending on Lucas Massey's claim to her inheritance from Drake.

Abel just wanted to know what the lawyer's message was about, since he'd been copied.

She considered her options, which of these gentlemen she wished to speak with first. *Clay Rocha.* Who hadn't messaged her. She tried him and got an auto-response:

Marshal Clay Rocha is on administrative leave, pending an investigation. Please contact Mahina Security.

They had no right to do that. If a marshal was suspended, only another settler could step in for him. Sass's heart started pounding in concern. Much of that concern was for Clay.

She read her messages from Security. Not one answered her most burning question — was Kendra Oliver calling the shots again?

In sudden decision, she started waking and mobilizing her crew and guests.

———

At a knock on the small lock, Sass set her breakfast plate aside and scoped out the scene using her tablet and the ship's external cameras. Just Josiah at the door. The next row of warehouses at the Schuyler loading docks stretched beyond him. She'd parked *Thrive* at one of Josiah's docks, sandwiched between two grocery haulers. No one bearing guns yet except for the gang kingpin's bodyguards. *Good.*

Sass buzzed Josiah in. Before he could say anything, she burbled, "Thanks for the loan on the grav carriers. Shall I let the ramp down?" She did so without waiting for a response.

Josiah pursed his lips at the three grav carriers, driven by Warwick, Benjy, Jules, and no Copeland. Atlas Pratt stood among them, bearing only his suitcase. Sass was supposed to deliver Copeland. Jules bore a fetching fruit basket atop her otherwise seemingly empty pallet. All the real goods were inside the pallets. "You'll explain, of course."

Sass shooed the grav carrier quartet before them, and led Josiah to follow down the ramp. "I'm having a small difference of opinion with Mahina Security today." The grav carriers dispersed. Jules and Benjy shot her a couple hurt backward glances before they vanished beyond the next transport. "Lovely personnel you've got. They're keepers."

"Huh. Girl looks a tad young," Josiah acknowledged. "Boy, too."

"My partner Abel planned to meet us here. I'd rather he didn't," Sass clarified, as Josiah pointedly frowned at the narrow space to the freighter next door. "You see, I hoped to surrender to your sheriff. You have a positive working relationship with your sheriff, don't you?" Sass winced hopefully. She couldn't call ahead to arrange this because Mahina Security would monitor her comms. She hadn't been free to confide her full plans to anyone.

"The sheriff is well-paid," Josiah allowed. "Where's Copeland?"

"His baby is in my auto-doc. It's doing wonders. We'd rather not disrupt that."

"Interesting. And the sheriff part?"

"Mahina Security seems to have arrested the marshal who was handling my case on a tricky matter —"

"Define tricky," Josiah demanded. The airy style of Sass's presentation was beginning to irritate him.

"Did you catch our livecast yesterday? Kendra Oliver promised to pay our guest Troy two thousand credits to jump to his death."

Josiah grinned. "Cash in advance, I trust."

"My reaction exactly. But no, she paid fifty credits down, then reversed the payment and tried to hide her tracks."

"Bitch."

"She is that. Anyway, last night the marshal — Clay Rocha — had Kendra in custody. He told me to bring everyone Pono-side for questioning. This morning, I suspect their roles are reversed. Mahina Security demands that I report to Mahina Actual. My position is they have no right to do that. They need to go through a marshal."

Josiah scratched under his chin. "A lot of demonstrations last night. Mahina Security invoked martial law. They claim they have absolute authority moon-wide. Why is it that martial law means there are no marshals?"

"They're spelled differently."

"I can read, Sass. I'm saying they've got everyone settler-side feeling a bit confused and ornery. Including our local sheriff, I imagine."

"I was hoping he wouldn't cost too much to accept my surrender."

Josiah's brows flew up in sudden understanding, and he laughed softly. "I'll see what I can do."

"Thank you! And the older guy with the suitcase used to run MA Medical. More recently PM3. He's our technical consultant on that future business venture we discussed. Please treat him well."

"Sweet!" Josiah pulled out his comm. Sass's own soon chimed happy receipt of his payment on delivery for the prison break.

She checked that point, ignoring another raft of messages vowing legal retribution. "I'd like those grav carriers back when this blows over. Abel should be around here somewhere. Copeland...is busy."

Josiah waved acknowledgment and strode away, collecting his goons in his wake. Sass blew out and retreated into *Thrive,* shutting the ramp again behind her.

So far so good.

About 20 minutes later, the Schuyler sheriff dropped by to accept the surrender of *Thrive* and whoever happened to be on board. Sass plied him with coffee and fruit cobbler and made friends. He was tickled pink to receive Kassidy's autograph on a photo of them together. The star was livecasting to her subscribers as usual, and gave the man ample opportunity to ham it up for his friends and family. He happily received a purple kiss on the lips. He claimed the wife would only be jealous she didn't get one.

In substantial relief at the quality of excuse for his actions, Sheriff Chumley solemnly agreed that baby Nico's medical treatment dictated that *Thrive* stay exactly where it was.

The logic of this was pretty damned thin, given that the child flew halfway around the globe overnight, and was presently parked in a grocery loading dock. However the excuse satisfied the sheriff. To Sass's surprise, he didn't even quote overtime pay and other complications that another bribe might defray. She figured Josiah kept the man on retainer. But his type usually expected more money should they need to do anything beyond 'look the other way.'

She escorted him cordially back to the small lock door, coffee and cake in his hands to fortify him until lunch. "Will you be needing any of us to drop by the police station? Make a statement or anything?"

"No, I don't think so." Chumley hitched up his belt. "No, I'm only accepting custody until a qualified marshal makes a lawful request. When you're satisfied, let me know. Then you're free to go."

Sass tamped down her grin. "And if Mahina Security should drop by?"

"They have no jurisdiction here, I'll tell you that," Chumley assured her. "Public demonstrations against Kendra Oliver might get out of hand." He winked at her and strode out. "I might be a friend of couple friends of yours, Sass. Josiah. Hunter Burke. Clay Rocha."

"I see." Sass didn't tamp her grin this time. "Pleasure to make your acquaintance, sheriff! Thank you for your assistance."

"We in law enforcement got to stick together, ma'am. Good day."

When he was gone, Copeland slipped out of the med bay.

"Is he always that agreeable?" Sass asked.

"Not by half," Copeland confirmed. "He's gung-ho for the resistance, though. Probably hoping for a shoot-out. May never have seen one before."

"Have you? Can you shoot?"

"Hell, yeah! Uh…" He glanced in consternation at the med bay door. Clearly the criminal engineer was still a bit befuddled by daycare coverage.

"Kassidy?" Sass called up to the catwalk. The celebrity and Eli leaned against the catwalk railing to observe the floor show in the hold. "Would you mind keeping an ear out for Nico in the auto-doc? Copeland is headed to the roof. I'll join him for a bit while I catch up on my correspondence." Depressing thought. The backlog of unanswered messages was growing rather extreme.

She yanked open the weapons cabinet by the ramp and selected a rifle and pistol. She invited Copeland to help himself.

36

Typically, it took years for a colony ship to debark its passengers, because the settlers had to build somewhere to live first, under trying conditions.

Copeland erected Jules' striped market awning atop *Thrive*, to cut down on the hot Thursday sun, while Sass sat dangling her legs through the hatch.

She really needed to respond to her message backlog. After thinking it through again, Sass chose to start with someone who hadn't contacted her.

"Tamber, MA Security? This is Sass Collier, captain of *Thrive*. We met in medical —"

"I remember, captain," Tamber agreed. Benjy landed in MA-Med only 6 days ago.

"I wonder if you could tell me where Clay Rocha is."

"Give me a moment to get somewhere more private."

Sass waited. Copeland wandered to the blunt rear of the ship, away from the loading dock, and glanced down. "Sheriff's erecting police lines," he reported. "Do not cross."

"Any sign of urb security yet?" Sass asked. The engineer shook his head.

"Sass?" Tamber resumed. "Rocha is locked in the same cell where he held Kendra Oliver last night. My guys and I were there. The mayor and city council flipped out over the demonstrations. They suspended charges against Oliver and reinstated her to restore order. First thing she did was throw Clay into a cell. We vamoosed before she could do the same to us."

"Who's Kendra's second in command?"

"Guy Fairweather, but he's in the cell next to Rocha. Seems he flipped on Kendra in exchange for immunity."

"Thanks, Tamber. If you hear any change in status, could you let me know?"

The cop hesitated. "Why?"

"Mahina Security asked me to turn myself in to them. I pointed out that only a marshal could ask that, and that marshal was Clay Rocha. In the meantime, in a show of good faith, I'm in the custody of the Sheriff of Schuyler."

"Too deep for me," Tamber commented. "Yeah. Rocha's a good guy."

"Shame he's a settler, huh? Guess he doesn't have friends in the city."

"He has all kinds of friends in the city," Tamber disagreed. "Guess I could reach out to a few, tell them his status."

"Could you? Thank you, Tamber!"

"No sweat. Tired of arresting citizens for nothing anyway."

After disconnecting from him, Sass recorded a statement of her current status in Schuyler custody and demand for Clay Rocha as her marshal. She mentioned baby Nico Copeland's medical treatment on board. She sent that off to her lawyer, parole officer Matt, Mahina Security, Abel and Eli, Atlas and Josiah.

Copeland noted, "You didn't mention the other three on board."

"Kassidy and Eli are urbs," Sass explained. "Subject to MA Security. You're an escaped convict from PM3. Nico and I are the ones in a legal grey area."

"I'm not a convict," Copeland replied. "Neither is Warwick."

Sass shielded her eyes from the sun to peer at him. "Why were you there? With a baby?"

"We got picked up in a harassment sweep at Josiah's brewery. Held without charges. Next thing I knew I was at PM1. The baby was due to graduate from the city creche. We had to accept him or lose him. They won't deliver unless the parents are together. I couldn't get out, so the wife joined me. Then she went nuts. The air was bad at PM1, everywhere. Tried to fix it, but I was fighting an uphill battle. Crazy crew, fruitcake foreman. Plant manager never left his quarters. He'd be lynched. The whole town is a gas chamber."

"Hold that thought." Sass yelled down into the hold, "Kassidy? I have another interview for you! Copeland, let's broadcast that story. Why were they harassing a brewery, anyway?"

She had to wait for her answer, because Copeland didn't care to tell it twice. She asked him again when Kassidy's interview reached that point.

"You know that swill they're selling now? The everclear and colored flutes, sweet beer soda instead of real booze? Yeah, all that syrupy crap is sold by Mahina Actual. I don't know if Kendra Oliver owns the outfit, or just runs enforcement for them. But they're driving all the other booze merchants out of business. Is how I heard it. There's no charges against me because they have no case. I was a facilities engineer. Brewing beer isn't a crime. And even if it was, do you arrest the guy repairing a fermenter? What kind of sense does that make?"

Kassidy interrupted. "Sorry, Sass, they shut me down. Not broadcasting anymore."

"Don't stop recording," Sass said, as the younger woman made to call in her drones. "Let's record it all. Unless you'd rather turn yourself in. Anyone down there yet to turn her in to?"

"Not yet," Copeland reported, after striding to the end to check the parking lot again. "Big crowd growing, through."

"Kassidy?" Sass asked softly. "This isn't your fight. You're an urb. You want out?"

Kassidy gazed at her blankly for a moment, then cocked a hip and a lopsided grin. She summoned in a drone for a closeup. "Screw that. My fans can't tell me what they want at the moment. They've been cut off by Kendra Oliver and her corrupt goons. But I think...no, I *know*. You want me to stick with *Thrive!* Am I right, fans? Of course I'm right! I know you! And I love you!" She blew the camera a kiss. "Besides, we have a deal, Collier. My 3,000 meter dive is on Dawn, five days from now!" She pumped a fist. "Can you stand it?"

Sass laughed. "Might skip the guests this time."

Kassidy shrugged a fair-enough. "Or drop them off below for the after party."

"Or skip them altogether."

"We'll negotiate!"

"Think about it, Kassidy," Sass urged. "Treason."

"I'm not guilty of a damned thing," Kassidy replied. "Neither was my dad, so far as I know. Or you. Dr. Bertram. Atlas Pratt. Or anyone else Actual exiled for so-called treason. Hey, one woman's opinion. But I celebrate Mahina. Urbs and settlers alike, to thrive together — that's not treason. Spiking the progress of terraforming — now that would be treason. Or would it be mass murder?"

"If you're sure," Sass said softly. She spent twenty years repenting one such hasty decision at leisure. She'd intended to keep Kassidy and Eli under wraps. Copeland's story was just too tempting and she forgot.

Kassidy checked her thrumming comm. "Ooh! We're back online again! Simultaneous transmission, settler and urb news! I love you, Mahina!" She kissed her fingers and threw them wide for the cameras. "I'll be back live in just a minute, folks! But first I want to replay for you the past few minutes." She bent to adjust something, then muttered, "Eat that, Kendra Oliver."

"Still recording?" Sass inquired.

"Absolutely," Kassidy confirmed.

"Incoming," Copeland reported. He sighted along his rifle.

"Copeland, put that down!" Sass ordered.

"Just using the optics," he claimed lazily. He did lower the weapon, though.

Kassidy announced, "I'm so wiggly, I must jump on your ship, Sass."

"Not again," Sass moaned.

Kassidy wasn't really using the ship as a trampoline, just a stage while she used her gravity generator. The thumps on Sass's hull these days weren't much worse than a ballet leap.

"Fun crew," Copeland said, craning his neck to watch Kassidy's mid-air somersault. "Need an engineer? I'm willing to work for room and board and daycare. You got the best air I've ever tasted. Though I wouldn't mind getting paid like that kid Benjy. I know how to do more than he does."

As she came down to rebound, Kassidy blurted, "Watch your feed!"

Sass frowned puzzlement for a moment, then hurriedly brought up Kassidy's drone feeds on her tablet and showed them to Copeland. The cameras held station near the top of her leaps, giving them an unobstructed view.

"Nice!" Sass said. "And yes. I'd love an engineer. And someone else who can fight. I'm an ex-cop. Abel was in commercial extruders."

"Not much future in that," Copeland said.

"Will Josiah mind?" Sass said, suddenly recalling that she hadn't kidnapped Copeland for herself. Much as she would love to have a fix-it man. Supervising all the work herself was getting old, and her skills were iffy. "Let's talk later."

Copeland chuckled. "Happy to audition in the meantime."

"I will keep that in mind," Sass purred. "Incoming."

Kassidy came down for a bounce. "Incoming," she echoed, and bounded up one more time to take a bow.

Sass's phone thrummed another kind of incoming. "Tamber! News?"

"Clay Rocha is out. A bunch of Directors demanded his release — Settler Commerce, Terraforming, Medical, Basic Research, don't know who else. I only reached the commerce lady myself. Rocha's next-door neighbor."

Atlas and Eli! Sass exulted. They must have pulled strings too.

Tamber continued, "The city council recalled Oliver and her forces from Schuyler. We'll see if they listen. Kendra Oliver and Clay Rocha are both relieved of duty pending investigation. Fairweather is reinstated to acting Director of Security. But he has a second-guessing committee sitting on him."

"I owe you, Tamber!"

He huffed a laugh. "I'm a cop. People watching is my kind of funny."

"You got that right," Sass agreed, and ended the call.

Clay's freedom was a weight of guilt off her mind. But Clay couldn't solve her immediate problem. He had no authority or forces. And crowd control wasn't his forte.

Sheriff Chumley, she realized. She made a quick call to convey the news that the urb forces here were ignoring a recall order from the city. She recorded the conversation and forwarded it to Josiah, Hunter Burke, and the rest of her crew. Copeland and Kassidy hung on every word.

THREE MAHINA Actual security flitters settled into the loading zone, with another circling on overwatch. If they expected cooperation from the locals, they got the opposite.

Schuyler dock workers were a rough crowd, often padding their paychecks freelancing for the mob. They poured into the plaza first, some bearing wrenches and crowbars. The Schuyler transit hub ground to a standstill. Curious civilians, angry demonstrators from last night, and resistance members sifted in as soon as they could reach the place.

Sheriff Chumley appointed himself spokesman for the Schuyler point of view. He held to their official position that MA Security had no business here. He demanded the flitters depart immediately. He was willing to talk to Marshal Clay Rocha. But Kendra Oliver was a criminal with no standing. If she dared show herself here, the sheriff implied her life would be forfeit and he shouldn't be sorry in the least.

Soon after Kassidy Wang's acrobatic show, acting Chief of Security Guy Fairweather sent an override message directly to each MA security trooper. He told them in no uncertain terms that orders from Kendra Oliver were illegal. They were recalled to the city. Anyone discharging their weapons against the settlers would face criminal charges. "We will have no Petticreek Massacre today."

The forces aboard two of the flitters loaded up and flew away. But two flitters remained, including Kendra Oliver's. She assumed the overwatch lieutenant above remained loyal to her. In fact, the overwatch checked with Fairweather, who agreed her team should remain in place to observe until Oliver withdrew. Her guns were hot and aimed at Kendra's vehicle.

Kendra sent half her cops, dressed in elderly riot armor, out onto the plaza to form a perimeter around their flitter. After receiving the recall order from Fairweather, a couple of them tried to withdraw into their vehicle. But they were locked out with imprecations to hold their ground. After a few minutes of these hostile interchanges, one decided to throw down his weapon. Hands in the air, he explained to nearby toughs what the issue was.

One of the dockers helpfully picked up the discarded weapon and blew a hole in the vehicle's door window. Others pitched in with wrenches and crowbars to widen the opening. Joining the spirit of the thing, the crowd converged to hammer on the flitter until it was forced to rise above the crowd. One of the men inside dared to aim his rifle downward, and it was shot out of his hands. The bullet continued onward through his faceplate for a shocking splatter of blood.

At that point, the flitter driver had enough, and headed back to the city. Kendra tried to wrest the controls from him and nearly crashed the vehicle before the others inside got her secured for delivery to the city.

In a series of slow and painstakingly polite steps, coordinated through Sheriff Chumley, the angry crowd withdrew to a ring around the deserted urb cops on the ground, none of whom retained a weapon by that point. The overwatch flitter landed to collect them. Overloaded, it lifted off to depart at a lumbering waddle that struggled to clear the heads of the crowd.

Sheriff Chumley waited a half hour to see if the crowd would disperse of its own accord. The dock managers requested anyone loading perishable goods get back to work. The rest were welcome to go home for the day. That got rid of most of the settlers. Dockers weren't interested in politics. Whatever came of this, they knew no one would consult them. The more casual onlookers drifted away after them.

A solid core of citizen activists remained to clog up the loading yard.

Chumley diffidently requested Kassidy Wang give another show and then ask them to disperse.

"Sheriff, with respect," Sass intervened. "These people have serious grievances. Somersaults are nice. But what can Kassidy tell them to do with their issues? They can't even post a comment on her livecast. Do you have a city council meeting or something you can refer them to?"

Chumley agreed to look into that. Kassidy assured him that she would be happy to deliver the message.

While Chumley was still figuring out what to tell the crowd, Clay Rocha simply walked to the small airlock and messaged Sass to buzz him him in.

37

One of the mysteries of the early Diaspora is where the colony ship crews went after depositing their settlers.

"Clay!" Sass cried. She leapt down from the catwalk as Clay stepped through the door into the hold. "I'm so sorry!"

Clay snorted. "No you're not. We wanted to take Kendra Oliver down from the moment we met her."

"True. You're underdressed," Sass noted. He looked strangely awkward in upscale weekend attire instead of his usual Fed suit. Compared to Sass's jeans and T-shirt, he still looked like a fashion model.

"I retired," Clay replied. "From Security, anyway."

"Oh. Clay, are you sure about that? I was hoping you might..."

"What, act as your puppet? Negotiate a better deal for settlers out of the uproar you caused?"

Sass pressed her lips flat. "I was hoping for another atmo tower at least."

He nodded ruefully. "We'll get that. And more. But my cover is blown as the settlers' inside man at Mahina Actual."

"You! Not Atlas."

"Me. And Atlas."

Sass frowned. "Atlas said he didn't know who else."

"He lied. So did I. So did you. But now that I've resigned, I get to tell everybody the whole truth for a while." He frowned in distaste, imagining those excruciating debriefs stretching before him. "Maybe I could set a daily limit on that. I have records for them to sift through." He shrugged.

"Come sit. Iced tea?"

"Sounds good."

Sass led the way. "So what happens now?"

"Now I need a place to live outside the city. I hear you rent out rooms."

"Really? As a marshal you didn't keep a settler place?"

"I did. I gave it to my ex-wife and my son." By then they were seated in the kitchen. Clay vented his irritation by swirling the ice wand through his tea in figure-eights.

"Oh. Sorry. Clay, I'm not sure how well you'd fit in here. For instance, you find me annoying. And it's my ship. Our ideas on what's legal, or wise — they're not always on the same page." And by that she meant never on the same page.

"Do they know how old you are?" Clay replied quietly. "Because I think that's the lie I'd most like to leave behind. At least in private. At home. And to be honest, Sass, your ship has the best air I've ever smelled on Mahina. I'll miss the botanical gardens and the animals. But not the urbs. Strange, but the inside of your crappy old skyship is the closest to that I can think of in the whole settler world. And you owe me for the last 24 hours."

"I owe you." Sass sighed. "Let's try one week and see how it goes?"

Clay's eyes narrowed. "Am I stuck in a bunk room?"

Sass laughed softly. "Atlas and the guys from PM3 stayed in Benjy's cabin last night, Kassidy's guests in the other one. I'm afraid housekeeping hasn't been up to our usual impeccable standards today. But my fourth cabin with private washroom is available. You and Atlas can flip for it."

"Good."

"So you're not here to take statements. There will be paperwork with the city."

"Not very much paperwork, for you."

"I kidnapped convicts. Oh wait — Copeland and Warwick weren't convicts." Sass mentally reviewed her crimes. She hadn't gotten caught for the worst of them yet, theft of scientific equipment.

Clay counted on his fingers. "Atlas was sentenced for life for the crime of caring what happened to the settlers. One could not ask for a more model prisoner, and he's already served 20 years. He's not going back to PM3. Copeland and Warwick deserve restitution for crimes committed against them. You didn't steal nearly enough trees. You should fix that. Whatever you had stashed in the pallets is Fairweather's problem, not mine."

"Scientific equipment for Eli," Sass supplied. "He's trying to find out why my plants grow better than his."

"Why do you do that? Just belt out crimes you're guilty of? Petty ones, too."

"Maybe there's more to it."

"Ah. Confess to the minor offense so as to distract notice from your real crimes. Speaking of. Sass, why did you buy a skyship?"

"It's a spaceship. Just needs a drive upgrade."

Clay leaned forward to listen intently.

Sass shrugged, grasping for words. "We could live forever, Clay. These people we live with, a one-way trip must seem unbearable. It did to us. But to us now it would just be...another. A fresh adventure again. See something new. More exciting than beer soda and rainbow-colored everclear. Kassidy makes a mint off of terminal boredom here. I could even come back someday and have Mahina be new. Somewhere out there they've solved these problems, Clay. Kassidy's dad, or his girlfriend, probably modified Benjy. I gave it to Atlas first to look into before I told you. But I guess you knew that."

"I suspected," Clay agreed. "Copeland has that gene splice as well, and the baby inherited it. Atlas sequenced their genomes. And I have to believe that whoever built our nanites is still out there somewhere. Why would we live forever, and he didn't?"

Sass nodded. "There would be no failure to thrive on Mahina, if everyone had our nanites."

"Hopefully improved so four out of ten didn't die," Clay said. "Wouldn't be many takers on those terms."

"I screamed bloody murder before they stabbed me with that thing," Sass recalled.

"You did. In my ear."

Sass raised her ice tea glass in salute. "And you took it like a man."

Clay rocked his head so-so. "Until I fell to my knees vomiting just like you did. And passed out in the mud with the rest. Let's stop this little trip down memory lane."

"Agreed."

"The urbs were so concerned with overpopulation when we came to Mahina."

"With good cause," Sass allowed. "But I don't want to spend the rest of my life watching the whole song play out, 99 bottles of beer on the wall. I don't want to be the last of the Mahinans. This world is so close to working."

She thunked her tea glass on the table in finality. "So? Get on with it, Rocha, make fun of me. For buying a skyship hoping to save the world."

He sat back and shook his head. "Pass. I figured it was something like that. Especially since the city's usual punishment is exile. I'd rather see the orbital again than Phosphate Mine 1. Your farm wasn't bad."

"I wouldn't get a farm for my second offense."

Clay grinned.

"Doesn't matter. I've barely scraped the taxes together to take ownership of *Thrive*. We have one more skydive for Kassidy. Then we could lose our only profitable client. I'm a long way from buying a space drive upgrade."

"Or a single sale," Clay countered. "I didn't go to jail like you did, Sass. I drew salary all this time. And saved religiously for my retirement. Which is now. Let's try a cabin for a month. I'm a hard sell."

Sass pursed her lips. Why did a decade of scrimping and saving sound easier than a month of Clay? "Alright. A thousand credits for the month. Room and board."

"Would it work for me to park my flitter on the roof?"

"I...have an engineer in residence today. I can ask him."

"Excellent. While you're at it, maybe you could ask how he and housekeeping can remove all the rust from my bulkheads and washroom before they paint. I trust you won't mind me sleeping in the bunk room until my room reaches move-in condition."

"Did I say a thousand a month? That's as-is. Pain in the ass condition is two thousand a month."

"Twelve-fifty. There are quite a lot of bulkheads that need shining."

"Maybe I like rust," Sass growled. "Seventeen hundred."

"I'm negotiable on which parts of the ship remain...earthy." He frowned at the kitchen. "A new galley is non-negotiable however. I'll help design it. Fifteen hundred."

Sass twisted in her chair to dolefully regard the corroded kitchen. One yellowed cabinet hung crooked from its hinge. Another looked like a grease fire survivor. Black grunge filled holes in a floor that looked like century-old linoleum. Jules worked on a cutting board laid over the grimy gaps in the counter and around the sink.

"Point," she conceded. "The ship is a work in progress. Fifteen hundred, agreed. Kitchen remodeling is expensive, though. I'll need to consult with my partner. And his wife. She uses it the most."

"Jules Greer. Housekeeping," Clay mused. "I also enjoy cooking. But I can schedule that with her."

"Why must you be so annoying?"

"Earth stopped transmitting. A few years back. Did they tell you?"

The news still hurt. "No. But Kassidy told me."

"I'm sorry. We have to make it work out here, Sass. That was always true, but. Something broke in me when I got that news. All the charades. The law, finding idiot criminals. Just doesn't matter. I want to get real again, but I've forgotten how. I doubt that makes any more sense than your decision to buy *Thrive*. Maybe I'm annoying because I don't remember how not to be. As though I consoled myself all these years about the big things by diving into minutiae."

"I have an assignment for you, Clay. Design a glorious kitchen for us. Get input from every person on board until we're all ooh'ing and ah'ing."

"Mm."

"Sell it to us, like it's your dream baby. But you want every single one of us to love it. Get all of our ideas incorporated in the new design."

"Hm."

"And then you pay for it."

"Knew that was coming."

Mercifully, Sheriff Chumley interrupted with an update. The Schuyler city council agreed to hold a sunset rally 8 days hence to follow up on grievances. Sass escaped up to the roof to give Kassidy the news, and stayed to watch her acrobatic finale.

Kassidy's announcement at the end was met with some grumbles and raised fists, but mostly applause for the acrobatics and thrown kisses. The crowd dispersed.

REPERCUSSIONS of the PM3 sky dive and prison break took weeks to unfold.

Guy Fairweather, acting Mahina Director of Security, collected up Kendra Oliver and his problem staff and sent them to await trial at Phosphate Mine 1. He suggested they address PM1's air quality issue while they still had brains left to figure it out.

Sass and Copeland were deeply gratified by the poetic justice.

On a 10-point scale for public confidence, Fairweather rated about a 5 at this point. Clay Rocha claimed that was for the best, because the urbs would keep an eye on him. He personally rated Guy even lower, but after decades of Kendra's misrule, there wasn't anyone better in Security.

Sass said Clay would be better. Clay shook his head. Older urbs still feared the more numerous settlers outside the city. Emotionally they required one of their own to protect them.

Atlas Pratt was less fatalistic. He capitalized on the news opportunity, unleashed from Kendra's bullying, to publicize his old proposal for satellite domed creches in settler areas. His successor as Director of MA Medical was infuriated at first. But Atlas, borrowing Clay's apartment in the city, was the more masterful at organizational politics. He reinvigorated MA-Med's research morale while making clear that he himself hoped to take a new position leading settler medicine, not to resume the Director role.

Sass herself was invited to a single public interview, on a settler news program. She dwelt on her upcoming tax day, and how it wouldn't be so bad if she knew how her taxes benefited settlers. But here she had this new water find suitable for another atmosphere factory, and the urbs didn't plan to build one. It was foolish for settlers to pay taxes to the urbs without input and transparency on what the urbs spent the money on.

That taped interview never aired. Sass's lawyer felt her comments violated her parole.

Josiah and Sass agreed that if Atlas could engineer support for publicly-funded mini-cities for settlers, the black market opportunity was moot. Josiah was less pleased that Copeland wanted to stick with *Thrive,* and Sass wanted an atmosphere factory more than a free-market water station.

During that edgy meeting, Abel diffidently asked whether Josiah had any advice for cutting their taxes. Sass confided their next-day deadline to pay about 140,000 credits, the lion's share of everything *Thrive* had earned so far. Josiah grinned crookedly and invited himself along to an in-person meeting. Abel and Sass didn't even realize a personal appointment was an option. Josiah invited Clay and their lawyer along, as well.

After two hours of these three heavy hitters putting the intimidated tax collector through the wringer, she meekly accepted a deal of 12,000 credits now to clear the title, with an estimated 40,000 of income taxes deferred to the end of the year. Sass and Abel owned *Thrive* free and clear.

"The income tax is still too high," Abel grumbled on their way out.

Josiah chuckled. "You still don't get it."

The lawyer winked at Abel. "Income is net after expenses. Including capital investment."

"New kitchen," Clay clarified. "Space drive. Old ship, in the hospitality business, needs sprucing up. And of course you pay Copeland and Benjy for the work."

"You don't owe squat," Josiah summarized. "You should have a nice cushy loss to carry into next year. A space drive, huh? Interesting."

"We're in the black," Sass said wonderingly. "We have a viable business. And without you guys, we would have handed over 140 grand today. We'd have walked out with pocket change."

Abel prudently paid kickbacks to Josiah and the lawyer. Clay claimed himself in it for the clean kitchen.

38

In most cases, the starship crews left their vast ships to be broken up to build human habitat. They departed on smaller vessels.

"What's wrong, Copeland?" Sass asked softly. She found the engineer in the dining room, sitting back to the wall, hands on knees. His expression of grim disgust reminded her of days when she took stock of her life and proclaimed it an epic fail. His toolbox lay open next to Nico's playpen, tools spread out beside it. The captain approached him gently, with a warm smile for Nico.

The baby blew bubbles in his own drool, bored behind bars. Baby Nico graduated from the auto-doc after four days, looking much healthier and interested in the world again. A bit too interested in his world. He didn't walk, but he crept fast and put everything in his mouth. Or, like his dad the engineer, he delighted to take things apart.

Copeland was a good engineer. But having to drag a playpen around with him and keep half an eye on Nico, he was far from quick. Engineering maintenance and baby care didn't go together. Jules helped sometimes, but she was busy with her market today.

Sass claimed another bit of wall, and sank to a seat beside the young man.

Copeland mopped his face on his shirtsleeve, and pulled himself together. His voice was husky with emotion. "This won't work. He tried to put one of my solvent rags in his mouth. Barely caught him in time."

"Maybe you'd be better off in Schuyler, back at the brewery," Sass replied. "Settled. Hire another mom to take care of Nico while you work regular shifts."

"Atlas says the creche can take him back. In Mahina Actual." Copeland swallowed. "They'd let me keep parental rights. Because of what happened. I could still see him. I can't stow him in a crate all his life."

"No. There's no family to help?"

"Only the wife's family. I don't trust them."

"No," Sass agreed. "Have you seen it? Inside Mahina Actual?"

"Nah. Went to the settler mall once. Pretty flashy."

"Nico is what, 18 months old?"

"Only 16 months. Yeah, got him 3 months ago. Hasn't gone too well."

Sass touched his arm. "The creche was Nico's home 3 months ago. They remember him. You lived there as a baby, too. It's a nice place. Why don't I take you to see it?"

"You'd do that?" Copeland canted his head back on the wall and squinted at her, face hard and untrusting. "Why?"

Sass shook her head. "Because it's the decent thing to do. Because it's easy. I have to go into the city anyway to make a statement to the cops. Copeland, I'd like to keep you as an engineer. But only if it's right for your family. Raising Nico in *Thrive*...it's not optimal. I'm willing to make it work. But check out the creche first. OK?"

She rose abruptly. "Pack up. Let's go."

When they reached Mahina Actual, Atlas met them at the entrance behind the food court. They stopped at Clay's apartment by the botanical gardens first. Sass coaxed Nico out of Copeland's arms and set him free on the grassy living room floor. Then she lured a baby goat to come play with him.

Copeland had never seen his child squeal with delight like that. The lazy slug even got off his butt and walked a few steps. He fell repeatedly. But he was so entranced by the goat that he clambered up again shrieking in glee to chase the animal again. The dad was terrified when the baby ate a flower. Atlas and Sass assured him the plants wouldn't do him any harm.

The engineer grew silent as they toured the creche facilities. A woman who looked 5 years younger than him, but was probably older, explained how he would be able to track Nico's daily activities and contact them with any concerns, as the urb parents did. Small children gamboled everywhere, well-supervised. The older kids were in school at this hour. Copeland's attention was riveted by the science and technology lab, presently occupied by eight-to-ten year olds peering at living soil microbes.

Nico's proposed bedroom was a cozy cheerful space with four cribs. The babies only went there to sleep the night, their guide explained. They napped on mats during the day. She led them out into the toddler play yard, shaded by trees neither spruce nor aspen. Balls and trucks and dolls and blocks abounded, among toddler-safe playground tunnels and slides.

"Nico!" another seemingly young man cried, scurrying to join them. "I hear you've had a setback, little man. Mr. Copeland, I'm Dr. Agassiz. How do you do?"

"You're too young to be a doctor."

"Ah…" Dr. Agassiz looked to Atlas for a ruling.

"No lies," Atlas ruled. "Copeland, the good doctor is around 50. Everyone you meet here looks about your age. They're not. All the pediatric facilities are located here in the creche."

"May I?" Dr. Agassiz asked, holding out his arms for Nico.

Copeland grudgingly handed the child over. They followed the doctor not to an exam room, but the toy bin. In the course of handing the child balls and blocks, tickling him and pumping his flaccid legs and arms, the doctor completed his examination. He set the child free to remove things from the bin and dump them on the grass.

"Is he OK?" Copeland asked guardedly.

"He's healthy. I see developmental delays from his toxic setback. Atlas sent his records." Dr. Agassiz pulled out a comms tablet to review, and jotted a few notes. "He's been gone four months. I'm seeing about one month's worth of healthy development. Nico was a bright child. I'd like to keep him here. See if we can't get him back on that track." The doctor smiled warmly to soften the blow.

"How?" Copeland demanded. "Is this something I could do at home?"

"Enriched activities. Talk to him a lot. Read to him. Play interesting games. Here I would have a physical therapist work with him. His muscles are lax. The bones aren't attenuated. He's just spent too much time being lazy. Find things that motivate him enough to get up on those stubby little legs and run. Right, Nico?" The doctor demonstrated by playing a brief round of keep-away with the baby, using a yellow bath duck. Nico could be coaxed into taking one step, rarely two.

"The goats, in the botanical garden," Sass murmured as a reminder.

Copeland reluctantly enlarged on this topic for the doctor's benefit. Then he explained the child's current living arrangements in the skyship. The engineer tended to digress into his shortcomings. Sass stayed at his elbow to coax out his strengths as a father. How he'd watched the toxins graph progress over the days Nico was encapsulated in the auto-doc. The child's daycare arrangements at PM3, and his attempts with Jules to persuade the little slug to walk between them.

"You're a great dad, John," Sass murmured. Copeland hated his given name. This lent it power.

Atlas squeezed his shoulder. "No one is saying otherwise. It's just a question of what's best for the child right now. And you, getting your feet back under you. We hope to give Nico's advantages in a creche to all settler children. Soon."

Dr. Agassiz nodded. "You'll be a trailblazer. We've never cooperated with settler parents before. Just hand the baby over at 12 months. We'll learn together. How to co-parent. We need a smart parent like you to lead the way."

Copeland scowled at the man. But the doctor seemed sincere. "He's my son."

"And always will be," Agassiz vowed. "My word on it."

Copeland turned his glower to Atlas, but there his brow furrowed in doubt.

"My word on it," Atlas echoed. "You know I'll do my damnedest."

"I do know that," Copeland whispered, and swallowed. "Alright." He pulled his posture out of its slump and gathered his strength.

"Don't make a big deal of it," Sass hastily advised. "Just a quick kiss, and I'll see you soon." Agassiz nodded wryly.

"You've had kids?" Copeland asked Sass, diverted. Unsure whether he was coming or going, the crew had been reticent to share the secrets of *Thrive*.

Sass nodded and dropped her eyes. Paul died long ago and far away.

Copeland picked Nico up for a quick peck on the lips and a squeeze, and deposited him back on the ground. "See you soon, sport." He waited until the baby was engaged in toys again, then they turned and walked away.

"The engineering in this place is incredible," he said after a few minutes. By then they passed through the temperate forest biome. He paused to study the light pipes on a tree. "Any chance we can tour around?"

"I shouldn't," Atlas said. "Eh, what the hell. Sass, promise you won't cause trouble. And meet me back at Clay's place within the hour."

"I promise." Sass tamped down a smile, wondering why anyone would believe her on that promise. Though she was sincere. It wouldn't do to let Copeland endanger his visitation rights with Nico on the first day.

In the event, they didn't stray from the direct route back to the botanical gardens before her timer went off. The engineer spent the first half of their hour deeply enthralled with how the light pipes worked in the forest, jotting ideas for shifting *Thrive's* tree collection into the hold.

Sass warned him when their time was half gone. But they only advanced to the next biome, the sanitation wetlands. Copeland ran across a kindred spirit there, a technician happy to answer questions. Aside from children's field trips from the creche, Sass imagined the man was overjoyed that anyone cared.

"We can buy these parts, right?" Copeland asked, as they picked up the pace to rendezvous with Atlas. "They're not urb-only restricted tech?"

"Lights and water? Sure, any farm supply store carries them."

"Think they'd let me take my kid out for a walk when I visit?"

"Most parents do."

Copeland gazed around the main plaza as they crossed it. "I see a lot of long walks with my kid in my future."

Sass smiled, happy for him. "Still want to work for us on *Thrive?*"

"Abso-rego-lutely. Pardon my fresh." He scowled at a passerby who scowled at him for swearing.

"French," Sass corrected automatically.

"Huh?" Copeland scratched the tribal tattoos running up his neck.

"Never mind."

39

If any colonial crews returned to Earth for a second load, they failed.

"Thank you for coming." Mahina Chief of Security Guy Fairweather stood from his desk to wave Sass and Clay to seats a week later. Appearing the standard 25 years old, Fairweather's face was fleshy and bland. Urbs could wear any face they liked, which made his chubby and forgettable looks a curious fashion statement.

Sass took a seat in silence. She had deep misgivings about this interview. Fairweather specifically requested the two ex-marshals not bring their lawyers for this 'exploratory' conversation. All she knew of Fairweather was second hand through Clay. He'd moved up the ranks after she took up farming as a convict.

"Good to see you again, Guy," said Clay. "Outside interrogation."

Fairweather quirked his lip in appreciation. "Computer, turn off all recording. You gave me a lot to think about, Clay, that night you arrested Kendra."

"Nothing that requires payback, I hope?" Clay's poker face was superb.

"Payback is an interesting word." Fairweather turned his eyes to Sass. "Captain Collier. Was this...stunt...at Phosphate Mine 3 a form of payback? For Ms. Oliver's recent attempt to hold your crewman hostage?"

"No."

"What exactly was the intent? Originally. I understand that the suicide attempt...changed things."

"A stunt. Kassidy Yang jumped from 2,000 meters in an interesting location."

"Don't insult my intelligence, captain. You intended from the first to liberate Atlas Pratt and several other inmates of PM3."

"Inmates?" Sass countered. "Atlas Pratt was General Manager. The other three were never convicted of anything. Merely forced to live on the sky-side at great risk to their health."

Fairweather's eyes flicked sideways at the word 'three.' Clay clarified, "Warwick, Copeland, and baby Copeland were the three."

"And your involvement, Clay?"

"None, until Collier and Pratt reported the suicide attempt."

Fairweather scowled. "Which you jumped on with great eagerness."

"That was payback," Clay allowed. "But not on you. Kendra was a bad actor, for a long time. Including many crimes against Sass — Captain Collier — and myself. As I shared with you that night."

"And now you live with Ms. Collier."

Clay shrugged. "I felt safer out of town after I tendered my resignation. We're not romantically involved. But we've worked together. Since long before I worked with you."

"He pays rent on *Thrive*," Sass added. "And he's remodeling our kitchen. Retirement project."

"Ms. Collier, you are on parole for your involvement in the last rebellion. And here you are, inciting public unrest again."

"Did I? Or did Kendra?"

"I believe it's clear you both did. And Clay. And most of all Kassidy Yang. Unfortunately she's fireproof. Too popular." Fairweather sighed annoyance. "You two are only popular with settlers, not urbs."

Skyship Thrive

Clay waved dismissal at that. "We're working entirely behind the scenes —"

"That too," Fairweather growled. "I want you two less visible. I need you to support the changes the city has agreed to. You must not call for further elaborations."

Sass pursed her lips. "The city hasn't agreed to build another atmo factory yet, has it?"

"No," Clay confirmed. "Still negotiating that."

Fairweather spread his hands. "Fine. I agree we need another spire. The mini-city creches for settler children. Nico Copeland and other at-risk settler children in the city creche in the meantime. Kendra Oliver is gone, and not coming back. But that's enough —"

"Trees," Sass interrupted. "The urbs are warehousing thousands of trees that were grown for settlers. Some of them remove toxins from the air. I have a couple. They're really good. Mahina Actual should release them for distribution."

Fairweather shook his head and made a note of it. "Trees. Fine. Quietly. Is that all?" His tone suggested it damned well better be all.

Sass traded a glance with Clay. "Benjy's genome."

"No," Fairweather said with finality. "Those crimes were committed by urbs upon unsuspecting settlers. The perpetrators are in exile. Ms. Collier, the point I'm getting at here is that I need peace between urb and settler to accomplish the advances we've agreed to. If you continue to escalate pressure, it all falls apart again. Mahina Actual will renege, the settlers will be outraged, and we're right back where we started. I need you to stop here and give it a rest for a while."

"Define 'a while.'" Clay's poker mask was on tight.

"Years."

"Twenty years?" Sass asked with an edge. "Sixty years? Ninety?"

Clay frowned. "I understood twenty and sixty. But ninety?"

Sass elaborated, "Mahina's original terraforming deadline."

"Ah!" said Clay. "Less than thirty years left on that? How time flies."

"A few years," Fairweather suggested. "Give us time to get the first settler creche up and running. Make it five years. Iron out the bugs. You know we'll hit some."

"And what you're asking in return?" Sass asked. "Keep our mouths shut? Or somehow engineer that the entire settler world stays quiet and obedient?"

"We don't have the power to deliver that," Clay said.

Fairweather's lip snarled briefly, but he tamped it back into place. "Clay, you're far higher in the resistance than you've admitted."

"If so, I'm a silent partner."

The security chief nodded. "A hell of lot smarter than Landau was. Smart enough to understand why I need what I'm asking."

"Granted."

"Actively pursuing peace and quiet," Fairweather demanded. "Retirement would be good."

"I am retired," Clay replied with a smile. "I'm thinking of travel. Off-world. Investigate a few leads that were exiled thataway." He pointed up. "Quietly. We could report back to Atlas Pratt and yourself, plus a settler representative. My son Hunter, for instance. But I insist on communications with all three. Not just you."

Fairweather narrowed his eyes, then turned them on Sass. "And you'd take this Kassidy Yang off-moon with you? And she squawks about all she sees?"

"Perhaps her broadcasts could funnel through you and the orbital," Sass suggested. "That's really between you and your urb citizen Kassidy Yang. I'm just the truck driver." She smiled. "I don't have a space drive to go anywhere except the orbital. This off-world excursion could be pretty short."

"They can build a space drive at the orbital," Fairweather claimed. "You pursue that agenda — quietly — and I'm willing to drop all charges. I know you don't respect what I did under Kendra —"

Clay interrupted. "Guy, I don't respect what *I* did under Kendra. I extend you the benefit of every possible doubt. You were caught between a rock and a hard place. Now you're not, and you're willing to make up for it. Some old habits may be harder to break than others."

"Fair enough. Are we agreed?"

Sass considered. "In five years we meet to review? And unless absolutely necessary, I hold any further issues and opportunities quiet until then. Is that what I'm agreeing to?"

Fairweather sighed. "Define 'absolutely necessary.'"

Clay took a stab at it. "Serious new crimes against settlers. Conditions putting human lives at risk."

"You pass those to me at any time," Fairweather said. "No need to wait. Rabble-rousing is what you agree to forgo."

Sass said, "Unless you ignore those crimes."

"I will not ignore them. I may not always choose to jump the way you want. But between Atlas, myself, and Clay's son, you will be heard."

Clay slipped a comm out of his pocket. "I didn't turn off my recording. You're welcome to delete it, Guy. But first let me cobble together the agreement."

He generated a transcript and dragged sections together, working on the desk where the other two could collaborate. They jointly paraphrased the aims and benefits of the accord.

When they were satisfied that the document captured the spirit of their terms, Sass sat back. "Do you have signature authority for this, Mr. Fairweather?"

"I do not," he confirmed. "I suggest we label it a memo. No signatures."

Clay agreed, and sent them copies. "Guy, shall I send this to Kassidy as well? You could use it as a foundation for your discussions with her."

"I'd prefer none of us forward it to anyone, nor discuss it except amongst ourselves."

"I prefer to discuss it with Atlas and Hunter," Clay replied mildly. "They are named, after all. Over drinks, perhaps, at my place. Or on board *Thrive*."

"Set it up. I'll be there."

Sass shook the security chief's hand in turn as they took their leave. She got away with it. They'd won significant quality of life improvements for the settlers, and had an agreement of honor to a next round in five years.

She won.

————————

A FEW DAYS LATER, Kassidy stepped out on the ramp to dive from 3 kilometers into the sunset, with only *Thrive* crew in attendance at the top. Sass let Benjy stay in the hold this time. She and the more authentically daring Copeland flanked the stunt woman.

At this height, they gazed into the top of the atmosphere. Sass had looked it up — Earth's atmosphere attenuated out for hundreds of kilometers. Mahina's, not so much. A gaseous skin based on ozone kept the atmosphere in place over a moon without enough gravity to hold air. The layers interacted with the low-angled sun to create fuzzy blankets of salmon, pure blue, and emerald green.

A big meteorite zapped down to the left, a brief tangerine ball of flame, a blue-white streak of lightning, then gone. Sass didn't envy Benjy on the bridge, sitting gunner's watch to disintegrate any meteor that approached too close.

The trio lay on the ramp edge to gaze on it all. Kassidy kept up a steady banter to build excitement in her fans. Sass tuned her out and inched forward to look over the edge. The moon was eclipsing below, the sunset line marching toward them to leave twilight in its wake. Kassidy only had a few minutes or she'd lose her moment. From this height, any illusion that Mahina was settled and green vanished. The captain wasn't sure she could identify a single settlement other than the one directly below. Kassidy would jump into Schuyler for her finale.

"There," Copeland said, pointing. "Mahina Actual just passed into sunset."

"Good eye," Sass murmured in wonder. Kassidy made a significantly bigger deal out of it. The lights of the city grew more distinct as the captain watched, a precious tiny few pinpricks compared to those old satellite images of Earth from when the cities and highways shone with light even from space. Earth's lights were doused before Sass could remember.

The sun line reached a wrinkle. Sass double-checked her geography by the faint craters. "Grand Rift?"

"Think so," Copeland agreed.

Kassidy skipped the rift in favor of the sky. Lights twinkled ahead, seeming to detach from the sun. "Fans, that's Mahina Orbital coming into view. So much brighter than Mahina Actual! Looks closer, but it's not! So, fans! Who thinks I should jump into the sky instead of the ground? Tempting! No, I'm pretty sure I can't aim well enough to hit the orbital."

"Definitely not," Sass confirmed, on a channel the audience couldn't hear. But *Thrive* could reach it. She felt like she was almost there. That was an illusion, of course, created by the satellite's prodigious solar collectors.

"It's time, boys and girls!" Kassidy pushed up and back from the edge, and strode to the base of the ramp for a running start. "Can you stand it? On three! One, two, three!"

She leapt up, jack-knifed, and dove straight down.

"Back in," Sass ordered, already pushing up as Copeland craned forward to look down.

"Aw, can't I jump, too? You could jump after to save me!"

"Comedian. Move."

Abel chimed in from the bridge. "Not funny."

Sass offered the engineer a hand up. Within minutes, they were inside, *Thrive* already nearing the ground by the time the airlock cycled. They stripped their pressure suits while watching the festivities outside on the big screen in the hold. The skyship landed half a kilometer away rather than stake out a parking spot against the crowds.

Kassidy beat them to the ground. But now she led the throng in jumping up and down pogo-style, playing with their grav generators. Many participated in jumps up to 2 meters or so. Kids did more than that on the playground every day. As the jumps reached 4 meters, most people dropped out. But a rare few of the ones who persisted had practiced mid-air somersaults as well.

Kassidy was so delighted that she egged them on to halt at zero gravity at the top of a leap. It took a few tries, then two fans managed to hover with her, poised 10 meters above the ground.

"Well, now you're up here, look around!" Kassidy invited. "It's kinda fun walking on air, huh?" She led them to mime walking above the crowd, moving nowhere. One, a teenage girl, tried her best impression of swimming and got major applause.

"OK, *be safe!*" Kassidy proclaimed. "Yeah, yeah, one of those lectures. Why are we standing 10 meters above the ground? If I do a somersault up here, and something goes wrong, I still have time to react and control my fall. And so long as I'm at zero g, I can't go anywhere here."

She demonstrated flipping forward to rotate around her belly button, then shot out an arm and twisted to spin on a diagonal. She pulled in her limbs to whirl faster, then threw them out to slow herself, gradually easing to a stop from friction. "Fun huh? Start slow."

Her volunteers gave hilariously botched performances, limbs flailing in sharp contrast to Kassidy's smooth practiced moves. She led a round of hooting applause for the other two, and invited them to fall carefully down.

"So gang! That was the end of my skydive series! Did you have fun? You know I had fun!" Massive applause. "What's next? Hm..." She rolled and looked up. "Think I could talk *Thrive* into visiting the orbital?" Even more enthusiasm. "Stay tuned, fans! I love you all to bits! Bye for now!"

40

Historians disagree on why the Aloha system rose to prominence.

"Please, *please* let me livecast from the bridge, Sass!" Kassidy begged one last time.

"No. We have a camera forward. Livecast that. Not us. Sorry, Kassidy. I need two gunners and a pilot, and we only have two seats. Into your cabin now, and seal the door." To assure the final word on the topic, Sass sealed the bridge before the stunt woman could wheedle any further.

"Ready guys?" she asked. Abel and Benjy had the two chairs for now. Sass leaned on the seat backs between them. "Remember I'm your backup. If you start getting frazzled, say the word and I spell you. Benjy, don't try to tough it out. Abel, we are in no hurry. Take it slow. Give yourself time to dodge, and your gunner time to aim."

The young men nodded somberly into the parking lot of Mahina Actual that spread before the cockpit windows. In addition to Kassidy's livecast income, this was a paid freight run to carry urb supplies to the orbital.

Besides, they had final business in the city. Copeland said good-bye to Nico. Kassidy endured a diplomatic dinner with Dr. Paripati. Sass, Clay, and Eli spent hours last night in a briefing with Atlas.

"Captain speaking. Departure check," Sass said ship-wide. Everyone on board reported their location and compartment sealed, pressure suits and emergency oxygen at hand. First mate Abel confirmed all compartments sealed, garden secured, fuel, water, and gases at full. Jules on Housekeeping reported food stocks replenished and all passengers accounted for. Engineer Copeland confirmed all major propulsion, gunnery, and life support systems at nominal in zero-atmosphere configuration.

"Captain acknowledges all systems are go. Mahina Actual, skyship *Thrive* is ready for departure."

"Skyship *Thrive,* Mahina Actual," Guy Fairweather replied, Mahina Chief of Security. Mahina didn't have air traffic control. "Your skies are clear. You are free to depart. Godspeed and a safe trip, Sass."

"Thanks, Guy. *Thrive* departing." Sass switched back to intercom. "We are a go. See you at the orbital. Captain out. Abel, let's go."

He blew out between pursed lips, took a deep gulp of air, and seized the controls. "Takeoff. Minus one half g external."

Once upon a time, astronauts had simulators and months of training to prepare for such maneuvers. In Earth orbit, they didn't have nearly the debris in orbit to contend with, at least at first. But Mahina was located in the planetary ring of a gas giant, chock full of bits of moon that never coalesced to the size of their big sisters. To leave the protective atmosphere was to fly straight into an asteroid belt. The workhorse *Thrive* wore a tough hull. Electrostatic shielding coped with particles up to the size of a house cat. Rendering bigger obstacles small was the gunner's job. The pilot dodged anything too big for the gunner.

The skyship manufacturer provided a 20 minute orientation video, filmed around Jupiter-Ganymede, not Pono-Mahina. The three of them reviewed the video five times this week, usually in slow motion. Benjy and Sass practiced their gunnery simulation drills.

On the plus side, their captain had made this trip before a couple dozen times. Sass sat as relief gunner twice, never pilot, half a century ago.

The ship rose, slowly at first but steadily gathering speed. From their view screens, the others had a great show of Mahina Actual dropping away beneath them.

The cockpit crew didn't look down. The moon couldn't jump up to bite them.

"Half atmosphere, gunner," Abel reported. He rotated the ship to point the forward guns up.

Benjy immediately blasted the forward guns. "Just a warm-up."

The computer prodded, "Did you water the plants?"

"Yes, plants secure," Abel assured the system. "I think."

Sass wiped sweat from her hands. She blew out softly, trying to calm herself, ready to step in as needed.

"Banking to aim for orbital," Abel said, swallowing. "Cutting acceleration."

Sass bit her lip. *Cut it more.*

"Slower, Abel," Benjy growled.

"Sorry. Leaving atmosphere in fifteen. No countdown." The training video was explicit on that point. The meteorite risk was already substantial. The gunner didn't need the stress of an irrelevant countdown.

Benjy stiffened. "Yours." He stuck a finger on the threat and flicked it sideways to highlight on Abel's display. Meanwhile, he got busy shooting smaller rocks in its neighborhood.

"Dodging to top left," Abel confirmed. Benjy adjusted his fire to that corridor.

"Whoa! Shit." Benjy hadn't seen another asteroid coming to side-swipe them until it was almost too late. He needed a dozen shots to neutralize its threat. The big one split into littler ones, that split in turn, while a rogue object snuck into the fray from another direction.

Abel dodged another that Benjy hadn't warned him about, a warty cigar shape the size of a house. Behind it four more threats suddenly appeared on Benjy's to-do list, and the computer pinged something approaching outside his view aperture.

"I've got the ping," Abel reported sweating, as one ping turned to a two-note warning. "Uh —"

"Slow, dodge right and down," Sass urged. "Benjy, second ping as it bears."

"Aye," they chorused. The 'second ping' asteroid was even larger than the last one, an object the pilot would normally handle. As his guns turned one threatening piece into 8, into 27, Benjy was dripping sweat.

He blasted the last threat and had a clear screen for a second. "Break." He slipped out of the seat to the right as Sass dropped in from the other side.

She no sooner grasped the controls than a flock of a couple dozen modest rocks came at her. She started blasting in priority order — the computer figured out that much for her, at least. But there were too many. "Abel, head right," she murmured. She flicked a half dozen rocks on the left for Abel to bypass, never letting up on the firing buttons.

Benjy stretched and breathed deep behind her, pulling his shattered nerves back together. He took a few gulps of water and ate some dried fruit for the sugar. Neck and shoulders unkinked one last time, he reported quietly, "Good to resume at will."

Abel jerked the controls to dodge three times in rapid succession. "Breather sounds good."

Sass shot the last of her rocks for a clean screen. "Ready. And now." She shifted into Abel's seat as he vacated it. Benjy resumed the gunner seat.

Their focused dance continued for over two hours. The orbital lay 150 kilometers above Mahina, 320 klicks from Mahina Actual at rendezvous. On the scale of space distances, they weren't going terribly fast, except for an obstacle course. Three rocks got through and hit the hull. Two bounced off, but one punched a thumb-sized hole into the ventilation system space near the bridge.

Copeland found and patched it in under 10 minutes. His chosen post for this trip was the hold, in a pressure suit. That put him no more than one door away from most pressure breaches. He'd advised

Sass to just evacuate the hold's air for safekeeping, but she overruled him. Skyships never did that when she lived on them early in the terraforming.

Of course, they didn't have amateurs driving the bus back then. They carried a couple hundred people without enough pressure suits in the hold. And they made the trip in one hour. Sass hadn't realized at the time just how little regard they'd shown for those lives in cargo. She resolved to listen more closely to her engineer's advice next time.

"Clear at last," Abel reported. He set his head back against its cushion with a huge sigh. "Captain, we are arrived at orbital interdiction."

The space station protected itself and its solar arrays with automated guns under control of an experienced AI. Its space was clear for a 10 kilometer radius.

Sass double-checked from the gunner's chair. Benjy was on break. "Clear skies confirmed. Jog pattern," she reminded Abel.

Abel winced. They needed a predictable zig-zag, lest they block the orbital's shooting. "Initiating jog at dead slow... To the front door?"

"Nah, just jog in place." Sass thumbed the comms. "Mahina Orbital, Skyship *Thrive* arriving. Captain Sassafras Collier speaking. Never done that before. We need a break. Mind if we get back to you in an hour or so?"

"Captain Collier, welcome to Mahina Orbital! Understood. Enjoy the view! Eager to meet you. Save room for dinner and drinks. Orbital out."

"You're on for dinner! *Thrive* out." Sass flicked the switch to intercom. "Now arrived Mahina Orbital near space. All hands stand down from pressure watch. Bridge crew on break before final approach."

Benjy unsealed the door. Sass stretched in her seat, fingertips to toes making a single plank, then relaxed into simple breathing and the view for a couple minutes. They faced the orbital side-on, with its huge shining tutu of solar collectors canted about 20 degrees. After a few more calming breaths, Abel reached out to the attitude control and brought the view level.

Sass started with a chuckle, and soon all three were laughing out loud.

"What's the joke?" Copeland inquired. He leaned in the doorway, detached pressure helmet held against his hip.

"Release from tension," Sass replied, as her chuckles died out. She swiveled and held a hand out to him to shake. "Glad we had you on board. Three of us wasn't enough for this."

"No," the ex-mob engineer agreed.

Sass pulled herself out of her seat and headed for the kitchen. The others made it there first.

In their gorgeous new galley, rich in dark rusty reds and nickel fittings, they gathered around the dining table to behold the view of Mahina on the big screen. An arc of the moon filled the top of the display, its scenery steadily marching across. The orbital took under a half hour for each circuit of the moon. The blue-green halo of Mahina's precious atmosphere stood vivid against the grey regolith and black of space. *Home.*

A city slid into the frame. "Mahina Actual?" Sass asked, pointing.

"Schuyler," Clay said. "Its fields are bigger than the city."

"Sweet," Sass breathed, lips curving unbidden into a smile. Clay broke into an outright grin. Last time they were in orbit, Mahina Actual was the only town visible to the naked eye.

Settlement had progressed. Some.

And they were in space seeking answers. "We'll be back, Mahina," Sass vowed.

ACKNOWLEDGMENTS

I'm deeply grateful to my test readers. The hard-working beta team for *Skyship Thrive* included Jim Hunt, Ron Kaminski, Jenniffer LaPointe, Karen Reinertsen, Barton Schindel, Jim Seals, Kate Travis, and WMH Cheryl. Thank you for sharing your time and insights, and especially for your friendship, and urging me on.

Thanks as well to the advance review copy readers, who read the almost-final manuscript, ready to post reviews for book launch.

And thank you, for reading my book. Without you, I couldn't do what I do, so I really appreciate that you give my work a chance. Drop me a line! I personally respond to all messages.

Books take a long time to write. Feedback is the fuel that powers the next story.

Ginger Booth
ginger@gingerbooth.com